THE MASKS OF IMOGEN

THE MASKS OF IMOGEN

The Strange Chronicle of Imogen Edwards

By

John Marriott

ISBN: 978-1-4269-6561-6 (sc)
ISBN: 978-1-4269-6562-3 (e)

Trafford rev. 12/19/2014

 www.trafford.com

North America & international
toll-free: 1 888 232 4444 (USA & Canada)
fax: 812 355 4082

Author's Note: Imogen pronounces the word "lieutenant" as though it is written as "leftenant."

CHAPTER ONE

Careful not to tread on the skirt of her gown as she walked behind her friend down the steps of the sloping aisle leading to the their seats in the front row of the first gallery in the opera house, the attractive dark-haired young woman was unaware of the pair of masculine eyes following her. Her friend was a very pretty blue-eyed blond, but the beauty of the almost statuesque, magnificently bosomed, dark-eyed brunette surpassed the prettiness of her companion.

Settled in the aisle seat, the dark haired beauty turned to speak to her friend. "Susan, it's really wonderful of you to bring me here to the opera this evening."

"Oh Imogen!" responded her friend. "I wanted to do something to thank you for being my accompanist all these years. But, come on, give the world a treat by taking off your stole so they can see those magnificent shoulders of yours. I can never understand why you try to hide the fact that you are a very beautiful woman."

"I feel embarrassed, Susan," said Imogen, shyly lowering her eyes. "I've never before worn a strapless gown—though I appreciate your buying it for me—it's lovely—but I feel half-naked in it, and my breasts are prominent enough already without being pushed up and thrust out like this."

"Half naked, Imogen! Good heavens! It's only your shoulders—which are magnificent—and I know lots of women who'd give their eye teeth to have breasts like yours."

"And I could tell them, they're no asset. They're all anyone ever notices about me."

"Well—I still think you should take off your stole. Look around at all the other bare shoulders. No one's going to notice one more pair. Do something a little bit daring for once in your life."

"Well, I suppose—"

Reluctantly, hesitantly, Imogen slipped off her stole and, after a minute of so, felt bold enough to glance about the opera house. As she did so, her eyes met those of the handsome man in evening clothes in a nearby box who had been ogling her from the moment she entered. Her own eyes widened, and her full lips parted as, for some moments, she sat transfixed, returning his gaze. Then, suddenly, she noticed that her handsome admirer's attractive female companion and turned away, feeling an unaccountable pang of jealousy. She tried to compose herself, but she could not resist the impulse to steal another look—noticing this time two rather grim-faced men, seemingly very uncomfortable both in their evening clothes and the circumstances, sitting behind the couple in the box and wondering who they might be. Her admirer flashed her a smile, whereupon, feeling the heat of a deep blush come over her, she again looked away.

"What's the matter, Imogen?" asked Susan, noticing her friend's agitation. "You're all aflutter."

"I'm not!" she said, without looking up. "It's nothing."

At that instant Susan also noticed the man gazing in their direction.

"Oh! You've attracted the admiration of a handsome man!"

" No!" Imogen replied a little too vehemently.

"Methinks thou dost protest too much, Ms Edwards. You're blushing!" teased Susan. Then her eyes narrowed and her forehead wrinkled as though she were trying to recall something. "Hm. Somehow I feel I should know that man, but I can't put a name to his face."

"You—you do, Susan?" Imogen responded. Then, trying to hide her agitation she said, "Maybe it's you he's looking at."

"No," said Susan, "He's definitely looking at you, Imogen. You've made a conquest."

"Oh," said Imogen, again feeling a blush come over her, "he's probably just flirting." She again glanced in the direction of her admirer and noticed him leaning over to whisper to his partner. "Anyway he's with a very attractive woman."

"Oh-ho! You're jealous!"

"No! I'm not!" protested Imogen.

"Oh now, Imogen. Thou really dost protest too much. And if he is flirting, his companion seems totally unconcerned by it." Again Susan screwed up her eyes. "Now, who are they? I should know them, and I think they're brother and sister."

Imogen blushed and said, "His sister?"

"Aha! You were jealous!"

"No, I was not!"

"Oh!" said Susan. "His partner is leaving the box."

Imogen looked up to see that indeed the woman was making her way to the rear followed by one of the two awkward looking men.

"I wonder where she's going—and why is that man following her?" she asked.

"I don't know," said Susan. "I wish I could place them. The man is still looking at you, Imogen."

Again Imogen blushed and looked away.

"I—I wish he wouldn't."

"Well, as you say, it's probably nothing. Too bad. The guy sure is handsome."

At that moment, with the hard-faced, expressionless man uncomfortable in his tuxedo close behind her, the woman from the box came down the aisle to where the Imogen and Susan sat.

"Hello," said the woman, holding out her gloved hand to Susan. "Miss Van Alstyne, I believe."

The woman's smile seemed quite genuinely friendly, though Imogen thought her eyes looked sad.

"Oh—yes," said Susan. "I feel I should know you, but I'm afraid I can't place you."

"I'm Ana-Maria Roselli—Andreotti, actually. I prefer to use my own name now that I'm divorced."

—Andreotti! Oh surely not—! thought Imogen, shocked.

"It—it's nice to meet you, Signorina Andreotti," Susan replied hesitantly.

"Please, just call me Ana-Maria. And I think your first name is Susan. May I call you that?"

"Oh—well—yes—I—I guess so."

"And who is this other very attractive young woman with you, Susan?"

"Oh—uh—excuse me. This is my friend Imogen Edwards."

"How nice to meet you, Miss Edwards—Imogen, if I may call you that" said Ana-Maria Andreotti, extending her hand to Imogen. "What a lovely name!"

"H—how do you do?" she replied, taking the outstretched hand hesitantly despite its owner's apparent graciousness.

"Do you live here in New York, Imogen? I don't believe I've ever seen you in East Clintwood. Mind you, I've been a way for a while."

"I—I am from East Clintwood—but I've been away at university, and I—I don't move in East Clintwood society. I—I'm here in New York by the favor of my friend Susan."

"Oh, I see. Well, my brother Manfred couldn't help noticing two such attractive young ladies, and since he knows Susan's father—which makes us almost like old friends...."

"Oh—yes. Every businessman in East Clintwood must deal with Manfred Andreotti," said Susan, embarrassed and emphasizing "must" for the sake of Imogen who had turned in shock to her friend.

"Well, yes—yes," said Ana-Maria Andreotti, showing some slight embarrassment. "But we wondered if you would join us in our box. It gives a splendid view of the stage. And I would really love it, too, if you joined us."

—Manfred Andreotti! exclaimed Imogen to herself. The crime boss of East Clintwood! Oh Lord no! Oh Lord! Oh Lord!

No longer did the man, handsome though he was, seem attractive.

Susan looked apprehensively at her friend. "Imogen?" she asked.

"Oh—I—" stammered Imogen.

"Oh, please do come, Imogen—and Susan," said Ana-Maria Andreotti. "Surely friends can share a box at the opera."

"Please, Imogen," Susan whispered imploringly, "say yes. For Daddy's sake, I feel I must."

"If—if you feel you must Susan," whispered Imogen in reply, anxious to please her friend, though fearing the consequences of doing so.

"Y—yes—we'd be—glad to join you," said Susan.

"Oh, I'm so pleased!" said Ana-Maria in reply to Susan. "And my brother will be delighted."

—That's what troubles me, thought Imogen. I certainly am not delighted, and I don't really think Susan is either. But the woman seems nice, and if Susan is with me, perhaps it will be all right—I hope it will be all right!

Her heart palpitating, she rose reluctantly with Susan to follow Ana-Maria up the aisle to the rotunda. Glancing toward the box which was their destination, she saw Manfred Andreotti direct toward her a triumphant smile, and she shuddered.

"I'm frightened, Susan," she whispered to her friend as they reached the rotunda and Ana-Maria walked on a bit ahead.

Susan turned to her and whispered in her ear. "I'm sorry, Imogen, and I'm not happy myself, but it's only while the opera lasts. I'm sure it will be all right. Manfred Andreotti controls everything and everyone in East Clintwood, so for Daddy's sake I've got to join them."

Again Imogen shuddered.

As they approached the entrance to the box, accompanied by the other awkward looking man who Imogen now realized was a body guard, Manfred Andreotti himself emerged and came toward them.

"Hey! Hi there, ladies. Good evening!" he exclaimed. "Real nice of you to join us! You are Miss Susan Van Alstyne, right?"

"Y—yes," said Susan. "That's right, and—"

But before she could introduce Imogen, Manfred himself addressed her, "And who, may I ask, is Miss Van Alstyne's gorgeous friend?"

Imogen dropped her gaze to the floor, embarrassed by Manfred Andreotti's intense interest in her cleavage.

—He's undressing me with his eyes! she thought. I know what he wants—as I feared!

"This is Susan's friend, Imogen Edwards," Ana-Maria responded to he brother's question.

"Hey Imogen! Nice to meet you!"

"H—how do you do, Signor Andreotti," said Imogen looking up briefly.

"Imogen?" said Manfred Andreotti, musing and still looking her up and down. "I never heard that name before—but I like it. It's nice. It suits you. A very pretty name for a very pretty woman."

"Oh! I—" stammered Imogen.

"Now, don't embarrass Imogen, Manfred," admonished his sister.

"Hey!" said Andreotti. "A woman as gorgeous as Imogen shouldn't be embarrassed by compliments! Anyway, Imogen, you're a friend of a friend, so compliments ain't out of place."

"Manfred," said Ana-Maria, "Your grammar."

"Oh yeah! Sis here's been trying to teach me to talk proper. But come on into our box. We got champagne on ice," said Andreotti, gently but firmly taking Imogen by the elbow and steering her into the box and to the seats at the front.

Nervously, Imogen noted that, whether by arrangement or design, Ana-Maria had seated herself on her brother's right side with Susan on her right, and that Manfred Andreotti had placed her on his left, isolating her from her friend and making her feel vulnerable.

"I take it you like opera, Imogen," he said as he turned toward her.

"Y—yes—I do," she said, cringing slightly, not really wanting to get into conversation with a gangster.

"Do you like Rossini?"

"Y—yes, I'm very fond of Rossini."

"Hey! Me too," he said. "*The Barber of Seville* is a real fun piece, but I prefer Verdi."

"Oh—uh—yes—Verdi," Imogen began hesitantly. "He—he's very rich, romantic and dramatic."

"Ah! You really know opera! Splendid!"

—Oh! she thought. I almost wish I did not know opera!

"Imogen's a very cultivated person," said Susan, leaning across.

"Yeah, I can see."

"And a very fine pianist."

"Yeah? I'd like to hear you play some time, Imogen. But, here, let's have some champagne," said Andreotti expertly popping the stopper of the champagne bottle and filling a glass which he offered to Imogen with what seemed to her an almost too friendly smile.

"Th—thank you," she said, almost inaudibly as she took the glass and immediately dropping her gaze to her lap.

Andreotti poured champagne for Susan, his sister and himself, then turned again to Imogen. "So you play the piano, Imogen."

"I—I'm no Martha Argerich or Maria-Joao Pires," she responded, again looking down. "Susan's the real musician—a splendid singer. She's going to London to study and to audition. In fact she has some concerts arranged already and will sing Cherubino in *The Marriage of Figaro* with the Royal Opera at the Covent Garden."

"Yeah," said Manfred. "She is real good. I heard her in East Clintwood as Violetta in La Traviata."

"Imogen helped me rehearse the part," said Susan, turning toward Andreotti. "She's a wonderful accompanist. She will be playing for me at my farewell recital in East Clintwood before I leave for England."

"Susan inspires the best in me," said Imogen.

—But, she said to herself, please stop praising me, Susan—not to this man!

"We intend to be at your recital, Susan, said Ana-Maria.

"Yeah!" said Manfred. "Wouldn't miss it for the world, but right now, let's have a toast," he said, raising his glass, "to two very attractive young ladies."

Inclusive though his toast was of Susan, Imogen knew by the way he looked at her that it was meant chiefly for her.

Just then the audience began applauding as the concertmaster of the pit orchestra made his entrance, checked the orchestra's tuning and took his seat at the head of the violin section. Almost immediately, to even more vigorous applause, the conductor entered, bowed to the orchestra and then to the audience, and as the house lights dimmed, turned and raised his baton. Soon the first notes of the scintillating Overture to *The Barber of Seville* resounded through the auditorium.

In the dark, Manfred leaned over to Imogen and whispered, "You're absolutely gorgeous, Imogen!"

"P—please, Mr. Andreotti," she said, reaching back to push his arm away from the back of her seat. "Please. You—you embarrass me!"

"I'm only telling the truth, Imogen" he said.

Imogen made no reply, but, very ill at ease in her mind and heart, tried to concentrate on the music and the action on stage. Manfred made no more advances, but kept glancing her way and smiling throughout the performance. Then, when the first act was over, he turned to her, and said, "How did you like it, Imogen?"

"I—I enjoyed it, Signor Andreotti," she said, though in fact in her agitation, her mind had been only half on the singing and the acting on stage.

"Great, but call me Manfred. Signor Andreotti's my papa, and Mr. Andreotti is too formal. I'm an easy going kind of guy."

"Oh, I—" she fumbled for words, not wanting to be on familiar terms with a criminal.

"That's a fabulous dress," he said, "and you look absolutely stunning in it."

"It—it's Susan's gift," Imogen replied. "She's my very best friend."

"And that's a lovely pearl necklace and earring set, Imogen," said Ana-Maria leaning over and speaking across Manfred. "A gift from someone special?"

"Oh—no. They were my mother's."

"And she gave leant them to you for the evening?"

"Oh—no. My mother and father were killed in an accident when I was only six months old."

"Oh, I'm so very sorry!" exclaimed Ana-Maria, and again Imogen thought she sounded genuine.

"Yeah," exclaimed Manfred Andreotti. "That's rough!"

"Yes," said Imogen sadly and looking down. "I wish I had known my parents."

"So who brought you up?" asked Ana-Maria.

"My uncle and aunt—my father's brother and his wife—and they've been very good to me. I could not have asked for better people to care for me."

"Though very strait-laced," said Susan.

"They have high standards," said Imogen, a bit reproachfully.

"Sorry Imogen," said Susan. "That was unkind, but still, you have to admit your uncle and aunt are rather reserved."

"Yes, I suppose so, but they do really care for me."

"Hey, that's good," said Andreotti. "I believe in family. It's good of your uncle and aunt to bring you up."

"Yes, it was—very good of them."

As they spoke, the conductor returned to the pit and raised his baton to begin the second act, and Imogen hoped that Andreotti would leave her alone, but his closeness to her and his obvious interest in her still made her feel uneasy, and again she found it difficult to concentrate on the opera.

At last, when the opera had ended and the singers had taken their final curtain call, Manfred asked his two guests, "Can we take you back to East Clintwood in our family jet?"

"Oh—uh—Thanks," said Susan, "but we're staying on a day or two, and I have my car."

Imogen was silent and looked down, but was inwardly glad they had reason not to accept Andreotti's invitation.

"Well, it's been so lovely to meet you both," said Ana-Maria, "and I do hope we'll meet again."

"I'll be leaving soon for London," said Susan.

"Oh, yes. I was forgetting," said Andreotti's sister. "I wish you all the very best in your career!"

"Yeah, that goes for me too," said Manfred.

"Thank you," said Susan.

"But how about you, Imogen?" said Manfred, turning toward her. "Will you be around East Clintwood?"

"Oh I hope so!" exclaimed Ana-Maria before Imogen could reply. "I'd really like to get to know you, Imogen. I'm hoping we might be friends."

Still looking down, she said, "I—I'll be around for a while. I—I want to go to graduate school eventually, but I have to earn some money first. I'll be quite busy over the summer with my job at the public library."

"Oh, but you'll be around East Clintwood for a while yet," said Ana-Maria. "Surely there will be time to see each other again. I do hope we will. Perhaps you'd have coffee with me some time?"

Imogen hardly knew how to reply. Though she thought Androtti's sister, despite her background, an attractive person and her friendliness quite genuine, she did not wish any kind of association with the Andreotti family, but before she could say anything, Manfred spoke.

"Yeah. You two should get together. I bet you've a lot in common. Ana-Maria's the artsy-craftsy type."

"You're so flattering, dear brother!" his sister replied with a mild, almost playful sarcasm. "You like those things yourself."

"Yeah, I do," said Manfred. "And mebbe I could take you out to dinner and to the opera again some time, Imogen?"

"Oh—th—that's kind of you, but—but I think not."

He looked at her hard.

"Yeah? Why not?" he almost demanded.

Imogen felt really frightened and blanched. "I—It—it's—I'd just rather not," she stammered.

Eyes narrowed, he stared at her in silence for some time as if trying to read her mind.

"Mebbe I can change your mind about that," he said. "I'm a very persistent guy and in the habit of getting what I want."

"Please, I—"

"Manfred," said Ana-Maria, "don't embarrass Imogen—and we must be going." Behind her, Imogen noticed, the body guards were becoming restless. "But please, do let us be in touch with you, Imogen," she said turning again to her. Then in Manfred's ear, she whispered, but Imogen overheard nevertheless, "Don't press her too hard, Manfred!"

Smiling and looking directly at Imogen, Manfred said, "A la *prossima volta, buona notte, Imogena!*—until the next time—" he said, smiling and almost possessively seizing her hand. Despite Imogen's attempt to withdraw it from his grasp, he planted a kiss on it, saying, "*Tu sei magnifica! Ancora, buona notte!*"

Though she understood Italian, Imogen was too dumbfounded by his compliment and his expression of an intent to see her again to respond and, completely speechless, stood staring at him for some seconds before uttering simply, "Oh—"

Manfred helped his sister into her cloak, donned his own, then turned to leave the box. Just before he stepped with Ana-Maria into the rotunda, he looked back at Imogen with a smile which, though not unfriendly, told Imogen that he would not refrain from pursuing her.

When they had gone, Imogen burst into tears and fell on Susan's shoulder saying, "Oh my God! Oh God, Susan! Oh God! What will I do?"

"Hey! It's all right. It's all right. It's probably all a big act and doesn't mean anything."

"Oh Susan, I wish I could believe that!"

"Oh, I'm sure it is," said Susan, though she sounded far from convinced. "Come on, Imogen. What you need is a good stiff drink. Let's go to the bar back at the hotel."

"No, Susan," said Imogen straightening up and wiping away her tears. "I don't want a drink. Let's just go back to our suite."

"Sure, Imogen, all right. Sorry the night turned out badly for you."

"It's not your fault, Susan, but now you see why why I don't like to look pretty. Something like this always happens when I do—but never anything this bad! I wish I could go home!"

"Okay, Kid, okay. We'll leave first thing in the morning."

Suddenly Imogen straightened up and looked Susan in the face. "No!" she said emphatically. "No. There are things you want to do in New York and I don't want to keep you from them, and I won't let this man get to me. I won't yield to him! I'll resist him with every fibre of my being! He won't have me! I won't be his! No, Susan, we'll stay."

CHAPTER TWO

Ever since she had found herself the object of unwanted sexual advances, first at high school and then at university, Imogen tried to disguise her beauty by dressing as unbecomingly as possible, to look, as Susan put it dowdy. And so, after her encounter with Andreotti, she began her first day of her summer job at the East Clintwood Public Library wearing her large round heavy—rimmed glasses—which Susan said made her look like an owl—and, in an effort to disguise her good figure and shapely legs and especially her full breasts, a very long and full skirt, an ample blouse, a bulky cardigan sweater and flat heeled shoes and tied her long dark hair into a tight bun.

—Surely, she thought, at the library I'll be free from Andreotti's attentions.

The day, spent in checking out books at the circulation desk, in fact, did pass uneventfully without any sign of Andreotti, and by the end of her shift Imogen felt some slight relief. Her relief, however, was short lived, for, as she began to descend the library's well-worn stone steps to the street to catch the bus to go home, a convoy of black cars, one of them a stretch limousine which the other cars appeared to be escorting, drew up to the curb. Dark suited men emerged from the front of the limousine to mount guard before opening the rear door. Knowing instinctively who would emerge through that door, Imogen turned and ran back up the steps toward the library entrance.

"Hey! Imogen!" a voice whose ownership she recognized only too well called after her.

She ignored the salutation and continued to run up the stairs. Behind her she heard the sound of pursuing footsteps and again the voice calling to her.

"Imogen! Wait! What's the hell's the big hurry?"

Still she did not turn back, but just as she reached the apparent safety of the library, a large group of school children who had been on a library tour came pouring through the exit, preventing her from reentering the building, and in that instant Manfred Andreotti caught up with her and grabbed her by the arm. The departing children turned to stare as he said, "Hey! Where you going in such a bloody hurry?"

Quaking with fear, but mustering up as much courage as she could, Imogen turned to face him.

"I have nothing to say to you, Mr. Andreotti."

"Yeah? But I want to say many things to you. Can I offer you a ride home?" Though his manner and words were polite enough, his manner of speech had a sinister undertone and he gripped her arm firmly.

Despite her fear, Imogen glared defiance at him as they stood staring at each other.

"No—thank you—Mr. Andreotti," she asserted as determinedly she tried to release herself from his tight grip. "I do not want to ride with you. I can manage quite well on the bus. Now let me go and stop bothering me."

"My car," he continued, still holding her tightly, "is more comfortable than the bus and will get you home quicker."

For several seconds he scrutinized her as though trying to read her mind and will, when, with a great effort, Imogen managed to disengage her arm from his grasp and caught the door handle to pull it open. Manfred as quickly caught hold of the door and tried to hold her back.

"Hey! Not so fast!"

"Let me go! I want nothing to do with you," protested Imogen, and, though fearful of what might ensue, to reinforce her determination, she kicked him sharply in the shin.

"Ow! Hey! Why you—! I oughta—!" he began, raising his fist.

"Hit me, Mr. Andreotti? Beat me up? That's how you get what you want, isn't it?" she said defiantly, though visibly trembling.

"No, I ain't gonna beat you up," he said, bending to rub his shin but still holding back the door to prevent her reentering the library. "Geez! All I want to do is talk to you. How come you gotta be so nasty?"

"I said I want you to leave me alone, and I mean it!"

At that same moment one of his body guards who had rushed up the stairs behind him made a move on Imogen.

"You want us to work her over, Boss?" he snarled.

"No, Al," said Andreotti restraining him. "That ain't the way." Then after a short pause during which he continued to stare at her intently, he said, "Okay, I'll leave you alone—for now. But don't worry. You'll come around. No woman's ever turned down Manfred Andreotti."

As he turned and made his way, limping slightly, down the steps to his limousine, Al said to him, "Feisty bitch, Boss. You shoulda let me—"

"No, Al. Messing her up ain't the way. I got more aces up my sleeve. She'll come round."

Trembling, Imogen entered the shelter of the library and watched through the glass door as Andreotti and the body guards reentered the limo and the cars drove away. Then she walked unsteadily to the reference room to sit down to try to control her agitation.

—What are the aces he has up his sleeve? she wondered as she sank back dejectedly into the chair. He's not going to leave me alone. What will I do?

When, somewhat later, she arrived home, her aunt, confined for the past year to a wheel chair after being hit by a car as she crossed the street, called out to her, "Come and see the lovely roses that came for you, Imogen."

"Roses?" she exclaimed. "Who would send me—" Then suddenly realizing that she knew who had sent them, she gasped, "Oh no!"

"I didn't read the card, of course," her aunt said as Imogen entered the living room. "I just had Tina put them in water in the vase. The card's there by the flowers." Then noticing her niece's agitation, her aunt said "Why are you so upset, dear, to receive such a lovely gift?"

"Because I think I know who sent them," said Imogen, stepping over to the mantel where the flowers had been placed, "and I don't want flowers from him."

Tina, the young woman from the social agency who stayed with her aunt when Imogen and her uncle had to be away from home, now entered the room, saying, "They certainly are beautiful. I've never seen such roses—and two dozen of them! I sure wish I had a fella who sent me flowers like that."

"I don't think you would roses from this 'fella,' Tina," said Imogen, opening and reading the card and finding what she had expected. "I certainly don't. They're from Manfred Andreotti, the crime boss! Oh! That man!" she blazed.

"How could he have found out where we live?" asked her aunt."

"Oh," replied Imogen, "he probably has spies for that sort of thing. He was at the library today and wanted to drive me home, but I made it plain I do not want his attentions. Now he sends flowers!"

Angrily she tore up the card.

"Oh dear!" exclaimed her aunt, for Imogen had told her aunt and uncle of her encounter with Andreotti at the opera in New York. "What are we to do?"

"I don't know, Aunt," said Imogen despondently. "I don't know." Then suddenly, she yanked the roses from the vase and dashed them to the floor. "Oh! Get rid of them! I don't want them!"

"I had such a hard time arranging them—and they're so lovely!" protested Tina.

"But the man who sent them is not!" said Imogen. "I'm sorry to destroy your work, Tina, but I don't want flowers from Manfred Andreotti!"

"There's many a woman in this town," said Tina wistfully, "who would give everything to receive flowers from Manfred Andreotti, Miss! They say he's real charming and spends lots of money on his women."

"Well, I want neither his charm nor his money, Tina. I hope you don't."

"I don't suppose he'd ever ask a girl like me anyway," said Tina, almost sadly.

Imogen for a moment glared darkly at the young woman; then stooping down to pick up the roses, she said, "Well, I'll take these out to the garbage. I wish I could get rid of him as easily. Ouch!"

"What happened, dear?" asked her aunt.

"Oh, one of the spines pricked me! I hope that's not an omen! Why is he so interested in me? I'm nobody. What does he see in me anyway? He knows I want nothing to do with him! I wish he'd leave me alone!"

Just as Imogen was about to take away the flowers, she saw through the living room window a black limousine draw up outside the house and body guards rush to open the rear door.

"Oh God!" she exclaimed. "He's followed me here!"

Her aunt turned in her wheel chair and Tina rushed to the window to look, but it was not Andreotti who emerged but his sister Ana-Maria, looking quite striking in a royal blue sleeveless dress with a deep V-neck and white collar, a broad red belt, white wide brimmed straw hat with a red band, and red four-inch high-heeled shoes and matching purse.

"My goodness! What an elegant woman!" exclaimed Tina. "Who is she? She must be very rich to wear clothes like that and drive around in a chauffeured limousine like that! Wish I could dress like that!"

"That's Andreotti's sister Ana-Maria," said Imogen. "Now what does she want? Is the whole family conspiring to get me to go out with him? Well, I'll still take these roses to the garbage!"

"You mustn't leave her standing outside, dear, no matter who she is," said her aunt.

"No—I suppose not," Imogen responded disconsolately. "I'll just throw the roses in the kitchen garbage can for now. But let me get the door, Tina."

Quickly Imogen ran to the kitchen, disposed of the flowers, and ran back to open the front door.

"Imogen!" said Ana-Maria. "I'm so glad I found you home!"

"Please Signora Ros—Signorina Andreotti, if you're here for your brother."

"My brother!" Ana-Maria said, a puzzled look on her face. "What makes you say that?"

"He—he hunted me down at the library today and sent me flowers."

"Oh! Did he ask you for a date?" she exclaimed, her eyes brightening. "I know he wants to. He really likes you, Imogen! He's done nothing but talk about you ever since we met you at the opera."

"Oh!" exclaimed Imogen in some consternation. "I—I didn't give him a chance to ask for a date, and I refused his offer to drive me home. I'm sorry, but I don't want to go out with your brother. So please—please—ask him to leave me alone."

"Don't judge him too harshly, Imogen. He's really quite nice," Ana-Maria replied, seemingly eager to defend her brother of whom she seemed quite genuinely fond. "He's a wonderful brother to me. I'd be so happy if he could be seeing a nice girl like you...."

"Oh...!" exclaimed Imogen, unable to find words to respond.

"But that's not why I'm here," Ana-Maria hastened to assure her. "I leave him to look after himself in such matters! I've so wanted to talk to you since we met at the opera, Imogen. May I come in?"

Imogen hesitated, not wanting to do anything that might encourage Andreotti, but she was too polite to refuse a request politely made, and Andreotti's sister seemed a sincere person.

"Oh—well—uh—" she stammered. "Y—yes. Please come in."

"Thank you," said Ana-Maria stepping across the threshold.

Imogen led her to the living room and introduced her to her aunt.

"I'm very pleased to meet Imogen's aunt," said Ana-Maria pleasantly, stooping to extend her hand. "Your niece is such a lovely young woman."

"Her—her uncle and I are very proud of her, M—Miss Andreotti," said Imogen's aunt, a little apprehensive about having a criminal's relative in her living room. "We've tried to do our best for her—and," she added emphatically, "we hope only the best for her."

"Oh, I'm sure you have and you do!"

"Uh—Please sit down, Miss Andreotti," Imogen's aunt invited her unexpected and not really wanted guest.

"Thank you," said Ana-Maria, seating herself on the couch and elegantly crossing her legs. Imogen seated herself across from her in the chair usually referred to as "the guest's chair".

"Imogen!" began Ana-Maria. "I do so want us to be friends!"

"Oh! I—" said Imogen, looking away.

"I know, I know. I suppose you can hardly approve of me—but I was not born into my particular family by choice. And I feel so alone sometimes. I have no friend who shares my interests—no one really cultivated and cultured like you."

"I—I don't know that I'm—"

"Oh you are! I don't get to meet and talk to educated people who love music. Besides, I think you're a very fine young woman, Imogen."

"We think she is too, her uncle and I," said her aunt, paying her niece an unwonted compliment. "But—but we didn't expect—Oh dear! I don't mean to sound unkind—"

"I know, I know," said Ana-Maria sadly. "You didn't bring her up to be friends with a—a—a Syndicate Princess—as I'm called." She paused, looked down at her lap. "It's a hell of a life being one, but I suppose," she continued almost mournfully, "I have to accept that I can't have friends like other people have—and a life like other people have. I'd very much like to open a fashion boutique, but...."

Imogen, noting the tears forming in Ana-Maria's eyes, recalled the sadness she had detected behind Ana-Maria's gaiety at the opera.

"I—I'm sorry, Ana-Maria," said Imogen, almost unaware that she had used the first name of this sister of the man whose atttentions she dreaded, "but I just can't—"

"I understand," said Ana-Maria, rising. "Well, I'm sorry to have intruded."

"It wasn't an intrusion," said Imogen, also rising, but not looking at her visitor. "It's not wrong to want friends. I'm sorry that—"

"It's all right. I guess I was a fool to think that you—"

Imogen was silent for a few moments before she again said, "I'm sorry."

"Yes," Ana-Maria said dryly, resignedly. "Well, good-bye then, Imogen—*arrivederci*."

She held out her hand, and Imogen, looking up with tears in her own eyes, for she did feel genuinely sorry for her visitor, took it briefly.

"Good-bye—Ana-Maria—*arrividerci*," she said.

She walked to the door with Manfred's sister and stood watching the young woman retreat down the walk. Just before she entered her waiting limousine, Ana-Maria turned and gave a sad wave of her gloved hand. Imogen waved back.

On her return to the living room, her aunt said, "You know, she seems a rather nice lady, despite what she is."

"Yes, she does," said Imogen. "And I think she probably is, but I don't want...."

"Oh, I didn't mean you should be her friend!" her aunt hurried to reassure her.

"Should be whose friend?" asked her uncle, a tall, strongly built, stern looking man, who had just come in through the back door. "Has that Andreotti fellow been trying to—"

"His sister was just here, Uncle," said Imogen.

"And such an elegant lady!" said Tina.

Ignoring Tina's comment, her uncle demanded, "And what did she want?"

"She wanted Imogen to be her friend, Arthur," said her aunt.

"Well, I should hope you turned her down!" her uncle asserted sharply to Imogen.

"I did, Uncle," his niece replied. "But I felt sorry for her, just the same."

"Sorry for her! Why?" he demanded.

"Well, I don't think her life's very happy."

"Hm." her uncle paused and stroked his chin. "No, I suppose life in that environment can't be the happiest for her," he said softening, for he was not an unkind or uncompassionate man despite his stern attitude and demeanor. "But," he said, a statement, not a question, "you did refuse."

"Yes, Uncle, I did."

"Well, that's good. But," he queried, "where did those roses in the garbage come from?"

"They're from Manfred Andreotti," said Imogen. "I don't want them, of course."

"I should think not!" he retorted sternly. "I hope he gets the message."

"So I do, Uncle," said Imogen, "but," she continued shaking of her head from side to side, "I'm not sure he will."

CHAPTER THREE

Indeed, Manfred Andreotti did not leave Imogen alone. The day after Ana-Maria's visit, flowers arrived again, and that evening he himself arrived at her aunt and uncle's door. Her uncle answered, and from the living room Imogen could hear the sharp exchange between them.

"Imogen does not want to see you, Mr. Andreotti," her Uncle asserted immediately on opening the door, "and does not appreciate the attention you are forcing on her."

"Hey! I ain't forcing my attention on her! All I'm doing is trying to make a date, and like any guy who likes a woman, I'm being persistent. What's so bad about that? You don't get nothing if you don't keep trying, and women like to play hard to get"

"My niece is not like that. When she says no she means no. She has told you in no uncertain terms she does not want to see you, Mr. Andreotti, so please leave her alone."

"I want to hear that from Imogen."

"Her aunt and I have raised her from a child, so I think I know her mind and can speak for her. She does not want to see you."

"Speaking of Imogen's aunt—your wife," said Manfred, his tone softening, "my sister says she's in a wheelchair like my papa. I'd like to help her get the best medical treatment."

"We've had the best advice available on that, Mr. Andreotti, and there's nothing can be done."

"Best advice in East Clintwood mebbe, but I can bring people in from New York or even London. Mebbe there is something can be done, and if there is, I'd be glad to pay for it."

"In other words bribery, Mr. Andreotti."

"Bribery! Geez, Mr. Edwards! I hate seeing my papa in a wheelchair, and in his case there really ain't nothing can be done for him. We had him looked at by the best specialists everywhere before we accepted that. But like I say, I hate seeing him like that, and so I hate seeing anybody like that. I'd like to help Imogen's aunt—your wife—if I can."

"But with Imogen as your reward."

"Hey! I want to date Imogen because I like her. But if I can help her aunt along the way, so much the better."

"Somehow, Mr. Andreotti, I can't believe your motives are disinterested. As I said before, Imogen does not want to see you, so please go away and leave her alone."

"Look," said Manfred, his tone becoming edgy, "I came here to talk to Imogen, not you, and I mean to."

Hearing that, Imogen herself came to the door.

"Please, Mr. Andreotti. Go away. What my uncle says is right. I do not want to see you.

He stared at her, as, struggling to control her fear and to hold back her tears, she stared defiantly back at him.

"Geez Imogen! All I'm asking is that you have dinner with me. What's wrong with that?"

"You want more than that, Mr. Andreotti."

"Okay, suppose I do. I'll give you lots in return. You'll have the best of everything. You'll be the best dressed, best treated woman in East Clintwood. You'll look and be treated like a princess."

"I don't want any of that, Mr. Andreotti, and I certainly don't want to be a syndicate princess, especially when it's all paid for with money extorted from honest people."

"Hey! I'm a business man."

"That's what Al Capone said, Mr. Andreotti," retorted Imogen's uncle.

"Capone was stupid and vulgar. Okay, so my methods are more direct, but don't tell me your businessmen don't use extortion."

"My friend Susan's father does not," said Imogen.

"Yeah, mebbe. But he's an exception."

"We earn our own bread, and don't interfere in other people's lives," said Mr. Edwards. "We're quite happy and quite content with our lot. We need nothing from you."

"My uncle's sentiments are mine, Mr. Andreotti," said Imogen. "Now will you please go and leave us alone!"

"Do you want to see your aunt walk again, Imogen? All that it would take is a date."

"There!" exclaimed Imogen's uncle. "You are trying to bribe us!"

"Call it what you want—but my offer still stands. I want to give Imogen the best life can offer, and I want to help her aunt walk. So why not do yourself and your aunt a favor, Imogen?"

"I—I appreciate your concern for my aunt, Mr. Andreotti," she said looking down, "but I can't accept the offer on your terms."

"That's right!" her aunt called from the living room. "I won't gain my health at the cost of my niece's freedom."

"Aw, don't make it sound so horrible, M'am," Manfred called back. "All I want her to be is my girl friend. I'll treat her real good. And I think you're all cutting off your noses to spite your faces."

"I don't want to be your girl friend, Mr. Andreotti," Imogen interjected. "I choose my own friends."

"So, do you got a boy friend?"

"No, I don't. I—"

She looked down.

"Aha! I hit a tender spot! You wish you did! So why—?"

"I don't want one at any price, Mr. Andreotti!" she said, looking up again. "Certainly not at yours. What kind of reputation would I have when you got through with me? So please leave me alone."

"Who says I ever want to be through with you?" Manfred said and fell silent for a moment before continuing. "Imogen, I've never met a woman like you. You got everything I ever wanted in a woman—beauty, brains, education, refinement—and you love music, like me. And nobody never stood up to me like you, and that makes me want you all the more. Okay, I'll leave you—for now. But I don't give up. I promise you, some day I'll find a way to win you over. You can count on it. And I'll say one thing for you, Mr. Edwards; you got guts, too, and I respect you for that. But remember, I can make things happen in this town, and I can make things not happen, too."

"Now you're threatening, Mr. Andreotti!" said Imogen's uncle. "I know your power and influence in the Clintwoods, but I for one do not intend to yield to it, and neither does my niece."

"Yeah, well think about this, Imogen. Whatever you think of me, my offer to help your aunt still stands. I don't like to see nobody confined to no wheelchair."

Then he turned and walked away to his waiting limousine.

"Uncle!" said Imogen, throwing her arms around his neck when Manfred was gone. "You were wonderful!"

Suddenly, the tension of the last few days being too much for her, she burst into tears, and in an unaccustomed gesture of affection, her uncle put his arms around her and patted her gently on the back.

"There, there, Imogen. There, there. Maybe we're not like real parents, your aunt and I, not like the parents you lost, but we've done the best we could for you, and we don't want anything to happen to you."

"You and Aunt have been wonderful to me, Uncle," Imogen sobbed. "Oh! I don't want to see him, but it would be wonderful if something could be done for Aunty."

"Imogen—!"

"Oh, don't worry, Uncle. I won't give in to him. But I can't help thinking about what he said. I would so like to see Aunt Ethel walk again."

"So would I, Imogen, but not at the price you'd have to pay."

"Nor I, Uncle. Not really."

CHAPTER FOUR

For several days after her confrontation with Manfred Andreotti at her home, Imogen received no more attention from him, and she began to feel that her determined resistance and her uncle's defiance had finally cooled his ardor. So on an evening some days after his visit, she felt it safe to visit her friends whom she had known since childhood, the Martinellis, owners of a small confectionery in the nearby district known as Little Italy. The childless Italian couple had been almost second parents to her. Whereas her uncle and aunt tended to be reserved and undemonstrative—though, Imogen knew, not unloving or uncaring—the Martinellis with their Mediterranean background were more outgoing and so provided an element of warmth to Imogen's life and personality which she might otherwise have missed.

"Papa Martinelli!" she called to the old man behind the counter as she burst into the little store.

"Gena!" he exclaimed. "Gena! Is-a that-a really you? Mama! Mama!" he called into the back of the store. "Coma quick. Our little Gena she'sa here!"

Almost on the instant a woman, considerably younger than her husband, plump but still quite attractive emerged from the back of the store.

"Gena! Imogena!" she cried running to Imogen and throwing her arms about her. "Isa so gooda see you!"

"It's good to see you, Mama Martinelli, and I'm so sorry I haven't been around sooner. So many things have happened since I got home.

Rehearsing for Susan Van Alstyne's recital, for one thing. And then she took me to New York for a few days—to the opera."

"Oh how nice-a! Susan, she nice-a girl. Notta stuck up lika lotsa richa girls."

"No she's not. She has been a wonderful friend, and I'll miss her after she leaves for Europe in a couple of months—but she has a wonderful career ahead of her. I just know it, and I'm happy for her."

"Si, si. She gotta beautiful voice," said Mr. Martinelli.

"Oh yes! And she's a true artist!"

"Ah, si, si. But how you lika Newa Yorka?" asked Mrs. Martinelli. "You enjoya da opera?"

"Oh—well—yes," Imogen replied without enthusiasm, remembering her meeting and ensuing troubles with Manfred Andreotti. "It was really wonderful," she continued, trying to convey what she would have felt had Manfred Andreotti not been there, "to see and hear opera live instead of just hearing it recorded or on the radio—or even seeing it on television."

"Isa wonderful," said Mr. Martinelli with a sigh. "In Milano when Mama she'sa young and I notta so old, I taka her many times to La Scala, but now, no chance to go."

"Not to be sorry, Papa," said his wife. "We gotta da happy memories. But Gena, now you back froma da university, and you coma see you olda friendsa!"

"How could I not come, Mama? I wish I could tell you how much you both mean to me."

"You say it by-a coma see us, Gena," said Mrs. Martinelli. "Others, they forgetta their olda friendsa, but Imogena she never forgetta. She always coma visit. But Gena, you such a pretty girl. We thinka university make you more sophisticata, dressa more attractive, but you not."

"Si, si," said Mr. Martinelli. "Mama righta. You shoulda weara da mini-skirtsa, da higha heels, getta da contact lensa, maka youself looka pretty. Why you not, Imogena?"

"Oh, Papa! Mama! I have contacts, but I hate putting them in. And if you knew what happens every time I try to look attractive—"

"Betcha Susan maka you looka nice for da opera," said Mr. Martinelli.

"Oh yes, she had me dressed up to the nines—unfortunately."

"Why unfortunata?" asked Mr. Martinelli.

"Oh—nothing, really," Imogen replied, regretting having given voice to her feelings. "I—I—uh—I don't like being stared at. But all the talks been about me. How are you? Is everything okay?"

"Si, si," said Mr. Martinelli, in a rather melancholy tone. "Everythinga okay."

"Is there something wrong?" asked Imogen, detecting the note of distress in the old man's tone.

"No, no. Nothing wronga."

But he did not sound convincing.

"Are you sure?" asked Imogen. "You seem upset."

"No, no," Mr. Martinelli protested with rather too much emphasis. "Notta upset."

"Just little problem," said Mrs. Martinelli, trying to sound reassuring.

"Can I do anything to help?" Imogen inquired, clearly worried for her friends.

"No, no. Everythingsa worka outa," Mrs. Martinelli replied.

"Si, si. Everythingsa be okay," said Mr. Martinelli.

"You're sure you're not in trouble?" asked Imogen, still concerned.

"We notta inna da trouble."

Just then, looking out the front window of the store, the Martinellis became visibly agitated.

"What is it?" asked Imogen, seeing their distress and turning in the direction of their eyes. Through the big plate glass window she saw three black automobiles, one of them a stretch limousine, draw up outside.

"Oh good Lord!" she gasped. "He's followed me here! How did he know?"

"Whatta you mean, Imogena?" asked Mr. Martinelli.

"It's Manfred Andreotti! He saw me at the opera in New York and has been trying to date me ever since. I thought maybe I'd dissuaded him. But he's traced me here. Can I never escape him!"

"Whatta! He after you too!" exclaimed Mr. Martinelli.

"You mean he's been troubling you!" cried Imogen. "I thought there was something! Oh Lord! Why would Andreotti want to bother you?"

"He wanta controlla everaboda, everathinga in dis-a town. *Picolla Italia* lasta place notta pay up."

"A shake down!" cried Imogen. "Oh God!"

"Gena, you go now," said Mrs. Martinelli.

"Si," said her husband. "You go outa backa way. He notta see you. And you notta go outa witha him. He bad man."

At that moment, two stocky men in dark suits and black fedoras entered the confectionery, the same two Imogen had seen at the opera and encountered at the library.

"Hey! Whatta ya know, Al?" said one. "It's the little lady from the opera and the lib'ry that the Boss takes such a shine to."

"Geez, Joe!" said his partner as they approached the counter. "How d'ya like that? The Boss'll wanta know about this."

As Imogen opened her mouth to speak, Mrs. Martinelli apprehensively and nervously addressed the two men.

"She just leaving. You notta bother her."

"Si," said Mr. Martinelli urgently, anxiously. "Gena notta involved. Is alla righta, Gena. You go-a home now."

"You seem in a great hurry to get rid of the little lady," said the one called Al, suspiciously.

"What do you want with my friends?" demanded Imogen, battling down her fear.

"That's between us and them, little lady," said Al, "and like they said, you ain't involved. Mebbe you better run on home—'cept like Joe says, mebbe the Boss'll wanta see you."

"I don't want to see him," protested Imogen, "but I won't leave! I won't stand by and let you hurt my friends!"

"Yeah? Whatta ya gonna do to stop us, little lady?" sneered Joe. "Call the cops? The cops work for the Boss. So you should mebbe step outside. Go talk to the Boss."

"No, no, Imogena!" Mrs. Martinelli protested. "You notta talka Mr. Andreotti. You go-a home."

"No!" protested Imogen. "I won't run out and let you be hurt!"

"We ain't here to hurt nobody, little lady. We just wanna do business with the Martinellis. If they co-operate, nobody gets hurt."

"The way Al Capone did business! You won't do that kind of business with my friends."

"Listen, little lady," said Joe, grabbing her by the arm, "you're in the way, and if you know what's good for you, you get out like we told you."

"I'm not a little lady—and let go of my arm!" cried Imogen, and before Joe knew what was happening, her knee hit him very hard in the groin.

"O—ow!" he cried, letting go of Imogen's arm and clutching himself. "Geez! You bitch!"

"Hey! yelled Al. "Whadda ya think yer—?"

But Imogen had already turned to him and drove the toe of her shoe into his groin.

"A—ah!" he screeched. "Damn you! I'll—"

Joe, still wincing and grimacing, straightened himself painfully, doubled his fist, and shook it in Imogen's face.

"Why you bloody little—!" he began, but a jar of pickles wielded by Mrs. Martinelli crashed down on his head before he could finish. "Ow! Hey!" he yelled, and turned menacingly toward his assailant. "So you want to play rough!" he said, reaching into his jacket for his weapon. "You ever been pistol-whipped?"

Al, also erect again though still showing signs of great discomfort advanced, though now rather more gingerly and with his pistol also drawn, on Imogen who, though still determined to resist Andreotti's henchmen, showed signs of real fright.

"Yeah," he snarled as he grabbed her by the arm. "Mebbe the little lady also needs the feistiness pistol-whipped outa her!"

"Let go of me!" she cried, struggling to escape Al's grip and, again kicking out, managing to land a glancing blow on his shin.

"You'll wish you never done that!" Al addressed Imogen and grasped his weapon by the barrel and raised it as though to strike her.

"Stop!" cried Mr. Martinelli in distress. "We paya da money! You leava Gena alone!"

Cringing before the impending blow, Imogen still managed to smash her heel down hard on Al's foot just as a commanding voice from the doorway shouted "Hey! Al! Joe! What the hell's going on here?"

Never had Imogen believed she would be glad, as she was at that moment, to hear the voice of Manfred Andreotti, for that's whose it was; but as she turned toward him, her face registered, not gratitude, but shock and horror, and he, on recognizing her, stared in open-mouthed amazement for several moments before speaking.

"Imogen! You? Wha—?"

"You notta touch her, Mr. Andreotti!" cried Mr. Martinelli. "You leava her alona. Alla she do is defenda herselfa."

"And from the looks of my boys, she did a pretty damn good job of it," said Andreotti. "Let her go, Al. And," he said turning to his men, "since you and Joe let a woman make monkeys outa you, I'd better take care of things in here myself. You wait outside."

"Uh—yeah, Boss. We was only—" stammered Al.

"Okay. Okay," said Andreotti. "Wait by the cars, and I'll join you later. Oh—and mebbe you better start wearing cans after this." Turning to Imogen, he said, "So how come I find you down here in Little Italy, Imogen?"

"It's really none of your business," she said, "but, if you must know, these are my friends, and I want you to leave them alone. You've no right to extort money from honest, hard-working people who have so little!"

He did not answer her question, but, through narrowed eyes, stared at her long and hard.

"Your friends, eh?" he said.

"Yes—my very good friends—and my uncle and aunt's friends—from when I was a child."

"So, they mean a lot to you," he said, meaningfully.

"Yes. They've been like a second mother and father to me—" Then suddenly she grasped the import of Andreotti's comments. "Oh!" she gasped.

"So what would you do for them, Imogen?" he said, looking deep into her eyes. "Maybe we can help them and help each other. I think you know what I mean."

"Oh God!" cried Imogen. "No!" She stared at him in silence, her mind racing.

"Well, it's either that or—"

"Yes—I know what you mean and what you intend," she broke in, and then speaking hesitantly and quietly, she continued, "It—it's not what I want, but if—if I do—what you want—will you—will you promise to leave my friends alone?"

"Gena!" cried Mrs. Martinelli. "What you do?"

"Nothing that'll be bad for her," said Andreotti turning toward the older woman and smiling triumphantly, "an' everything that'll be good."

"I don't know about that," said Imogen, looking Andreotti straight in the eyes, "but," she said turning to her friends, "don't be upset, Mama and Papa Martinelli. It's—it's all right." Then she turned back to Manfred. "Y—yes, Mr. Andreotti, I—I'll be your—your girl friend—provided you—"

Triumphantly elated, Andreotti responded almost gleefully, "You got my word on it, Imogen! Geez! Geez! This is the happiest day of my life! And Imogen—you won't regret this!"

"Gena! No!" cried Mrs. Martinelli. "You notta do this." Then turning to Andreotti she pleaded, "You leava Gena alona, Mr. Andreotti. We pay whatta you wanta."

"Si, si!" seconded Mr. Martinelli. "We pay! We pay! You leava Gena alona!"

"No, Mama and Papa Martinelli," said Imogen. "I want to do this for you. I won't let you be used by this man. Rather than that, I'll be his—his mis—his mistress." Then turning to Manfred, she said, "I've given you my word, Mr. Andreotti, and I'll keep it—provided you keep yours. But Mr. Andreotti, I want your solemn promise—"

"Hey!" exclaimed Andreotti. "How many times do I gotta tell you? I gave my word, and I'm a man of my word."

"I've no other choice but to accept it, Mr. Andreotti, but if I ever find that you've gone back on it—"

"Imogen," he said, taking her by the shoulders and looking deep into her eyes, "when I give my word, I keep it. I won't go back on it."

For some moments Imogen returned his gaze, and to her own great surprise, she responded, "Somehow, Mr. Andreotti, I believe you. But," she hurried to add, "there's one condition."

"Yeah?" he said, his eyes narrowing. "What's that?"

"That everyone in Little Italy is included in the deal—that you leave all of them alone. They are all my friends."

For several moments he stared at her in utter astonishment, his brow wrinkled in consternation as though trying to reach some quick resolution of the conundrum with which Imogen had confronted him.

"You drive a hard bargain, Imogen."

"In exchange for what I'm giving you, Mr. Andreotti, I don't think the price is too high."

He continued to stare at her for some moments, seemingly still uncertain how to respond. Then suddenly he broke into a smile of seemingly unbounded joy. "Okay," he said. "Okay. I can handle that. It's a deal! But hey!" he added. "We're gonna be friends! Call me Manfred!"

"I—I'll try to," she said limply, all her stamina drained away by the trial of wills she had just undergone.

"Imogena!" cried Mrs. Martinelli. "You notta do dissa for us."

"Yes, Mama Martinelli," responded Imogen, sadly but resolutely, "I will do this. Because of all you've meant to me, I can't do less."

"Hey folks!" said Manfred. "Nothin' bad ain't gonna happen to Imogen by being my girl. In fact, she's gonna have nothing but the best. She's gonna be treated like a princess, and next time she comes back to see you, she's gonna look like one!"

"As I said once before, Mr. Andreotti, I've never wanted to be a princess, and certainly not a syndicate princess," said Imogen ruefully, "but from now on I guess my role is to enhance your image—to make you look good."

"Hey, Imogen! You *are* a princess! All I'm gonna do is make you look like what you are."

"I'm hardly from your stratum of society."

"Geez! Who gives a shit about that!"

"Well, if, as it seems, you don't, Mr. Andreotti—and I can't do anything about it—I guess I'm yours to do with as you please."

"Hey! I wanna see you look good—like you looked at the opera! Better, even! Like you should look! And hey, like I said, call me Manfred."

"Gena! Gena!" cried Mrs. Martinelli. "Thissa notta right."

"No!" protested her husband. "Is notta right whatta you do to our younga friend, Mr. Andreotti, itsa notta right at alla."

"Geez, folks! Don't you worry about your friend! I'm not doing nothing bad to her, just giving her a life of glamour and wealth and fun—the life she deserves. But hey, Imogen? You got a nice dress or something you can put on and some high heels—and contact lenses?"

"I—I don't have a very extensive wardrobe, Mr. Andre—M—Manfred," she responded apprehensively. "Wh—why do you ask?"

"Because we're going out for coffee, and I want you to look nice and not like an old fashioned school marm."

"We—we're going for coffee—to—tonight—already?"

"Sure. Why not? You're my girl friend, so I'm taking you out for our first date. No point wasting time."

After a pause, Imogen replied, "If that's what you want, Mr. Andreotti, I guess I've no choice—and I'll try to make myself look reasonably attractive, though not, I'm afraid, quite the trophy girl friend you want. But first, give me just a few minutes to say good-bye to Mama and Papa Martinelli."

"Hey, sure. No problem."

Imogen turned to the Martinellis and embraced them as they stood weeping in each other's arms.

"Oh Gena! Gena!" cried Mrs. Martinelli. "This-a da saddest daya oura lifa."

"Si, si," said her husband. "Is-a terrible day. Itsa terrible whatta happena you."

"Try not to be sad, Mama and Papa," she said. "I'm a big girl and know how to take care of myself. I'll be all right." Turning to look at Manfred she said, "You saw how I handled myself with your men, Mr. Andreotti. Just remember, mistresses have been known to be very vengeful and to kill their lovers in their beds."

Taken aback by this defiant warning, Manfred stood for a moment staring at her wide-eyed and open-mouthed. But he quickly recovered his cocksure composure and said, "Hey! hey! You got the wrong idea about me, Imogen. I won't do nothing that'll make you want to do that. An' you're not my mistress, you're my girl friend, an' you're gonna enjoy being my girl friend—you'll see! And, folks," he said to the Martinellis, "when I bring Imogen back to see you, you'll see that this is the best thing that ever happened to her."

"We notta believa that, Mr. Andreotti," said Mrs. Martinelli.

"Hey folks! You're Italian, I'm Italian. Would an Italian lie to his fellow Italians?"

"We think you lie-a lotsa people, Mr. Andreotti," said Mr. Martinelli.

"Okay, okay. So you don't believe me now, but I'm soon gonna prove you wrong. But come on Imogen, time for our first date."

Again Imogen embraced her friends, this time each separately.

"Please don't worry about me," she said, though her eyes filled with tears. "I'll hold him to his word, and I will be back to see you." She kissed them each on the cheek and then turned to Manfred. "All right, Mr. Andreotti, I am yours to command. Let us be on our way." Then she turned back to her friends who once again held each other while the tears streamed from their eyes. "*Arrivederci,* Mama and Papa. I'll be all right, and I won't forget you."

Smiling triumphantly, Manfred extended his arm, and, after a moment's hesitation, Imogen took it gingerly, turned briefly to wave to the Martinellis and to give them what she hoped was a reassuring smile, and walked on Manfred Andreotti's arm out of the confectionery and into the night. Was that, she wondered, significant of the future on which she was embarking?

CHAPTER FIVE

Al and Joe stared in astonishment as their Boss emerged from the Martinellis' confectionery with Imogen on his arm. Imogen looked over at the two henchmen, lowered her gaze momentarily, looked up again and on a sudden impulse withdrew her arm from Manfred's and stepped over to them.

"Al—Joe—" she said. "I—I've agreed to be your boss's girl friend so—"

"Wha—?" exclaimed Al. "You—!"

"Geez!" gasped Joe. "I'll be damned!"

"I know, after—after—what happened back there, it's probably hard for you to believe, but—but I—I have, so—Al and Joe, we—we'll be seeing a lot of one another, and—I—I hope that—that what happened between us, that you'll—that, in spite of everything, we can be friends."

"Uh—geez, Miss!" said Joe. "You really got guts an' none o' the Boss's women never said they wanted to be friends before! Geez!"

"Geez! no, Miss!" exclaimed Al. "Geez! You sure ain't like his usual floozies—uh—I mean, you ain't no floozie Geez!"

"Yeah, like, holy shit—uh—pardon me, Miss—but hell!—I mean— We just ain't used to this, Miss. Geez, Boss!" Joe said, looking at Manfred, "You picked a real lady this time!"

"Yeah!" said Manfred. "Now mebbe you know why I worked so hard to win her over. She is a lady, so I want you to treat her real special."

"Geez! That won't be no trouble!" said Al. "Like, yeah, Miss. I mean, like, what you did in there, it was, like, self-defence. I mean, like we'd a' done the same, like—so yeah—sure—we can be friends."

"Yeah," said Joe. "Like Al says, if it'd 'a been me, I'da probably done just like what you done. So yeah, Miss, glad to be friends with ya. Geez!"

"You guys just don't want to get kicked again where it hurts most," said Manfred, half-humorously.

"I don't think it's only that, Manfred," said Imogen. Then, smiling shyly at them and holding out her hand to them, she said, "You really do want to be friends, don't you, Al and Joe? I think we can be."

"Yeah, Miss, yeah," said Al, after a moment's hesitation taking her hand. "Like Joe said, glad to."

"Yeah," said Joe, taking her hand after Al had released it. "Yeah."

"I'm glad," said Imogen, smiling at them again.

"All we need now is the violins," said Manfred sarcastically. "And I don't want to stand here all night neither. So let's be on our way. Take us to Imogen's uncle's house, Al. You know the way." Then after handing Imogen into the passenger compartment of the limousine, he asked as he slid onto the richly upholstered seat beside her, "So how about you and me? Can we be friends?"

"Oh—!" exclaimed Imogen, taken aback by the question and uncertain how to answer. "I—I—" she began. "W—well—since we've been brought together willy-nilly, Mr. Andre—Manfred—I—I'll try to be friendly—but—but please don't expect me to find it easy."

"So why is it so easy to be friends with the boys and so hard with me?" he asked.

"I—I don't have to s—sl—sleep with Al and Joe."

"Huh? Yeah—well, there ain't nothin' wrong with sleeping with your boy friend."

"I would have preferred it to happen by mutual consent, M—Manfred. I know it's what you want—and I will—but—but I—I hope it won't be tonight. I—I'm not ready—"

"How do you mean not ready?"

"I—I need some time to—to prepare myself, Manfred," she said. "I—I've not had any experience."

He stared at her in astonishment.

"Holy Shit! You ain't a virgin!"

"Yes, Manfred," she said almost inaudibly. "Strange as it may seem in this day and age—I am."

"Geez! Geez! Well I'll be—Geez!" Then suddenly Imogen began to cry, and Manfred demanded, "Hey! Geez! What the hell's the matter?"

"It—it's nothing," she sobbed. "Just that I—I suppose you'll think me a—a square—or whatever the current slang is for people like me—"

"I donno—but geez! Nobody your age—it's the last thing I ever expected! I didn't think nobody over thirteen was a virgin nowadays. Geez!"

"I know, Manfred, I know. I—I was brought up an Anglo-Catholic, and—and I was saving myself for—for—"

"Your husband? Geez! That idea went out with bloomers. And what the hell's an Anglo-Catholic?"

"A high church Episcopalian, or Anglican—"

"Huh? You got me there. Anyway, I don't want to talk about religion. I'm a straight Catholic—so there ain't nothing to discuss anyway. But geez! A virgin!"

"M—Manfred, just agreeing to be your girl friend is all I can handle emotionally right now—so—for tonight—please!"

Manfred screwed up his face and looked at her through half—closed eyes.

"Okay," he said after a moment or two. "Okay—but just for tonight."

"Yes—Just for tonight," she agreed without enthusiasm. "Just for tonight. I—I promise. Afterwards..."

Tears in her eyes, she left the sentence unfinished.

"Well, I hope at least you'll let me put my arm around you."

"A—all right..."

As he moved close to her and put his arm across her shoulder and drew her to him, she shuddered as she was being enclosed in his arms, having a terrible premonition that she was being enclosed in his world, a world totally alien to hers, and from which she might never escape.

"What's the matter?" he asked "You're trembling."

"I—I don't know—I'm frightened, M—Manfred."

"Frightened!" he exclaimed. "Frightened! Hey! What's to be frightened about!"

"The future, Manfred."

"The future! Geez, Imogen! We're going to have a great future—you'll see. Nothing bad's gonna happen to you and everything good!"

"I—I'm sorry, Manfred," she said, again bursting into tears. "Th—this is all so unexpected and—and alien to me, I—"

"Hey! Hey! Imogen," he said. "The way I feel about you, I wouldn't do nothin' to hurt you or let anything bad happen to you!"

At just that moment Al's voice through the intercom announced their arrival at Imogen's uncle and aunt's home. The limousine came to a stop and Joe hurried around to open the door to let them out.

"Th—thank you, M—Manfred," she said as he handed her out of the limousine. "And thank you, Joe."

"Uh—yeah. Geez! You're welcome, Miss!" said Joe, still unused to being addressed politely.

"You're gonna have the boys eating outa your hand before long," said Manfred. "You'll spoil them."

"Good manners are never out of place, Manfred. You gave me your hand to help me out of the car just now—so you must put some value on them."

"Oh—yeah—well, my Mama kind of drilled it into me always to use good manners with a lady. She's one herself. But come on, I'll take you in."

"I—I think I should do this alone, Manfred. Uncle and Aunt won't be very happy that—that—with what has happened."

"Yeah, well I could sort of reassure them."

"I—I'm not sure they'd find you reassuring, Manfred. I—I'm sorry."

"Geez! What's so horrible about a guy and a girl going out together?"

"You're not just any guy, Manfred—not the sort they'd hoped I'd meet. They'll find it hard to accept that—that—"

"That you're going out with a crook, as they probably think of me."

"I didn't want to say that, Manfred—but, yes, that's what they do think. So—so I think I'd better do this by myself."

"Okay, okay. But at least I can walk you to the door."

"I guess that will be all right—"

As they reached the porch steps, Imogen's uncle emerged from the house.

"What's going on here?" he shouted. "What are you doing with my niece, Andreotti? I told you to leave her alone."

"Imogen's not a girl I can leave alone," said Manfred, also advancing. "She's got under my skin. But hey! I'm just taking your niece out for coffee, Mr. Edwards. Nothing to get upset about.""

"What! Imogen!" he uncle exploded. "You didn't agree to have coffee with this man! Don't tell me . . . !"

"Please, Uncle, let's go inside, and I'll explain everything," said Imogen.

He stared angrily at Manfred and then uncertainly at his niece.

"This better be good," he said.

"It ain't nothing bad," said Manfred.

"That I can't believe—not about anything you have to do with, Andreotti."

Before Manfred could respond, Imogen intervened: "Uncle—please. Let's go in." Then turning to Manfred, she said, "I—I'll be back as quickly as I can."

"Yeah," he replied, "don't be too long."

As soon as they were inside the house and the door closed, Imogen burst into tears and fell onto her uncle's shoulder. "Oh Uncle!" she sobbed. "He's won!"

"Imogen!" he replied. "How—? I thought we'd discouraged him."

"So did I, Uncle," she sobbed, "but I guess we were naive to think we could. But let's go into the living room so I can tell both you and Aunty together."

In the living room, where she seated herself beside her aunt on the sofa and took her hand, Imogen gave as clear and concise an account as she could of the events at the Martinellis', but without mentioning her scuffle with Al and Joe.

When she had finished, her uncle said, "Imagine that crook taking advantage of your decency and good nature like that!"

"I—I just didn't know what to do, Uncle. I couldn't let him take advantage of the Martinellis like that."

"Surely there's something we can do, Arthur," said her aunt, distress written all over her face. "Couldn't you talk to your friend Lieutenant Wolinski?"

"Please don't cause trouble, Uncle! I'm in enough as it is!"

"Don't know that it would do any good anyway. He's about the only honest cop on the force. Everybody knows Andreotti has the chief and the rest of the force in his pay. Whenever Wolinski gets anything on the criminal element in this town—which is basically Andreotti—the chief always squelches it. But I'm very upset by this whole business with you and Andreotti, Imogen—and very angry."

"I'm not happy about it, Uncle—but I've got to go along with it. As you say, he holds the power in this town."

Her aunt sighed. "It's just all so wrong, Imogen, that a man like him should have that power."

"But he has, Aunty. Susan told me even her dad—and we all know what a fine, decent man he is—has to come to terms with him."

"There's so much evil in the world!" sighed her aunt, dabbing her eyes with her handkerchief. "But oh! Why has this all happened to you of all people, dear?"

"I don't know Aunty. It seems I'm jinxed. I always attract the wrong men—but never men like Andreotti. Why a criminal found me so desirable and pursued me so, I can't understand."

"Yes," said her uncle, rising and pacing back and forth the length of the room, "with so many women of easy morals, you'd think he could leave a decent girl like Imogen alone."

"It's all so horrible," said her aunt.

"It is, Aunty, but I don't know what I can do about it—and he'll be getting impatient, so," she said rising from the sofa, "I'd better get ready."

"Get ready!" exploded her uncle. "What's wrong with the way you look now?"

"I'm to be his trophy girl friend to enhance his image, Uncle. I have to look glamorous. I don't have a glamorous wardrobe—though in time he'll probably provide me with one. Until then, I'll have do the best I can."

"I just don't know what's going to happen to you, dear," sighed her aunt, again dabbing away her tears.

"I know exactly what's going to happen to me," said Imogen as she started toward her bedroom. "It happened to most of my friends years ago, so I guess now it's my turn. I'm long overdue."

In her bedroom, Imogen seated herself on the bench before her dresser and buried her face in her hands.

—Yes Aunty, why did this have to happen to me? And what will happen to me? Yes, Uncle, of all the women in East Clintwood why did he have to pick on Imogen Edwards? Why? Why? Why? But I suppose if I could answer that, I'd have solved the riddle of existence, and I don't suppose it would change anything even if I could answer it. So I suppose I'd better make myself look pretty—as pretty as I can.

She rose and walked to her closet and examined its contents.

—What on earth have I got that will please him? Not that I want to—

She took a white blouse from its hanger and a grey suit.

—These are the best I have right now. He'll probably think them too prim or prudish or prissy or something. He probably likes his women half-naked. Well, not tonight, Mr. Andreotti!

She stripped down to her slip and took up the blouse.

—And he'd probably prefer me bra-less and slip-less—to coin a new word—but again, not tonight, Mr. Andreotti! Except this bra is a size too small and hurts. Well, bra-less but not slip-less.

Quickly she donned the blouse and her suit.

—Wear high heels, he said—commanded. Again, she said looking in her closet, not much to choose from. The gold one's Susan got me to go with the gown for the opera would be out of place, so I guess that leaves the red four-inch heels and the red purse she persuaded me to buy to attend the matinee performance of Arthur Miller's *After the Fall*. She said I needed more color in my wardrobe and they'd go well with my grey suit. Actually, I suppose they are rather nice, but... Hm.

She slipped her feet into the shoes and seated herself again at the dresser.

—And now, she thought, for these wretched contact lenses! Putting them in always makes me nervous!

She laid aside her glasses, took a deep breath and, after a couple of failed attempts, got the lenses into her eyes and wiped the resultant tears away with a tissue.

—I suppose he'll expect a bit of make up. Hope I can remember all the tips Susan gave me about applying lip gloss.

Make up applied, she unfastened the ribbon which had tied her hair back in a pony tail and combed out her long dark tresses. As she did so, her eye fell on the framed wedding picture of her parents which had sat on the dresser since she was a little girl. She picked it up and gazed at it.

—You died so young Mother and Father! I never knew you. You were both very good looking, and Mother, I never really noticed before, but you had very full breasts like mine. I almost wish you had not passed on your genes for good looks to me. I'm sure you would never have wished your daughter to become a gangster's mistress because of them. So, Mommy and Daddy, if you can hear me, pray for the daughter you hardly got to know and who never knew you. Pray for your little girl.

She sighed and then rose resolutely from before the dresser.

—Well, she thought as she picked up her red purse, I guess this is it. It's time meet your destiny, Imogen. Oh God! I have a sinking feeling that my life can never be the same again.

Just as she returned to the living room, there came a loud banging at the outside door and Manfred's voice shouting, "Hey! Imogen! What's taking so long? I wanna take you for coffee tonight, not next week!"

"I'll go," said Imogen to her uncle who had started, angrily, to rise, and hurried to the front door. "Manfred," she said on opening the door to him, "you don't have to break the door down, and you're disturbing the whole neighborhood. I told you it would take time to explain everything to Uncle and Aunt. But—but," she said hesitantly, "please come in for a just minute. At least you won't find us so ill-mannered as to make you stand on the porch."

He stepped across the threshold and surveyed her critically.

"Is that the nicest thing you got to wear?"

"It's the best I've got. I told you I don't have an extensive or glamorous wardrobe. I'm sorry you don't like the way I look."

"You look okay—though sorta like a lawyer or an accountant, mebbe. But hey! I like the red shoes. Red's my favorite color!"

—Oh dear! If I'd known that—

Entering the living room, Manfred said cheerily, "Hi there, Folks! I'm taking your niece out for coffee, and I promise I'll take real good care of her."

"We certainly hope so, Mr. Andreotti," said her uncle sternly. "We're not pleased about this."

"I can take care of myself, Uncle," interjected Imogen to prevent an argument.

"Yeah, she sure can!" said Manfred, no doubt thinking of the events at the Martinelli's confectionery. "But I mean to do more than just take good care of her, Mr. Edwards. I'm gonna treat her like royalty. She'll be the envy of everyone in both East and West Clintwood."

"I think she'll more likely be the scandal rather than the envy of East Clintwood," said her uncle.

"Hey! Geez!" protested Manfred. "What kinda guy do you think I am anyway! I treat my women good!"

"Let's not have an argument, Uncle and Manfred," said Imogen. "I never wanted to be a princess, Manfred, and I'm not sure I'm suited to the role or that I can live up to your expectations—but I guess my role from now on is to be a fashion plate to enhance your image."

"Hey!" said Manfred. "All I want is for the best looking woman in East Clintwood to dress like the best looking woman in East Clintwood!"

Imogen could not help blushing at the compliment, though she wished it had come from someone other than a gangster. To Manfred she said, "I prefer to dress simply."

"You'll change your mind when you see how glamorous you can look," he said.

"Well, we'll see. But right now I suppose we should be on our way. I—I hope we won't be too late getting home," she said, hoping that if she stated her wishes clearly and in the hearing of her uncle and aunt, Manfred would, at least for this evening, comply with them. "I have to work tomorrow."

"Yes, Mr. Andreotti," said her uncle. "Please at least get our niece home in good time."

"Don't worry, folks. You can trust me. Manfred Andreotti's a man of his word. But now, let's go, Imogen."

"I'll say just good-bye to Uncle and Aunt first."

"Oh, yeah, sure."

She leaned over to kiss her aunt, whispering, "Try not to worry, Aunty. I'm a big girl and can take care of myself."

"I certainly hope so, dear," her aunt whispered back tearfully.

Then she went to her uncle and threw her arms about his neck.

"And don't you worry, Uncle. Remember, I'm your niece, and you taught me how to take care of myself."

"Just be sure you do, Imogen. We don't want any harm to come to you."

"I'll be all right, Uncle," she said, stopping his mouth with a kiss. "Oh dear!" she said as she stepped back. "I've got lipstick on you! I guess I didn't blot my lips well enough. Here," she said, taking a kleenex from her purse, "I'll wipe it off. But I'm glad, Uncle, that you were the first man on whom I smeared lipstick!"

"Yes—well—Imogen—I'm flattered. I—"

"Uncle!" she exclaimed, seeing the tears form in his eyes. "I—I've never seen you cry before. Please don't. You'll make me cry too." She wiped her own eyes, and then her uncle's. "There." She forced a smile. "I'll be all right, Uncle. As I said, I'm your niece." Then turning to Manfred and taking his extended arm, she said, trying to sound nonchalant. "Signor Andreotti, I'm yours to command."

"Hey! That's supposed to be my line! But goodnight folks," Manfred said as they stepped outside. "And don't worry. I'll take good care of your niece."

"It will be hard not to worry, Mr. Andreotti," her aunt called after them. "She's like a daughter to us."

"Yes, we'll expect you to keep your word, Mr. Andreotti," said her uncle.

"Hey!" he called back. "I believe in family too! That's why I'll take good care of her."

CHAPTER SIX

For a few moments the quiet of the evening was disturbed only by the tak-tak-tak of Imogen's heels on the cement pathway as they walked toward the limousine. Then Manfred asked, "You're sure that suit is the nicest thing you got to wear, Imogen?"

"It's the best I have," she said. "I can't help it if it doesn't meet your approval."

"Yeah, well, like I said, you look okay but a bit too buttoned up, sort of strait-laced."

"Rather like a lawyer or an accountant, I suppose" she said, sarcastically.

"At least you could have left off the jacket, or worn the jacket without the blouse."

"If you want someone in skimpy attire, why don't you go down to Front Street and pick up a hooker?" she protested indignantly."They dress skimpily enough! Perhaps you'd rather I came nude."

"Yeah, that'd be all right. Bet you look great nude! But hookers I don't need. Not when I can have someone like you."

"Well! Thanks for the compliment!"

"Hey! Geez! I mean they're cheap. You ain't cheap. You're class. I'd just like you to look more glamorous. But let's not quarrel on our first date. We're out to have a great time together! Here's the car. Let's be on our way."

He gave directions to Joe who held the door for them to enter before he slid in beside her. When they were settled into the plush upholstery, he said "Now, relax! Enjoy yourself!"

"I'm not here voluntarily, remember, Manfred, and I hardly know you. I'm not sure I'll be able to relax and enjoy myself."

"Okay, okay, so I took advantage of you a bit, but you'll never regret this, Imogen, when you get to know me better." Then, making a real effort to be friendly and conciliatory, he said, "Your aunt and uncle are nice folks, and I really like it that they're fond of you and concerned about you. Like I say, family's important. My family are real important to me."

"And Uncle and Aunt are very important to me, and I don't like to see them upset. They took me when my parents were killed and raised me as their own child. They are my parents, for, as I told you, I never knew my real parents. So they're naturally upset by my entering a relationship with the crime boss of East Clintwood."

"Hey stop this crime boss business. I'm just like every other guy. I like to date attractive women."

"To collect scalps, Manfred? But since we're going to have a relationship, let's make it an honest one. You are the crime boss of East Clintwood."

"Yeah, yeah. Okay. Okay. But don't call me that all the time."

"I'll try not to, but I can't forget that's who you are."

"Well, do try. And maybe you will in time."

"I still don't understand why you want me to be your girl friend. I'm sure I'm not your usual type of woman."

"That's exactly why I want you—because you're not like my usual type of woman. I never met anyone like you."

He leaned over toward her.

"Wh—what are you doing?" she protested, drawing back.

"You're my girl friend, after all. Guys have a right to kiss their girl friends."

"A right! Since when? And I've been your girl friend for only about an hour, Manfred," she said rearing back form him. "Isn't it a bit soon? To me a kiss means something."

"Hey, come on! Where have you been! A kiss ain't nothing. Everybody kisses. And with lips as luscious as yours—"

But before he could act on his wish, there was a beeping sound. Manfred drew a cellular phone from his inside jacket pocket.

"Yeah?... Yeah... Okay... Good. Take care of it."

He replaced the phone, turned to Imogen and said, "Sorry. Business."

—Yes, she thought, shuddering. What kind of business? Take care of what? A drug shipment? A drug deal? A shakedown? Some one to be—rubbed out—as they say? Who is this man I'm sitting beside and to whom I've surrendered my life? And I suppose, whether I want to or not, I'll have to kiss him. Oh God!

"What's the matter?" he asked. "You're trembling again."

"Oh—n—nothing."

"Here," he said, putting his arm around her shoulders and drawing her to him. "Isn't this nice? There's nothing to worry about. I'm really not such a bad guy. Now how about that kiss?"

"A—all right," she said. Against her will, she let him draw her close to him and press his lips against hers.

"Come, on," he said. "It's a two way street. You're supposed to get involved too."

"I—I'm not used to it, Manfred."

"Hey! Come on now. Wet your lips a bit and pucker up."

"I—I..."

He brought his mouth down on hers again, and she managed to make a bit of a response.

"Well, that was a little better. Come on. Try again."

Just then, however, Al's voice over the intercom announced their arrival at their destination.

"Huh? Oh, yeah. Okay, Al."

"Wh—where are we, Manfred," said Imogen. "You never said where you were taking me."

"La Neapolitana," Manfred replied. "It's a great place."

"La Neapolitana!" exclaimed Imogen. "Isn't it very expensive?"

"You don't think I'd take you to a greasy spoon, would you?"

"No," she said after a moment's thought, "I suppose not. I'm just not used to going to places like La Neapolitana."

"You'll like it."

"I—I'm sure it's quite splendid."

"It is, and, hey! At least take off that jacket before we go in."

"Oh—a—all right," she said, slipping off her suit jacket, "since you don't want me to look like your attorney."

"Hey! No bra! But why the slip?"

"Oh! What kind of woman do you think I am! Do you want me to look like a floozy!"

"Okay, okay. Point made. But all kinds of women go bra-less today."

Manfred slid out of the limousine when Al opened the door, held out his hand to help her out and then offered her his arm to lead her to the restaurant.

"Thank you," she said, though rather mechanically, anger in her eyes.

"Hey! You're welcome!"

"You at least have the manners of a gentleman, Manfred," she said, her manner softening a bit, "and I appreciate that. Uncle always handed Aunty out of the car when she could still walk—and me too when I got older."

"Yeah, well, like I said, my Mama taught me how to behave with a lady. But let's go in."

—For all his manners, I'd prefer to be walking on the arm of just about anyone else, she thought. Still, good manners are something I never expected from him.

On their approach, the smiling doorman, with a slight formal bow, opened the restaurant door for them and said, "Mr. Andreotti! Good evening! How nice to see you again!"

"Hi Giovanni!" said Manfred. "Nice to see you."

"And good evening to you, too, Miss," he said to Imogen.

"Oh—G—good evening—Giovanni," said Imogen. *"Buena sera."*

She lowered her gaze as she passed through the doorway into the restaurant.

—Does everyone know him? she wondered. I suppose it will soon be all over town that Imogen Edwards is Manfred Andreotti's mistress. I wish, like Elizabethan ladies, I could be wearing a mask—or a veil like Arab women!

"Ah! Signor Andreotti!" said a voice. *"Benvenuto!"*

Imogen looked up to see a very jovial little man of a swarthy Italian complexion greeting them.

"Posso presentarie Signorina Imogen Edwards, Beniamino" said Manfred. *"La mia ragazza nuova."*

"Benvenuto Signorina!" said Beniamino, perusing Imogen with a critical and somewhat puzzled eye.

—I suppose, thought Imogen, he thinks me a strange choice for Manfred's 'ragazza'.

Aloud she said, *"Grazie, Signor Beniamino. Piacare."*

"Ah! *Signorina parla Italiana!"* said Beniamino in response to Imogen.

"Un po," she replied.

"Yeah!" said Manfred, proudly. "She's a real smart lady. She's been to university—a big change from the bimbos I usually ally get hooked up with, eh Benny?"

"*A l'universita! Madre di Dio!*"

"Yeah, she's got class."

"*E moltissima bellezza!*"

Imogen blushed at hearing she was exceptionally beautiful.

Manfred responded, "You can say that again, but let's speak English, okay. No need to show off."

"*Si*—I mean yes, Mr. Andreotti. You would like your usual table?"

"Of course. What do you expect?"

"Beniamino's only being polite, Manfred," Imogen whispered to him, "not showing off. I think he speaks Italian to you because he likes to share his heritage with another Italian."

"Huh? Yeah? Okay, mebbe, you're right." To the proprietor he said, "*Si Beniamino. Grazie.* Thanks."

"Right this way then, please, Signor Andreotti e Signorina Edwards."

As he led them down the aisle toward the far end of the restaurant, customers looked up from their coffee cups, and a buzz of conversation arose.

"Isn't that Manfred Andreotti?"

"Yeah, but Geez! Who's the dame with him?"

"Doesn't look like his usual type."

"Yeah, she's got more on, for one thing."

"She's good-looking, though, and sure well endowed up front."

"That's for sure!"

Imogen, greatly annoyed, blushed deeply.

—My "frontal endowment" again! And even though Manfred makes much of my education, he just likes to bask in its glow and glory in his conquest. It's really my breasts he likes!

The manager stopped at a table in the far corner of the restaurant, drew out the chair for Imogen, and said,"*Per piacere sedersi*, Signorina. Uh—Please be seated, Miss."

"*Grazie, Signor Beniamino*," she replied, forcing a smile.

"*Il menu.* The menu."

"*Grazie*," said Imogen again.

"Yeah. Thanks, Beniamino," said Manfred.

"I will send one of the girls along to take your orders. *Arrivederci, Signor, Signorina.*"

"*Ciao*," said Manfred.

As he turned to leave, the manager leaned over to Manfred and whispered, just loudly enough for Imogen to hear, "*Gentile fanciulla, Signor Andreotti.*"

"*Si, molto gentile*," replied Manfred. "A real lady." Then to Imogen he said, "You'll be a real hit around here, Imogen. None of my other women spoke Italian. Though you don't have to; everyone speaks English. Beniamino just likes to put on the dog."

"It is his native tongue, Manfred, and he knows you speak it. As I said, perhaps he only wishes to please you."

"Yeah, I suppose. He still likes to put on the dog."

"I really don't think that's it at all, Manfred."

"Do you always look on the good side of everything?"

"I try to, Manfred. I suppose you don't."

"No, because there ain't any good side. Everyone's out to get you, so you've got to get them first."

"Is that how you think of me? Am I out to get you? To me it seems the other way around. You chose me!"

He was suddenly silent, almost shocked.

"Huh?—No—you're different." He continued to stare at her. "I believe I can trust you," he said. Then he asked, "What would you like?"

"Oh—I—uh—I don't know," she said, looking down at the the menu. "Everything looks very appealing."

"*Buona sera, Signor Andreotti*!" said a female voice.

"Hi, Traci," said Manfred turning in the direction of the voice.

"Oh!" gasped Imogen as she looked up. Her mouth dropped open and her eyes widened on seeing the attractive young waitress nude to the waist.

"Oh! Oh my goodness! Manfred, you didn't tell me..."

"Huh? Oh. That the waitresses are topless? I forgot, I guess."

"You should have warned her, Mr. Andreotti," said Traci. "I take it you've never been here before, Miss. He comes here all the time, so he takes it for granted. You'll get used to it. Like the old joke says, 'You've seen two, you've seen 'em all.'"

"I'm not sure one should get used to it. But it was a bit of a sho—a surprise," said Imogen.

"This is our first date," said Manfred. "Traci, meet Imogen Edwards."

"H—how do you do, Traci," said Imogen.

"Hi, Imogen," she replied. "Sorry to shock you. But you know, you don't look like Mr. Andreotti's usual girl friend—if I may say so."

"So everyone says, and I'm sure I neither look nor am like his usual girl friends," said Imogen. "I still don't know why he wants me to be."

"I'd say it's probably because you're gorgeous, Imogen," said Traci.

"I been looking for someone with class and not a gold-digger like I usually get hooked up with, and Imogen has got class," said Manfred. "She's a university graduate."

"A university graduate! Boy, that sure is different from Mr. Andreotti's other girls! How did he find you!"

"You mean I ain't good enough to have a university graduate for my girl friend?" snarled Manfred. "That I don't go to places where university graduates go?"

"I—I didn't mean..." stammered Traci.

"Yeah, Okay. We met at the opera."

"Oh! The opera! That *is* class!"

"I was there only because a friend took me," said Imogen, "otherwise I couldn't have gone—though I like opera."

"Yeah. And she plays the piano, too. But maybe you'd like to take our orders? We came here for coffee and a little private talk."

"Oh—yes. What would you like, Miss—Imogen."

"Oh—well," said Imogen, still embarrassed by Traci's semi-nudity and by all the discussion of her beauty and "class", "I—I—think a *caffe latte*."

"That's different, too. Most of Manfred's girls like something with a bit of a kick in it—like Russian or Spanish."

"Hey!" said Manfred "Bring the lady what she wants. But *I'll* have Spanish."

"Yes sir, Mr. Andreotti. Coming right up. Nice meeting you, Imogen."

"N—nice to meet you, Traci," Imogen responded. Then after the girl had left, she demanded, "Manfred, why did you bring me here—to a topless restaurant?"

"Huh? Like she says, I always come here. Besides, what's so strange about it? Lots of places have topless waitresses."

"Yes," she said, "I suppose that's so. I don't get around very much, and I suppose this is the sort of place a gangst—some—one like you would frequent."

"Hey! What's that supposed to mean? We did meet at the opera, remember. I go to all sorts of places, and I was coming here before the girls went topless because they make good coffee. Besides, I own the place."

"You—you own it?"

"Hey, I own half the town, and what I don't own, I control. Nothing happens in this town without my say-so."

"No—I guess not. So were the topless waitresses your idea?"

"A lot of the customers wanted them, so, yeah, we figured they might be a good selling point. What's the matter with it anyway?"

"It's degrading, Manfred. It's degrading to women to have to expose themselves like that just to please men. We're not your playthings, you know."

"You are some sort of women's libber, aren't you?" said Manfred, glaring at her.

"I'm not militant, Manfred, but I believe in their basic ideas. Women *are* men's equals, you know."

"Not where I come from they ain't. Women do what they're told."

"And you expect of me to do what you tell me."

"Hey! Geez! I came here thinking you'd like it, hoping we'd enjoy ourselves—and all I get from you is a fight! Geez!"

"Maybe you're regretting choosing me for your girl friend."

"No, no, I ain't. You can't cut me off that way. But Geez! I wish you'd let up a bit—relax and enjoy yourself."

"It's hard to relax in circumstances not of one's own choosing, Manfred, but, I suppose, when all's said and done, I belong to you and have to be what you want."

"Damn it, Imogen! Stop talking like that! Can't you get it through your head that I want you for my girl because I like you? What's wrong with a guy liking a woman and wanting to date her? I've wanted you to be my girl ever since I saw you at the opera, and one way or another I was determined you would be my girl. There's women in this town would give their eye teeth to be my girl friend, so mebbe you should try to realize how lucky you are and be happy about it."

"Lucky! To be coerced to be the mistress of—of—How can you possibly expect me to be happy about this situation, Manfred? I'm doing this only to help my friends, remember, not because I want to. And after all, it's all happened just tonight, so I've hardly had time to get used to the situation—or to know you. So how can I possibly relax? All right. I'll try to be as pleasant as I can. But you've got to give me time."

"Okay! Okay! Geez!"

She lowered her gaze. "I'm sorry, Manfred," she said, and then her eyes filled with tears.

"Geez!" he said. "You don't have to cry about it. Geez!"

"I—I can't help it. Please try to understand. It's hard for me to accept what has happened. We're from totally different worlds, Manfred, and I find it hard to bridge the gap between them. I'll need time. Please give it to me—at least a little. That's all I ask."

For several moments he stared into her eyes.

"Yeah, yeah. Okay," he said. "Okay. I understand—I guess."

Just then Traci returned with their coffee.

"Here we are," she said. "Let's see. *Caffe latte* for you, Imogen, and Spanish for you, Signor Andreotti."

"Thank you, Traci," said Imogen. Managing a smile, she added, "And—and I'm sorry I was upset at first. I have to get used to this new world I've entered."

"Yeah, I suppose so. Lots of women around this town would give their right arms to be his girl friend, so you'll be envied."

"So I've been told," said Imogen with a wry smile and a glance at Manfred.

—It's my soul, she thought to herself, that I worry about though, not my right arm or my eye teeth.

Then, aloud she said to Traci, "You *are* very attractive, Traci."

"Hey! Thanks! It's not usually the women who say that. And to tell the truth, it took me a while to get used to going topless. But then, I said to myself, 'Hell, I figure I've got a pretty fair set of hooters, so, why not show them off?' Still, I hardly expected another woman to compliment me on them."

"I mean, Traci, that you are a very pretty woman, not just that you've nice breasts."

"Oh—gee. Thanks." Then, looking closely at Imogen, Traci said, "You know, under that blouse you've got a great pair of hooters yourself."

Imogen blushed, but managed a smile, "I guess I should take that as a compliment, Traci. But," she added, "I don't think I'll become a topless waitress."

"Lots of girls do it—or strip—to put themselves through college."

"I know, Traci. I feel sorry for them. Fortunately, I didn't have to."

"Yeah, it must be nice to have money."

"I don't have money, Traci. I won a scholarship. Otherwise, I could never have gone."

"Then it must be nice to have brains. Wish I did."

"We all have different gifts, Traci. Don't sell yourself short. Always think the best of yourself. You're probably a lot smarter than you think and have many talents."

"Yeah? Well, thanks. Enjoy your coffee."

Manfred had remained silent, staring at Imogen throughout her conversation with Traci. She looked back at him, took a sip of her coffee and in an effort to draw him out of his silence, said, "It is excellent coffee, Manfred."

"Yeah, glad you like it. Wish you liked me better."

She set down her cup and dropped her eyes. "I never said I didn't like you, Manfred."

"No, but you don't act like you do."

She looked up and took another sip of her coffee before she spoke.

"I don't mean to, Manfred, but, as I said, it's hard for me to get used to being the girl friend of—of—"

"A crook. Geez! Can't you get it through your head I'm just a guy."

"Perhaps, I'm too blunt. I'm sorry. But as I said before, if we are to have a relationship, and I suppose that's what we are to have, we should build it on honesty. And surely, Manfred, you have to confess that you're not the usual sort of 'guy' most women expect to date. But then, you said yourself you were looking for a different sort of woman, and guess in me you've found one."

He stared at her in silence for a few moments before he said, "You know, I kind of like the way you don't gush, but say what you think. It's kind of refreshing. You're a challenge."

"A challenge!" exclaimed Imogen, laughing for the first time that evening. "Well! Now that is really very remarkable. I guess you're also a challenge to me."

"Huh?" Again he stared at her. "Yeah, I suppose I am," he said. "But hey! It's nice to hear you laugh!" Then he too laughed. They looked at each other in silence. Then he exclaimed, "We'll get along just fine, Imogen!"

"Oh—well—as I said, Manfred, I'll try to get along well with you." They again stared searchingly in silence into each other's eyes. Then, again to make conversation, Imogen asked, "How is your Spanish coffee?"

"Good. You should try it next time."

"Perhaps. Why is it called Spanish?"

"Because it's tequila in it."

"Oh—I've never tasted tequila. In fact, I don't know very much about liquor at all."

"Is that so? You ain't a teetotaler, I hope."

"No, Manfred," she said, with a wry smile," I do take a drink now and then, but I'm not a connoisseur—nor am I a complete Goody Two Shoes."

"No, but you don't ever seem to have kicked over the traces."

"No, I guess not—perhaps because there have been no traces to kick over. Uncle and Aunt, though they are always concerned about me and gave me good advice and guidance, have never been restrictive. But," she said, again with her wry smile, "perhaps there is dark as well as light in all of us. Who knows what might lie hidden in the dark depths of my soul waiting to come out."

Looking at her through narrowed eyes, he said, "Are you afraid something dark might come out?"

She was silent for a moment before she said, "I don't know."

"Well here. Start kicking over the traces by sipping a bit of my Spanish coffee."

"All right, Manfred," she said, "if you'd like me to."

"Yeah, I would. Maybe you'll find you like it. Here."

He passed the glass across to her, and she took a sip.

"It is very tasty," she said.

"Shall I order one for you?"

"No, thank you—not tonight. The latte is fine. But perhaps another time. It *is* nice."

Again they fell silent. Manfred kept looking at her, making her feel rather embarrassed, so that she averted her eyes.

"What's the matter?" he asked.

"Nothing—it's just the way you look at me—as though you were trying to read me like a book."

"Mebbe I am. I'm trying to figure you out."

"Hamlet had something to say about that. I really don't think there's much to figure. I'm just simple Imogen Edwards—but—but—as I told you, I'm not your type."

"Okay, so like I said, you're a challenge. The minute I saw you, I knew you were someone special. I said to Ana-Maria, 'That girl's no ordinary woman. She's something special.' And Ana-Maria said, 'Yes. She's got distinction written all over her.' And I knew right then that I wanted you."

"You're sure it wasn't my hooters, as Traci calls them?" she asked, again smiling wryly. "You were certainly eying my cleavage that night at the opera."

"Well, your dress kind of drew attention to it. And let's face it, since you insist on honesty, you got great knockers!"

"Oh, now they're 'knockers'! Well, the dress was Susan's gift. I had to wear it. But I wish I could be appreciated for more than what I've got up front. I have a mind, Manfred, as well as breasts. I'll graduate *summa cum laude*. And I've a bit of musical talent. I play the piano well—well enough to accompany Susan, at least. Those are the things that I prize most about myself."

"Hey! That's what I mean! Your special! You got class, refinement, talent and taste. But geez! Don't be ashamed because you're well endowed!"

"I'm not ashamed of my breasts, Manfred, but they're only containers for my mammary glands, just a matter of genetic inheritance—biology. Why are they so special because they're bigger than most women's?"

"I don't know, but they are very nice, whatever you may think. But it's not just your knockers—"

"Breasts, Manfred," she protested.

"Okay, okay. Breasts. Geez! But you are gorgeous, and you're talented and smart. You got everything! I think mebbe I always been looking for someone like you."

She blushed as she said, "Well, thank you, Manfred. I guess I should feel flattered, but I think you've too high an opinion of me."

"Hey! Don't run yourself down! Like you told Traci, always think the best of yourself!"

"I guess I'm just not used to compliments om my appearance, Manfred," she said, looking down.

"Well, you better get used to them because you're gonna get lots of them—especially on your looks! Don't knock the fact that you're gorgeous!"

"I'll try not to, Manfred," she said, blushing.

"Good!" he said. Then noticing her empty cup, he asked, "Another latte?"

"Oh—no thanks. But it was very, very good. Thank you. I—We told Uncle and Aunt I'd be home early. So—so would you mind taking me back now, Manfred?"

"Huh? Oh, yeah. Okay but I'm not used to breaking up a date so early—"

"It's just our first one, Manfred, and hardly a real date."

"Yeah. Okay. Our first real one is on Friday. I'm taking you out for dinner and dancing."

"Do you always give orders to your girl friends, Manfred?" she asked. "But all right. I'm sure it will be quite splendid—but I'm not a very good dancer."

"I thought you were a musician."

"I play the piano with my hands, wrists and arms, not my feet and legs, Manfred. But if you give a good lead, I think I can follow well enough."

"Hey! No problem. I'm a good dancer. My mama made sure of that."

"She sounds like an extraordinary person, Manfred," said Imogen at Manfred's second reference to his mother's influence on him.

"She's an Italian dona—a lady. You'll meet her soon. She'll like you, I know. You'll meet her in about another week at Papa and Mama's anniversary. You're invited, of course."

"Oh dear! I'm just a girl from the working class, you know, Manfred, not from high society."

"You act like a lady. And you can look like one too. You'll knock everybody's eyes out! When do you get a day off?"

"Uh—the day after tomorrow. Why?"

"So we can fix you up with a nice dress for Friday and a formal for the anniversary. I'll meet you at Chez Madeleine's at noon."

"Chez Madeleine! That's very exclusive and very expensive!"

"Of course it is! Do you expect me to dress you in stuff off the rack at the Sally Ann thrift store, or something? My girl gets the best."

"I never expected—"

"Hey! Quit worrying, will you? Manfred Andreotti's women never look anything else except great, and Imogen Edwards is going to knock the spots off every other woman in East Clintwood. But okay, let's go for now. I said I'd get you home early, and I'm a man of my word."

"Like a good Boy Scout," she said as she rose from her seat.

"Boy Scout!" Manfred exploded. "Boy Scout! Geez! Well," he said, holding out his arm for her, "here—if you're not too proud to let a Boy Scout help you across the street."

"Why, thank you, Sonny" she said, adopting a croaking voice in imitation of an old woman.

"Hey! That's the spirit! You got a good sense of humor. Use it more. Treat life as joke!"

"I'll try—and I appreciate your keeping your promise to Aunt and Uncle."

"Like I said, I'm a man of my word."

Manfred tossed two twenty dollar bills onto the table as they left. Traci, who had been standing by, called out, "Oh Mr. Andreotti! Thank you! Thank you very much!"

"Hey, don't mention it, Traci," he called back. "You deserve it."

—Everyone makes a fuss over him! thought Imogen. Don't they know what he is? But perhaps it's because they do know what he is that they're so deferential. Maybe they're afraid of his power—as I am! Or is it that his money—which isn't his, which he extorts or obtains through selling drugs—buys him gratitude and appreciation. And now he's going to lavish his extravagance, which he calls generosity, on me. And I know what's expected of me in return! Strange though, I think perhaps he does really like me—but that doesn't make my situation any easier or better.

Once again lowering her gaze, she walked on Manfred's arm into the rotunda.

"*Buona notte, Signor Andreotti, e grazie,*" said Beniamino. "*E buona notte, Signorina.*"

"Oh—yes—*si. Buona notte, Beniamino,*" Imogen replied.

"*Per piacere tornare.*"

"Oh—*si, si. Grazie.*"

"Yeah, we'll be back lots, Benny," said Manfred.

He walked her to the limousine where Joe held the door for them to enter. As before, Imogen thanked him, and as before, Joe was embarrassed.

"You really are going to spoil my boys," said Manfred.

"Maybe they deserve a bit of appreciation, Manfred. I imagine they do a lot for you. But you said back there that I'm different—that you think you can trust me," said Imogen when they had seated themselves inside.

"Yeah, yeah, I do. I can just see it in you."

"Maybe there are others who are different and can be trusted too."

"I never met any. Besides, like Leo Durocher said, nice guys finish last."

"And you want to finish first."

"Sure. Everybody does. Don't you?"

"What does it mean to be first, Manfred?"

"Huh! What do you mean, 'What does it mean to be first?'? Everybody knows what it means. It means to be on top. It means not to have anyone else bossing you. Didn't you say you're going to graduate—what did you call it? Summit something?"

"*Summa cum laude*. It's Latin for 'with great distinction'. And I earned it, but I wasn't striving for those words on my diploma, Manfred. I wanted a good education, and so I studied hard. It's what I've learned that's important to me, not the honor."

"I bet you don't mind the honor!"

"No, but I wasn't seeking it."

"Yeah, well you got it. But, hey! I said I didn't want no fights. So don't, okay?"

"All right, Manfred. I don't mean to quarrel with you, but questions just come into my head, and I like to ask them. It's the kind of mind I have."

"Yeah, well sometimes what you don't know don't hurt you. And mebbe you could try to look on the good side of me."

"I thought you said nobody had a good side, Manfred. But you know," she said, somewhat to her own surprise, "sometimes you behave rather like a very nice person."

"Huh? Thanks a lump! But all these questions, all these comments, they get me all mixed up. I don't like being mixed up. I like things simple."

"I'm sorry, but I guess I'm kind of mixed up myself by all this, too."

"Well, don't be. Like I say, Just relax and enjoy everything."

She fell silent for a while before she said, "I'll do my best, Manfred."

"Good!" he said emphatically. Then, as he put his arm over her shoulder and drew her to him, she stiffened. "Hey! You make it hard for a guy close to you."

Almost inaudibly, she answered, "Closeness needs time to develop, Manfred."

"Time! Time! Time! You're always wanting time! Live for the moment, I say. And at this moment I want to kiss you. And this time don't be like a cold fish. This time see if you can be like a woman!" To her surprise, she felt hurt by his harsh disapprobation. She turned on him and slapped him fiercely across the face.

"Cold fish, am I!" she exclaimed, her face red with anger.

"What the...?" he exclaimed, putting his hand to his cheek. He stared at her, surprise and amazement as much as anger written on his face.

Amazed at her own temerity and fearful of his reaction, Imogen stared open-mouthed and wide eyed at Manfred. Then as his rage came to the fore, and he removed his hand from his cheek and raised it as though to strike her, plucking up her courage, her eyes flashing outward defiance, though her veins pulsed and her heart pounded in fear as she awaited the imminent blow, she shouted, "Go ahead! Go ahead, hit me! That's what you do, isn't it? That's how you get what you want—by bullying and intimidating, by battering and killing?"

He glowered at her through narrowed eyes.

"Why you little..!" But he did not finish his phrase and the blow did not fall.

"Bitch, Manfred? Is that it? Is that what I am?" she demanded.

He continued to stare at her, his furrowed brow and narrowed eyes seeming to reflect an internal conflict.

"You know," he said, speaking calmly and lowering his hand, his anger giving way to perplexity, "underneath that prim and proper outside, you're a real tiger."

"And tigers have claws!" said Imogen.

"I don't know why I let you get away with that!" he said. "I wouldn't let anyone else!"

"What would you do—beat them!"

"No—but I'd sure let them know they'd better not do it again."

They stared at each other in silence. Then Imogen said, "I suppose I am prim and proper and also a—a cold fish—but mostly it's from lack of experience—"

"Then mebbe it's time you got some experience. All I'm asking for is a kiss."

"J—just so long as that is all you're asking—tonight—Manfred. On—on Friday night, I promise, I—I'll give you what I know you want."

She let Manfred take her into his arms. He brought his mouth down hard on hers.

"Relax!" he whispered. "Let the woman in you come out."

He began to stroke her leg, and in spite of herself, she found herself yielding to him as his left hand moved under her skirt and his right to fondle her breasts, and then to unfasten the buttons of her blouse.

Then she reacted in shock at what she was feeling.

—Oh Lord! What's happening! I've got to break this off before...

"Manfred! Manfred!" she cried aloud and struggled to free herself. "Stop! You promised—! You said just a kiss!"

To her relief, the limousine drew to a stop and the voice over the intercom announced their arrival at her uncle and aunt's home.

"Damn!" said Manfred. "Just when things were beginning to get nice."

"You took advantage of me, Manfred!."

"Hey! Geez! What's a guy supposed to do when he's with a gogeous woman! It was only a bit of heavy petting. Surely you've... But, no I guess you haven't. Geez! You're from another era—and mebbe another planet!"

"Do you want another slap across the face!"

Grasping her by the shoulders, he stared at her, then threw his head back in laughter.

"Hey, tiger!" he said. "Hey!" Then in a quiet voice he said, "Imogen, somewhere in there between the cold fish and the hot-blooded tiger there's a real, warm-blooded woman who wants to get out. I could feel her struggling in there while we were kissing. So don't be afraid to let that woman out."

Perplexed, confused, frightened, she stared at him unspeaking.

"I—I'd like to go in now, Manfred," she said at last.

"Yeah. Okay. But don't forget your promise about Friday night."

"I—I won't—Manfred."

Al and Joe took up their stations and Al opened the door. Manfred helped her out of the car and she thanked both him and Al. Manfed walked her up the path to the house, the silence again broken only by the tack-tack of her heels on the cement. Manfred walked up the steps with her to the door.

"It's customary for the guy to kiss his girl good-night," he said.

"A—all right," she said, "as long as you..."

"Behave like a gentleman? I can if I have to," he said and took her into his arms.

He held her close and his lips against hers were warm, and again she felt the intensity of his passion hard to resist. Then he released her and said, "Some day, Imogen, you're gonna fall in love with me, and fall very hard."

"Manfred," she said, looking away, "you can't make a woman love you or buy her love."

"No, but I can win it," he said. "And I will. But for now, good night, Imogen—until Friday,"

"Y—yes," she stammered "G—good night—M—Manfred."

He turned to walk away down the path, but then turned back.

"Oh! Hey! Don't you forget to be at *Chez Madeleine* on your day off."

"Oh—n—n—no. I won't. I—I'll be there."

Again he was about to turn and walk to the limousine, but instead he turned back to her again.

"Ana-Maria's right. I don't talk too good, do I? I got bad grammar."

She stared at him a moment. "Strange you should bring that up, Manfred, but you—you have to be yourself."

"It ain't—it isn't that I wasn't taught better, I just never bothered to learn. But with a university graduate for a girl friend I should talk better."

"You don't have to on my account, Manfred."

"Yeah, I do. I wanna—want to talk better. It's got more class."

"I think speaking well is a skill to be acquired simply for itself, Manfred, and for good communication, not for class, as you call it."

"Okay—but it's still got class. I'm gonna—going to—work on it. But good night for now. See you at Chez Madeleine's on Thursday."

"Y—yes. G—good night."

She stood immobile watching him go.

—Because of me he wants to speak better! I suppose that's a compliment, but his grammar's not what I worry about!

She turned to enter the house.

—What I feel when he kisses me frightens me! It makes me feel things I've never felt before and it's exciting—and frightening. Oh Lord! Oh Lord! I've fallen into a dark and dangerous sea. Oh God, help me to swim—or at least to tread water!

CHAPTER SEVEN

Attired in a black strapless dress with a sequined bodice and very short skirt, black patterned hose, and black four-inch stiletto-heeled shoes, the long dark locks of her hair falling voluptuously to her bare shoulders, Imogen submitted herself to her friend Susan's perusal.

"You look great, Kid!" said Susan.

"I feel half naked," said Imogen.

"That's the whole point."

"Yes, I know. It's just the preparation for later on," she said, "when I'll be completely naked."

"At least, Kid, you've got your eyes wide open. You're not naive, but I'm still amazed that you've remained a virgin so long."

"Maybe it's because I'm not naive that I have—but I won't be a virgin much longer. I'm the last of a breed, I know, so look your last on the last virgin. It's not that I put any special store by virginity itself, but—well—to put it crudely, I didn't want to be laid if I wasn't loved—and I certainly didn't want to lose my virginity to a gangster!"

"The guy I lost mine to was a real creep, Kid. Worse things could happen."

"Oh, I suppose I could be drowned in a malmsy butt like the Duke of Clarence in *Richard the Third,* or, as is more likely to happen, end up in a pair of concrete shoes at the bottom of the Clintwood River."

"Don't be so melodramatic, Imogen. From all I can see, the guy really goes for you."

"That's what frightens me, Susan. He says he loves me—how on so casual an acquaintance I don't know—and that sooner or later I'll fall in love with him. So what have I got myself into? What kind of pressures will he put on me? How will it end? When will it all end? Will it ever end?"

"I don't know, Kid," said Susan, lowering her gaze away from her friend. "I don't know. I'm sorry all this has happened—and it's all because of me."

"Oh no, Susan," said Imogen, taking her friend in her arms. "Don't blame yourself. How could you have have known he'd be at the opera or that he'd be attracted to me?" Then, burying her head in Susan's shoulder as she suddenly felt the desperateness of her circumstances, she cried, "Oh God, Susan! You'll soon be gone! What will I do without you to turn to?"

"Hey, Kid!" said her friend, patting and stroking her back. "You're a lot stronger than you think you are. I wish I were as strong."

"You've always seemed the strong one to me, Susan."

"I'm just sophisticated and probably a bit cynical. That's not real strength. You're the really strong one, Imogen."

"But you've more *savoir faire* than I. I'm not naive, but I'm a neophyte in this sort of thing. I don't know how to handle myself. What do I do?"

"Just be yourself, Imogen. That will carry you through."

"I hope you're right Susan. I wish I could be as confident in myself as you are," she said, standing away from her friend, "but I guess I just have to face this ordeal as best I can."

"Maybe it won't be an ordeal. I've heard it said he's really a nice guy with his girl friends." She paused as though reflecting then she asked, "What if you do fall in love with him?"

"Oh Susan! Don't say that! It can never happen!"

"No, not likely," said Susan, and fell silent for a moment. Then, smiling to try to lighten the situation, she said, "Darn you! After all the work I put into making you look gorgeous, you've smeared your mascara. Here, let me fix it up." Then, as she reapplied makeup to Imogen's eyebrows and eyelashes, Susan said, "Oh Imogen—maybe I'm just trying to deal with my own guilt feelings—but somehow—I don't know how—but somehow, I know you'll come out of this on top."

"I don't see how I can, Susan. I have very bad feelings about it all. I'm sure there will be irrevocable consequences. If I come out at all, I won't come out unscathed."

"Hey, Imogen. You're overreacting. Guys like him are blowhards, and they get bored easily. He'll eventually get tired of trying to make you love him and dump you—not that that's exactly a pleasant experience."

"I'd be happy if he'd dump me. I tried to make him see that I'm not his kind of woman the other night, but not even slapping his face would deter him. He says I'm a challenge."

"You slapped Manfred Andreotti's face!" cried Susan, throwing up her hands in amazement. "And you got away with it!"

"Yes—"

"Gosh Imogen! If you can do that, you will come out of this on top! Maybe you'll reform the guy."

"I doubt that. He was born and raised in a criminal world and knows nothing else. But even if I do come out of this intact, who'll want me afterwards? Who'll want a gangster's cast-off mistress?"

"Oh, probably lots of guys will find you fascinating. And if you keep dressing like the beautiful woman you are, the men will be falling all over themselves to get to you."

"But what kind of man will want me? But," she said, looking away, "if I think of the future, I'll go mad."

"Yes, Imogen, take it a day at a time."

"I'll try, Susan, I'll try. Oh please, Susan," Imogen pleaded, holding out her hands to her friend, "please keep in touch with me! At least writing to you will help—except I really shouldn't burden you with my problems."

"What do you mean burdening me?" said Susan taking Imogen's hands in hers. "We've been friends since we were kids, Imogen, and we've always shared everything. Of course I'll keep in touch. I'll want to know how everything's working out for you."

"You're the best of friends, Susan. I'll miss you—now even more. But here I am thinking of myself. You're embarking on a great career—and I'm very, very happy for you."

"Thanks, Imogen, thanks."

Again the two friends fell into each others arms and held each other close for several moments until, noticing by the elegant watch Manfred had bought for her that it was but a few minutes before his intended time of arrival, Imogen said, "Oh good heavens! He's due here shortly. I'd better go out to the living room to meet him when he comes. But oh, Susan! I'd give anything not to have to!"

"You'll handle the situation, Imogen—better than I could."

"I don't know about that—but I certainly hope I can bear up. Right now, I hope I can stand up to Uncle and Aunt's criticism. They won't like to see me bare-shouldered and displaying all this leg."

"Let's face it, Imogen, they're a bit old fashioned. Anyway, I'll be there to fend off their criticism. And they're good people. Their disapproval will pass."

"I rather like them old fashioned. Strait-laced they may be, but their values are right. Anyway, the real trial comes later. But let's go. It's coming to the moment of truth for Imogen Edwards."

"The moment of truth is for the bull, Imogen. Maybe you're the matador—the matadoress—matadora?—Anyway, maybe you'll be the winner."

"Sometimes the bull wins, Susan."

The two young women left the bedroom and walked the few steps down the hallway to the living room. As she passed the long mirror in the hall, Imogen caught sight of her full reflection.

"Is that really me?" she asked, stopping to look.

"It sure is, Imogen. As I said, you look great."

"I—I do look really glamorous—thanks to you, Susan—but glamorous for Manfred Andreotti—!"

"As I said, there'll be others after him to look glamorous for."

"Maybe..."

As Imogen expected, her uncle and aunt greeted her appearance with shock and dismay.

"Great heavens!" cried her uncle. "You're not going out dressed like that!"

"I'm afraid I am, Uncle. It's what he expects."

"That dress barely leaves anything to the imagination!"

"It's the style now, Mr. Edwards," said Susan, trying to be helpful. "I think she looks great. Imogen's got the figure for it."

"I don't think a girl should dress to flaunt her flesh like that," said Imogen's uncle.

"None of this is what I want, Uncle."

"We live in a much freer age, Mr. Edwards" said Susan.

"Well, I still don't like it. She looks like a hooker—especially in those heels and showing all that leg!"

"Surely you don't wear things like that, Susan," said Imogen's aunt from her wheelchair.

"Yes—similar. But I don't look as well in them as Imogen."

"Oh, Susan! Stop making me out to be Helen of Troy or the goddess Aphrodite. You're very attractive."

"Nature didn't endow me the way she endowed you."

"I wish she hadn't endowed me quite so abundantly. I'd much rather have your musical ability than my—endowment."

"Don't knock looks, Imogen. Besides, you play the piano brilliantly."

"I'm no Alicia de Laroccha or Maria Joao pires, whereas you're in the same league as Renee Fleming and Elisabeth Schwartzkopf."

Just then they heard the sounds of automobiles drawing up outside. Imogen looked out to see Manfred's shiny black limousine with its two escorting cars at the curb.

"He's here!" cried Imogen. "Oh Lord! This is it!"

"Hey, Imogen, you'll be all right," said Susan, embracing her.

"How can you say that when she's going on a date with a gangster, Susan?" said Imogen's aunt. "Who knows what might happen?"

"Imogen knows how to take care of herself, Mrs. Edwards. She's a tough nut."

"Justifying your confidence in me, Susan, won't be easy," said Imogen.

At that moment they heard footsteps on the veranda followed by an imperious knock on the door.

"That's him!" said Imogen. "I'll go, Uncle," she said to her uncle who had risen.

She opened the door to Manfred in his tuxedo, and once again, much to her chagrin, she found herself thinking how handsome he looked. His admiration of her was unmistakable.

"Wow! You look terrific!" he exclaimed finally. "Boy! Do you do things for that dress!"

"Th—thank you, Manfred," Imogen stammered, once again pleased in spite of herself to be complimented on her appearance. "But you've already seen me in the dress at the store."

"Yeah, well, you look even better tonight."

"Probably it's because Susan helped me with my makeup—my war paint. W—will you come in? I just have to get my wrap and say good-night to everybody."

"Oh, yeah. Sure." He stepped in and greeted everyone. "Evening, folks. Nice to see you again. Hi there, Susan. You did a great job with Imogen's makeup—not that she needs any," he said. "She don't need nothing—I mean anything—gotta talk proper with Imogen—to make her gorgeous."

"I just enhanced what nature's already given her," said Susan.

"Hey! Yeah! That's what I tell her I'm doing. The nice clothes and everything—they just show off what's already there." Then turning to Imogen's aunt and uncle, he said, "Doesn't she look terrific, folks?"

"This dress certainly shows off too much of me, Manfred," said Imogen. "My uncle thinks I'm flaunting my flesh and look like a hooker."

"Hey, folks! Hookers ain't got Imogen's elegance and class. And it's the twenty-first century. Times and fashions have changed. All the women dress like that—except they don't look as great as Imogen."

"I must say, Mr. Andreotti," said Imogen's uncle rather reluctantly, "she does look rather like a fashion plate, but that's not the Imogen we've grown to know."

—And I won't be that Imogen when I come back, she thought.

"Hey!" Manfred responded to Mr. Edwards. "Imogen's a beautiful woman and she looks the way a beautiful woman oughta look! And here," he said presenting to Imogen the orchid corsage he had been carrying, "for the most beautiful woman in the world—though it don't do you justice."

"Oh—why, it's lovely, Manfred!" she said, quite genuinely impressed. "Thank you! Isn't this a beautiful orchid, everybody?" she said showing it around. "But I'm not sure where I can wear it on this dress."

"Here, at your left breast," said Susan. "I'll pin it on for you," she said and helped Imogen fasten it to her dress.

"I don't know what I'd have done without you Susan—really."

"Looks great there," said Manfred. "But it's time to go. Are you ready, Imogen?"

"Yes," she said, "I guess I am."

—As ready as I'll ever be, she thought.

From the back of the chair where she had laid it in readiness, she picked up the cashmere stole Susan had bought her for their evening at the opera, arranged it about her shoulders, and said, "I'll just say 'good-night' to everyone."

She leaned over and kissed her aunt who, her eyes filled with tears, grasped her by the hand.

"Please don't worry, Aunty," she whispered. "I'll be all right."

"Oh, I hope so, dear, and I'll try not to worry," her aunt whispered in reply, "but it won't be easy."

"My goodness, Uncle," Imogen said when she turned to see him also with tears in his eyes. She went to him, stood on tiptoes and kissed him on the forehead. "There, I didn't get lipstick on you this time. Susan showed me how to blot it better."

"Take care of yourself, Imogen," he said, his voice choked.

"I will, Uncle" she said. "As I said before, remember I'm your niece."

Then she threw her arms around Susan.

"Thanks for all your help, Susan."

"As they say in the theatre, Kid, 'Break a leg'."

"Thanks, Susan. I understand what you mean, but I'll try not to take your advice literally," she said forcing a smile. Then, with a brave face and trying to sound casual, she turned to Manfred and said, *"Bene, Signor Andreotti. Andremo?"*

"Si—I mean yeah, let's go. Uh—good night every body. And don't worry about your niece folks," he addressed Imogen's uncle and aunt. "I'll take good care of her."

CHAPTER EIGHT

After they left the house, Manfred offered Imogen his arm into which, after a moment's hesitation, she slipped hers, and they walked down the path to the limousine, for a few moments the only sound being again that of Imogen's heels making their staccato tattoo on the cement pathway.

"Well, here's the car," said Manfred as, after only a minute or so, they arrived at the limousine where Joe held the door for them. Manfred gave directions to Al who was to drive. As she got in, Imogen thanked Joe.

"Huh? Oh—yeah. Uh—You're welcome, Miss," replied Joe, still unused to gratitude.

As he settled in beside her and the limousine pulled away from the curb, Manfred said, "I've waited a long time for this. Our first real date."

"Yes," said Imogen somewhat diffidently, "I guess it is."

"First of many."

"I suppose so," said Imogen, "till you get tired of me and find someone else."

"Hey!" he said. "Like I said, there ain't never—there isn't never—isn't ever?—going to nobody else—anybody else! You're everything I always wanted in a woman!"

"You hardly know me Manfred!" she protested. "How you can say that?"

"I just know, that's all. I just know."

"It just seems so—so strange—so impossible," she said, looking him straight in the eyes. "We're from such different worlds, Manfred. You might think differently when you know me better."

"No, I won't."

"I don't know how you can be so sure."

"It's something I feel in my guts. But right now we're just a guy and his girl on a date. So—"

He took her into his arms, held her very close, and kissed her long and hard. Imogen neither resisted nor responded.

"Geez!" he said. "I wish you could let yourself go! Loosen up a bit!"

"So you keep saying, but please, Manfred, give me time."

"Yeah, yeah. And you keep saying that. How much time is enough?"

"I don't know, Manfred. A woman likes to have some choice in the matter."

"Okay, okay! But when a guy wants something bad enough he'll do anything to get it—and I want you real bad."

"I still don't know why."

"Geez! Do I have to keep telling you?"

"No," she said. "In fact, I'd rather you didn't."

"Then stop asking."

"All right, I will."

The next few moments were spent in silence as the limousine rolled through the streets. Then, remembering her resolve to follow Susan's advice and to take everything a day at a time, she asked, "Where are we going for dinner tonight, Manfred?"

"The Café Napoleon."

"The Café Napoleon?" she responded in surprise.

"Yeah. Don't worry. The waitresses are fully clothed."

"Oh, I wasn't thinking about that. But it's a French restaurant."

"Yeah? So what?"

"Well, you're Italian. I expected you'd take me to some place Italian."

"Sometimes I like a change. Anything wrong with that?"

"No, not at all. Of course not. I was just surprised, that's all."

Just then Al's voice over the intercom announced, "We're there, Boss."

"Okay Al," Manfred replied. To Imogen he said, "You'll like this place."

"I'm sure I well, Manfred. I hear it's very select. Not the sort of place frequented by Imogen Edwards from the slums."

"You ain't—you're not from the slums!" objected Manfred. "Your uncle and aunt got a nice little house, and you're a very select lady, and a select restaurant is where you oughta go."

After stepping out of the limo, Manfred extended his hand to Imogen to help her out, and in thanking him she managed to smile and also to thank Al who stood by and like Joe was flustered.

"Uh—geez, Miss," he said. "You're welcome! Geez!" Then, as Imogen took Manfred's arm to walk to the entrance, she heard him say to Joe who had also come up and the two of them followed a few steps behind, "The Boss sure picked a winner this time! She's real polite. And geez! Is she good looking!"

"You ain't just whistlin' 'Dixie,' Al!" said Joe. "But she ain't no pushover neither, if you remember the other night. The Boss may have his hands full with her."

"Yeah, but he's got a full house, and all she's got is a pair of deuces."

"Yeah, but I bet she plays them deuces for all they're worth."

As she walked on Manfred's arm along the red carpet that extended under the long canopy from the curb to the entrance of the Café Napoleon, Manfred said to her, "You're really going to spoil my boys if you keep thanking them like that for everything."

"It's only good manners, Manfred," she said. "A little politeness never hurts."

"I pay them good salaries."

"Yes, but a bit of the human touch does wonders sometimes."

"Yeah? Yeah, mebbe you're right."

As they approached the entrance to the restaurant, another couple preceded them, and Manfred called out to them, "Hey! Lootenant Wolinski! What brings you to the Café Napoleon?"

"Andreotti!" said the man addressed, turning to see who had spoken. "If I'd known you'd be here I'd have made reservations elsewhere."

"Hey! Lootenant," responded Manfred. "That ain't very nice. It's always a pleasure to see you."

"Yeah, I bet it is!" replied the Police Lieutenant.

—Lieutenant Wolinski! thought Imogen, greatly agitated by the identification of the police officer. Uncle Arthur knows him! What will he think of his friend's niece being on a date with Manfred Andreotti!

"So what brings you here, Lootenant?" asked Manfred. "This isn't you're usual sort of greasy spoon."

"It's our wedding anniversary. I thought it would be nice to take my wife to a nice place for once in her life. She hasn't exactly lived a life of luxury since she married me."

"I've never regretted it a moment of it, Stan," said the policeman's wife, a very attractive woman in her early forties.

"Mrs. Wolinski!" said Manfred. "A pleasure to meet you. And I'd like you to meet my new girl friend, Imogen Edwards."

"Imogen Edwards!" exclaimed the Lieutenant in surprise. "Not Arthur Edwards's niece?"

"Yes, Lieutenant," said Imogen, averting her eyes, "I am."

The Lieutenant stared at her.

"Well I—How on earth does a girl like you—a young woman of your upbringing—get mixed up with a guy like Andreotti?"

Manfred turned to look at her, seemingly apprehensive of what she might say.

"He—he asked me," she said almost inaudibly.

"What!" exclaimed the policeman. "And you accepted!"

"Yes," she whispered in reply, still looking down.

"Just like that? You just said yes? What kind of intimidation did you use on her, Andreotti?"

"I guess you could say he chose me, Lieutenant," said Imogen, wanting to avert an unpleasant exchange and looking up at the policeman, "but—it was my decision to accept."

"There's something fishy here," he said, staring at Imogen, who managed to hold her gaze on him. "I can't imagine Arthur Edwards' niece simply agreeing to on her own accord become the girl friend of a crook like Andreotti."

"He was very persuasive, Lieutenant."

"I bet he was."

"Stan," said the Lieutenant's wife, "I think you're making this young lady very uncomfortable. After all, we're all here to enjoy a pleasant evening. Let's not spoil it either for us or Mr. Andreotti and his young lady friend."

Imogen looked gratefully at her, and they exchanged smiles, Imogen's shy.

"Yeah, okay," said Wolinski, responding to his wife's admonition, "but I mean to get to the bottom of this."

"Hey, Lootenant," protested Manfred. "There ain't no bottom to get to."

"Yes, please, Lieutenant," implored Imogen. "I assure you, everything is all right. I—I'm here willingly."

The Lieutenant looked hard at her for several moments.

"Okay," he said incredulously, "if you say so."

"Yeah," said Manfred, "she does say so. And maybe you should believe her, Lootenant. She comes from an honest, hardworking family."

"When did that sort of thing ever matter to you, Andreotti?"

"I appreciate family, Lootenant."

"Come, Stan," said Mrs. Wolinski as her husband was about to make some response, "let's leave these young people to enjoy themselves." Then she spoke quietly to Imogen, "You look very nice, dear. I hope you have a pleasant evening." Imogen blushed as she smiled her thanks as the lieutenant's wife said, "Good—night Imogen and Mr. Andreotti.

"Yeah, good-night, Mrs. Wolinski, and happy anniversary to you and the Lootenant. You know, Ma'am, I really admire this husband of yours."

"I do too, Mr. Andreotti. He's a wonderful man."

"And, if I may say so, a great cop."

"Yes, he's that too. It's too bad—well, I'll leave you to imagine what's too bad. I don't think I really need to tell you."

"Yeah, well you know, you could get out to the Café Napoleon more often if he'd let me help him out a bit."

"Accept bribes, you mean, Mr. Andreotti."

"Hey, Mrs. Wolinski, I like to be generous."

"We won't accept your—'generosity,' Mr. Andreotti, not at the price of our souls."

Hearing that, Imogen winced and looked away, and even Manfred said nothing for some time. When eventually he spoke he said merely, "Well, like you say, we're here for a pleasant evening—and I hope you have one too."

"We will, Andreotti, in spite of your being here," said the Lieutenant.

"Hey, Lootenant. That still ain't—isn't very nice."

"Since when did you start worrying about your grammar, Andreotti?"

"Since I met Imogen. She's *summa cum*—what is it again, Imogen?"

"*Summa cum laude*," she said quietly, blushing.

"Yeah. *Summa cum laude* in English literature from Princeton."

"Well, certainly not your usual type of woman, but if she improves your English that's something at least—not much, but something."

"Oh, Stan," said Mrs. Wolinski, "lay off! And Imogen, congratulations on your achievement."

"Th—thank you, Mrs. Wolinski," said Imogen again managing a smile in response to the friendliness of the Lieutenant's wife.

"I don't know how you managed it, Mr. Andreotti," she said, "but you seem to have found a very remarkable young woman in Imogen, so take good care of her."

"Hey! Don't worry, Mrs. Wolinski!" said Manfred. "I intend to take very good care of her!"

"Good-night again," said Mrs. Wolinski as they turned to enter the restaurant, and Imogen heard Mrs. Wolinski say to her husband, "She's a nice girl, Stan. Don't get her into any more trouble than she's in already. And who knows, maybe she'll have a good effect on Andreotti."

"Huh?" responded her husband. "Okay. I'll do my best, but I just don't understand it, because, yes, she does seem like a nice girl. But I'd be more afraid that Andreotti'll have a bad effect on her."

As Manfred led Imogen into the foyer of the Café Napoleon after the Wolinskis, Imogen was too troubled in mind to notice the fish pond with its fountain, the plants, the plush furnishings, or the large reproduction of David's painting of the coronation of Napoleon or Manfred's and her reflection in the large mirrors.

Her reverie was interrupted when Manfred said after the hostess had led the Wolinski's through the curtained doorway and out of earshot, "Hey! That was great the way you handled Wolinski!"

"Wha—? Oh—I—uh—I bent the truth a bit, Manfred," she said. "I didn't lie, but I didn't tell the whole truth. I don't want any trouble for Uncle Arthur or the Martinellis."

"There won't be no trouble. Wolinski's boss does what I tell him."

"You really do control this town, don't you?" said Imogen in a tone of disapproval.

"It's either control or be controlled in this world, Imogen. Better control than be controlled. Better to be the hammer than the nail, the enforcer than the enforced."

"Are there no other options?"

"Not that I ever heard of. Except to be on the good side of the one in control—like you, Imogen. Funny about Wolinski, though. He doesn't seem to see it that way. I can't bribe him."

"Maybe he has principles."

"Principles are for idiots."

"I like to think I have—or had—a few principles, Manfred. Does that make me an idiot?"

"Huh?" Manfred was silent for a moment. "No," he said at last. "No, you ain't no—you're not an idiot." He looked at her in puzzlement. "Geez!"

"I don't think the Lieutenant is either."

"Huh?" Manfred breathed again, his face expressing puzzlement. "Huh?" Then he asked, "Hey! Why did you call him 'Lieutenant,' not 'Lootenant'?"

"My British background, I guess."

Just then, the manager advanced, effusively welcoming Manfred, and again Imogen marveled at the deference accorded him.

"*M'sieur Andreotti! Quel plaisir! Bienvenu encore au Café Napoleon!*"

"Always nice to come here, Pierre," responded Manfred. "Meet my girl friend, Imogen Edwards."

"*Mademoiselle* Edwards!" said the manager, seizing and kissing Imogen's hand. "*Bienvenu au Café Napoleon! Quel honeur a faire la connaissance de la tres belle petite amie de M'sieur Andreotti!*"

"*Merci, Monsieur,*" replied Imogen blushing.

—Of how many of Manfred's *petites amies*, she wondered, has the *maitre d'* had the honor of making the acquaintance?

"Ah! *Mademoiselle parle francais!*"

"She knows everything, Pierre."

"Ah! *Mademoiselle a du talent! J'espere que Madeoiselle trouvera ici tout a son gout!*"

"*Merci, Pierre,*" Imogen replied. "*Je suis bien sure que tout sera bon.*"

"*Eh bien, Mademoiselle, Monsieur, voici Yvette. Elle vous conduit a votre table preféréé, M'sieur Andreotti. La champagne et prete en glace, et, comme vous avez commande, M'sieur, c'est de la meilleure.*"

"Thanks, Pierre—I guess" said Manfred, whose expression had been a mixture of pleasure at the *maitre d's* admiration for Imogen and annoyance at his speaking French to her. "But cut the French. I don't understand none of it.

"He said the champagne is on ice and everything is as you requested, Manfred," said Imogen.

"*Je vous demand*—I ask your pardon, *M'sieur. C'etait*—It was for Mademoiselle. She speaks French so beautifully."

"Yeah," said Manfred, regarding Imogen with the pride of possession. "Ain't she—isn't she something? And since she understands, I guess everything's okay." Then turning to the pretty blond young waitress, who had just arrived, he said, "Hi there, Yvette! You're looking great this evening."

"Oh, *merci*, Mr. Andreotti, *et bon soir*. But I bet you say that to every woman."

—I bet he does too, thought Imogen.

"Only the pretty ones, Yvette," said Manfred.

—I bet he says that to all of them, too. He can certainly turn on the charm!

"I'd like you to meet my new girl, Imogen Edwards," said Manfred.

"Ah! *Bon soir, Mademoiselle*," said Yvette, surveying Imogen critically, perhaps with a touch of personal vanity, but apparently finding everything to her approval.

"*Bon soir*," said Imogen. "*Il me donne plaisir de faire votre connaissance, Yvette.*"

"Oh—uh—" stammered Yvette, embarrassed, "I just happen to have a French name. I don't speak French. Pierre likes us to greet the customers with '*bon soir*'."

"Oh, I see. Well, I'm happy to meet you Yvette."

"Oh, well, thanks—uh—*merci*," said Yvette. "It's nice to meet you, Ms Edwards. Now, if you'll just follow me, *M'sieur* Andreotti and *Mademoiselle* Edwards, your table is ready."

As they followed Yvette, several of the patrons looked up from their meals to stare, and there arose a quite audible buzz of whispers.

"Hey! Who's the woman with Andreotti? I never saw her before. But boy! Is she something!"

"Yeah, she's sure a knockout whoever she is!"

"Yeah! Look at the build on her! Is she ever well stacked!"

"Especially those headlights. Wow!"

—Headlights! thought Imogen. I've never heard them called that before! And I've never before heard that I'm well stacked!

"Yeah, and great legs, too!" said another voice.

"And a nice little tooshy with a very provocative wiggle!"

—Good Lord! A provocatively wiggling tooshy now! I suppose that's the effect of these heels. That, and to show off my legs, is probably why he wants me to wear them. I really am his trophy girl friend.

To her surprise, however, Manfred rounded on the nearest group of commentators and snarled, "Mind your own business!"

A sudden hush fell over the restaurant, and Imogen turned to gave him an appreciative smile and to whisper, "Why, thank you, Manfred!"

"Bunch of ignorant cruds!" he said to her. "Nobody talks like that about my girl—about you. No, not about you, Imogen!"

—Well! she thought. Well!

Meanwhile, Yvette had ushered them to a corner table at the far end of the restaurant. As she held the chair for her Imogen thanked her, and then, when she was seated across from Manfred, said, "It's nice to sit! It's hard to stand in for very long in these stiletto heels. They're well named 'stilettos.' Wearing them is a bit like walking on daggers."

"Wait'll you try five inches!" said Yvette. "They're brutal, but, boy! You sure give the guys goose bumps when you wear them—but even four inches can have that effect."

"Yes, and I hear," said Imogen with a wry smile, "that they give our tooshies a very provocative wiggle."

"Uh—yeah," said Yvette. "I guess they do that." Then turning to Manfred she said, "I'll let you sample the champagne." Deftly she popped the stopper, brought the bubbles under control, and poured a small amount of the effervescent liquor into Manfred's glass. He rolled some about in his mouth, swallowed it and pronounced it satisfactory. Yvette filled both glasses and said, "I'll be back in a few minutes to take your order."

On the waitress's departure, Manfred raised his glass and said, "Here's to us and to great times together."

"Oh—" said Imogen, taken somewhat aback by the toast. "Oh—to—to us."

After she had sipped her champagne, he added, "And to the most gorgeous girl in the world."

"Oh Manfred! Please!" Imogen protested, blushing with embarrassment and proceeding to make a show of examining the menu.

"I wish you'd get it through your skull that you are gorgeous," he said, "and stop being so embarrassed when I pay you a compliment."

"As I said, Manfred, I'm just not used to them."

"Well, you're going to get a lot of them; so you better get used to it." Then turning to the menu, he asked, "See anything you'd like?"

"I hardly know what to choose. I'm afraid I'm not used to such gourmet fare. Your taste, I'm sure, is far better than mine. Perhaps you should choose."

"Okay. How about a *Chateaubriand* for two? It's great."

Imogen found it in the menu. "Oh—It does look wonderful, Manfred. If that's what you'd like—"

"Hey! I'm asking if you'd like it."

"If you say it's good, Manfred, I'm sure I will like it" she said closing her menu and laying it on the table.

"You will. It is good," he said, and turned, snapped his fingers, and Yvette almost on the instant reappeared to take their order.

"An excellent choice, Mr. Andreotti," she said. "Henri, the chef, will prepare it right here at your table."

"I can hardly believe I'm with such a gorgeous and cultivated woman as you," said Manfred staring at her across the table after Yvette's departure.

"I can't get over the fact that I'm here with you, Manfred; but I still don't understand—Oh! Sorry. I said I wouldn't bring that up any more."

"Well I don't mind telling you that I never met a woman before who's got so much going for her as you! You've been to university, you like opera and play the piano! And to top it all off, you're gorgeous!"

"Anyone would look gorgeous in an expensive and glamorous dress like this."

"The hell they would! The dress doesn't make you, you make the dress."

"Oh Manfred! All kinds of women would look glamorous in this dress."

"Not like you."

Imogen made no reply, for at the moment Henri wheeled up the trolley with their Chateaubriand kept piping hot by a brazier of glowing coals.

"Ah! *M'sieur* Andreotti," exclaimed Henri. "'Ow nice to see you again. *Et Mademoiselle! Elle est tres charmante*—she eez very charming, *M'sieur, et tres belle*—veree beauteefool!"

"You don't have to translate that, Henri. Even I know what 'tray bell' is. The problem is getting her to believe it. But she's more than just pretty. She's brainy and talented too."

"*Vraiment, M'sieur*? Ah! Eet eez eendeed a plaisure to meet Mademoiselle."

"*Je suis heureuse de faire votre connaissance, Henri*," Imogen responded.

"Ah! *Mademsoiselle parle Francais*! Mademoiselle speaks French *parfaitement*—perfectlee."

"*Merci, Henri.*

"Yeah, Henri," said Manfred. "She not only speaks French but Italian too—fluidly."

With great difficulty Imogen repressed a laugh and whispered almost voicelessly behind her hand, "That's 'fluently', Manfred."

"Huh? Oh—yeah. Of course, Henri, I meant 'fluently.' Slip of the tongue there."

Again Imogen could hardly repress a laugh and had to put her hand to her mouth and turn aside.

"Ah! *Mais c'est merveilleux*! Zat eez marvelous" said Henri. "*La Francais et L'Italien aussi*!

"Like I said, Henri, she's really something special."

"*Vraiment, M'sieur*—trulee."

All the while Henri had been carving the meat and distributing the portions with the vegetables and tiny potatoes onto the plates which he placed before Imogen first and then before Manfred.

"*J'espere que cela sera a son gout, Mademoiselle.*"

"*Merci, Henri. Je suis bien sur que ce sera tres savoureux.*"

"Ah! *Merci bien, Mademoiselle*," said Henri, refilling their champagne glasses. "*Bon appetit, M'sieur, Mademoiselle.*" Then after bowing formally, he departed.

"Yeah, Imogen," said Manfred. "Like he said, *Bon appetit*. I know what that means too."

"Oh—yes *Bon appetit*, Manfred. It certainly looks and smells delicious." Then tasting a bit of the meat, she exclaimed, "Mmm! It *is* delicious!"

"I told you you'd like it."

"I didn't doubt it, Manfred. You're far more of an epicure than I."

"Epicure?"

"Oh—a person with a taste for—who savors—the best pleas—ures."

"Oh—yeah—well, from now on, Imogen, you're going to know the best—the best food, the best clothes, the best entertainment, the best of everything!"

"I—I'd rather you wouldn't spend a lot of money on me, Manfred."

"Hey! I never do anything by halves. I always do things in a big way. I don't know how to do it any other way. So you'll just have to get used to it."

"I—I suppose I will, Manfred, but it still embarrasses me."

"Well, it's the way you should be treated—like the high class woman you are."

"I'm really a member of the *lumpenproletariat*, Manfred," she said with a sardonic smirk.

"Huh? There's nothing lumpy about you!"

Again Imogen could not help a smile at his misunderstanding. "That's not what it means. It's German and means something like ragamuffin workers—people of the very lowest class. But what about my knockers? Aren't they rather lumpy?" she said with a slight laugh.

"Breasts," he said.

"Oh—thank you, Manfred!" she exclaimed, gratified by his correct usage. "I appreciate that!"

"Yeah, well, I'm catching on. But they ain't—aren't lumpy. They're terrific. But hey! Glad you got a sense of humor!"

And again Imogen could not help smiling. "I rather think I'll need one," she said.

"Huh? Uh—yeah. Okay. Still glad you got one."

They ate in silence for several minutes. Then Imogen was taken totally by surprise by Manfred's saying, "You would like to see your aunt walking again, wouldn't you, Imogen? Now that you actually are my girl, mebbe—maybe—you'll believe I ain't—I'm not saying it to get you to go out with me. I really would like to help."

"Oh—Why Manfred! That—that's very generous of you, and I'd like more than anything to see Aunty walk again, but—as you saw the other day, my uncle and aunt are very proud. And they—they—don't like—they think that—"

"They think my money 's dirty. Well, I just give people what they want—"

"Like drugs?" asked Imogen. Then somewhat belligerently she continued, "People want them because criminal organizations push them."

"Yeah? Well what about the tobacco companies? That stuff's bad for you too. Causes cancer. And what's advertising if it ain't pushing? Look how much of it is directed at kids! And the people who sell liquor—Do they care whether people become alcoholics? So why's what I do so much worse?"

"I don't like what they do either, Manfred, but they don't use intimidation and violence."

"Oh yeah! They can be pretty ruthless. You accused me of getting my way by violence. Well, who the hell do you think wanted that poet executed in Africa? The oil companies, that's who because he was a threat to their interests."

"He was concerned for the health and well-being of his people, and yes, what they did to him was horrible, but—"

"But nothing! Some of your most respectable citizens are the biggest crooks around. They get around government regulations and do all kinds of dirty tricks and under-the-counter deals. But they're called captains of industry. Because I'm more direct in my methods, I'm called a crook. But don't you call me a crook, Imogen, and don't call my money dirty because all money's dirty. There's no such thing as clean money!"

"Unfortunately, Manfred," she said looking down in some embarrassment that she had touched such a sore nerve, "there's truth in what you say, but I don't think two wrongs make a right. However, I don't mean to quarrel with you, either. I would dearly love to see Aunt Ethel walking again if it were possible. I—I'll talk to my uncle and aunt and try to persuade them. And—and—Manfred—thank you for offering to help."

"Hey, look!" he said, somewhat calmed. "I want to do this. I don't like to see people in wheelchairs. Like I said to your uncle, I wish there was something could be done for my Papa, but there ain't—isn't. We've been to the best specialists."

She looked up at him and saw that there actually were tears in his eyes. "I—I'm sorry, Manfred—and I'm sorry I upset you."

"Hey, forget it—and thanks. So, since I can't help Papa, let me try to do something for your aunt. It'd really make me feel good if I could help her."

"As I said, Manfred, thank you for your offer. I'll talk to Uncle Arthur."

—Oh! If something good could come of all this—if he really could make Aunt walk again—I'd feel this was almost worthwhile!

After they had eaten a while in silence, Imogen asked a question that had been much on her mind.

"Manfred—you—you never married?"

"Huh? No. I mean, yeah. Yeah I did. But hey!" he said as Imogen dropped her fork with a clatter on her plate, shocked at the revelation. "I ain't—I'm not—cheating on my wife. This ain't an affair, Imogen. I ain't—I'm not like that. We've been separated for five-six years now."

"Oh—I—I'm sorry."

"I'm not. We hated each other—at least, we never got along. Nothing I could do pleased her. East Clintwood wasn't good enough for her. Thought it was small time, and I was small potatoes compared to her papa who's in the big time in Philadelphia. Yeah, I know East Clintwood's a bit of a side show compared to New York, Boston, Philadelphia, New Jersey, but hell, we got up to New York lotsa times for the opera and stuff. And besides, I got ambitions. Takes time that's all. But she couldn't wait."

"Why did you marry her?"

"Not because either of us wanted to. It was all arranged between our families."

"Did you have to marry her? Didn't you have any choice?"

"Not if you want to stay on the good side of the godfather. It was his idea."

"Then how were you able to separate?" she asked. "Didn't the— godfather object to that?"

"Believe you me I have to pay one hell of a separation allowance!"

"Oh—And—were there any children?"

"Yeah. Yeah." He looked off wistfully into the distance. "A little boy. She's got him. Guess he's not so little now." Imogen looked straight into his eyes as he turned back toward her and saw real sorrow in them. "I kind of miss him," he said, again looking away.

Imogen's eyes widened and her mouth dropped open slightly when she heard that.

—Why—why beneath all the bluster and bravado and the tough exterior there's a residue of humanity! What a strange, contradictory man he is.

Without thinking, she reached across the table and laid her hand on his.

"Manfred, I'm sorry," she said.

He took her hand between his and pressed it firmly.

"Thanks," he said. "Geez! Thanks! Nobody else 'cept Ana-Maria and my Mama ever cared a damn about my feelings."

She stared wide-eyed at him in this further totally unexpected and probably unwonted revelation of his humanity. For several moments they just stared at each other in silence.

—He really has feelings! But what a horrible world he lives in! thought Imogen. Nobody has any control over his or her own life! If Manfred controls East Clintwood, what must be the power of the one who controls him, the one they call the godfather?—and what will happen to me in that world?

Her reverie was interrupted by Yvette making her routine check. "Is everything all right here, Mr. Andreotti?" Then seeing their hands locked, she said, "Oh! Sorry!"

"Uh—yeah, yeah, Yvette," said Manfred. "Yeah everything's just great. Right Imogen?"

"Oh—yes—indeed," said Imogen, quickly withdrawing her hand from his. "The meal is absolutely superb."

"Great. Well, sorry to intrude," she said, quickly making her exit.

For several moments Imogen and Manfred refrained from looking at each other and ate in silence. Then Manfred said, "My sister Ana-Maria really wants to get to know you now that we're dating."

"She—she seems very nice," Imogen responded.

"Yeah, she's okay. My older sister—older than both of us—is something else, but Ana-Maria's okay. We used to be very close before I took over the business. That night at the opera was the first time we could get together in a long time."

"I—I think I'd like to get to know Ana-Maria."

"She's really looking forward to it."

"That—that's very nice of her." Then Imogen asked another question. "But something has been puzzling me. Why are you called Manfred? It's a German name, but you're Italian."

"Yeah, well, it's really *Manfredo*, but I like Manfred better. More macho."

"Oh—I see. It is a very masculine sounding name, I guess. There was a medieval king of Sicily of that name—son of the Holy Roman Emperor Frederick II, and so the great grandson of Frederick Barbarossa."

"Yeah? Geez! You know everything, don't you."

"I suppose that's kind of trivial pursuit knowledge. Mostly I think of the hero of a dramatic poem by Lord Byron."

"Yeah? What's it about?"

"Well, it's about a man, somewhat in rebellion against his society, who yet feels guilty about something which turns out to be his incestuous love for his sister Astarte whose death he has caused. And—"

"Incest with his sister! That's sick."

"Well, I suppose it is—I mean it's wrong, I know, but it happens, and literature is about human life and experience in all its complexity. Literature, as someone said—I forget who—allows us to entertain an idea without seeing it as a call to action."

"Yeah? Well, there's some things that shouldn't be written about, and that's one of them. Do they actually teach that kind of garbage at university?"

"It's not garbage, Manfred. It's a poetic exploration of an aspect of human nature. Incest has been a concern of human civilization almost from the beginning, and it's a problem we still have with us today."

"I still say writing about it is sick."

"What about pornography, Manfred? You can pick it up on the news stand. I think that is sick—though I don't believe in censorship. But I'm surprised you're so angry about something like Byron's poem."

"It's about something that's against the laws of God!"

"Against the laws of God!" exclaimed Imogen, completely taken aback by his protestation. "But isn't theft, isn't extortion, isn't bribery—aren't they against the laws of God?"

"Hey!" he said angrily. "I don't want you talking about that sort of thing! That's none of your business."

"I—I don't want to know all about what you do, Manfred, and I don't mean to give offence, but—but if I'm to be your girl friend, we should be open and honest with each other."

"It's got nothing to do with us going out together and having a good time, so I don't want you asking me anything about it! Like I said, it's none of your business. Is that clear?"

"Yes, Manfred," she said, staring him angrily in the eye, "it certainly is. Very clear."

"Okay. As long as you know that, we'll get along fine."

"I hope so."

"Anyway, to answer your question, I go to confession."

Again Imogen reacted in surprise.

"To confession! Do you actually tell your priest everything you do?"

"No, but I confess to telling lies. So that makes it okay."

"I thought," she replied coldly, "that confession and absolution were supposed to lead to amendment of life."

"We give big donations to the Church and build community centres and gymnasiums and things like that for people."

"To buy yourselves off."

"Hey!" he stormed. "Look! I said you stay out of our affairs. Anyway, you're not a Catholic, so you don't understand."

"Not a Roman Catholic."

"Whadda you mean not a Roman Catholic. You're either a Catholic or you're not."

"I see. Well then, I guess I'm not a Catholic."

"What are you, if I might ask?"

"I could tell you it's none of your business, Manfred." She continued to look him steadily in the eye, forcing herself not to flinch before his angry gaze. Completely taken aback by her sharp response, he fell silent. "However," she said, "I'm an Episcopalian."

"Episcopalian? Isn't that the Church started by Henry the Eighth?"

"We don't see it that way."

"Yeah? Well, there's only one church, and that's the Catholic."

"That's what we say in the Nicene Creed."

"Huh? Look," he growled. "I don't want to talk about religion. There ain't nothin' to talk about anyway."

"I see. Well, all right. We won't."

They fell silent. Imogen took a few more mouthfuls of her food, but found she had lost her appetite and pushed her plate away. Apparently Manfred had lost his also, for he too pushed his plate away with an angry motion.

"I thought we agreed not to quarrel," he said, glowering at her.

"I wasn't trying to quarrel, Manfred. I only asked a question. It was you who got huffy."

"You shouldn't have asked what you asked."

"It just seemed natural to do so, Manfred. How was I to know? As I've said before, I'm not from your world. To me it just seemed a natural question to ask."

"Okay. Now forget it."

"I'll try."

Again they fell silent.

—I've got to walk on eggshells! thought Imogen. Then suddenly, as from nowhere, a humorously incongruous notion struck her, and in spite of herself she burst out laughing.

"What's so funny?" demanded Manfred.

"Oh! Something rather silly occurred to me."

"Yeah, well let's hear it."

"Well, I was just thinking—please don't take offence—I was just thinking that when I'm with you I've got to walk on eggshells—you know—be careful what I say—and the thought of walking on eggshells in four-inch stiletto heels struck me as rather incongruous—rather bizarre."

"Huh? Yeah," he said, though without laughing, "I guess that is sort of funny, when you think about it. Yeah, I can just see your spikes crunching into all those eggs and the yolks squirting all over the place."

"That wasn't quite the picture I had. I saw myself trying to tread on the eggs ever so lightly on tiptoe so as not to break them."

"Hey, yeah!" he said with a sort of a smirk. "That's kind of funny too."

"But I would have to be careful, come to think of it, not to go down on my heels," she added to try to allay his irritation.

—He's not really laughing, she thought, but maybe the tension is broken—for a little while.

At that moment, Yvette reappeared. "Are you folks finished? Can I get you some dessert? You seem happy about something, Ms. Edwards."

"Oh, I had just thought of something rather funny, Yvette," said Imogen. "And please call me Imogen. But I don't think I could eat another mouthful, thanks—though it was all delicious."

"Yeah, I'm full too," said Manfred.

"Then perhaps you'd like coffee?"

"Yes," Imogen responded. "That would be very nice—that is, if you'd like some Manfred?"

"Yeah, I wouldn't mind a cup of coffee. Hey," he said, almost elated. "I see the band coming on stage. We'll be able to dance pretty soon."

"Yes, in about another ten minutes or so," said Yvette. "Meanwhile, I'll bring your coffee."

While they drank their coffee, the dance band began to play, and couples rose to dance. Imogen, thinking about her lack of skill on the dance floor, sipped her coffee slowly to delay having get up.

"Could you hurry, Imogen? I want to dance," said Manfred.

"As I said, Manfred, I'm not very good. On the dance floor I have two left feet," she joked, "both made of concrete."

"You'll be fine," he said.

So as not to annoy him further, she drank the rest of her coffee quickly, and Manfred rose and held out his hand to her. Setting down her empty cup, Imogen took his hand and rose to her feet and swayed a bit, forgetting the unaccustomed height of her heels. "Oh dear!" she said. "I hope I can do it all right and not step all over your feet."

"I'll hold onto you. Just follow my lead. I'm a good dancer," he said leading her to the floor where he took her in his arms and began to lead her in step to the beat.

She shuddered briefly as she noticed Al and Joe moving along the edge of the crowd, keeping close watch on the dancers, ready to move into the crowd at the first sign of trouble. Manfred, however, seemed completely unperturbed.

"Hey! You dance okay," he said after they had been around the floor a few times.

"You *are* a very good partner, Manfred. It would be hard not to do well with your lead. And actually, these shoes keep me up on my toes and my step light." Then she added with a smile, "Maybe I could walk on egg shells in them, after all—or dance on them perhaps."

"Huh? Oh, yeah. Anyway, I love to dance, so I'm glad you're getting on okay."

"I—I'm enjoying it. It's nice to dance with such a good partner."

—Even, she thought, if he is a gangster!

"Hey Lootenant!" called Manfred who had spotted the Wolinskis over Imogen's shoulder. "Nice to see you enjoying yourself for a change. Seeing you off duty gives me a whole new slant on you. I wouldn't have thought you'd be such a good dancer."

"Because I'm a flatfoot, is that it Andreotti?" snarled the police officer.

"Naw. That's a myth. Just didn't think there was any place in your life for anything so pleasant as dancing."

"Thanks to guys like you, Andreotti, there isn't much time for it."

"Hey! That's not nice. But I'm not like you. I take regular times off. You should try it."

"You can afford too, I can't."

"Come on, Stan," said the lieutenant's wife. "Let's not get into an argument. Remember, we're here to enjoy ourselves."

"That's what I say, Mrs. Wolinski. And you're a very good dancer, by the way."

"Why thank you, Mr. Andreotti. I enjoy it. How about you Imogen?"

"Well," said Imogen blushing in embarrassment at her situation, "I'm not very good, but I must say, Manfred is a very good partner and gives me a very good lead."

"Well, watching you, I'd have thought you very good," said the policeman's wife. "If what you say is true, you certainly follow well."

"Oh, thank you. Manfred makes it very easy."

"You know, Wolinski," said Manfred, "you and your wife make a good looking couple."

"I knew what I was doing when I chose this lady," said the lieutenant.

"And you think I didn't choose you, Stan?" said his wife with a smile.

"No. But I'm glad you did."

"And so am I, Stan."

"Well, for tonight anyway, enjoy yourself Andreotti—and you too, Miss Edwards."

"Thank you, Lieutenant," said Imogen, rather surprised to realize that at least on the dance floor, she was enjoying herself.

"You know, Stan," Imogen heard Mrs. Wolinski say as they danced away into the crowd on the floor, "They make a rather attractive couple."

She did not hear the lieutenant's reply.

The music came to an end, and Manfred said, "There. Your feet aren't made of concrete, and you didn't step on my toes once."

"It's a real achievement, Manfred, but I think you, and maybe the shoes, deserve the credit."

"Practice for Mama and Papa's anniversary. There'll be lots of dancing there, and all eyes will be you. You'll be *la prima donna d' il ballo*."

—Though not *in maschera*. If all eyes are to be on me, as they probably will be, I wish I could be *in maschera*.

"But there's the music again. Let's take another turn around the floor."

"Yes, if you like—and I'd like to. I—I'm really enjoying it—more than I thought I ever would."

"That's great."

He drew her very close against him, and she winced when she felt the hardness of his revolver under his jacket.

"What's the matter?" he asked.

"I—I felt your gun!" she said. "It—it frightened me."

"Hey! Nothing to be afraid of. It won't go off."

"It's not that, Manfred—I just don't like them, that's all. But I guess they're part of your stock in trade, and we agreed not to talk about such matters."

"Right. We're here to enjoy ourselves—like Mrs. Wolinski said."

"She seems like a very fine lady."

"Yeah, she does. Well preserved too."

"She's very attractive. I think she's one of those women who gets better looking as she grows older. I hope I look as well when I'm her age. Not that she's very old."

"So you finally admit that you're gorgeous!" said Manfred.

"How do you mean?"

"You said you hoped you looked as well as her when you're her age. That means you know you're good-looking now."

"Oh—well—I suppose I am rather pretty."

"Pretty! Geez! You're absolutely stunning! I've never met anyone as gorgeous as you!"

"Well, if you say so Manfred. I—I guess I should feel flattered."

And in spite of herself, she was beginning to enjoy the compliment.

Again he drew her close, and they finished the dance in silence.

"Now," he said when the dance was ended, "let's go."

Though she knew his reason, she had hoped he would have waited longer for it and was quite shocked at the suddenness of his desire to leave.

"So soon?" she said.

"What's the matter? It's not all that early."

"Isn't it?"

"No, so let's go then."

"A—all right," she said.

—Since it must be, I suppose it might as well be now. As Hamlet said, "The readiness is all"—and I guess I'm as ready as I'll ever be. But oh God!

Manfred called for Yvette and handed her a number of bills of large denomination. "That should cover it," he said. "What's left over is for you and Henri."

"Oh! Mr. Andreotti!" exclaimed Yvette, staring wide-eyed at the money. "Thank you! Thank you very much!"

—Again! thought Imogen. His money, no matter how ill-gotten, certainly seems to win him a lot of favor and good will.

As she entered the rotunda on Manfred's arm and caught a glimpse of their reflections in the large mirrored section of the wall, she was realized that, yes, she herself was a very attractive woman, perhaps even gorgeous, as Manfred said, but was quite shocked to see that, as Mrs. Wolinski had said, she and Manfred did indeed make a very handsome couple.

—Oh! she thought. If only he were not—

CHAPTER NINE

In the car he drew her close, but again she did not yield to him.

"What's the matter?" he demanded.

"Nothing. Nothing's the matter."

"You're stiff as a post."

"Oh—"

"Are you afraid, or something?"

"I—I guess so."

"What are you afraid of?"

"Of—of what's coming."

"What do you mean you're afraid of what's coming? What the hell is coming? You mean making love?"

Though Imogen did not regard what would happen to her in bed with Manfred as making love, she declined to dispute the issue and merely said, "Yes."

"Why?"

"I—I didn't want it to happen—this way."

"Whadda ya mean not happen this way? What way?"

"Please, Manfred, please."

"Whadda ya—"

She held up a hand to silence him.

"Please don't press me, Manfred. I'll go through with it."

She buried her face in her hands.

"Damn! What the hell! Geez—!"

"Manfred," she said, looking up, speaking firmly and drying her eyes, "I agreed to be your girl friend knowing what it entailed. So, let's forget about my inhibitions and reservations. Somehow I'll overcome them."

Any further comment was forestalled by the voice of Al over the intercom just at that moment to say, "We're here, Boss."

"Yeah, okay Al," Manfred responded.

Until that moment, Imogen had been so full of anxiety that she had been unaware that they had crossed the river into West Clintwood. She looked through the limousine's one way windows to see the imposing facade of West Clintwood's luxurious Imperial Hotel.

"Wh—why have we come here, Manfred?" she asked, turning to him.

"I have the whole upper floor here," he said. "A special private place of my own for times like this. I own the place."

—Is there anything in the Clintwoods he doesn't own? wondered Imogen.

"Oh—"

Two of Manfred's men posted themselves at the main door of the hotel as the uniformed doorman bowed profusely in admitting Manfred and Imogen.

"Good evening, Mr. Andreotti!" he said. "Good evening, Miss."

"Oh—good evening," she said, hardly looking up. "Th—thank you."

"You're welcome, Miss."

"Ah! Mr. Andreotti! Good evening!" said the clerk when Manfred had led her across the carpeted and plushly furnished foyer to the main desk. "You'll find everything ready as you requested."

Whereupon he produced a key from a drawer under the counter which Manfred handed to one of his men. "Take Gus up with you and check everything out," he said, a comment which reminded Imogen again how dangerous were the circumstances into which she had entered, and again she shuddered.

To the clerk Manfred said, "Meet Miss Edwards, Sidney."

"A pleasure, Miss Edwards."

"G—good evening, Sidney," answered Imogen. "I—I'm happy to meet you."

At that moment a well-dressed couple entered the hotel and glanced toward Manfred and Imogen as they crossed to the elevator.

"Manfred Andreotti, I think," the man said underneath to his partner, "and one of his floozies."

"A very elegant floozie, if you ask me," said the woman as they stepped onto the elevator.

—So now I'm a floozie, thought Imogen. Well, I guess if I'm Manfred Andreotti's woman, I'll become known as his floozie to every functionary at every establishment in the twin cities of East and West Clintwood.

When Gus returned to say everything was all right in the apartment, Manfred ushered her to the elevator, and the three of them mounted to the topmost floor where Manfred led her to a door across the hall from the elevator where the other of the two men stood guard.

"Did you check the balcony?" Manfred asked the guard.

"Yeah. Nothing there, Boss."

"Okay, Imogen" he said motioning her to enter. "Come on in. Hey! Don't worry," he added, seeing her anxiety and putting his arm around her shoulders and drawing her to him. "Everything's okay. I've a close watch kept on the place, but it never hurts to be careful."

But her physical security was not her concern.

She hesitated a moment, swallowed hard and preceded Manfred into the apartment when he opened the door for her.

"Pretty nice place, hey," said Manfred with a kind of smug satisfaction,

The luxurious furnishing and the many fine paintings and sculptures, all tastefully chosen, did indeed astound her.

"It—it's really quite elegant, Manfred."

"Glad you like the place. I spent a lot of money on it to make it nice. Nice to find someone who appreciates it."

"Why," said Imogen who had wandered over to take a closer look at some of the paintings, "these are all originals!"

"Yeah, yeah," he responded rather too off-handedly. "Ana-Maria had a lot to do with deciding which ones to keep—choose. She has excellent taste!"

—How naive can you be, Imogen! This is all stolen art! He's an art thief too—or a dealer in stolen art.

Clearly anxious to change the subject, Manfred said, "Come out on the balcony. It's a great view."

He led her to a large curtained window, pushed aside the draperies, released the lock, slid aside the glass panels and led her onto the large balcony fully appointed with outdoor table with a large folded umbrella and chairs, and a variety of potted plants and small trees. Below them spread the lights of the city of East Clintwood across the Clintwood River, a silver band in the light of the moon, a view so impressive that Imogen could not help exclaiming, "Oh! It is a splendid view, Manfred! And," she said, looking up, "what a wonderful view of the stars! I can identify so many constellations up here above the city lights."

"And I can see them in your eyes," he said taking her into his arms. "In the moonlight, you're more gorgeous than ever."

"Oh, Manfred! Please! You embarrass me!"

"Why? Why should you be embarrassed by the truth? The best thing that ever happened to me was meeting you that night at the opera."

"Manfred, please, I can't give you—"

"I know you don't agree and don't feel anything for me right now, but you'll come round."

"You're very sure of yourself, aren't you."

"Yes, I am, and as I said, I always get what I want." He pressed her to him and kissed her hard. Then lifting her into his arms, he said, "We can look at the stars some other time."

He carried her back into the apartment. Clearly he'd had lots of practice closing and locking the sliding panels with a woman in his arms, for he did so now quite deftly. Equally deftly, he unfastened the zipper at the back of her dress.

"M—Manfred—I'll undress myself. Please let me down."

"I always like to undress my women," he said.

"I'll undress myself, Manfred!" she said firmly. "I want to have at least that much control over my life."

"Huh? Geez! Well, if you insist—" he began as he set her on her feet again.

"I do, Manfred," she said.

"Okay, but there's something I want you to do when we make love."

"Oh? Wh—what's that? If it's anything like wearing handcuffs or being chained to the bed, I refuse—"

"Hey! nothing like that. Geez! What kind of pervert do you think I am? All I want you to do is wear your spikes. A naked woman in spikes really turns me on."

"Oh! I see you like your sex a bit kinky."

—And maybe you'll find me a bit kinky, she thought.

"You'll use a condom, won't you? If you don't have one—" she began, reaching into her handbag.

"Hey! What's the matter? Think I got AIDS or VD or something! Geez! Who the hell do you—"

"No, Manfred, and I'm sorry if I gave offence, but I don't want to become pregnant and then get dumped."

"Hey! I'd never dump you. Anyway, I always use a condom, and I'm very careful who I sleep with."

"I—I appreciate your consideration in using a condom—but I just wanted to be sure."

"Yeah. Okay, now that we've got all them things squared away, let's get down to making love."

"Y—yes—I guess it's time. Wh—where is the—the bedroom? I want to undress alone."

"Geez! Geez! Geez! You sure as hell are fussy—but it's back through that door there," he said indicating a doorway slightly ajar behind her. "Turn on the blue light by the bed when you're ready. It's very romantic."

—Romantic is not what I feel, Manfred! she thought.

But aloud she said, "A—all right." She walked to the bedroom door and just before entering she turned back and said, "I—I'll call you when I'm ready. I won't take long."

She closed the bedroom door behind her and fell backward against it.

—Oh Lord! Help me through this—and forgive me!

She walked to the bed and sat down.

—Well, Imogen, the moment of truth has arrived. Time to get laid.

She rose and slithered out of her dress and laid it over a chair and slipped off her shoes to remove her panty hose and her G-string. Then she looked about her for the bathroom door, walked to it, opened it and switched on the lights which showed an attractively appointed powder room.

—Well, he certainly has everything very elegant and well appointed for his floozies!

—I should pee first.

That done, she returned to the bedroom where she slipped her feet back into her shoes and then opened her handbag and removed a mask and held it to her face.

—I don't imagine he'll like me wearing this, but I don't think I can go through with this without it. It's silly, I suppose, but somehow it makes me feel I'm keeping something back—preserving something of my integrity.

Perhaps it will say to him I'm not giving myself to him completely or willingly and that I'm doing this under protest.

She drew the mask over her face.

—Oh Lord! she gasped suddenly. What a strange feeling, as if somehow I'm becoming a different person—as though some drastic change coming over me, that I'm no longer Imogen Edwards. But that's silly. I'm the same person under the mask as I am without it, and I'll go mad if I think about such things. Right now, I have to do what the rest of American womankind does all the time, so Manfred says, and I guess it's mostly true—so here goes—the gangster's masked mistress.

She turned on the blue light by the bed and walked to the bedroom door and turned off the ceiling light so that only the dim glow of the blue light illuminated the room.

—Very romantic, I suppose, if this were really love making, but it's not, it's just fucking, to put it crudely. Well, Imogen, time to get fucked.

She put her hand on the door knob, opened the door slightly, and called, "Manfred—would you turn off the lights—please?"

"Huh? I want to see you."

"You will—but not right away—please."

"Geez! You're squeamish! But okay." When the lights went off, he called, "Come on out."

She, took a deep breath, opened the door fully, and stepped into the darkened room. She stood a moment silhouetted in the door frame and Manfred came to her an took her into his arms. She received a shock on realizing he too was naked, and in feeling the bare flesh of his chest pressed against her naked breasts and his erect penis burrowing into her pubic hair.

"Oh—!"

"What's the matter?"

"You—you're naked. It—it gave me a—a start."

"You don't expect me to make love with my clothes on do you?"

"No—it—it's just I've never been naked with a naked man before."

"I still find that hard to believe, but never mind. It's kind of an honor that I'm the first with you."

With one arm about her shoulders, he bent down and placed his other behind her knees, and lifted her into his arms.

"Oh—I—I guess I'm supposed to comment on how strong you are."

"Not if you don't want to. But I've never had anyone as nice as you in my arms before."

He carried her into he bedroom and then, by the blue light, in the room he saw her mask.

"Hey! What the hell! What's with the mask!"

"I—I hope you don't mind, Manfred. For—for now, I—I need it. The mask will help me overcome my inhibitions about this. It—it's the only way I can go through with it."

He continued to stare at her.

"Geez! You sure are making a hell of a big fuss about what everybody else does every night of the week practically. Dunno why I put up with so much from you, but well, if you want it, it ain't gonna—it isn't going to interfere none. But talk about kinky sex!" He lay her on the bed and looked down on her. "Hey!" he said after contemplating her for a few seconds. "You know, the mask makes you look real sexy! And it really sets off those great dark eyes of yours! Great idea!"

—Oh Lord! thought Imogen. That was hardly what I had in mind!

"And geez! I figured you had a great body, but never till now did I realize how great!"

"I—I hope you see me as more than just a body."

"Oh, hey! I do, but there ain't nothing wrong with having a great body too."

She looked on apprehensively as he drew the condom he took from the drawer of the bedside table over his erect penis.

"Bet you've never seen a cock like that before," he said, obviously proud of its large size.

"I—I've never seen a—a cock at all, Manfred—except in pictures."

"O yeah. I forgot."

She trembled as he lay down beside her.

"Manfred—please be gentle. It is, after all, my first time."

"Don't worry, Imogen. Don't worry. This is meant to be pleasant, and it will be." He leaned over and kissed her lips below the lower edge of her mask and began stroking her thighs. "Your skin is so soft and smooth," he said. "And you're so beautiful. That mask doesn't hide the fact that you're the most beautiful woman I've ever known."

As he stroked her thighs, she was at first unnerved by his touch on her naked flesh.

—What did the Victorian mothers tell their daughters? Think of England? What should I think of? The text of a poem? A score of a Beethoven sonata?

When he cupped her breasts with his hands and began to stroke them, she again felt unnerved, but gradually under his surprisingly gentle caressing she let herself go and to relax and yield to him. Then his hand went between her legs and touched her vagina.

"Oh!"

She tensed a bit, but his touch remained gentle, and again she found her resistance overcome and her vagina become soft and moist.

Then he parted her legs, lifted himself on top of her and entered her.

—Oh God!

He began to move inside her, gently at first, then more urgently.

—Oh Lord! This is horrible!

Then she felt a very sudden sharp pain as her hymen broke, and she let out a scream.

—Oh God! I knew it would be painful—but—but—not like—Oh! This is horrible!

Only momentarily distracted, Manfred continued to move within her with renewed and ever increasing ardor and passion, and suddenly she thought, Oh! I've never felt anything like this before! No, no! This is not horrible! I could never even have imagined it would be like this! It's not horrible! It's—it's—Oh God! This tension—it's almost unendurable—but oh! Oh! It's exciting, it's ecstatic! I—I—like it! It's wonderful!

"Oh!" she cried aloud. "Oh! Oh!"

And then, when she thought she could endure the tension no longer, it suddenly broke, almost like an explosion, and her whole being became suddenly relaxed in a way she had never felt before, exhausted but calm. At almost the same moment Manfred's face became distorted as his upper torso rose above her, and then he too went suddenly limp and collapsed on top of her as though he too were exhausted.

"Oh! Oh!" she sighed. "Oh!"

He slid face down beside her, one arm still over her body and then turned his face toward her.

"Did you enjoy it?" he asked, almost weakly. "Was I good?"

"I—I—yes—yes—I did enjoy it—so—so I guess you were good. I—I had heard that gang—that—I thought you'd just jump on me and force your way into me, but you didn't. Oh! I did like it!"

"I told you you would. Now you know what you've been missing."

"Yes—"

Suddenly tears began streaming down her face flowing from under her mask, and she turned away from him.

—Oh God! Why did such a wonderful thing, the most wonderful that I've ever known, have to happen with a gangster? Oh God! Oh God! Why?

"Hey!" he said raising himself on one elbow and staring down at her. "What's the matter? I thought you said you enjoyed it!"

"I did, Manfred. That's what—It's nothing, Manfred," she sobbed. "I—I can't explain. I guess I'm just a silly woman."

For several minutes she sobbed uncontrollably.

"Hey! Hey!" said Manfred. "Imogen! Geez! No other woman ever reacted like this."

"I—I'm not like other women, I guess, Manfred. I—I'll be all right in a while."

"Geez! I wish I knew what the hell was wrong."

"I—I hardly understand myself, Manfred. Nothing like this has ever happened to me. It's so completely unlike anything I ever experienced."

He touched her gently.

"Well, hey!" he said. "Next time it'll be easier."

"I—I suppose so, Manfred—but that's not—As I said, I can't explain."

"Geez! You sure are a strange one!" He remained leaning over her for a few moments, then sank back. "I'll never understand women!" he said.

Imogen stopped sobbing, lay silent for a moment, then turned to him.

"What a wonderfully original thought, Manfred!" she said, with mild sarcasm. "But," she hurried to add, "even though it is a cliche, maybe it's right. You can't ever fully possess me, ever fully enter me. I'll always be a mystery to you. Maybe, subconsciously, that's why I wanted to wear a mask."

"Huh! That's too much for me. And this is hardly the time and place to get philosophical."

"No," she said, rolling onto her back and staring at the ceiling. "I suppose not."

"You can take the mask off now," he said reaching over to do so.

"No!" she protested, slapping his hand away. "Not while I'm naked!"

"Well, as I say, you look real sexy in it, so okay."

She was silent for a while before saying, "I—I'm lying in my own blood—and it's soaking into the bedspread."

"That ain't nothin' to worry about. I'll get it cleaned."

"Well," she said, getting up from the bed, "I want to get cleaned up."

"Yeah. So do I. We can take a shower together."

"No!" she said, staring down at him through the openings of her mask. "No! It's enough that I've made love with you! For now, that's all! I'll clean up in here!"

"Ah geez! You take the fun out of everything!" Manfred shouted after her as she grabbed up her clothes and rushed to the powder room. "But geez! I love to see you naked in high heels!"

"Well," she called back as she shut the door and locked it behind her, "you'll just have to live on the memory for a while!"

—Oh Lord!, she said to herself when she was alone. I never realized how frustrated I was! And now what do I feel? Released? Aroused? Dirty? All three?

She turned on the tap in the wash basin and soaked a wash cloth.

—At least I can make myself physically clean. And I suppose now I should take off this mask. As she was about to she caught sight of her reflection in the mirror and leaning on the edge of the sink, she stared at herself for a while.

—Eighteenth century prostitutes wore masks to identify what they were. Maybe the mask is appropriate, for I feel rather like a whore.

Still contemplating her reflection she fell silent.

—What if I should like being a whore? Oh God!

Quickly she removed the mask, returned it to her handbag, cleaned herself up and dressed. She left the powder room, looked about for Manfred, and not seeing him, called his name.

"In here," he called from the living room. Looking at her and shaking his head as she emerged from the bedroom, he said, "You're a very strange woman. But how about we cap the evening off with a glass of wine on the gallery?"

"All right, th—thank you—but then I—I think I'd like to go home right afterwards, Manfred."

"Huh? The night's hardly begun!"

"Aunt and Uncle will be worried, and—and I—I feel I need to be alone."

He paused and stared at her some moments, but then he said, "Yeah. Okay. I promised to take care of you and to bring you back safely, and I want your aunt and uncle to know I keep my word—but after this, I want you to be prepared to stay the night with me."

"Oh—yes—I—I suppose that's also implicit in our deal."

"I wish to hell you'd stop referring to it as a deal! You're my girl friend, my woman, And it's because I love—like you. I want you, Imogen. I need you!"

She looked at him anxiously, but also sorrowfully and compassionately.

"I'm sorry I can't see things your way, Manfred."

"I can wait," he said, "for however long it takes."

"You may wait a very long time, Manfred—maybe forever."

"You'll come around sooner than you think," he said.

She looked away, then said, "Let's have our wine—and then we should go," she said.

A bit later, as they drove home, she let Manfred put with his arm about her shoulders and draw her to him. She relaxed in his embrace but was very silent.

"Why so quiet?" he asked.

"Sometimes a woman likes to be quiet, Manfred. It's been such an eventful evening for me—probably the most eventful of my life—that I want to think about it—reflect on it—that's all."

"Hey! it wasn't so bad, was it?"

She remained silent for some moments before she said "No," she said at last. "It wasn't. In many ways it was very pleasant. That's why I want to think."

"Geez! Geez! I just don't understand you!"

"Well, I'm glad I'm not completely transparent, Manfred. We—all of us—are and always will be mysteries to each other—you to me as much as I to you. We can't ever fully know one another. We're mysteries even to ourselves."

"Geez! Geez! You sure got some deep ideas. You get me thinking too. I'm not used to having to think about my women."

"That troubles you, doesn't it?"

"You're a new experience for me, and like I said, a challenge"

"You're a new experience—and a challenge—for me, too, Manfred; so I guess that makes us even."

"Yeah," he said, seemingly thoughtfully. "Yeah. I suppose it does."

They both fell silent for a while.

Then eventually, Imogen said with a smile, "And I think it also sort of makes us equal. It is the era of equality between the sexes, whether you like it or not."

"You seem determined to make me like it."

Again she smiled and said, "As I said, you're a challenge to me, Manfred."

"Hey! Touche!" cried Manfred and broke into a laugh in which Imogen found it impossible not to join. At almost the same moment the limousine pulled up at her uncle and aunt's home, and Manfred walked her to the door. They stood looking at each other for some moments before Imogen spoke.

"Well," she said with a wry smile, "it has been an interesting evening, Manfred. I certainly learned a lot."

"Huh?"

"And I enjoyed dinner—and dancing. I hope another time we'll spend more time dancing, for I really enjoyed it. For the rest—well, my head is full of confused thoughts which I want to try to sort out."

"Geez—!"

"Don't be upset," she said, again with a wry smile and touching her finger to his lips, "I won't burden you with too many disturbing philosophical ideas."

A look of utter amazement came over his face as suddenly she threw her arms about him and kissed him, though not passionately.

"Hey!" he said. "I wasn't expecting you to do that—though I sure as hell ain't complaining!"

"Women's Lib says the woman can take the initiative if she wants to. That's to say 'thanks' for the interesting evening, Manfred."

"I wish you had said 'enjoyable evening' or 'pleasant evening'—but maybe someday you will. And hey, if Women's Lib says what you say it does and makes you act like you did, maybe it ain't—it's not—so bad after all, and you're going to be all right, Imogen!"

"Well, we'll see. For now, Manfred, good night. It was an enjoyable evening."

"Yeah. Yeah. Good night, Imogen. I'll be in touch. We need to get you a dress for Mama and Papa's anniversary."

"Oh—yes. I guess so. Well—good night."

He turned and descended the steps, then turned back and waved to her. She nodded in acknowledgement, then turned and unlocked the door to enter the house.

"Is that you Imogen?" called her uncle from the dark hallway.

"Yes, Uncle, it is."

In his pyjamas and dressing gown, he turned on a light and looked earnestly at her.

"Are you all right?"

"Yes, Uncle, I'm all right. I'm not the same Imogen who left here a few hours ago, but I'm all right."

"Oh God! he didn't—!"

"Yes, he did, Uncle—yes we did. Did you really expect we wouldn't?"

"Well, your aunt and I sort of hoped against hope." He paused a moment. "What do you mean 'we did?' You let him have his way without protest?"

"I let him know I wasn't doing so willingly, Uncle, but I didn't want to be raped."

"No—no, I suppose not. And he didn't use force?"

"No, Uncle, he didn't. And I won't become pregnant. He used a condom."

"Well, that's one blessing. I just wish it had not happened at all." Again he paused, puzzled. "You seem awfully blase about it."

"Do I, Uncle? Well, I guess since it has to be, there's no point getting upset."

"Well, no, I suppose not—but—"

Then suddenly, all her pent up emotion gave way, and she burst into tears and fell on his shoulder.

"Oh Uncle!" she sobbed. "Oh Uncle!"

"Imogen! Imogen!" he said, patting her back and shoulders. "I feel as though somehow I've let you down—betrayed my trust from my brother and sister-in-law—to your father and mother. This was not what they'd have wanted, and certainly not what your aunt and I wanted!"

She stood back and wiped away her tears and kissed him very tenderly and affectionately on the cheek..

"Don't blame yourself or feel guilty, Uncle. It's not your fault. As Conrad's Marlow said, 'It's always the unexpected that happens'—and this has happened, that's all." Then after a moment she asked, "Is Aunty all right?"

"She couldn't sleep worrying about you. She wanted to know that you were all right. So did I, of course."

"Well, I'll try to persuade her not to worry. I'm all right, and if he's like he was tonight—he was actually rather nice, a gentleman in many ways, believe it or not—and I stand up to him as much as I can—and if I do—I'll continue to be all right."

"Lord, I certainly hope so."

"I will be, Uncle." She was about to kiss him good-night when she remembered Manfred's offer to help her aunt. "Oh, Uncle," she said, "he wants to send a doctor around to see if Aunt can be helped. He says he'll pay for everything. I know how you feel about—"

"I certainly don't want to have your aunt cured with stolen money, extorted money, money from the pushing of drugs, and—"

She put her finger to his lips to stop him from speaking further.

"Uncle, I understand. I don't like having that kind of money spent on me. But remember what General Booth said—"

"General Booth? Oh yes. Founder of the Salvation Army. What did he say that relates to all this?

"He said he'd take the devil's money and use it for God's work, and surely God wants Aunty healed and made able to walk—and we certainly do. Oh Uncle! Please! Let something good come of all this unhappiness—please, Uncle! Then maybe I'd feel that it was worthwhile."

Her uncle stood staring at her in silence for some time. At last, he spoke.

"Oh Imogen—Imogen! My poor girl! Yes, I see. Okay. I'll tell your aunt what you said and try to persuade her."

"Thank you, Uncle. And now I'll just go and say good-night to her and assure her I'm all right. Then both of you try to get some sleep."

Back in her own room a bit later, Imogen sat contemplating her reflection in the mirror on her dresser.

—Maybe I am, as Manfred says, gorgeous—and sexy—and maybe, after all, I like being gorgeous and sexy. And oh Uncle! I couldn't tell you this, but I feel suddenly that I'm a real woman—a fulfilled woman—and I like the feeling—but why, why did it have to be a gangster who awakened me to my womanhood? It makes me feel like a whore. And yet—and yet, now that it has happened, I want it to happen again. I feel as Marie Louise must have felt when, after Napoleon—whom she'd come to think of as the Corsican ogre—first made love to her, she said, "Do it again!" If it has to be with a gangster, then I'll be a whore! But oh God help me! God forgive me!

CHAPTER TEN

The following Sunday, Imogen rose before her uncle and aunt to attend the early Eucharist at St. Aidan's Episcopal Church. She wore the grey skirt belonging to her suit, a white blouse, her red four inch heels, carried her red purse and, in preference to her glasses, wore her contact lenses.

—I'll go, she thought, as the new Imogen Edwards. It's she who wants to see Father Daniels.

"Imogen!" exclaimed Father Richard Daniels, the rector, when he met her at the door after the service. "I hardly recognized you! How attractive you look! The way you should look, if I may say so."

"I hardly expected to hear anything like that from you, Father," she said, embarrassed and rather taken aback by the priest's unconscious agreement with Manfred Andreotti.

"Oh, I know. Priests are not supposed to have human feelings, but I'm afraid we do. And it's the Manichean heresy that denigrates the human body, not Christianity properly understood."

"Didn't St. Paul have something to say about outward adornment?"

"If First Timothy is Paul. But he speaks of seemly attire. I don't think that means unattractive."

"Hm. I'm not sure how seemly my attire was the other night," she said.

"Oh—? What happened the other night?" asked the priest, rather perplexed.

"Something happened of which my attire was only a minor part—but I—I wonder if I could make an appointment to see you, Father? Are—are you free on Wednesday?"

"Hm. I hope this is nothing serious."

"Serious enough, Father—but I don't think this is the time or place to talk about it. It—it's about a relationship—that's all I can say just now."

"Oh? A relationship? Well—Hm. Let me see—" The priest fumbled inside his cassock and produced a little appointment diary and a ball point pen. "Yes, Wednesday is fine. Is ten o'clock all right?"

"Yes, that would be fine. I'm sorry to be so enigmatic."

"Well, I'm sure you'll enlighten me on Wednesday."

"Yes, Father. I'll see you then—and thank you."

"That's why I'm here, Imogen."

And so on the following Wednesday at ten o'clock, Imogen sat before her parish priest in his office and told him the story of her relationship with Manfred Andreotti.

The priest, his brow furrowed, apparently deep in thought, leaned back in his swivel chair and for some time looked at her in silence.

"My goodness, Imogen!" he said at last. "I don't know what to say. I've never had to deal with a problem like this before. I'm deeply sorry this has happened to you. Dear me! Dear me! I wish I could think of something you might do, but at the moment nothing occurs to me."

"I don't know if there's anything anyone can do, Father. He has great power in this city."

"I'm only too well aware of that, Imogen. It's really shocking that it should be so, but I'm afraid it is so."

"I guess, Father, I just wanted to be able to tell someone that I could trust and whom I respect."

"Why, thank you, Imogen. But, yes, it does help to share the burden with someone—even if there's no immediate way of lifting it."

"I'm afraid it's a terrible burden, Father. I'm sorry to trouble you with it."

"No, no, Imogen. As I said on Sunday. That's why I'm here. I only wish I could be of more help."

"You helped by listening to me, Father." She was silent for a moment, then spoke hesitantly. "Father—I—I—Part of what is bothering me is that—well—first, if it weren't for what he is—he is very nice and treats me well—I—I could almost like him—"

The priest stared at her some moments before he spoke.

"Hm. Yes. I've heard he can be very charming, but be careful, Imogen."

"I—I'm trying to be, Father—as much as I can in the circumstances—but—but—it was my first sexual experience—strange as that may seem in this day and age—and—and, Father—I enjoyed it!"

Again the priest contemplated her silently for a few moments.

"The sexual experience itself—" he said at last, "the sexual act in and of itself—if we can isolate it from its circumstances, which I'm not sire we can entirely—but if we could, the experience is not in and of itself wrong, and it is meant to be pleasant and enjoyed. It is good. Though I uphold the view that its right place is in the marriage bed—particularly for Christians—but I don't think sexual intercourse out of wedlock is so very horrible if the people really care about each other and have some sort of commitment."

"I—I'm surprised," she said looking at him in some astonishment, "to hear you speak like that, Father."

"Some of my brother clergy—less so my sister priests—don't agree with me. But we live in an increasingly secularized society, and we can't impose our standards on non-believers—though there are those who think we can and should. I guess I'm a bit of a heretic, Imogen."

"I'd say you were an understanding and compassionate human being, Father."

"Thank you again, Imogen. But I sense that you're troubled because you're not really happy about how you feel about your relationship with Andreotti—that it's not a caring relationship."

"Yes, Father, it's not—at least it's not caring on my part. He says he loves me—I don't know how he can on such a brief acquaintance—and he says I'm very special—but the circumstances, Father—out of wedlock and with a gangster—! "

"Yes," he mused. "And you've made no commitment on your part?"

"No, Father—except for what I've told you—though—though I—I don't hate him. He—he's very nice to me—as I said."

"Well, we are not to hate people—not even people like Andreotti—just what he does. But this is a most difficult situation for you, Imogen."

They sat staring at each other for several moments.

Finally the priest said "Your situation reminds me somewhat of Isabella's in Shakespeare's play *Measure for Measure*. I'm sure you know it."

"Oh, yes, but you know, I never made the connection—and—and Isabella didn't yield her virginity to Angelo as," she said looking down in embarrassment, "I did to Manfred Andreotti."

"I'm not judging you, Imogen. Many find Isabella's attitude to her brother Claudio rather unfeeling and lacking in compassion—though I don't think Shakespeare thought she should surrender to Angelo. But she had the Duke on her side, and she agreed to his scheme to arrange the liaison with Mariana in substitution for herself."

"Angelo and Mariana were betrothed, Father," said Imogen, looking up again, "and in those days it was considered all right."

"Yes that's true, but the scheme still seems sneaky and a bit sleazy."

"Yes, I guess that's right. Many do see it that way."

"However, I'm thinking more of the way Angelo tried to manipulate Isabella to gratify his lust. And strangely enough, Angelo—rather like Andreotti, according to what you say—wanted Isabella because in her way she too was a very special sort of person. Also, I think in that play Shakespeare was trying to show—if we can make a moral preacher out of him—that in this world, we just can't always act in strict accord with rigid moral principles. It's a messed up world we live in, Imogen, with the good and the bad often incredibly and inextricably intertwined." Again he fell silent. "Damn!" he exclaimed at last. "Oh—sorry, Imogen. I'm not as holy as I should be."

"As I said, you're human, Father," she responded looking up at him and smiling.

"All too human, I'm afraid. It's hard to control at times."

"It's because you're human that I feel I can talk to you."

"Well, thank you, Imogen. There was a time when I forgot my humanity. Almost all of us do. We think ordination automatically makes saints of us, or angels, or something. Some of us, I'm afraid never get rid of the idea. But all this literary and theological discussion, however enlightening about the world and humanity, isn't helping you in your circumstances. As I said earlier, I wish I knew what to tell you to do—how to help you."

"It helps to talk about it, and you've listened, Father."

"That's easy enough to do and doesn't cost much. Well, Imogen, you've acted to help your friends—and I'm sure God will take that into account. It's the motive more than the deed that He looks at."

"The trouble is, Father, that in some ways this whole mess is rather a good deal for me. He buys me very attractive—if a bit too revealing—clothing and I—I find that I like looking attractive," she said, blushing.

"And why shouldn't you? Both my wife and I have often wondered why you didn't dress better."

"Oh—yes—your wife is very attractive, Father, and she dresses well. I should have thought of her example, perhaps, more than I have."

"I don't know what I did to deserve a woman like her, Imogen—a good Christian and a beautiful woman to boot. But, about the matter you mentioned first—that you thought you could almost like him—We have to believe, don't we Imogen, that there is good in everyone, no matter how deeply it's buried under the surface. Even gangsters are human beings made in God's image and are redeemable—somehow." He fell silent. When at last he spoke, he said, "I know you're in very difficult, unsavory and unenviable circumstances. And so, Imogen, though I can't come up with any brilliant solutions right now, I'll certainly be praying for you."

"Thank you, Father, but sometimes—I'm sorry, Father—it's very hard to understand how prayer works or to believe that it does."

"Oh, I know, Imogen. You're not alone. I've had some very dark times, too. I don't know how prayer works. I know God doesn't force himself on anyone. Unlike the medieval church, I don't believe grace is irresistible—not because God can't overcome the barriers we set up but because, unlike many of us—too many—He respects our boundaries, and so He won't. He has to look for openings, and he has to work with a lot of rather ornery people and with a lot of badly messed up situations—and sometimes, I guess the openings don't occur. I don't think it's easy being God. Well, enough theological speculation. I haven't been much help, I'm afraid."

"It has helped to talk, Father. Thank you for listening to me, and for your prayers—and for your wisdom."

"Wisdom! Well, I don't know how wise I am, Imogen. I often feel I just blunder around. But remember, for what it's worth, I'm always here for you."

"Thank you, Father. But now—would—would you hear my confession?"

"Certainly I will, Imogen."

"I—I'm afraid I can't exactly promise amendment of life."

"I'm sure God will understand. You acted from a good motive. Like Asa, your heart is right."

"I—I hope so, Father."

CHAPTER ELEVEN

In a white, very full skirted backless evening gown with only two panels of material rising above her waist and crossing in a V over her breasts and clasped behind her neck, gold earrings and necklace, white gloves reaching above her elbows and gold shoes with five inch heels and a gold handbag completing her ensemble, Imogen stepped from the limousine and stared in wide-eyed, open-mouthed astonishment at the large, two storied, white mansion with its long flight of stairs up to the colonnaded terrace which ran the full width of the building, and large palladian windows and second storey balconies. Although she knew it had all been made possible by stolen and extorted money and illicit trade, she was nevertheless impressed.

"Pretty nice place, hey?" said Manfred standing at her side after handing her out of the limousine.

"It's magnificent, Manfred!"

Embarrassed as much by the unaccustomed splendor of her attire as by its exposure of her flesh, she felt even more embarrassed as well as angered by the low, lewd whistles with which the male guests chatting, smoking and drinking on the veranda greeted her as, on Manfred's arm, she mounted the steps.

"Hey, Manfred!" called out one of the men on the terrace. "Where'd you find the gorgeous broad?"

"Yeah, Andreotti," called another voice. "She's a living doll. Has she got a sister for me?"

As Imogen had anticipated, another commented on her "great pair of hooters," and admonished her to "be careful they don't fall out of that dress you're almost wearing!"

"Shut up, you clowns!" Manfred retorted angrily. "She's one of a kind, and she's not a broad. And she has breasts, not hooters. You guys need a lesson in taste and discrimination. This is a very educated, cultivated lady, so keep your lecherous thoughts to yourselves."

Imogen, as pleased as she was surprised by Manfred's rebuking his friends and associates for their remarks, looked at him appreciatively, smiled, and whispered, "Thank you, Manfred!"

A chorus of adverse reactions followed them as they walked past.

"Geez! What's with Andreotti all of a sudden?"

"Yeah! How come he's so touchy about this dame?"

"She must be some woman if she can wrap Andreotti around her finger like that. Holy shit!"

"Holy fuck, I'd say."

"Knock it off, you bunch of yahoos!" Manfred called back at them as he led her into the lavishly furnished foyer of the mansion. Here several couples and other groups sat or stood about, talking and sipping cocktails, but, as she passed by with Manfred, they all turned their eyes on her.

"Who's that with Manfred?"

"Dunno, but she's sure a beaut!"

Down one of the two long flights of curved stairways which led to the gallery above the foyer a small boy about four years old came running toward them.

"Oh *Zio Manfredo*!" he cried, stopping in his tracks in front of them. "Your new girl friend's booful!"

"Hey Luigi! You're developing a good eye already," said Manfred ruffling the child's hair affectionately, a gesture which again surprised Imogen but which she felt revealed an an unexpectedly appealing aspect of his personality.

"Manfred!" she exclaimed. "What a delightful little boy? Who is he?"

"This is Luigi, my nephew. My other sister Rosina's kid. Luigi, meet Imogen."

Imogen knelt down to the child's level and extended her hand.

"How do you do, Luigi. I'm very happy to meet you."

Tongue-tied with embarrassment, the little boy looked down.

"Hey, Luigi!" said Manfred. "Where's your manners? Cat got your tongue? Can't you say 'How do you do?' to Imogen?"

"How do do, Immy-jean," said Luigi, looking shyly at her.

"How do you do, Luigi. What a handsome and charming young man you are," said Imogen, "and not because you said I'm beautiful. You just are."

"Oh! Oh!" cried the little fellow, and turned and ran away, seemingly uncertain whether he was happy or embarrassed. "Mama! Papa!" he cried. "Come see *Zio Manfredo*'s booful girl friend!"

"Hey! You've really got a fan!" said Manfred as Imogen stood erect again.

"He's a lovely little boy, Manfred! How could anyone not like him?"

"Yeah, he's okay. Nice to have him around," he said. "Makes up a bit for not having my own kid here."

Imogen heard the sadness in his voice, and laying her free hand on his arm, responded "I think it's really sad that you can't see your son, Manfred."

"Thanks," he said, a catch in his voice, gratitude in his eyes. "But hey!" he said, resuming his somewhat artificial tone of joviality, ashamed almost, Imogen thought, at having let his humanity reveal itself. "Let's go in. I want you to meet my Mama and Papa. It's their party, after all, and they've been dying to meet you."

"Oh dear, Manfred! You've been talking out of class. You've probably built me up so much in their imaginations that the real me will be a let down."

"I doubt it," he said.

From the foyer, Manfred led her into a large ballroom where couples were dancing under the crystal chandeliers hanging from the ornately decorated ceiling to a Johann Strauss Waltz played by the hired professional orchestra seated at the far end of the room. Rich draperies adorning the large windows completed the opulent decor, and again Imogen found her breath taken away by the splendor of her surroundings.

"How magnificent!" she exclaimed.

"Yeah, it's a pretty nice room, all right," said Manfred. "Mama and Papa are over there," he added, indicating with a nod of his head a family group on the right and directing her steps that way. "Oh—don't mention to Papa how we got together in Little Italy."

"You mean they don't know Manfred? Why?"

"Papa thinks I'm too soft on people some times. He wouldn't like to hear I let your friends off the hook, even though I've put the squeeze on some other clients to make up for it."

"Oh—"

"Yeah. I run the operation, but Papa's still the real boss."

"Oh—I—I see."

—I'd hardly have thought him soft, she thought, but I suppose by the standards of his world, his action was soft, and that means he took a risk and put himself in danger in making me his girl friend! Why does he think I'm worth it? And what will be the consequences for him—and for me?

Manfred had now led her, again under the appreciative scrutiny of many eyes, across the ballroom to where a grey-haired, wizened, leathery looking man sat in a wheel chair, and by his side stood a tall, erect dignified, almost regal woman, younger than he and still quite handsome despite the grey in her hair and the lines at the corners of her eyes. On her right in a becoming pale blue strapless gown stood Ana-Maria, all smiles and eager when she saw Imogen. On the old man's left stood a good-looking but hard-faced woman in an unbecoming pink gown, whom Imogen assumed was the other sister, Rosina, and a rather smug-looking man, no doubt her husband. With them stood Luigi who became very excited on seeing Imogen again.

"Oh!" he cried. "There she is! There she is! *Zio Manfredo*'s booful lady!"

Rosina looked at her with a very critical and unfriendly eye, and her husband, Imogen thought to her discomfort, with a rather lecherous one.

"Mama! Papa!" said Manfred, his voice resonating with pride. "This is Imogen."

"Hey! Hey!" said Manfred's father from his wheel chair. "*Manfredo* say you a reala gooda looking woman! He notta lie!"

"*Piacere, Signor*," said Imogen, dropping a slight curtsy.

"Hey! She speaka *Italiano*!" cried the old man.

"I told you," Manfred almost crowed, "she was smart and talented as well as a real beauty like you'd never seen before!"

Just then, with a formal bow, Manfred's mother spoke. "*Buona notte, Signorina. Benvenuto a la Casa Andreotti*. My Manfredo speaks very highly of you, *Signorina Imogena*, and I can see that you have the manners of a lady."

"*Grazie, Signora Andreotti*," Imogen responded dropping a deep curtsy. "*Piacere e felice anniversario. Congratulazioni.*"

"*Grazie, Signorina*. And You speak Italian very well," said *Signora Andreotti*, apparently both impressed and pleased by Imogen's speaking to her in her native language.

"Hey!" exclaimed Manfred. "Didn't I tell you she was really something!"

"Indeed, indeed," said his mother. "How did you acquire such facility, *Cara*?"

Reassured by the affectionate "*cara*," Imogen replied, "I grew up next door to Little Italy and with many Italian friends, and I studied Italian as my minor in university where I read some of Dante and Petrarch, Ariosto, and Tasso in the original."

"Who they?" asked the old man.

"Oh goodness, Papa!" said Ana-Maria, speaking for the first time. "They're some of Italy's greatest writers."

"There, you see again!" said Manfred. "Didn't I tell you she knows everything. Graduated *summa cum laude* from Princeton."

"Oh Manfred!" protested Imogen. "I hardly know everything!"

"*Di nuova, Benvenuto, Signorina Imogena*," said Manfred's mother, obviously warming to her son's new companion. "*Benevenuto, et grazie*."

"I told you you'd like her, Mama," said Manfred and then continued the introductions. "Ana-Maria you've met. This is my older sister Rosina and her husband Giorgio."

"How do you do?" said Rosina, with a curt nod, not extending her hand. "So you're what all the fuss has been about."

"I—I hope Manfred hasn't been making too much of me—though it seems that he has."

"He's talked of nothing else. Well, now at least we know who you are."

"If you ask me," said her husband with a smarmy grin, "Manfred hardly said the half of it."

"No one asked you," snarled his wife, turning an angry look at him.

As though to relieve the tension, Ana-Maria stepped forward and took Imogen's hands in hers.

"Imogen! Imogen!" she exclaimed. "I'm so glad to welcome you to our home and so happy that we can be friends after all!"

"I—I look forward to it, Ana-Maria."

"Manfred, you simply must spare us a little time tonight to be together, woman to woman."

"Oh, yeah," he said. "A bit of hen talk. Should be possible. But first I want to dance with my beautiful and talented girl friend. Imogen?" he said, offering her his arm.

"*Sì!*" cried the elder Andreotti with a lecherous laugh. "You dance witha you lady, Manfredo. But you lucky I in thisa wheela chair. Otherwisa you notta getta mucha chance."

Taking Manfred's arm Imogen walked with him to the dance floor.

"Your mother's very gracious, Manfred—as you said, a true lady—and so is Ana-Maria, but your older sister doesn't like me," she said as he enfolded her in his arms to dance.

"Don't worry about Rosina" Manfred responded. "She doesn't like anybody—except herself."

"And—and your brother-in-law—I—I don't like the way he looks at me."

"You don't need to worry about him. He's a wimp. All talk and no action. He pees sitting down."

"Oh—"

"So," he said, leading her in the waltz, "forget about them. We're here to dance." After only a few steps, he said, "Hey! Your dancing's even better tonight than the other!"

"Why, thank you, Manfred, but I still think it's because I have such a good partner, and these five-inch heels really get me up on my toes—but oh, what a time I had learning to stay upright in them. But how do you come to be such a good dancer? You're a far better dancer and give a better lead than anyone else who ever partnered me—not that I've had all that many partners."

"Well, Mama figured since the family'd become so important we should get a bit of culture and social graces. She's from the Italian aristocracy, you know."

"No, I didn't Manfred! How is it—if it's not impolite to ask—that she married your father?"

"Her Papa, the count, had dealings with the Syndicate. That's how they met. The family needed money. So Papa was able to cut a deal."

"Oh—!" Imogen exclaimed, horrified at the thought of a matrimonial business transaction.

"But it wasn't all business," said Manfred, interpreting her thoughts. "They were in love. In fact, she was pregnant with Rosina at the time. Anyway Mama hired people to teach us stuff like dancing. I just sort of took to it, I guess, and enjoyed it."

"Is that why you go to the opera—because of its social prestige?"

"Yeah, partly. But all Italians love opera. It's in our blood."

"I suppose, in a way of speaking, it is. Do you like other kinds of music—the symphony, piano, violin, chamber music—?"

"Yeah, but not as much as opera. But hey! I want to hear you play the piano! Susan says your great, and there's a real nice grand piano in one of the other salons. None of us really took to it that much—Ana-Maria a little. I never even tried. I bet you'd make that piano sound great. I'd love to hear you."

"I don't know, Manfred. Perhaps some day."

"Maybe we'll find time this evening at one of the intermissions."

"Oh—well, I didn't really come here to entertain—"

"Not for everybody, just for me."

"Well—"

The music stopped, and Manfred said, "We'll talk about it again. Right now lets get a drink."

He led her to a long table where many varieties of alcoholic beverage and the appropriate glasses were set out. Behind it stood another table bearing a huge, many-tiered anniversary cake.

"My goodness! What a magnificent cake, Manfred!"

"Yeah, well it is their fiftieth anniversary, after all. What would you like to drink?"

"White wine would be very nice."

"Sure. Any kind in particular?"

"Oh heavens, Manfred! I hardly know one wine from another."

"Well, here, try a bit of *Pinot blanc*. It's French. You'll like it."

"I'm sure, if you say it's good, I will. Your taste in such matters, Manfred, is excellent."

Manfred called to the bartender, "A *Pinot blanc* for my lady and a Bourbon and branch for me, bartender."

"This is very nice, Manfred," said Imogen when she had tasted her wine.

"Thought you'd like it. Then, looking past her, he said, "Well if it isn't Rosina and Giorgio. I knew you couldn't stay away from the bar for long, Giorgio."

"Speak for yourself, Manfredo."

"Yeah, well I know how to hold it better than you do."

—Clearly there's no love lost between the brothers-in-law, thought Imogen.

"So," sneered Rosina, "this is the skirt Manfred picked up in the suburbs."

"Hey!" snapped Manfred. "Who are you calling a skirt? She's got more class that you'll ever have, Rosina. And we met at the opera."

"Well, I suppose she is a rather pretty little thing," said the obviously jealous Rosina, eyeing Imogen's decolletage, "especially in a dress which leaves so little to the imagination."

"The dress was Manfred's choice," protested Imogen.

"You can't stand to see a woman better looking than you, can you Rosina?" taunted Manfred.

"Manfred," said Imogen. "It's all right. Please let's not have a quarrel."

"Yeah," he replied. "Right you are. Try not to spoil the evening, Rosina—for Mama and Papa's sake if for nobody else's. This is supposed to be a happy occasion."

"Well if you're going to bring a little slut like this—"

Seething with anger, Manfred raised his hand and struck Rosina very hard across the face making her stagger backwards.

"Nobody calls my girl friend—especially not Imogen!—a slut."

Gasps of amazement rose from those standing about, then a stunned silence and then by a buzz of whispering.

"Manfred!" cried Imogen. "Please! If—if I'm going to be the cause of so much trouble, please take me home. I don't want—"

"You're not causing the trouble. It's this bitch of a sister of mine!"

"Hey, now!" spoke up Giorgio. "That's my wife you're talking about."

"It's about time you came to my defence, you wimp!" said Rosina. "You let him get away with hitting me!"

"Please! Please! Manfred, do take me home," cried Imogen. "I don't want to be the cause of friction in your family. Clearly they don't like me."

She broke into tears.

"Hey! Hey, Imogen!" said Manfred putting his arm around her. "See what you've done!" he barked at Rosina. Then to Imogen he said, "It's all right, darling, it's all right."

"'Darling'!" snorted Rosina. "Already she's 'darling'!"

That he had called her "darling" had not registered on Imogen in her agitation. In fact, she would have assumed that all his women were "darling" were it not for his tender solicitude which both astonished her and evoked her appreciation.

Ana-Maria now came hurrying across from the other side of the floor and intervened.

"What's the matter? What's going on here? Why is Imogen crying?"

"Aw!" said Manfred in disgust. "Rosina's just being her normal self."

"Rosina!" protested Ana-Maria. "Imogen's our guest. You know how Mama and Papa feel about that. Imogen," she said, grasping Imogen's hand, "I'm sorry."

"I—I'd like to go home," Imogen said again.

"Oh, no, no. You mustn't do that!" protested Ana-Maria. Then turning to her brother, she said, "Maybe if I took her up to my suite for a while, Manfred?"

"Yeah. Good idea. You go with Ana-Maria for a while, Imogen and have a nice chat. It'll make you feel better."

"Yes, please do," coaxed Ana-Maria. "I've been hoping we might have some time to talk—you know, girl talk—woman to woman. I so want to get to know you!"

"Well—"

"Come on, then" said Ana-Maria, almost tugging her away, giving Imogen little choice but to go with her.

"Yeah. You girls have a nice chin wag," Manfred called after them. "See you in a while, Imogen."

Ana-Maria first went to explain to her parents.

"Why did Manfred hit his sister?" demanded *Signora Andreotti*.

"It seems she insulted our guest—Imogen," replied Ana-Maria.

"Thatsa notta nice," said the old man. "No waya talka pretty woman lika you. We maka her apologize."

"No. Please, Signor Andreotti," said Imogen. "It's all right. I—I'm sorry for the trouble."

"It's not your fault, *Cara*," said Manfred's mother. "We're sorry that Rosina was impolite to you. You're *Manfredo*'s friend and our guest, and she should treat you well. But even so, *Manfredo* should not hit his sister."

"I—I really think I should leave," said Imogen once more. "I don't want to be the cause of trouble in a family."

"No, no," cried Signor Andreotti from his wheelchair. "You notta leava. Rosina acta bad. You stay. She apologiza."

"Yes, you must stay, Imogen," said Ana-Maria. Then to her parents she said, "I'm taking her up to my rooms for a nice heart-to-heart chat."

"Thatsa gooda idea," said the old man. "You go talka Ana-Maria, Imogena. You feela better. Then you coma back."

"*Si, si*," said Manfred's mother. "A nice visit with Ana-Maria is just the thing."

"Come on, Imogen," said Ana-Maria, again tugging her by the hand and leading her away across the ballroom toward an arched exit. "Really, something's got to be done about Rosina—though I don't know what. She's vicious. She's the eldest and thinks she ought to rule the roost around here, and I believe she even thinks she should run the business instead of Manfred."

They entered a large salon where Imogen saw the grand piano Manfred had mentioned, and, because in times of distress she always found relief and consolation in music, she wished she could sit down and play it. However, Ana-Maria led her up a long curving flight of stairs to the second floor and down a hallway to her apartment where she ushered her into a comfortably and tastefully furnished sitting room.

"This is lovely!" exclaimed Imogen despite her distress and tears.

"It's my own private retreat," said Ana-Maria. "I don't know what I'd do if I didn't have this place. Please sit down, Imogen. I'm sorry all this has happened, but I'm so glad we can have this time to chat. I've so looked forward to it!"

Imogen seated herself in the comfortable armchair indicated and buried her face in her hands.

"I—I'm sorry," she sobbed. "I'm very upset by all this."

"I understand, Imogen, but don't let Rosina get to you. As Manfred said, she's just being Rosina. But what did she do to make Manfred hit her? It's not like him to do that."

"I felt like slapping her myself," said Imogen, looking up. "She called me a slut."

"Oh! That bitch! You *should* have slapped her! That's the only way to treat her. You have to stand up to her. She had no right to call you that!"

—Except, thought Imogen, sleeping with Manfred—even if it's not by choice—almost does make me a slut—or a whore—especially since I enjoyed it and want to do it again.

"He shouldn't have hit her though," Imogen said, resuming the discussion.

"Manfred defends those he cares about, Imogen," said Ana-Maria. "When we were kids, Rosina always picked on me—I don't know why except maybe because I'm the youngest—and Manfred always came to my aid and stood up for me against her. He and I have always been good friends—except that he's so busy all the time now that he runs the business. So you see, he acted in character. It shows how much he cares about you."

"I—I appreciate his coming to my defence, but I still don't think he should have hit her."

"Well, no, I suppose not. I'll speak to him. But," said Ana-Maria brightening, "I'm so glad we can be friends, Imogen. Manfred really thinks you're wonderful—and I agree with him."

Imogen looked down and blushed.

"It's funny, you know," Ana-Maria continued, "Manfred and I are fairly easy going, but we've not had good success at marriage—Oh!" she exclaimed, putting her hands to her mouth in consternation. "I hope he told you."

"Oh, yes. He did on our first real date," said Imogen. "It's sad he doesn't see his little boy."

"Yes. He really misses him, but I'm glad he told you about his marriage. Rosina's very hard to live with, but she manages to hold onto Giorgio. Probably has him too frightened to try to break away." Then suddenly she burst into tears and cried, "Oh God, Imogen! I hate this life." And she leaned forward from her chair to grasp Imogen's hands. "How I hate it! I rattle on to try to keep from thinking about it. Please, please, Imogen, be my friend!"

"I—I'll try, Ana-Maria." said Imogen sympathetically pressing Ana-Maria's hands in hers. "I'd like to be your friend. I think I'll need a friend in all this, too."

"We can cry on each other's shoulders," said Ana-Maria looking up. "There's no one else with whom I can cry. I hate being a syndicate princess! I feel so boxed in. I can't be myself.

"I'm sorry, Ana-Maria," said Imogen, beginning to understand the sorrow she had seen in Ana-Maria's eyes at the opera and feeling genuine pity for her. "I—I think I can understand how you feel."

"Oh, I manage all right. You don't grow up in this environment without learning to be tough—but I wish I didn't have to be. And I wish Manfred didn't have to be."

On hearing that, Imogen looked wide-eyed and intently into the eyes of her new friend.

"He was brought up to be tough and ruthless," Ana-Maria continued, "and he puts up a good front, but it's only partly him. I worry about him. Oh, he's efficient. He runs everything very well. He can put pressure on people, but I wonder if he's got that last bit of ruthlessness. So far the

Andreotti name is enough to frighten everyone, but I wonder—if people were to know he's not completely ruthless—" She paused. "I—I shouldn't talk about this."

Imogen continued to stare at her, now utterly confused about the man who had coerced her into being his mistress. She had heard and seen so much that had the effect of softening her toward him.

"That he wanted you for his girl friend," Ana-Maria went on, "shows, I think, what kind of man he is at heart. He sees you as very special—beautiful, intelligent, talented and cultured. He's never found anyone remotely like you before—nor have I. That's why I've wanted you as a friend."

Imogen feeling embarrassed and not knowing how to respond, the two women sat some moments in silence looking at each other. A knock at the door interrupted the silence and Manfred's voice called from behind it.

"Hey! Are you gals going to talk all night?"

Ana-Maria went to the door to admit him.

"Oh Manfred! You're so impatient."

"Yeah, well I don't like being away from my woman. How is Imogen?" he asked as he entered. "Is she all right again?"

"Yes, I'm fine again, Manfred," she said managing a smile. "Ana-Maria and I had a good talk."

"Good, but everyone's wondering where you disappeared to, and it's getting on toward the time for toasts and cutting the cake, and I'd like another dance before that."

"Yes, come on Imogen," said Ana-Maria. "Let's go back."

Imogen rose to meet Manfred, seeing him, after Ana-Maria's revelations about their childhood and Manfred's less than ruthless nature, in a different, though not yet clear, light.

"What is it?" he asked.

"What do you mean, Manfred? What is what?"

"You're looking at me funny."

"Oh? I didn't realize." Then she added, partly to cover her own embarrassment, "Funny peculiar, or funny ha-ha?"

"Huh? I don't know. But come on. Let's go back and dance."

"I'd like that, Manfred."

As, followed by Ana-Maria, he led her down the hall toward the stairs, she said "I wish you hadn't hit your sister, Manfred, and I think you should apologize."

"Geez! She deserved it! She shouldn't have talked to you like that."

"No, but I'm afraid people will say unfavorable things about me, Manfred. As your girl friend, I won't be immune from gossip. So please apologize to her."

"Okay, if you want me to."

"I do, Manfred, but you should do it whether I want you to or not. But I'll go with you when you do. And do it soon."

"Okay. Right. If you say so. Yeah—yeah, you're probably right, I should."

They reached the bottom of the stairs where the magnificent grand piano stood.

"I want to hear you play before the evening's over," said Manfred.

"I'll be happy to play for you some time. It looks like such a wonderful instrument." She broke away from him and walked over to look at the piano. "My goodness!" she exclaimed. "A *Boesendorfer*! I've never played a *Boesendorfer*!"

"Is that supposed to be good?"

"Some people say it's it's the Rolls Royce of pianos—a better piano even than the Steinway. I don't know about that, but I do know it's a very fine piano."

She lifted the cover and touched a few chords.

"It has a lovely tone!" she said.

"Hey! The music's just stopped in the ballroom. Why don't you sit down and play something?"

"Oh, I don't know—"

"Please do, Imogen," said Ana-Maria. "I'd love to hear you too."

"Well—"

Manfred having already raised and propped up the lid, she found the temptation to play such a fine piano too strong to resist.

"All right," she said, drawing out the bench and seating herself at the keyboard and peeling off her gloves. "Let's see. But if I'm to work the pedals," she said kicking off her gold five-inch stiletto heels, "I don't think I can do it in these stilts you expect me to wear."

She thought for a moment and then began to play the meditative B-flat Impromptu of Schubert's first set. Her fingers caressed the keys bringing forth from the instrument the beautiful song-like melody and its gently undulating accompaniment, and, head thrown back, staring into vacancy, she lost herself in the music.

When she had finished, Ana-Maria said, "Oh Imogen! That was lovely!"

Manfred stared at her in amazement.

"Yeah!" he said. "Yeah. Geez! Susan was right! You really do play beautifully!"

"Thank you," said Imogen. "Thank you both, but on a piano like this—"

"Hey! Geez! There you go again. The piano's only as good as the person who plays it."

"A good piano also inspires good playing, Manfred."

"Please play something else!" said Ana-Maria.

"Oh, but shouldn't we get back?"

"We still got time," said Manfred. "Play something else—please."

"Well, this really should have come before the other," she said and launched into the rapid runs of the Second Impromptu in A-flat. Her fingers rippled over the keys, and she played the impassioned middle section with an intensity she had never given it before. To her amazement a burst of applause greeted the final chords, and she looked up to see a considerable number of the guests gathered around.

"Oh—!" she exclaimed. "Th—thank you all. I—I didn't realize I had an audience."

"We just couldn't stay away when we heard you," said someone.

"Hey! And it was great!" said another voice.

"Yeah! You really found a talented lady there, Manfred."

"Didn't I tell you she was something special," he said, almost gloating in his pride.

At this moment little Luigi burst from the crowd and ran to her.

"Oh Immy-jean! You play p'ano booful! Just like you booful!"

"Why Luigi!" she said putting her arm around him "Thank you! Just for that I will play something else specially for you."

The audience murmured ascent and approval.

"Yes, yes. Do play again."

"Do you know," Imogen asked Luigi, "the song 'Twinkle, twinkle, little star'?"

"*Zia* Ammaria sing it for me."

—But not your mother, she thought. How sad!

"Well," she said aloud and looking down at him, "this is what a man called Mozart did with that song—only he called it '*Ah! Vous dirai-je, Maman*'. It's really a French song. It means, 'Ah! I want to speak to you, Mama.'"

And she began to play Mozart's Variations. Occasionally she glanced down and smiled at Luigi who stood rapt in wonder as she played.

Again applause greeted the conclusion of her playing, and Luigi said, "Oh! That boofull, Immy-jean! Play again!"

"Oh, Luigi, not just now. I've played enough for tonight. We should all get back for you grandpapa's and grandmama's party."

"Can you play *Liebestraume?*" asked Manfred.

"*Liebestraume?*" she said, taken aback by the request. "By Liszt?" she asked, knowing full well he meant the popular third piece of that title.

"Yeah. That one."

"Yes, but don't you think—"

"Everything can wait. I'd like to hear you play *Liebestraume*—please," he said.

"Yes! Yes!" said the other voices. "Do play again."

"Well—a—all right—"

—Why has he asked for this? she asked herself as she started to play. Why?

With the last hushed chords, a hush also fell over her listeners who all seemed to feel that something unusual was happening here, and Imogen looked up to see Manfred leaning on the end of the piano, an enraptured gaze fixed upon her. She sat for a moment staring back at him, her lips parted in deep consternation.

"I think he's in love with her," she heard one of the women whisper.

"Maybe he is," whispered the woman standing beside her. "The title means `Love's Dream'."

"That was just beautiful!" said Manfred gazing at her with that same wondering, admiring gaze with which he had first looked at her at the opera. "Beautiful—like you. Luigi's right. You play like you are."

"Oh!" she said, almost inaudibly and looking away in confusion. "Manfred, please! You embarrass me!"

Ana-Maria came to her rescue saying, "I think we really should get back now, though I could listen to you play all night, Imogen."

"Yeah," said Manfred, coming back to his surroundings. "Me too, but it is just about time for the toast and the cake-cutting." He came over to Imogen and held out his hand to her.

"I—I have to put my shoes on again—"

After slipping her feet into her gold pumps and pulling on her gloves, she rose and diffidently took his hand.

"You really do play beautifully, Imogen!" he whispered in her ear.

"Th—thank you," she said as they walked back toward the ballroom. "I—I appreciate your saying so, but you really embarrassed me."

"Sorry, I just can't help it. You are beautiful—and I love you."

"Oh Manfred!" she exclaimed in shocked surprise at the intense feeling with which he spoke. "How can you?"

"How can I not love a woman as beautiful and talented as you?"

"If—when—I'm loved, I want to be loved for more than my looks."

"I do love you for more than that. Haven't I been saying how smart and talented you are? I can't explain, but, like I said, I knew as soon as I saw you that you were more wonderful than any woman I ever met before, and that I wanted you like I never wanted any other woman before."

"I—I don't know what to say, Manfred. I—I can't return your feelings—"

"Maybe not now. I won't pressure you," he said, "but at least let me love you."

"I—I feel I'll only cause you pain, Manfred."

"We'll see."

As they spoke, they reentered the ballroom and were immediately confronted by Rosina who said, "So she plays the piano, does she? The way Luigi talks about her, she's a female Paderooski."

"Rosina," said Imogen looking Rosina directly in the eyes. "I'm sorry you don't like me, but I'm also sorry Manfred struck you, and so is he."

"Yeah. Yeah. Sorry about that, Sis."

"Well you should be!"

"He is, Rosina," continued Imogen. "Since Manfred has chosen me to be his girl friend, then we have at least to try to tolerate each other."

"Yeah, Rosina," said Manfred, "you better accept Imogen. Like she says, I chose her to be my girl friend, and I don't want anyone else, so you're going to see a lot of her."

"Hm! Well, there's no debating over taste, I suppose," Rosina snorted. "Okay. I'll put up with you, Imogen, but stay out of my way, that's all. And quit trying to steal my kid away from me."

"Steal your—steal Luigi!" Imogen almost exploded. "It was he who came to me. But if you don't want me to be friends with him, I'll not be. But don't accuse me of trying to steal him!"

"Yeah, and when do you ever show him any affection, Rosina?" said Manfred. "Ana-Maria gives him more love than you ever do, so I don't know why you can't let him be friends with Imogen."

"Never mind, Manfred," said Imogen. "It's her right as his mother, and I don't want the little fellow to be the centre of a storm or torn this way and that. Come, Manfred," she said, and this time she led him away. "Good night, Rosina."

"Hey! You really stood up to Rosina!" said Manfred admiringly as they walked away. "That's what she needs."

"In your world, Manfred, I can see I'm going to have to learn to hold my own."

"Well you sure did with Rosina! But let's not talk about that now. Let's get back to Mama and Papa. The New Jersey godfather is going to propose a toast."

"Oh—the—the godfather's here!"

"Yeah. He and Papa are old cronies. But come on. They want the family all gathered around."

"I'm not family, Manfred."

"You're my girl. That makes you family."

He led her to where the family were gathering about his parents.

"Is she going to be in this?" demanded Rosina.

Before anyone could reply, Signor Andreotti spoke: "You be quiet, Rosina. She'sa Manfredo's lady and has the manners of a lady, so she'sa welcome here."

"There, you see, Rosina" said Manfred.

Rosina scowled and grit her teeth.

The godfather, greying and somewhat frail, but nonetheless, Imogen felt, still rather sinister-looking, stepped forward, wine glass in hand, to speak.

"*Amici*," he began, "Friendsa. Whatta wonderful occasion is-a this. My olda frienda Alessandro and his-a lovely wife, theya married fifty years. Is a longa tima..."

Imogen, however, did not really hear the speech, for her heart was troubled by Manfred's profession of love for her—a love she felt she could never return. Yet the glimpses of another Manfred behind the criminal, the Manfred who missed his son, who showed affection for Luigi and fondness for Ana-Maria, who rebuked those who made snide comments about her and defended her against Rosina persisted in forcing their way into her mind. Was there more to Manfred than the criminal? But how, born and raised in a world of criminals, could he have avoided becoming anything else? But his mother seemed of a very different sort. Had she had some sort of ameliorating influence on him? And how did Ana-Maria come to be so pleasant a person? But a criminal Manfred was, for all that, and—

Suddenly aroused from her reverie by the applause following the godfather's speech, Imogen became aware of a waitress in a short black dress and white apron, black nylons and black high heels offering her a glass of champagne from a tray.

"It's for the toast," said the young woman.

"Oh—yes," said Imogen. "Thank you—*gracie.*"

Manfred standing beside her also took a glass as the godfather raised his.

"So heresa da toasta to Alessandro and his-a Giulietta. May they have anothera fifty yearsa!"

"Alessandro and Giulietta! Fifty more years!" everyone shouted.

Though she did not join in the shout, Imogen raised her glass to the elder couple and mouthed the words "Happy anniversary."

Then, excusing himself to Imogen, Manfred stepped forward.

"Thanks, godfather. *Grazie.* Thanks very much. Thanks everybody for being here for Papa and Mama. And now another toast, this time from Ana-Maria and Rosina and me to the best parents in the world. Mama and Papa Andreotti!" he cried, raising his glass. And again the crowd echoed him.

"And now," he said, "for the cake cutting."

He wheeled his father, his mother walking beside him, over toward the table with the great cake. The cake cutting was a poignant event as Manfred lifted his father to his feet and held him erect while he and his wife, jointly holding the knife, made the first cut into the cake. There was again loud applause. With people milled about, Manfred became lost from Imogen's view.

"So you're Manfred's new woman," said a voice beside her.

"Oh—!" she exclaimed in shock on turning to see the speaker, a young woman wearing a dress of a filmy transparent material with nothing on underneath.

"My dress?" asked the woman. "Too risque for you? Well, I've got the figure for it, and I'm the godfather's daughter-in-law; so I can get away with it."

"Oh—I—I—uh—suppose you can—but on our first date Manfred took me to a topless restaurant, so I realize this sort of thing is part of the world into which he has introduced me."

"I bet you wouldn't dare wear a dress like this."

"Probably not, but until I met Manfred I never thought I'd dare wear a dress like the one I'm wearing now. So, who knows."

Just then Manfred reappeared with two plates of cake.

"Well, Andrea," he said on seeing the godfather's daughter-in-law. "I see you're letting yourself be seen in public. I take it you've met Imogen. She'd do a lot more for that dress than you do."

"Hmph!" she snorted. "But really I must go and find Arturo."

Turning on her stiletto heel, she marched off.

"You were not exactly polite to her, Manfred," said Imogen.

"You don't know her. She's a cat."

"I hope you don't expect me to dress like that!"

"You could bring it off," he said. "But I'm only making a comment, not a suggestion. Have a slice of Mama and Papa's anniversary cake."

"Mm!" she said after she tasted it. "It's delicious, Manfred."

"Yeah. We got a great chef. But I got another duty to perform," he said stepping back to the table, but this time steering Imogen along with him. "I think many of you have brought presents," he called to the assembled throng. "So I guess now's the time to bring them up."

As she stood by and watched as people brought forward their expensive gifts, Imogen suddenly became aware of Rosina's husband Giorgio standing beside her.

Sho," he said, his voice rather thick from drink, "you're Manfre"s new wom'n."

"You're the second person in the past ten minutes who's made that comment, so I guess I must be," she replied.

"I c'd real' go fra woman like you," he said, drunkenly eyeing her decolletage.

"You have a wife, Giorgio, whom I think may be prone to jealousy. It's she you should 'go for'."

"She's a bidge," he said. "A har' nose' bidge. The Syn'icate an' ar fam'lies forced her on me."

"I'm afraid there's nothing I can do about that, Giorgio. I'm an outsider."

"You cou' be my frien'. Know wha' I mean?"

She turned on him angrily. "I don't like what I think you're suggesting, Giorgio, and I don't want to hear any more talk along these lines! In fact, I don't want to talk to you at all. You're drunk."

"Hey! Who you callin' drung?" he said rather too loudly.

Whereupon Manfred stepped in demanding, "What's going on here?"

"Nothing, Manfred, ol' boy. Jus' talging t'yer girl frien'. S'anything wrong wi' tha'?"

"There is in the way you were talking to me, Giorgio," said Imogen.

"Yeah, I can imagine!" said Manfred. "You leave Imogen alone. She's my woman, and you've got one of your own, even if she is Rosina. So you stay away from Imogen if you know what's good for you."

The note of menace in Manfred's voice visibly frightened Giorgio, but he tried to maintain a brave front.

"Ha ha! Lizzen a who'sh dalking! You don' scare me, Manfred?"

"Listen to the booze talking!" said Manfred. He placed his hand on Giorgio's chest and gave him a push, causing him to stagger back. "Get out of here, wimp, and sober up."

At that moment, Rosina who had been occupied with the presentation of gifts to her parents, stepped forward angrily.

"What the hell's going on here?" she demanded.

"Just teaching your husband a little lesson in manners, that's all," snarled Manfred.

"What's that woman been up to?" Rosina stormed. "She's nothing but trouble."

"I've been up to nothing!" Imogen flared back, anger flashing in her eyes. "It's your husband who's the trouble maker, not me. Ask him what it's all about if you want to know."

"This is all your fault, Manfred," flared Rosina, "bringing this hussy in here!"

"Who are you calling a hussy?" demanded Manfred. "Imogen's behaved like a lady ever since she came—and Papa and Mama accept her. It's your jealousy that's causing the trouble, not her!"

"Manfred," said Imogen. "You'd better take me home. I'm not making trouble, but I certainly seem to be the occasion for it."

"No," said Manfred. "Why should you have to go when it's this bitch of a sister of mine that's causing the trouble?"

Ana-Maria now stepped in from the sidelines where, by this time, the squabble had become the centre of attention of the assembled guests.

"I agree with Manfred, Rosina! What gets into you anyway? Why must you pick on poor Imogen?"

"Poor Imogen!" retorted Rosina. "Poor Imogen! Yes! Poor Imogen from the slums dressed to the nines by Manfred and introduced into our society as though she were a princess—as though she belonged!"

"Hey!" shouted Manfred. "Hey! Who are you to say I can't bring my girl here if I want to? Imogen's got a right to be here if I want her here because she's my woman, and she's ten times the—"

"Manfred!" interrupted Imogen. "I can't stand this! I can't stand this quarreling. Please! Take me away, please!"

"Oh, Imogen, Imogen!" said Ana-Maria placing her arms around Imogen's shoulders. "I'm so sorry all this has happened, but don't go, please. Don't give in to her. It's what she wants."

Imogen fought back her tears. "I don't like being the cause of dissension in a family," she said. "For one thing, it's spoiled your parents' anniversary celebration."

"Hey! Hey!" It was the voice of the elder Andreotti. "Rosina, you stoppa that! Imogena nice-a girl. She girl witha lotsa spirit! I lika that!" Then turning in his chair to look at Imogen, he said, "You notta worry, *Imogena*! We lika you."

The old man's interjection was like a bombshell and caused complete silence to reign for several seconds before murmuring spread through the crowd. Imogen released herself from Ana-Maria's embrace, whispered a word of thanks to her, and stepped over to the senior Andreottis.

"I'm sorry for all this, Signor and Signora Andreotti," she said. "If I'd known it would happen, I wouldn't have come."

"You're our guest. Our *Manfredo* invited you," said Signora Andreotti. "You have a right to be here. Rosina should know better. Ignore her. And Rosina, you behave yourself!"

"*Si! Si*" said her husband. "Imogena, youa welcoma here. You coma back lotsa time. Manfredo choose gooda when he choosa you."

"Th—thank you—*gracie*. And—and I have a small gift for you," said Imogen reaching into her handbag and drawing forth a small package which she presented to Manfred's mother. "It's not very much—I can't afford expensive gifts—but I hope you'll like it."

"Hey! Geez Imogen!" said Manfred who had come over to stand beside her. "You didn't have to do this."

"No," said Ana-Maria also stepping to her side. "But what a gracious gesture on your part!" Then turning to Rosina, she said, "Do you see what kind of person she is!"

"Hmph!" snorted Rosina, but made no further comment.

"I couldn't not bring something," said Imogen. "It is your parents' anniversary, and they were—kind and—and gracious enough to include me among their guests."

By this time, Signora Andreotti had opened the parcel and was staring at Imogen's gift. "It's lovely, *Imogena*. A bust of someone."

"It's a replica of the bust of the Egyptian Queen Nefertiti," said Imogen noting the older woman's puzzlement. "I got it at the museum."

"Queena Neffa—who?" asked Manfred's father.

"Nefertiti," Imogen replied. "She was a queen of ancient Egypt, the consort of Pharaoh Akhenaton, the pharaoh who tried to establish monotheism—belief in a single God—in ancient Egypt. In fact, some think it was really her idea."

"She was Catholic?" asked Manfred's father.

"Oh no. That was long before Christianity. It was an idea before its time. It didn't take on."

"I notta understanda," said Signor Andreotti, a look of perplexity on his face.

"It's ancient history, I know, but it's a very famous bust, found at Amarna in Egypt but now in the museum in Berlin."

"I never heara her," said Manfred's father holding the little statuette, "but she kinda gooda looking. Is nice. But how she beieva in-a one-a God if-a she notta Catholic?"

"Well, there are many who do, the Jews for example, and the Moslems."

"You Catholic?"

"Well—I'm an Episcopalian, or Anglican. We believe we are part of the Catholic Church—the universal church."

"You believa inna da Pope?"

"We don't recognize his authority."

"*Manfredo*, your lady-frienda notta Catholic."

"I know, Papa, but I don't care. When a woman's as wonderful and gorgeous as Imogen, who cares whether she's Catholic, Protestant, or Greek Unorthodox."

"Yes, Papa," intervened Ana-Maria. "Where will you meet a nicer woman than Imogen? You've said yourself what a lovely person she is."

"*Si, si*. She very nice-a, beautiful younga lady. Better if she Catholic."

"I'm sorry, *Signor Andreotti*. I was brought up in the Episcopal Church. It's my spiritual home, and I believe it a true Church."

"Oh Papa!" said Ana-Maria. "Catholics are not the only nice people in the world. In fact, I know a few Catholics who are pretty horrible and some Protestants who are very nice—like Imogen."

"She wasn't born to the aristocracy either," intervened Signora Andreotti, "but she's a well-mannered lady, Alessandro. That is very much in her favor."

"*Si, si.* Thatsa trua. Okay. *Manfredo* lika her, so is-a okay. She gooda looking girl, so who care if she not Catholic."

"That's what I say, Papa," said Manfred. "Now the music's starting again, so I think I'd like to dance with my beautiful Episcopalian. Come on, Imogen."

He grabbed her hand and was about to lead her onto the dance floor when Signora Andreotti called them back. "*Imogena,*" she said. "Papa really likes you, but he has some funny notions some times. You are *Manfredo*'s friend, and we all like you. You are welcome. *Benvenuto.*"

"*Grazie, Signora,*" replied Imogen. "I'll always try to deserve your welcome." Then, on the dance floor, Imogen said, "Are you sure, Manfred, that you did right in making me your girl friend and in bringing me into your home?"

"More right than I've ever been about anything. And hey! Like Mama says, Papa gets some funny notions. After a while he won't care if you're Catholic or Mohammedan. Ana-Maria thinks of you almost as a sister, and that's a real plus. And Luigi thinks you're the cat's whiskers."

"Poor little fellow; he seems lonely and wanting a friend."

"Yeah. As a mother, Rosina's the shits. The only person she cares about is herself. But don't worry about her. You make me happy—happier than I've ever been in my life."

"I don't know what to say, Manfred."

"Don't say anything."

For a while they danced without speaking, Manfred holding her very close.

"You know, in some ways, Manfred," said Imogen at last, "I feel sorry for you."

"Sorry for me! Geez! Nobody ever said that to me! And why the hell should you feel sorry for me? I got everything—power, wealth. With those you can have anything you want."

"Can you, Manfred? Can you have real love and real friendship? How worthwhile are relationships based on coercion—or that you buy? Are you ever really wanted, cared about for yourself?"

"Huh?" He was silent for a few moments. "Look, if you're talking about how I..."

"No, I wasn't thinking of that, Manfred, but of your whole way of life."

"Which you disapprove of."

"There are many things I like in you, Manfred," Imogen said after a long silence. "You—you've been very nice to me—and—and I'm very grateful to you for paying for Aunt Ethel's operation, and so I'm puzzled. Somehow you don't fit the pattern of—of the world you live in. You don't seem fully to belong."

"Where the hell else can I belong! I was born and brought up in this world. Do you think I can just get up some morning and walk out of it and get a nine-to-five job somewhere? Neither the cops nor the Syndicate would let me do that. I wouldn't last till noon!"

She said nothing for a while, thinking. When she spoke at last she said, "I'm sure that's true, Manfred. For you there's no escaping it. I guess that's why I feel sorry for you. You're a prisoner. You can't lead an ordinary life. Everywhere you go you have to have body guards. You can't trust anyone, and you can't ever feel safe."

Now it was his turn to be silent for some time before saying, "Mebbe that's why I gotta be first—why I got to run everything, be in control. Anyway, who wants to be ordinary?"

"I'm ordinary and I don't mind."

"You are not ordinary!" he protested loudly. "You're special!"

Imogen fell silent.

—And what of me? she wondered to herself. Will I escape? How safe am I?

After they had danced in silence for a while, Manfred said, "You say I don't trust anybody. I trust you."

"Do you Manfred? Why?"

Again he was silent before he spoke.

"I don't know. I just do. You just seem trustworthy."

Again Imogen fell silent. Then she said, "Well, Manfred, believe it or not, I trust you. You don't seem like a person who can be trusted, and I don't know why, but I do trust you—at least in respect to me."

"Not sure how to take that, but I'm glad you do, because you *can* trust me."

Again they danced a while in silence before Manfred asked, "When does your aunt go into hospital, by the way?"

"She goes the day after tomorrow. I—I want to be able to spend as much time with her as possible."

"Hey! I understand. I'll be up to see her as much as I can too. I really hope they can help her."

"Oh, I certainly hope so, too—but even if they can't, Manfred, I'll always be grateful to you for trying. But your doctor said he thought there was at least a fifty-fifty chance. It took a lot of X-rays to find the problem, but they think it's one they can deal with—though it will be tricky."

"Doc Savage knows his business. If he thinks it can be done, it'll be done. And like I said, I hate to see someone laid up like that, so if I can help your aunt, it'll make me happy."

"It is very kind of you, Manfred."

"Hey! I like to help people."

—He is full of so many contradictions and incongruities! thought Imogen. In his twisted way, he really does seem to have something of a generous spirit.

The music ended, and Manfred said, "Let's go out on the terrace and get a bit of fresh air."

"Oh—yes—if you like. That would be pleasant."

They found many couples, perhaps also seeking fresh air, gathered on the terrace, and so Manfred led her through them and out onto a flagstone pathway leading into the rose garden.

"What a lovely fragrance!" exclaimed Imogen. "The scent of the roses is like a balm on the air! It must be lovely to see this garden in the day time!"

"Yeah, and you will some time," he said. He stopped, turned to her, and took her into his arms. "At last we're alone."

Imogen let him draw her to him, but she turned her face away.

Manfred was silent for a moment, looking off into space.

"You're really wonderful, you know."

Imogen said nothing in reply, and he pressed her very hard against him.

"Haven't you anything to say?" he asked.

"I don't know what to say, Manfred. I'm not used to effusive compliments—as I've said before—and I don't know how to take them. I'm not sure I'm wonderful—just a bit different."

"It's not just that you're beautiful, play the piano, like opera, and have been to university. There's something special about you."

"I don't know what that is, Manfred."

"Neither do I, but it's there." He turned her face toward him, placed a hand under her chin and raised her head. "Who needs an explanation anyway," he said as he brought his lips down hard on hers. Then he said, "Come on. Let's make love."

"Now, Manfred?" she asked in surprise. "The party's not over yet, and don't you have to see he guests leave? You're the host, aren't you?"

"Ah, they'll be here till morning and most of them'll be too drunk to know anything anyway. Half of them will have to be dragged or carried to their cars."

"Oh—I see. Well—

—In fact, now that you've awakened me sexually, Manfred, I'm as eager as you. I can't get enough! I *am* a slut and a hussy!

Lifting her into his arms, he said, "There's a way up the back where no one will see us."

He carried her up a flight of stairs and down a hallway to his suite of luxuriously furnished rooms and into the bedroom where stood a large, king-sized bed.

—How many mistresses have shared this bed with him, wondered Imogen, but strangely, I don't care!

She reached into her handbag to extract her mask, but Manfred prevented her.

"Not that one," he said. "I've had this special one made for you."

"You—What?" Imogen began as he reached into the drawer of a bedside table from which he produced a gold mask trimmed about the edge and the eye holes with tiny diamonds.

She gasped, and then exclaimed, "Oh Manfred! It's absolutely gorgeous—and again, it's too much! You're always trying to spoil me. But," she said, putting the mask over her face and smiling at him, "I'll wear it for you."

Looking across at herself in the mirror.

"Oh my! It's so elegant—and makes me look so very mysterious and sexy!"

* * * * *

Later, with Imogen lying naked and masked beside him, Manfred said, "You were good tonight."

"Was I?" she said, somewhat distractedly.

"Yeah. More involved—as though you were enjoying it. Were you?"

"Yes—yes, I was."

"That's good." He said nothing more for some moments. "Even though I kind of like it and it does make you look real sexy, are you sure you need to wear a mask?"

"Yes, Manfred," she said. "I'm sorry. I still need it."

"How come?"

"I—I can't explain—except that I feel sort of as though I've become a different person. I feel confused and uncertain about what's happening to me, and until the confusion is gone—I don't really know why, but I feel I need the mask."

"Well, I guess if it helps you make love, okay—for now. But I'd like to know I was making love to you, not to some woman of mystery."

"As I said, Manfred. we're all mysteries to one another."

She sighed deeply.

"What's the matter?" he asked.

"Hm? The matter? Nothing, Manfred."

"Why'd you sigh like that?"

"Did I sigh? I wasn't aware of it. I don't know why. I—I'd just like to be—quiet, I guess, Manfred."

"Yeah? Well, it is kind of nice after making love."

He drew her close to him and within a few minutes, fell asleep.

—What a strange, bizarre situation I'm in—mistress to a gangster who says he loves me and makes love to me. But is it really love-making? You say you love me, Manfred, so maybe to you, it is making love. But what am I doing? Just fucking? If so, I like it. Something dark and libidinous has been awakened in me. Who am I really? Who is Imogen? I thought I knew. Perhaps that's why I wear the mask—because I no longer know who I am. And who is Manfred? He treats me with respect and stands up for me. And he really seemed to appreciate my piano playing—and my other accomplishments—and that means a lot to me. I think I could almost like him—I almost do—if only he were not—but as he says, how can he ever be anything else? Oh God! Oh God! I'm so mixed up, so confused!

CHAPTER TWELVE

With her uncle, Imogen entered her aunt's hospital room and was astonished to see it adorned with a huge display of flowers.

"My goodness Aunty! Where did all these flowers come from?"

Then she knew the answer before her aunt gave it.

"They're all from Mr. Andreotti, dear."

"Yes, I should have known. It's like him to do something extravagant like this. He does nothing on a small scale."

"And paid for with stolen money," growled her uncle.

"Yes, I suppose so, Arthur," responded his wife, "but they are lovely just the same."

"Yes," said Imogen, "in his way he's being kind."

"Imogen!" exclaimed her uncle. "I'm shocked to hear you say that."

"I am too, Uncle—but I've come to see that he's a person of many contradictions. He knows no other way to show he likes people than to spend money, and I think, in his way, he really means everything kindly."

"He spends too much money on you, Imogen," said her uncle. "I get worried you're being taken in by it. You're not, are you, Imogen?"

"I know what he is, Uncle."

"That's good. Don't forget," he said as he leaned over to kiss his wife and Imogen drew a chair up to the side of the bed and sat down.

"How are you Aunty," she asked reaching out to take her aunt's hand. "They tell us the operation was a success."

"I still feel groggy from the anesthetic, dear, but they made me sit and stand for a while in spite of that."

"Stand Aunty! You could stand!"

"I felt very shaky, but yes, I could stand."

"Oh Aunty! That's wonderful!" cried Imogen, bursting into tears and falling on her aunt's shoulder.

"Is that really true, Ethel?" said Imogen's uncle, his voice choked with emotion and grasping her hand.

"Yes, Arthur, it is. They say tomorrow they're going to have me take a few steps."

"That is good news, Ethel. I can hardly believe it, but I thank God for it—and—and I guess I also have to thank Mr. Andreotti—much as I'd rather not."

"God works in mysterious ways, Uncle," said Imogen, sitting up and looking at him, smiling.

"He certainly does, but I never thought He'd work this way."

"Nor I Uncle."

"Yes, I'm sure we do have be thankful to Mr. Andreotti," said Imogen's aunt.

"Did I hear my name being taken in vain?" said Manfred entering the room at that moment.

At the sound of his voice Imogen rose to meet him.

"Oh Manfred! The operation was a success and Aunty actually stood up for a few minutes! They're going to start her walking tomorrow!"

"Hey! That's great!" he responded enthusiastically. He stepped over to the bed. "That's great news, Mrs. Edwards," he said taking her hand in his. "I'm really happy to hear it."

"Why thank you, Mr. Andreotti," said Imogen's aunt. "I don't know how we can thank you enough for what you've done."

"Hey! No thanks necessary. You're Imogen's aunt!"

"Uh, yeah, Mr. Andreotti," said Mr. Edwards, rising and after a moment's reluctance and hesitation, extending his hand to Manfred who seized it and pumped it hard. "We appreciate what you've done. Don't know what we can do to thank you."

"Hey Mr. Edwards! For anyone connected with Imogen, I'm happy to do anything I can, so just knowing Imogen's all the thanks I need."

"We're very grateful to you, Manfred," said Imogen, blushing, and then, quite spontaneously but to her uncle's dismay, threw her arms around him and kissed him. Then she suddenly drew back and hung her head in blushing embarrassment.

"Hey! Hey! I liked that! Do you have any more aunts I can help so I can get another kiss like that?"

"I—I do have to thank you for that Ferrari, Manfred," said Imogen, "but it's too much. I—I wish you could arrange some way to send it back."

"Why?" Manfred turned an almost hurt look to her. "Don't you like it?"

"Oh, no. That's not it, Manfred. It's a wonderful car, but it's too much for me."

"Hey! You're a classy woman. You should have a classy car."

"Oh my goodness!" exclaimed Imogen's aunt from her bed. "He bought you a Ferrari?"

"Yes," said her uncle. "A brand new bright red *Ferrari* arrived this morning. It's bought, paid for, and registered in Imogen's name. They had all the papers right there. And, yes, it is too much—too much like a bribe."

"Hey! It's no bribe! I like spending money, especially on the people I like. So I don't want any more argument about it. Okay?"

"Well—all right, Manfred" Imogen said, almost resignedly and at the same time blushing and looking away. "You seem determined to make me a woman of class, but I'm really just a girl from a working class suburb."

"Geez! What does that matter? You got more refinement and class than a hell of—Oh! excuse me, folks!—than an awful lot of women born rich."

"We tried, Mr. Andreotti," said Imogen's uncle, "to give her the kind of upbringing and education we felt her parents would have wanted her to have."

"Well, you did a great job. She's a great girl!" Manfred said, putting his arm around Imogen's shoulders. "You've got every reason to be proud of her."

"We are, Mr. Andreotti," said her uncle. "We want only what's good for her."

"Hey! Me too, Mr. Edwards."

"You're all making me embarrassed," said Imogen, blushing again. "But I think this is all very tiring for Aunty. I think perhaps we should go—not that I want to, Aunty."

"I am rather tired, dear. It was nice of you both to come—and you too, Mr. Andreotti. Oh—and thanks for all these lovely flowers!"

"Hey! For Imogen's aunt, nothin's too much. And you couldn't keep me away!" Manfred reached out and took her aunt's hand as Imogen bent over to kiss her. "Glad the news is so great!"

"I'll be in again tomorrow, Aunt Ethel," said Imogen. Then she turned to Manfred. "I think Uncle would like a few minutes alone with her, Manfred. Maybe we could step out in the hall."

"Hey! I understand."

As her uncle went to the bed to kneel beside his wife, Imogen stepped with Manfred into the hallway where the two ubiquitous body guards stood on duty outside the door.

"I—I really do appreciate this, Manfred, and I want to show my appreciation."

"Hey! You don't need to do that!"

"I want to, Manfred. It can't be anything lavish, of course, but at least—in a couple of nights' time—let me take you for coffee."

"Huh? Yeah, well, okay, sure. That'd be okay. Yeah. That's nice."

"And—and after that," she said, lowering her head and blushing, "if you'd like to go to your place across the river—"

Oh! Hey! Yeah! I'd really like that!"

"Not," she said looking up, still embarrassed, "for a few days though until we know exactly how things are going. I want to give Aunty as much of my time as possible."

"No problem. I understand—though it's hard to wait."

—Oh Manfred! Imogen shamefully confessed to herself. If you only knew how hard it is for me to wait too!

CHAPTER THIRTEEN

"You wanted to see me, Miss Schwartz?" asked Imogen as she entered the office of the head librarian.

"Er—yes, Imogen," said Miss Schwartz looking up at her over her half-moon glasses. "Sit down—please."

Miss Schwartz, Imogen reflected as she seated herself at the opposite side of the desk from her superior, was one of those old-fashioned librarians who regarded the library as her personal fief to be guarded at all costs from predation and detraction, and so she felt she knew the reason for her summons. For some time now since she had been seeing Manfred, she had become aware of of a growing coolness in the attitude of her colleagues in the library toward her; and the way they would look away when she would look up from her work and their whispering together in little groups of two or three told her that she was the subject of gossip.

Miss Schwartz cleared her throat, apparently in some embarrassment. "I don't really know how to begin, Imogen," she said, "but we've been hearing some rather distressing things about you."

Miss Schwartz's "we" was a kind of royal "we" she used when she felt the the interests of the library were at stake. Imogen, however, managed to maintain her composure.

"What sort of things, Miss Schwartz?" she asked calmly.

"Well—er—we've heard that you—I hope you don't think I listen to gossip—but it has come to our attention that you—er—you have been seen in public with—with—ah—"

"Manfred Andreotti," interposed Imogen, beginning to lose her patience.

"Uh—yes. I—uh—"

"My personal life is my own affair, Miss Schwartz," she responded firmly, keeping her growing anger and hostility under control.

"Ah—yes, indeed, but—well—some of our clients are rather upset you know—"

"I don't think they've any cause to complain about the way I serve them."

"Uh—no, no, but—well, they don't like to think that—that—"

"They're being served by a gangster's girl friend? I don't see why my relations with Manfred Andreotti are of any concern to them if I do my work conscientiously and serve them efficiently and courteously, which I think I do."

"Oh—yes, yes, you do—but as I'm sure you're aware, a woman is judged by the company she keeps, and—er—well—er—it gives the library a bit of a bad name, you know."

"I don't see why it should. What I do outside is of no consequence to anyone or to the library. The library is the library, and my personal life is my personal life. I know that at least some of the girls are living out of wedlock with their boy friends, but no one complains. I'm not doing that."

—At least not yet, she thought to herself.

"Yes, but, well—something of—of what—of Mr. Andreotti's reputation rubs off, as it were, on the library, don't you see."

"No, I don't, but it quite obviously rubs off on me."

"Imogen I never thought—you of all people—would be the one to date the head of the East Clintwood crime syndicate. I—I just don't understand! Somehow, Imogen, I just can't think you'd do this voluntarily."

Imogen looked down at her skirt for some moments, embarrassed.

"It's really none of your concern, Miss Schwartz," she said at last, raising her eyes again and looking straight into those of the head librarian, "but even if it were, it's a very complicated story."

"Well, I—uh—I don't mean to pry, Imogen, it's just that I have the reputation of the library to think of, and people have been speaking to me. They've also commented on those very short skirts and very high heels—"

"Miss Schwartz!" said Imogen angrily and rising from her chair. "How I dress, as well as my private life, is my business." Seething inwardly, eyes ablaze, she rose from the chair in front of the desk. "Good morning, Miss Schwartz."

She turned and strode from the office and past a group of her colleagues who looked up in surprise and embarrassment as she walked by. She stopped and turned on them.

"Yes," she flared, "I'm Manfred Andreotti's mistress, but what I said to Miss Schwartz, I say to you: my personal life is none of your concern!"

They stared at her in open mouthed astonishment as she turned and strode out of the building and down the front steps. Walking very briskly to find relief from her anger, her high heels hammering angrily on the pavement, she made her way down the street away from the library. So intense was her anger she hardly noticed two young men coming in the other direction or heard their long, low whistles.

—The nerve of her! The nerve of them all! I'll date Manfred Andreotti if I want to! I'll wear high heels and miniskirts if I want to! And since everyone knows I'm a gangster's mistress, I'll show the world what it is to be a gangster's mistress! I will come to the library bra-less! I'll come topless! I'll come completely nude! I'll set a new standard for gangster's mistresses! I'll be the gangster's mistress to end all gangster's mistresses!

She walked on for some time time before turning around to return to the library.

Miss Schwartz, hands on hips, confronted her as she entered.

"Where have you been, Imogen!" she demanded.

"Out," Imogen retorted defiantly.

"You left your post, you know."

"Yes, I know."

"You can be fired for this."

"Then fire me."

Miss Schwartz's mouth dropped open and she seemed to go limp in the face of Imogen's defiance.

"Imogen, I really don't know what's got into you," she said at last. "You're not like the girl you used to be. You were never so—so belligerent before."

"People change, I guess, but I'm only standing up for my right to keep my personal life private, Miss Schwartz."

"Oh Imogen! That's true, of course, but you do have to admit that— that this is all very—very much out of the ordinary. At first, I couldn't believe what I heard, but it seems it's true, and it's all so perplexing!"

Imogen softened toward her superior.

"Yes, I suppose it is, Miss Schwartz—and it has been perplexing for me. I'm sorry if I seem touchy. Still, as I said, it is my life we're talking about."

"Yes—yes—dear me! I know, really, that what you do outside the library is your business, but when people complain to me—well I don't know what to think or do."

"Perhaps," said Imogen, "you should tell them that so long as my work at the library is acceptable they should leave well enough alone and mind their own business."

"Yes, yes. I—I suppose you're right. You do do your job very efficiently and courteously—as I said—but—oh dear! Oh dear!"

"Well," said Imogen, "right now, I'd better return to the circulation desk."

When she left the library at the end of her shift Manfred was waiting outside for her in his limousine.

"Hey Imogen!" he called

"Manfred!" she cried and stepped over to the curb to talk to him.

"Get in," he said opening the door. "We'll drive you home. But hey! You look mad as a boiled owl. What's up?"

"I had a run-in with the head librarian a bit earlier," she said as she slid in beside him, "and it still rankles."

"Huh? What about?"

"About you!" she said, as the limousine drove away.

"About me!"

"Yes, about you. She's heard that I'm seeing you, and she's all in a huff about it."

"What the hell bloody business is it of hers?"

"That's what I told her—not quite in those words."

"Yeah. You'd be too damn polite about it."

"Oh, I don't know how polite I was, but I didn't lose my temper—well, maybe I did a bit—but I was very firm, Manfred, and very angry!"

"Hey! Good for you," he said, laying his arm across her shoulder. "And I don't blame you. Geez! I oughta—"

"No, Manfred. Don't you do anything. I'll fight my own battles."

"Well, there's one thing I can do," he said, taking her in his arms and kissing her. "Mebbe this'll make you feel better."

"Yes," said Imogen, rather to her own surprise when her released her, "that does make me feel better."

"Yeah? But you know, you don't need that job in the library. You should quit—"

"Or they might fire me."

"Well, what if they do? I want you to come and live with me. I want you with me all the time, Imogen. I can't live without you."

She had been expecting such a request since the beginning of their relationship, but still, it took her aback.

"Oh—oh—Manfred—I—I guess I should be flattered that you want me so much, but I don't think I'm ready to live with you—not yet."

"Why not?"

"I—I want to be at home when Aunty comes back from the hospital, and there's Susan's final recital. I promised to accompany her—"

"Yeah, okay, okay. But think about it."

—And now that there's no point worrying about my reputation, because I've already lost it—or acquired a new one, yes, I will think about it!

"Here we are at Miss Imogen's house," said Al's voice over the intercom.

"Oh—yeah. Okay, Al."

"Thanks for the ride, Manfred," Imogen said as she made ready to get out. Then she asked, "Will I see you tonight at the hospital?"

"You sure will!"

For the first time since her interview with Miss Schwartz, Imogen smiled.

"It's nice of you to give so much time to Aunt Ethel, Manfred."

"Hey! She's *your* aunt."

"She's also a wonderful person."

"Hey! Yeah, she is. I know that."

"Well—I'll see you later, then."

"Looking forward to it!"

Again as on the previous night at the hospital, Imogen impulsively threw her arms about him and kissed him, and then as suddenly broke from him, jumped out of the limousine and ran along the path and up the steps and into the house.

CHAPTER FOURTEEN

When Manfred arrived at the hospital, Imogen carrying a red handbag and wearing red five-inch high heels, a full red skirt, and a white blouse over which she wore a blue jacket to hide her bare shoulders and her lack of a bra, walked with her aunt who was on crutches, she on one side, her uncle on he other.

"Hey Mrs. Edwards!" Manfred almost shouted as he approached. "They've got you up and around! That's great!"

"I have to be on crutches for a while," Imogen's aunt replied, "until I get the strength back in my legs, but yes, it's wonderful to be able to move about on my own even like this—and we have you to thank for it, Mr. Andreotti."

"Hey! Like I said, it makes me feel good to do something like this! And seeing you walking is all the thanks I need." He fell suddenly serious. "I wish my Papa could walk again."

"That's very sad, indeed, Mr. Andreotti," said Mrs. Edwards. "I feel almost as though I've received what should be his."

"Oh, hey!" he responded, brightening again. "Don't think of it that way. You help the one's you can, that's all."

—Oh Manfred! thought Imogen. You seem like two people in one, each a contradiction to the other! If only that good side of you could gain the upper hand, I think I could almost l—! Oh! Oh! What am I thinking!

Imogen reddened and turned away. Noticing her sudden change, Manfred asked, "Hey, Imogen! What's up?"

"Oh—nothing, Manfred. I—I guess I was feeling, like Aunty, the irony that you can't help your father, but you can help my aunt. It is sad."

"It's nice of you to think about Papa. There's a lot of people who don't give a damn—uh—sorry, folks—give a hoot," he replied. "But that's the way the cookie crumbles. He can't be helped, so forget it."

"You're fond of him, Manfred," said Imogen. It was a statement, not a question.

"Yeah—like you are of your aunt. That's why I wanted to help her if I could."

—Oh Manfred! Is this an act to gain approval, or do you really mean it? Somehow I think you really do.

She looked down.

"You're looking terrific tonight," said Manfred, changing the subject. "I like your red shoes, skirt and handbag. Like I said, red's my favorite color."

"Yes, I know," she said, still looking down.

—It's partly why I wore them, Manfred—but only partly.

Her uncle, who earlier had commented unfavorably on the fact, frowned.

"You've had quite an influence on the way Imogen dresses since she's been going out with you," he said. "She doesn't seem like the Imogen we used to know."

"Hey, Mr. Edwards," Manfred declaimed. "I just want her to look like the great looking woman she is. And red looks real good on her."

"It—it's—appropriate," said Imogen very quietly, still looking down.

"Yeah. Goes great with your coloring."

—That's not what I meant, Manfred. I'm wearing red because I'm a whore. Uncle says I've changed since I met you, and I have, and I'm ashamed to say, I'm enjoying the change.

Looking up again, she said aloud, "I think we should get Aunty back to her room and into bed. She's been up for quite a while, and we shouldn't tire her."

"No," said her husband, "you shouldn't overdo it, Ethel, though no one's happier than I to see you walking."

"I *am* feeling a bit tired," said his wife. "Thank you all for being so considerate."

Later, as she walked with Manfred down the corridor to the elevator, having left her aunt and uncle alone in the hospital room, Imogen said,

"Oh Manfred! It's the most wonderful thing in the world to see Aunty on her feet again—and—and it is all because of you. I can't thank you enough."

"You're my girl. That's all the thanks I need."

"Though it's not why I became your girl friend," she said looking down and finding it hard to say the words, "I—I'm glad—for Aunty's sake—that—that I did—because otherwise, this would never have happened. So—so—I know it's not much—but that's why I want to take you for coffee tonight—to show my appreciation."

"Like I said, you don't have to, but hey! It's a real nice idea!"

"I thought we might go to a place in Little Italy this time—not as posh as the places you take me, but very pleasant, and they serve first rate coffee and the best pizza in East Clintwood. At least I've never tasted better."

"Yeah? Okay. Let's go and find out."

Down in the main floor rotunda, Imogen said, "I really like the Ferrari, Manfred—though it's too much—and I brought it tonight. I thought that since I'm inviting you out this time, you might like a ride in the car you bought me—that it would be a—a—well, a pleasant change if I were to drive you."

"You want to drive me?" he said, turning to look at her but seeming more to be searching within himself than inquiring of her.

"Yes, Manfred. Is—is there something wrong with that? Don't you want me to?"

"It's too dangerous, Boss," said Al who, with Joe, as always, hovered near. "That car ain't bullet proofed."

"Oh—yes—I see," said Imogen, once again receiving a harrowing glimpse into the world with which she had become so closely associated.. "I—I should have thought—"

"Hey!" said Manfred. "Who's to know? No one expects me to be riding in a red Ferrari."

"I still don't like it, Boss," said Al.

"I suppose it is better you didn't come with me, Manfred" said Imogen. "I'll just follow along."

"Naw," said Manfred. "That's no good either. Al, you stay here. Joe, you and the others check around outside. We'll use the back entrance. When everything's okay, Imogen can bring up her car and then you quys can bring up all others. Soon as we're well on our way and we're sure no one's following, the limo can turn off down a side street somewhere and head for home."

"If you say so, Boss, but I still don't like it."

"You worry to much, Al."

"That's what you pay me to do, Boss."

"Okay, okay. And don't think I don't appreciate it. There'll be a nice bonus at Christmas."

"You treat us real good, Boss. That ain't the problem."

"Yeah, well I've got this town completely sewed up. Nothing happens here, nobody comes or goes that I don't know about. And you guys are good and know your jobs. So don't worry, Al. I trust you to see that everything is okay."

"I hope we do, Boss. An' I hope it will be."

"Hey! I put a lot of faith in you guys!"

They followed the procedure Manfred had laid down and set off toward Little Italy.

"Do you see now why I feel sorry for you, Manfred?" Imogen asked as they drove off.

"Huh? What do you mean?"

"All the precautions you have to take. You can't just walk out the door, get into your car and drive where you want to go. You're not really free, Manfred, for all your power."

After remaining silent for a while, apparently lost in thought, his facial expression puzzled, even troubled, Manfred said, "You come up with some of the damnedest ideas sometimes."

"I just say what comes into my head, I guess," Imogen said. "It's hard not to, but I'll try not to say things that upset you."

"I ain't—I'm not upset. You just make me think about things I never thought about before, and, yeah, that does sort of bother me I guess. But like I said the other night at the party, I can't change what I am."

"I know, Manfred," she said sadly. "And that's why—Oh!" she exclaimed, seeing an opportunity to change the subject, "We're nearly there. Over there. That's it in the middle of the block on the right—Gabrielli's—after the Italian Renaissance composer."

Manfred signaled the other cars to pull over, and Imogen parked the Ferrari in front of the little café.

"Hey!" he exclaimed, "This does look like a nice place!"

"It is," said Imogen, slipping off her jacket just as they got out. "And so are the people who own it. They've created a warm, friendly atmosphere."

"Hey!" exclaimed Manfred. "Hey! Bare shoulders! I like that, but I never expected you—

"The dresses you buy me reveal a lot more flesh than just my shoulders, Manfred," she said, blushing. "But this is your night. I wanted to please you. You like a bit of bare flesh as well as red shoes and skirts, and Susan's right; I do have splendid shoulders. There. See how vain I've become!"

"Hey! Why shouldn't you be. And wow! you're not wearing a bra!"

"Oh you!" she said with a whimsical smile. "All you're interested in are my knockers. But, yes, I've become very naughty, Manfred, and I'm starting to like and accept my full breasts."

As they entered the little cafeteria, the proprietor stared incredulously at Imogen without her glasses, her dark hair combed out long, her shoulders bare, and wearing very high heels, but nevertheless he greeted her warmly.

"Gena! Hey! Issa longa tima we notta see you! You looka reala good!"

"*Grazie*, Bernardo. It's nice to be back in East Clintwood again."

"Itsa beena too longa, Gena."

"I know, Bernardo," responded Imogen, blushing. "I'm sorry. A—a lot of things have been happening. Uh—Bernardo, this is Manfred Andreotti."

Bernardo's eyes almost started from their sockets.

"Manfredo Andreotti!" he exclaimed in disbelief. "You go outa witha Manfredo Andreotti!"

"Yes, Bernardo, I do."

"Hey! Bernardo!" said Manfred holding out his hand to the incredulous and dumbfounded proprietor who took it automatically but unenthusiastically, still too amazed to know what to think or say. "Always good to meet a fellow Italian. Yeah, me and Imogen met at the opera. It was hard work to persuade her to be my girl, but I finally managed it. Best thing that's ever happened to me. And hey, Bernardo! You got a nice little place here."

"Oh—*Grazie, Signor Andreotti*," said Bernardo, still dismayed.

"Manfr—Mr. Andreotti has paid for an operation for Aunt Ethel," said Imogen to try to relieve the tension, "and she's going to be able to walk again."

"Oh! *Madre di Dio!*" exclaimed Bernardo, clapping his hands together. "Thatsa very good. *Si,* thatsa wonderful. But you—"

"I told Manfred you make great coffee and best pizza in East Clintwood, Bernardo," said Imogen cutting him off to avoid possible further embarrassment.

"Oh—*Grazie, Imogena*. We trya keepa uppa da tradition of *la vecchia patria*—da olda country."

"Yeah, that's great, Bernardo," said Manfred. "So let's try out the coffee, and hey! I wouldn't mind a slice of your pizza, either. Make it pepperoni."

"*Si—si, Signor Andreotti*," he said, then called into the kitchen to his daughter. "Maria! Here's Imogena coma back."

Bernardo's daughter, a plumpish but rather pretty dark haired young woman, appeared from the back.

"Imogen!" cried Maria on seeing Imogen running over to her. "*Mama mia* it's nice to see you again! But gee! You look so different—but very nice. Golly!"

"Thanks, Maria, and it's good to see you, too."

"Is this a friend from university?" Maria asked, looking somewhat dubiously at Manfred.

"No—this is Manfred Andreotti."

The girl's mouth dropped open and her eyes started.

"M—Manfred Andreotti! *Mama mia!* Not—"

"Yes, Maria. I'm his girl friend."

"Oh! *Madre di Dio*! You—you go out with Manfred Andreotti?"

"Yes, Maria."

"Hey! Nice to meet you, Maria," Manfred broke in jovially. "Any friend of Imogen's is a friend of mine!"

"I—it's nice to—to m—meet you, Signor Andreotti," stammered Maria.

"Hey, Maria! Like I said to your papa, we Italians should get to know each other better."

"I'm not Italian, Manfred," said Imogen with a humorous smile.

"Imogen, you don't have to be," said Manfred.

"Maria," said Bernardo, "you showa Imogena and Signor Andreotti to a booth and bringa them coffee—and a pepperoni pizza for Signor Andreotti. Gena, you want pizza too?"

"Not tonight, thanks, Bernardo, but I will some other time."

"How about we sit in that booth down at the back?" said Manfred.

Maria led them to the back of the little restaurant and as Imogen and Manfred seated themselves, said, "I—I'll bring coffee right away—and—and your pepperoni pizza—*Signor Andreotti.*"

"Yeah, thanks, Maria" said Manfred. Then as the young woman departed, he said, "Nice friends you got, Imogen."

"They are the best. I grew up around here, as I told you, Manfred. I've known them all since I was a child. They're very important to me. It's wonderful to have such good friends. That's why," she said blushing and looking down, "I wanted them not to have to pay protection money."

"Hey! No problem! And I'm glad we're friends now, Imogen. We get along pretty good—pretty well."

To her own surprise she said, "Yes—yes we do."

"Surprised?"

"Yes, I guess I am."

—And I'm even more surprised that I enjoy being your mistress. It's exciting. But how will it end?

Just then Maria returned with two coffees and on a plate a large slice of piping hot pizza for Manfred.

"Boy!" exclaimed Manfred when he saw the pizza. "That really does look good—and smells good to!"

"I—I hope you like it," she said, and stood by.

Manfred mixed sugar and cream into his coffee, tasted it and exclaimed, "Hey! You were right, Imogen! This is great coffee!"

"I'm glad you like it," said Imogen. "I told you it was the best in town."

"Yeah, and I think you're right. Now, if the pizza's as good as the coffee—" He broke off a portion with his fork and tasted it. "Hey! You're right about that too, Imogen! This is really great pizza!"

"Also the best in East Clintwood."

"I—I'm glad everything is all right," said Maria and turned to leave.

"Maria!" he called after her as she departed. "Tell your papa I'll be back for more of this!" Then looking over at Imogen, he said, "Geez! I'm glad you brought me here, Imogen! Who'd have thought anything would be so good down here in Little Italy!"

"Sometimes simple is best, Manfred," said Imogen, "and Little Italy's a wonderful place."

"Well, they sure make great pizza!"

He ate in silence for a while as Imogen sipped her coffee.

"These people really are nice folks, Imogen," he said finally. "I can see why you stood up for them, and you can rest assured, they'll not come to any harm. Your friends are my friends, Imogen."

"Oh—th—thank you, Manfred," she said.

—Though God knows, she thought, people have a right not to be harmed simply because of who they are, not because they're friends of a gangster's girl friend. Refraining from harming them is simply civilized and decent.

"I really mean it," he went on. "Like your aunt. I mean, geez! I almost feel like she's my aunt."

"You've certainly been good to her, Manfred," said Imogen, looking into his eyes.

"Imogen, I'd do anything to make you happy."

Imogen blushed. "Don't, Manfred," she said. "Please don't. I wish you wouldn't say things like that."

"Why? Why not?"

"I can't explain, Manfred, I can't explain. I don't know why. I just wish you wouldn't, that's all. I really don't want you treat me as someone special."

"But you *are* special—but you're also the strangest woman I ever met—but I guess that's partly why I like you. Still, I wish you'd accept that I think you're the greatest, most beautiful, most wonderful woman in the world."

"The world's a big place, Manfred. And that's just why I find all this extravagant praise hard to accept. You make too much of me."

"Geez! It's time someone did make a lot of you! And it's time you realized what a great girl—woman—you are."

"You overdo it, Manfred. It's too much."

"Well, if it embarrasses you—but hey! I'm like that. Always have been. I always do things in a big way."

—Yes, and God knows, thought Imogen, I'm really beginning to like all the praise!

They were both silent for a while, and then he asked, "Finished your coffee?"

"Oh—yes—almost. Just a couple of mouthfuls."

When she had drunk them off, he said, "Shall we go?"

"Yes—let's. And I'm glad you liked it. I'm glad I could treat you—even though nothing like the way you do me."

"Hey! Like they say, it's the thought that counts. And remember that whatever I do, there's thought behind it. I do things because I want to and because they make me happy." He rose, slipped a twenty dollar bill under his plate for Maria, and together they walked to the front of the café. When Imogen had paid the bill, Manfred said to the owner, "Real nice place you got here, Bernardo. And that was great coffee and pizza. Imogen was right. You do make the best in East Clintwood. We'll be back."

"Yes, Bernardo," said Imogen, "we will. It won't be so long next time."

"*Grazie, Imogena, Signor Andreotti,*" said Bernardo. "*Buona notte.*"

Imogen felt Bernardo's cheerfulness was forced, and after Manfred was seated in the Ferrari, she looked back to see father and daughter standing at the window looking after her in uncomprehending amazement and some consternation. She smiled and waved at them, but their responding wave was diffident.

—What must they think of me! she thought as she seated herself beside Manfred, buckled the seat belt, turned on the ignition, put the car into gear, and drove away from the curb.

"You know," said Manfred once they were underway, "you think too much, always looking for reasons, always bothered about everything. You should just take life as it comes."

"Is that what you do, Manfred?" she responded. "Don't you have to think things out, and make careful plans for everything you do?"

He paused a moment.

"Yeah," he said at last, "for some things. Not about people. I either like them or I don't, and I don't worry about why. And I like you. I wish you'd just accept that I do."

"I know you do, Manfred. I just can't understand it. But I guess that's what you're saying isn't it? I'm not sure I can ever stop wondering, Manfred, but I won't ask about it any more."

"Good. Just let yourself go and enjoy everything."

"I enjoy many of the things we do, Manfred. I never thought I'd enjoy dancing so much."

"Yeah. You're a good dancer. I don't know why you thought you weren't."

"As I said, Manfred, I've never had so good a partner."

—And you're good in bed, and perhaps to my everlasting shame, I enjoy being there with you. I can hardly wait until we're there again! How is it that I've lost all my shame and my inhibitions and enjoy sleeping with a gangster? All I know is that I like what you do to me. Maybe you're right. Don't look for reasons, just accept the flow of life.

They sped over the bridge and into West Clintwood, and soon arrived at the hotel. When, after the cars were parked and the body guards made their inspection and they ascended in the elevator and entered Manfred's suite, Imogen gasped.

"Oh! Manfred! A grand piano! A *Boesendorfer*!"

"Yeah, it's for you," he said. "You said it was the best kind."

"Why—Manfred, once again, it's too much—but thank you!"

"Yeah, well I want you to play for me when we come here. I like to hear you."

She went over to it and touched a few chords.

"Oh! It has a beautiful tone—like the one at your parents' home!"

Almost automatically she sat down and began to play, and Manfred took his place at the other end of the piano and gazed down at her.

"That was real nice!" he said when she finished. "What's it called?"

"'Fantasy Impromptu.' It's by Chopin."

He came around to her, took her hand and raised her to her feet.

"You're wonderful," he said.

"Oh Manfred—"

"You are," he said, pressing her to his body.

He began to stroke and kiss the exposed flesh of her shoulders.

"That's nice," she said without thinking.

"You never said that before when I touched you. What's happened? Tonight you seem changed—different."

"Perhaps I am, Manfred."

—Yes, I am. Manfred. Oh! How I've longed for your body all these days during Aunty's hospitalization! You satisfy my need, Manfred, as much as I satisfy yours. God forgive me! I am a whore, and I'm no longer ashamed to be one.

"Your shoulders are so soft and smooth," he said.

"They're rather broad shoulders for a woman's," she said, teasingly, enjoying his arousal of her by his caressing. "But then I need them to hold up these cantaloupes of mine. And I have broad hands with rather long and strong rather than dainty fingers," she added raising her hands and spreading them out. "Paws, you might say. They're what makes it possible for me to play the piano so well."

"Yeah, well you sure do that. But hey! Your hands ain't—they're not that big, and your shoulders aren't too broad—they're great—and so are you. But what's that got to do with the present moment?" he said, nibbling at her neck.

"Nothing. It just means that I'm not your perfect classic beauty."

"Who cares about that?"

"I don't," she replied. "I never have." From her hand bag she drew a red sequined eye mask and put it on.

"Sorry not to be wearing your gold mask, but red goes with the rest of my ensemble."

Then she pushed yoke of her blouse down even farther to bare her breasts. "Maybe I should be like the young Elizabethan ladies. They masked their faces but exposed their breasts."

"You seem to be loosing your inhibitions."

"I am, Manfred."

"Then why do you still need the mask?"

"I wear it because I'm a whore, Manfred—a shameless, sex-starved whore. That's also why I'm wearing red. Red in the old plays is a whore's color, and a whore is what I've become."

"You're ain't no—you're not a whore!" he protested, standing back and staring at her.

"Yes, I am. I'm your whore, Manfred, and I like being your whore. You said the mask makes me look sexy, and I like looking—and feeling—and being sexy—and it makes me feel empowered. So don't ask questions," she said, giving him a quick kiss on the mouth. "Just take life as it comes, and me as I come. But really I hardly need the blouse," she said, pulling the garment over her head to expose herself to the waist, for the first time, suddenly realizing the previously only dimly perceived power of her sexuality. "Or for that matter, anything else." She unzipped her skirt, let it fall to the floor and stepped out of it, clad only in panty-hose and her high heels. "I've become quite shameless," she said as she threw herself into his arms.

"Imogen! What's happened to you?"

"You have, you big, oversexed, arrogant, super-macho two-bit tin-horn crook! So, lover, are you going to make love to me or not?"

CHAPTER FIFTEEN

"Father Daniels," said Imogen, sitting across the desk from her parish priest in his study, "I don't know what's happening to me. I feel I'm becoming another person—someone totally different and shameless."

"What do you mean, Imogen?" asked the priest, frowning slightly. "Tell me about it."

"I like being Manfred Andreotti's mistress."

The priest stared at her.

"Well, you have dropped a bombshell, Imogen. I am rather taken aback."

"I was sure you would be, Father. It all seems so very strange. I can't understand it myself. I can't explain it. It's as though I'm kicking over the traces, except there are no traces to kick over. Uncle Arthur and Aunt Ethel are a bit old fashioned, but they've never tried to dominate me, though they have certainly made it plain to me that there are things of which they disapprove. They've always been kind, and I've always respected their counsel. Yet now—now—well, there has not been much excitement in my life—everything has been so safe and sane without any risks—and I find it exciting being Manfred's girl friend—his mistress, I'm afraid I have to say."

Again the priest stared at her in silence, before saying, "I think I understand what you're saying, Imogen, but—"

"But there are better ways of finding excitement. I know that, Father, but—but—You—you said, Father, that there is good in everyone. Is there also evil?"

The priest stared at her again in silence before he said, "Yes, we're all capable of it. Do you feel you are evil, Imogen?"

"I—I don't know, Father. I just feel an attraction—something impelling me—I suppose it's the fascination of forbidden fruit."

"Maybe, Imogen. We all are attracted that way some time. Be careful."

Imogen was silent now, thinking.

"At first, as you know, the very thought of being a gangster's mistress horrified me, but now—Father, he is very nice to me."

"Don't be taken in, Imogen. People like him can be very charming."

"I know—at least I think I do, but somehow I feel he is genuinely fond of me."

"And you Imogen? How do you feel about him?"

"I—I don't know, Father. I certainly don't hate him—or even dislike him—especially after what he has done for Aunt Ethel. It would have been ages before Uncle Arthur and I could have saved enough—and it might have been too late by then."

"And you feel you have to pay him with sexual favors?"

"No—no. Before I agreed to be his mistress, maybe the offer was bait, but he didn't withdraw it after I'd become his girl friend, but made it again on our first date—so I think he genuinely wanted to help. And he really seems to appreciate me—to respect my education and my piano playing—to take pride in it even."

"Are you sure this is not just flattery to—"

"To take advantage of me, Father? I've already let him do that, and— and now, it's no longer a matter of taking advantage. I—I want it—I like it. That's really wicked, isn't it, Father?"

"To enjoy sexual intercourse? No, Imogen, as I think I said before, that is not wicked—not in itself, at least."

"But he's not my husband—and I think that's half the reason why I enjoy it—half the fun. I enjoy being naughty. I've been too much of a goody-goody. If I've been repressed, it's because I've been repressing myself." She was silent a few moments, then said, "He—he wants me to come and live with him, Father—and I said I would—after my graduation and Susan's farewell recital—both of which occur in the next few weeks— so it's almost time."

Again the priest was silent for some moments.

"Do you want to do that, Imogen? Is he pressuring you into it?"

"He—he has pressed me, Father, and at first I resisted, but—but now—Yes I want to," she replied. Then hardly above a whisper and looking the priest in the eye, she added, "If for no other reason than that I can be in bed with him every night. I'm sure that shocks you, Father."

"Yes, it does, I'm afraid, Imogen. But if you're so determined to do this, why have you come to me?"

"I—I don't know, Father. I just felt I needed to talk about it, I guess—not, certainly to ask your approval, for I know you can't give it, but—to—to get it all out in the open—to see it in the light of day, as it were. Obviously, because I've no desire to do any differently, I can't make a confession and ask absolution. Unlike the woman taken in adultery, I intend to sin again and again."

The priest sighed.

"I can't control your life, Imogen, and it's not for me to judge you, though I'm not happy with your decision—and I fear for you. I don't imagine I need point out the dangers—moral, spiritual—and physical—of what you intend to do. I'll certainly continue to pray for you, and remember, Imogen, I'm always here, no matter what."

"Oh Father!" she almost sobbed. "I don't deserve your concern. You've been so good and so kind, and now I feel I'm throwing dirt in your face."

"Jesus allowed a woman who may have been prostitute to wash his feet, Imogen. Forgive me—I don't mean to imply that's what you are."

"I feel I am, Father—not in the sense that I sell myself—though I suppose in a way, I do."

"Let me put it differently. Jesus rejected no one, and I do not reject you, no matter how unhappy I feel about what you've decided to do."

"I—I know that, Father. You're the most wonderful man—"

"No Imogen, just a humble servant of our Lord—at least I hope I'm humble—and a servant."

They were both silent for some moments, looking at each other. At last Imogen lowered her eyes.

"Well," said the priest, "if you're determined to do this—"

"Then I guess there's nothing more to say."

"No, there isn't."

"Thank you for listening to me, Father."

"I'll always be here to do that, Imogen."

Imogen rose from her chair.

"Good-bye, Father," she said.

"Good-bye, Imogen. God bless you, my dear. Go in peace."

"God bless you, too, Father."

She walked to the study door with the strange, unsettling, sinking feeling that her ways and those of this good priest were parting—perhaps forever—that she was embarking on a path that would take her in a direction that led away from everything the priest represented and which she had once valued. When she turned back to try to speak again, the priest's head was bowed over his folded hands in an attitude of prayer. Quickly she turned away and, with a heavy heart, left quietly.

CHAPTER SIXTEEN

Imogen clad completely in red—dress, shoes, gloves, even hose—with rubies about her neck and at her ears, entered the university ballroom on Manfred's arm. A sudden hush, several gasps, mostly female, and then a buzz of voices, mostly, male, greeted their arrival. Some of the comments she overheard caused Imogen to smile with a kind of perverse satisfaction, for the effect was just what she had hoped. As they stopped to have their tickets checked, a chorus of whispers arose.

"Good Lord!" said a voice. "Is that really Imogen Edwards! She looks absolutely terrific!"

"And did you see her at the ceremony!" said another. "Red five-inch heels and a skirt that barely covered her ass!"

"Yeah. I always figured she had great bazooms even if she tried to hide the fact, but I never knew she had such great legs. Nice ass, too!"

"Who's that with her?" asked a female voice.

"I don't know," said another woman, "but he's sure good looking. How'd she find him I wonder?"

"Or where's she been keeping him!" wondered another.

"Yeah," said one of the men. "She always cold-shouldered us guys when we were at school like maybe we had AIDS or something. Now we know why. All the time she's been having a secret love affair."

"Well, I heard a couple of guys did date her, but she kneed them in the nuts when they tried to get her into the sack."

"Somehow I think I should know who that guy is," said one of the men. "I've seen him, or his picture, but I can't place him."

"Yeah, he looks familiar to me, too. But boy! I never thought she could look like that! It's as though I'd never really seen her before."

"Well, you're certainly seeing her now," said a woman. "She's practically nude to the waist in that dress."

The dress, except for the color, was the same as the one she had worn to Manfred's parents' anniversary. When Manfred had insisted she should have a new dress for her graduation, she had asked Madeleine "Do you have a red one like that white one Manfred got me before?"

``Rouge! Mais oui, Mademoiselle. Bien sur!`` exclaimed Madeleine. ``Avec vos cheveux bruns, Mademoiselle aura l'aspect tres frappante dans rouge! Tres charmante! J'ai une robe rouge comme ca—si vous la voulez!``

``C'est ce que je veux, Madeleine,`` said Imogen.

"Red!" exclaimed Manfred as Madeleine turned to go to the back for the red dress. "How come red? Not because of what you said the other night—"

"Because it's your favorite color, Manfred, and because I rather like it myself. And I've been thinking that I want my former fellow students to see me as they've never seen me before—dressed to the nines as they've never seen me dressed."

``Ah, M'sieur! Mademoiselle aura l'aspect tres magnifique dans une robe rouge,`` exclaimed Madeleine when she returned with the dress.

"Huh?"

"She says I'll look magnificent in a red dress, Manfred," explained Imogen.

"Magnificent, eh? Well, yeah, okay," Manfred reflected. "You looked terrific in red shoes and skirt the other night. So in a gown—yeah. Magnificent. And, yeah, it is my favorite color."

—And "Charmante" is not how I would describe the gown, nor is charmante what I wish to be. ``Frappante, oui. Mais plus, provocatrice, ou, peut etre, choquant, scandaleuse? How delicious it will be to see the looks on my former fellow students' faces and to hear their exclamations at the transformation of dowdy Imogen Edwards and to see their shock when they learn that she is Manfred Andreotti's mistress! Oh Imogen! You don't have a curl in the middle of your forehead, but you are becoming a very horrid little girl—well not so little, but certainly horrid! But revenge, they say, is sweet.

And so, now, as they entered the ballroom, Imogen said "We're causing quite a sensation, Manfred. A rather new experience for me—and I'm rather enjoying it. Would you like to meet some of these people I took classes with?"

"Sure, if you want me too."

"Shall I tell them who you are? That will certainly cause a sensation."

"As long as you don't mind."

"No, I don't mind," she said. "Word will eventually get around. I just wondered if tonight you want to be known."

"Half the State knows me already—or who I am at least—so a few more won't matter."

They walked over to a group of Imogen's former classmates.

"Imogen!" said one of the young women. "My goodness! Look at you!"

"Hello, Betty," she said. "Hello, everyone—and congratulations, fellow graduates." Then turning her head to indicate Manfred, she said, "I'd like you all to meet Manfred Andreotti."

Eyes popped and mouths dropped open at the shock of Imogen's introduction of her date.

"Hi, folks," said Manfred cheerfully. "Happy to meet Imogen's friends. Any friend of hers is a friend of mine."

"Manfred Andreotti!" one of the male graduates whispered to his partner. "She's been the woman of the crime boss of East Clintwood all these years!"

"Golly! Who'd have believed it?"

"Yeah. Posing as a poor girl all the time!"

Imogen overheard the exchange, smiled to herself, but did not comment on or correct the assumptions.

Betty, who had been as close to being a friend as Imogen had during her university days, having overcome her initial astonishment, said. "Imogen! You're—you're Manfred Andreotti's girl friend?"

"Yes, Betty, I am," Imogen replied, quite without discomposure.

"And you've been his girl all the time we were at school?"

"No, only since the end of this term, Betty."

Betty stared in astonishment.

"But how—?" she began.

"He asked me," responded Imogen to the question Betty seemed unable to complete.

"Just like that—and you accepted?"

"Not right away, but he was very persuasive," Imogen said, turning to smile mischievously at her partner. "Weren't you, Manfred?"

"Yeah," said Manfred. "She played hard to get for a while. I had to work pretty hard to persuade her. And make some concessions," he added, with a sardonic smile of his own.

"I did drive a hard bargain," said Imogen.

The young men and women turned to each other, their faces studies in incomprehension.

"But hey folks!" said Manfred. "There's the music starting. Let's not miss out on the dancing. Maybe a little later we can have champagne—on me of course—to toast your graduations. Nice meeting you. Come on Imogen, let's dance."

"Hell! I didn't think she liked dancing," said one of the young men as Manfred led Imogen out onto the dance floor.

As Manfred took her into his arms to begin the dance, Imogen said, "We certainly did cause a sensation."

"And you enjoyed it."

"I did, Manfred, I did."

"How come?"

"Formerly dowdy Imogen Edwards is enjoying the new experience of people's taking notice of her and of shocking the people who used to look down on her. Aren't I horrible, Manfred?""

"Naw. It'll do them good to see a new side of you."

"In this dress," she said with a whimsical smile, "I'm letting them see quite a bit of both sides of me." Then, after a few moments, she changed the subject. "Manfred, it was really very thoughtful of you to bring Uncle Arthur and Aunt Ethel down here in your limousine with me and put us all up at that lovely hotel. It was very important for Uncle and Aunt to be at my graduation."

"Well, geez! Of course. We couldn't leave them behind in East Clintwood. And hey! I'm glad to see your aunt walking again."

"Oh yes, Manfred, so am I! And it's all thanks to you. She still needs her cane sometimes, but it is really wonderful to see her able to move around on her own. I can never thank you enough. And I'm really happy that you're my escort to the ball this evening—and not just so I could shock my former fellow students."

"Hey! I wouldn't have missed it! It's another opportunity to dance with my girl."

"You even came to the ceremony. I hope you weren't bored."

"Hey! I wouldn't have missed seeing you go up to get your degree. And you looked great. Knocked the spots off everyone around."

"Thank you," she said, and couldn't help a smile, "but I think the dress you bought me helped."

"Couldn't see the dress for that black gown they made you wear."

"Then it must have been the red five-inch spikes. But you know," she said, "I'm getting quite vain. I'm starting to enjoy receiving your compliments."

"It's time you did, especially when you're *Summa cum*—what? I can never remember."

"*Summa cum laude*, Manfred," she laughed. "It's Latin. When the universities began in the Middle Ages, Latin was the language of learning."

"Yeah? And it means pretty damn good, right?"

"More or less, Manfred. 'Pretty damn good' about sums it up—but 'with the highest praise,' to be precise."

"And you deserve it. Beauty and brains! Geez! "

"It took four years of hard work, Manfred, and beauty didn't have much to do with it—especially since I tried very hard to hide it—which I no longer want to do."

"And I'm sure as hell glad you don't," said Manfred.

Imogen fell silent as they danced, and after a while Manfred asked, "Why so quiet? Aren't you enjoying yourself?"

"Oh—no—I mean, yes I am, Manfred. I was thinking how one stage of life ends and another begins. For four years our whole life centred in this place. It was books and lectures and essays—and now it's all over, and we leave it all behind to start something new, and probably we'll never see one another again."

"I never thought of that. Are you sad about leaving?"

"I don't know Manfred. A little, I guess."

—And what will my future hold? Will becoming Manfred Andreotti's mistress just be a passing episode, or will it change the direction of my life forever—as I fear it may? But it's best not to worry about the outcome. Right now, I'm enjoying the evening being his mistress.

The orchestra concluded the first number in the sequence, and with the rest of the dancers, Imogen and Manfred circled the floor. From across the floor, Betty waved at them and Imogen waved back.

"Do you think Betty is very pretty, Manfred?" she asked as the music resumed and they began to dance again.

"Yeah, but not as pretty as you. You're gorgeous."

"So you say, but Betty was the Freshman Beauty Queen in her first year."

"You don't say? How come you weren't beauty queen? You're ten times better looking."

"I don't know about ten times, but I didn't enter the competition, Manfred, and no one nominated me. I was dowdy Imogen Edwards in those days."

"Yeah. Putting yourself down as usual."

"Wanting to be seen as more than just a pretty face and a sexy body, Manfred. But I have to confess, now that I've proved my abilities, I rather like looking glamorous. I'm glad to recognize that I am beautiful. Maybe, as you say, it is time I did. And Manfred, I appreciate the fact that you value my intelligence and learning as well—although," she added with a teasing smile, "I think you admire them because you think having a beautiful, intelligent, educated mistress makes *you* look good."

"Well, yeah, but—Oh, hey. The music's ended. Let's get a drink."

He led Imogen to the bar and as he ordered Bourbon for himself and white wine for Imogen, Betty and her partner approached. "Hi!" said Betty. "Gee, you two look really great on the dance floor!"

"Manfred's a very good dancer," Imogen said. "I just follow."

"I—uh—I don't suppose you'd like to change partners for the next dance?" asked Betty hopefully.

Imogen stared at her in astonishment. "Oh—why—I don't mind, Betty, if Manfred doesn't. What about you, Geoff? Do you mind?" she said turning to Betty's partner.

"Yeah, well," he said, feigning reluctance but looking at Imogen's decolletage rather too eagerly and almost lecherously, "she seems to want to, so it's okay by me, I guess."

"Manfred?" queried Imogen, turning to him as he returned with their drinks, "Betty would like to have the next dance with you. Would you?"

"Huh? Yeah. Sure," he said, "if you don't mind."

"Oh," said Imogen, deciding to make light of the situation. "I'm terribly, terribly jealous. You want to dance with her because I told you she was First Year Beauty Queen. I'm not sure I can trust you with her."

"You could have been beauty queen, Imogen, if you'd entered and worn a dress like that," said Betty. "That's why Geoff wants to dance with you," she teased.

Geoff gulped and turned red.

"Yeah, that's what I say," said Manfred. "I mean that she could have been beauty queen. But sure, Betty, I'd be happy to dance with you—if your date doesn't mind."

"Geoff says he doesn't mind being stuck with me," laughed Imogen. "So I guess it's settled."

"Oh gee!" exclaimed Betty. "Thank you!"

"Let me buy you both drinks first," said Manfred. "What'll it be, Betty?"

"Oh, thanks. I'd like a Singapore Sling."

"What'll it be for you, Geoff?"

"Uh, yeah. Thanks Mr.—uh—Andreotti. I'll have a Bourbon and branch water."

"Right"

"He's just dreamy!" whispered Betty to Imogen as she looked over toward Manfred as he ordered the drinks at the bar. "I'm so excited! I'm just dying to dance with him! I've never danced with a gangster before! Thank you for letting me!"

"Well, be sure you don't call him a gangster—and," Imogen added, in a mock-serious tone, "be sure you return him to me all in one piece. You have a way with men."

"Surely you're not in love with him!" said Betty.

The question struck Imogen like a bombshell and completely dumbfounded her.

"Wha—! No—no! Of course not!"

"Methinks thou dost protest too much, Imogen Edwards."

"Don't be silly. How could I be in love with a gangster?"

"There've been women who have. But here he is."

—How strange! How strange, thought Imogen as Manfred handed their drinks to Betty and Geoff. Betty wants to dance with him because he's a gangster, and I didn't want to have anything to do with him for the same reason. I became his reluctant mistress, but—I'm not reluctant any more—but surely—surely I'm not in love with him?

Imogen was silent most of the time as the others chatted and sipped their drinks. Then the music began again, and Geoff asked, a little too eagerly, "Are you ready to dance, Imogen?"

"Oh—uh—yes—As ready as I'll ever be, Geoff." Then to Manfred she said, again adopting a bantering manner, "Enjoy your dance with Betty, Manfred. She's a much better dancer than I. And you have fun, too, Betty. Come on, Geoff. I'll try not to step on your toes."

"She won't, Geoff," said Manfred. "She's a lot better dancer than she makes out."

"Yeah, I think so too," said Geoff.

When they got out on the dance floor, Geoff said, "That's a really great dress you're wearing, Imogen. I never thought I'd see you in such a dress. You really look terrific in it."

"Well, thank you, Geoff. And until a few weeks ago I never thought I'd wear such a dress."

"You mean until you—until you met Andreotti?"

"Until I met Manfred, yes. But don't hold me so close, Geoff. You're Betty's boy friend, remember. The dress hides my great legs," Imogen said with a mischievous smile, "but it gives a tantalizing glimpse of my terrific bazooms. So if you step back a bit you'll be able to see my cleavage better."

"Aw, hey, Imogen!" he said as he moved back from her. "You don't have to rub it in! None of us ever thought you could look so gorgeous—I mean—I don't mean—"

"It's all right, Geoff, I didn't know myself."

"And you *do* have great breasts—if I may say so."

"Everyone does, Geoff, so I guess you may too. They were all anyone ever noticed about me in the four years I was here. I was the poor girl on scholarship who had great boobs. A lot of guys thought I'd be an easy lay. I wasn't. My uncle taught me how to deal with mashers."

"You're uncle?" said Geoff in surprise. "How come it was your uncle taught you that?"

"I was raised by my uncle and aunt after my parents were killed in a traffic accident when I was a baby."

"You—you mean you're an orphan?"

"I suppose I am, but I never think of myself as one. I never knew my parents, and my uncle and aunt couldn't have been better to me than my real parents."

"Gee. I didn't know."

"Well, I didn't proclaim it from the roof of the library, but on the other hand, no one really wanted to know anything about me—just to get me into bed."

"Uh—yeah—I—"

"Don't worry about it Geoff. That's all in the past now."

"Uh—yeah." He fell silent for a while as they danced. Then he asked, "How did you come to be Andreotti's girl friend. When you were here—"

"I was a goody two shoes, I know. But how I became Manfred's mistress is not something I feel free to talk about, Geoff. It's come about, that's all."

"Did—did he threaten you?"

"If he did I wouldn't tell you now, would I? But no, he didn't threaten me. But I'm afraid, Geoff, you'll just have to live with the mystery."

"Yeah, okay—but what's he like? What's it like being a—a—"

"A gangster's mistress? To tell you the truth, I find it exciting. He's not as bad—to me at least—as I thought he might be. In fact, he's very nice."

"Holy—! I don't know—you seem a different person, Imogen. You seem—I don't know—more poised, self-assured—or something."

"How about brazen?"

"Oh, I wouldn't—"

"I would, Geoff. If I'm to be a gangster's mistress, I have to be—at least a little bit. Better to play the role to the hilt than go around looking glum and gloomy all the time. I've had to adapt."

"I—I guess so."

Again they danced in silence, Geoff seemingly bemused by all he had heard.

At last, Imogen interrupted his reverie and said with a whimsical smile, "The music has stopped, Geoff. Maybe we should stop dancing."

"Oh—uh—yeah," said Geoff with a start. "I didn't notice."

"I know, I'm such a fascinating person."

"Uh—yeah, well, you are. I never realized—Uh—yeah. Well—uh—thanks for the dance. I'll see you back to Andre—to your partner."

"If he hasn't run off with yours," Imogen teased.

"Huh? Well if he has, I—Uh—no—there they are."

"Oh good! Caught them before they made their escape!" Then in a more serious tone as they walked across the floor in the direction of Manfred and Betty, she said, "Thank you for the dance, Geoff. I did enjoy it."

As they joined the others, Manfred was saying, "It was nice dancing with you, Betty."

"I bet you enjoyed dancing with her more than with me," Imogen bantered. "Geoff got off all right. I didn't step on his toes once."

"Uh—you're a very good dancer, Imogen," said Geoff.

"You bet she is!" said Manfred.

"Thank you," said Imogen with a little curtsy of feigned gentility. "Thank you both. How did you enjoy dancing with my date, Betty?" asked Imogen

"Oh—it was—" she began rather too enthusiastically. "I—uh—I really enjoyed it," she said. Then she whispered to Imogen, "He's a dream, a real dream, Imogen!"

"I'm glad you enjoyed him," Imogen replied aloud. "I don't lend him out very much. Only to special friends."

"You're sure you're not in love with him?" she whispered, but then seeing Imogen's discomfiture, she said, "Well, thanks for lending him to me. It was really nice dancing with you—M—Manfred."

"Hey! you're welcome," said Manfred. "Can I get us all another drink?"

"Uh—not for me," said Geoff, seemingly worried for his own date and realizing he had scored no points with Imogen.

"I—I guess not," said Betty, pouting slightly in disappointment.

"Imogen?"

"No thanks, Manfred. Perhaps a bit later, but not just now."

"Well," said Manfred. "I enjoyed meeting you folks."

"Oh! Same here!" said Betty.

"Yeah," said Geoff, less enthusiastically. "Likewise."

"I'm sure we'll have a chance to talk again before the end of the evening," said Imogen.

"Oh, I hope so!" exclaimed Betty.

"Right," said Geoff, none too eagerly. "Uh—see you."

"*Au revoir,*" said Imogen.

Imogen walking on his arm as they perambulated the ballroom, Manfred asked, "So, how was the dance with Geoff?"

"It was all right," she replied, "but I'd rather dance with you."

"Hey! It's nice to hear you say that."

"I'd forgotten how vacuous some of these guys are. They were not here for an education, but just for the status and prestige of having been here."

"Yeah?"

"Yes. It's sad. So much they could gain from the experience."

"Uh—yeah. I guess. I never went, so I don't know. Anyway, you're my education, Imogen. I've learned about more things from you in the few weeks I've known you than in all the rest of my life."

"It's nice of you to say that, Manfred, but I'm sure it's not true."

"Hey! It is true. I like to hear you talk about things."

"I appreciate that, Manfred. Most men don't"

"Yeah?. But there's the music again," he said. "Let's dance."

"I'd love to, Prince Charming," she said.

"Prince Charming!"

"Well, you have transformed Cinderella."

"Meaning you?"

"Meaning me. And I'm glad you have."

"He-e-ey!"

"Though I don't suppose Cinderella wore a dress as revealing as this. She was in a different kind of fairy tale."

"She wouldn't have looked as great in it as you do. You've got what it takes to wear it."

"Maybe she did too, but was too modest—as I was once," she said as Manfred took her into his arms to dance. "Everyone's been staring at me—at us—and whispering. Word has got around that Imogen Edwards is Manfred Andreotti's mistress. Between the dress, Manfred, and being here with you, I've become quite notorious—and I'm enjoying my notoriety."

—Oh yes! It has been a moment of triumph for me—and it's all because of Manfred. But—but surely Betty is not right that I'm in love with him—is she?

CHAPTER SEVENTEEN

Susan's farewell recital was a resounding success. Embracing her friend backstage after the last encore—Schubert's *An die Musike*, a song which for both of them expressed their own love of, and joy in, the art of music—Imogen, wearing the gown Susan had bought her to go to the opera on that fateful night when she had met Manfred, said, "Susan, you were splendid! I don't think you've ever sung better!"

"Thanks, Imogen. I really felt inspired. But you—you were brilliant yourself. Your accompaniments were more sensitive than I've ever known them. I've never had an accompanist like you. And your solos were marvelous!"

"I played them for you, Susan. But one of these days you'll be accompanied by someone like Dalton Baldwin or even someone like Alfred Brendel, for you deserve the very best. But tonight I wanted to do my best for you. And I guess maybe I caught some of your inspiration."

"Don't underestimate yourself, Imogen; you're a fine pianist—and a great person. You've been a wonderful friend."

"Oh Susan! I'm the one who's benefited most from our friendship. I'm going to miss you."

"Hey Kid! Even though it won't be as often, we'll see each other again."

"Oh, I hope so, Susan! But your career is going to occupy your whole time and become your whole world."

"I'll still get back now and then, Imogen."

"I hope so, Susan, but now this is your night. You must go out and meet your public. "

At the reception, the two friends were soon separated as well-wishers crowded around Susan. Waiting for Manfred to find her, Imogen noted that many people in the crowd whispered to one another as they glanced her way.

—Everyone knows I'm Manfred's mistress! How could they not! I've sacrificed whatever good name I ever had, and I'm now the subject of scandal. Well, let them be scandalized! Why should I care? The cream of East Clintwood society—except of course Susan and her family—always looked down on me. Gangster though he is, Manfred respects me far more than any of them ever did. So let them look down as deep as they want!

Suddenly she was was surprised and a bit embarrassed to be greeted by Father Richard Daniels who, accompanied by his attractive wife, had made his way to her through the crowd.

"Oh—Father Daniels!" she said. "How—how nice to see you. It—it's very good of you to come—for Susan."

"Only a pastoral emergency would have kept me away, Imogen," said the priest. "You know my wife?" he asked.

"Oh—yes—I mean, I know who you are, Mrs. Daniels. I—I don't think we've ever met formally."

"Well, it's a pleasure to meet you now, Imogen," said the priest's wife. "And I want to say that you are a very fine pianist."

"Oh—Thank you. I love to play—and especially to accompany Susan. She brings out the best in me."

"She has a beautiful voice," said Mrs. Daniels. "And she's a real artist."

"Oh, yes, she is! And I'm so happy for her that she's embarking on a solo and operatic career—but I'll miss her terribly."

At this moment, Manfred, with his ever present body guards hovering near, approached them through the crowd.

"Oh—Manfred—I—I'd like you to meet my—my parish priest and his wife. Father and Mrs. Daniels—"she hesitated, embarrassed to introduce a priest to a gangster—"Th—this is Manfred Andreotti."

Without batting an eye, though his wife was somewhat taken aback, Father Daniels extended his hand.

"How do you do, Mr. Andreotti."

"Huh? Oh—Uh—yeah," said Manfred, himself a bit nonplused at the priest's apparent unflappability, "How do you do, Reverend—uh—Father. Nice to meet Imogen's priest—and you too, Mrs. Daniels. Imogen says you're a great guy, Rev—Father."

"Imogen tends to underrate herself and overrate others," said the priest, "but, since it comes from her, I appreciate the compliment."

"Yeah, I know what you mean. I've had a hard time convincing her she's beautiful."

"I for one am glad you have, Mr. Andreotti, for both my wife and I have always thought she was and should make more of the fact that she is."

Imogen, who despite her new-found self-awareness, nevertheless blushed at hearing herself praised for her good looks both by and in the presence of her priest.

"Yeah? I didn't think you people thought things like that," said Manfred, responding to the priest's comment.

"And why do you think I chose such a pretty wife, Mr. Andreotti?"

"Uh—yeah. I—uh—yeah. You sure did, Rev—Father."

Imogen was surprised to see Manfred at such a conversational disadvantage. To try to put him more at ease she said with a mock pout, "Manfred, I'm jealous!"

"Uh—well, Geez! you know what I mean."

"We've been telling Imogen what a fine pianist she is, Mr. Andreotti," said Father Daniels to change the subject.

"Oh hey! Yeah!" said Manfred, perking up. "She's great, isn't she? I love to hear her play. I could listen to her all night."

"Then you must have very good taste, Mr. Andreotti," said Mrs. Daniels.

"He does, Mrs. Daniels," said Imogen. "In fact, we—we met at the opera in New York."

"Yeah, and I'm real proud to have a beautiful girl friend who's educated and smart and plays the piano like nobody's business," said Manfred. "But I was going to take Imogen over to get a drink. Maybe you'd like to join us."

"No, thanks," Mr. Andreotti," said Father Daniels. "Not this time. We've friends to meet. Glad to have met you, though."

"And I, Mr. Andreotti," said Mrs. Daniels. "Good evening. Good night, Imogen."

"Good night Mrs. Daniels, Father," said Imogen.

"Hey! Yeah, good night," said Manfred. "Nice to have met you folks!"

As Manfred steered Imogen toward the refreshments table, he said of the priest and his wife, "Real nice folks."

"Yes they are. Father Daniels has been our parish priest since I was a teenager, Manfred. He prepared both Susan and me for Confirmation. "

"Yeah? Funny, though. Most folks get all hot and bothered when they meet me, or all gushy and want to kiss my boots. They didn't."

"He sees the world as it is, Manfred. It takes a lot to unnerve him. He simply treats everyone equally—as a fellow human being. I don't think Father Daniels—or his wife—would ever lick anyone's boots."

"Yeah. I sort of respect people like that. Refreshing to meet such folks. Like you say, he is a great guy—and has a lovely wife."

"They're wonderful people, very worthy of respect, Manfred."

"Yeah? Yeah. But here we are. How about some champagne?"

"Yes. To toast Susan. That would be very nice, Manfred," Imogen replied.

When Manfred handed her a glass of champagne, he said, "Yeah. Here's to Susan and her success."

"To Susan. Oh Manfred! I'm so happy for her!"

"Yeah," said Manfred. "She'll do great. I'd like to hear her sing Verdi—La Traviata some day, or Aida for example."

"And Mozart and Rossini!" said Imogen.

"Yeah, them too," agreed Manfred.

"This is nice champagne, Manfred. Thanks to you, I'm beginning to develop a more discriminating palate for such things."

"Yeah, well didn't I tell you being my girl friend wouldn't be such a bad thing?"

Just then, another voice addressed them.

"Miss Edwards. You're still hanging around with Andreotti, I see."

"Now Stan, don't be uncivil."

"Oh—" said Imogen, taken by surprise. "Hello Lieutenant Wolinski and Mrs Wolinski. It's—it's nice to see you again."

"Hey Lootenant," said Manfred. "What brings you out tonight to such a cultural event? Afraid some one's going to kidnap the soprano?"

"Now Manfred!" admonished Imogen.

"It would never occur to you, of course, Andreotti, that my wife and I might like classical music and appreciate fine singing, or that I might know Miss Van Alstyne's family. You probably don't think I have any friends—or any taste for the life's finer things."

"Hey, Lootenant! Hey!" said Manfred throwing up his hands in protest. "I was only joking."

"Okay, okay! And I hope you're treating this young lady well."

"He is, Lieutenant," said Imogen, blushing. "Very well."

"Huh!" exclaimed the lieutenant, astonished. "You almost sound as though you like being his girl friend."

"I—I—" stammered Imogen, again taken aback by the suggestion that she might feel affection for Manfred. "He has been very nice to me, Lieutenant."

"Well, I'll be—"

"There's a good side to everyone, you know, Stan," said the policeman's attractive wife. "But my! Your friend Susan sang very beautifully tonight, Imogen, and—"

"Oh yes! Susan's a great artist!" exclaimed Imogen. "It has been an honor to be her accompanist."

"I was going to say, Imogen, that you played very well. And your solos were lovely."

"Imogen's the greatest, Mrs. Wolinski," said Manfred. "Beautiful, talented. Having her for my girl's the best thing that ever happened to me."

"Better than you deserve, Andreotti," said the Lieutenant.

"Now Stan!" said his wife. "Try not to spoil the evening for these people. You're not on duty."

"Yeah, yeah. Okay. Right. But I still think, Miss Edwards, that you—"

"Stan!"

"It's okay, Mrs. Wolinski," said Manfred. "For once the Lootenant and I agree. Imogen is better than I deserve."

"Yeah," said the policeman as Imogen blushed, "and don't forget it. Well, nice to see you again, Miss Edwards. Just watch yourself, Andreotti."

"I always do, Lootenant."

"Good night, Imogen," said Mrs. Wolinski. "It has been nice to see you again. Good night Mr. Andreotti."

"Good night Mrs Wolinski," said Imogen. "And good night Lieutenant."

"Yeah. Good night Mrs. Wolinski. You too, Lootenant," said Manfred. "Take care."

Before the Wolinskis were out of earshot, Imogen and Manfred heard the lieutenant say to his wife, "How come you always take his side?"

"I don't take his side, Stan," said his wife. "I just don't want that nice Miss Edwards to be upset."

"I'm concerned about her too. I'm afraid she'll be hurt, because somehow I'm going to get Andreotti."

"Geez!" said Manfred. "The guy never lets up."

"It's his job, Manfred, and you shouldn't antagonize him."

"I suppose not, but he didn't come on all that friendly. But now, how long are we going to stay around here? You know your promise."

"Yes, Manfred, I know. But I want to stay until Susan is ready to leave. She is my best friend, after all, and I'm her accompanist—and this will be the last time I see her in a long while. And also I should go home first with Uncle and Aunt."

"Yeah. Okay, I guess, but I've been waiting for you to come and live with me for a long time."

"I know, Manfred, I know. You've been very patient," she said. "It won't be much longer."

"Yeah, yeah. Okay."

—And oh Manfred! How eager I am too! But oh! It's so sad—and how terrifying—to turn my back on my old life and on those I love. Just how nice is Imogen Edwards, Mrs. Wolinski?

"But, hey!" said Manfred, breaking into her reverie. "It looks like things are breaking up now. Let's go and say good-bye to Susan so we can be on our way."

"Oh—yes—all right."

They made their way to where Susan stood saying good-bye to her well-wishers.

"Imogen!" cried Susan as they approached. "I was afraid you'd left, and I so wanted to see you once more!"

"I'd never have left without saying good-bye to you, Susan."

"No, I didn't think you would. But oh Imogen! How can I say good-bye to you?"

"Or I to you, Susan? You've been my best friend ever! I hate to see you go. I'll miss you so!" She embraced her friend and held her close. "But Oh Susan! This is the right thing for you. I can hardly wait to read of your triumphs at Covent Garden and *La Scala* and the Met. The very best of everything, Susan."

"Oh," protested Susan in mock reproof, "you've got it all planned out for me, I see."

"How can it be otherwise, Susan? It's your destiny."

"Well, it's certainly my hope—but it's all very frightening to contemplate."

"Nothing can stop you, Susan."

"In my heart I know I can do it—but it's still a great challenge."

"Susan, you've got what it takes to meet the challenge."

"Thanks, Imogen, thanks. You've always been my greatest supporter. I'll miss you—but I'll never forget you. I owe so much to you. Don't think your accompaniments didn't help get me where I am."

"As I've said, Susan, you inspire the best in me, but you're the one with the talent. To have been your accompanist has been one of the greatest joys in my life."

"When I come home on holidays, we'll get together and do lieder all day and night."

"I'll look forward to it, Susan." Then, tears in her eyes, Imogen said, "I wish we didn't have to part, but the world is waiting for you. You've got to go and meet it and embrace your good fortune—and I have to let you and wish you every success."

"Oh Imogen!" said Susan, also tearfully, "I could never have had a better friend than you!"

"Nor I than you, Susan."

Again they threw themselves into each other's arms and embraced for a long time. Almost like lovers the two friends kissed each other on the mouth, and then Imogen broke away.

"Good-bye, Susan," she said, tears now running down her cheeks, "I—I should go—and let you go."

"Not good-bye," said Susan, wiping away her tears. *Au revoir.*"

"Yes—*au revoir.*"

Then, unable to hold back her tears, Imogen turned and hurried away.

"Hey! hey!" said Manfred catching up to her and putting his arm about her shoulders after hurriedly saying good-bye to Susan and wishing her well. "Don't take it so hard. You'll see her again."

"I know, Manfred, but we've been the best of friends for a very long time—since childhood. It's hard to think she won't be here any more to see almost any time I want to. But," she said, brushing away her tears, "I'm happy for her, so very happy for her."

"Yeah, that's nice," he said. "That's real nice."

"And now," she said, tears again coming to her eyes, "I've got another good-bye to make. I'll go home with Uncle and Aunt," she said. "I want to say good-bye to them there where I lived with them since they took me in when my parents were killed—and, Oh! That won't be easy either. Uncle and Aunt are pretty upset."

"Geez! They've no need to be," he said. "Coming to live with me's not the end of the world—and this is the twenty-first century."

"I know, Manfred," replied Imogen, "but they're old-fashioned. They never expected I'd do something like this."

"They gotta keep up with the times."

"They're not naive, Manfred. And I rather like them for their old-fashioned ways. There's something very good in what they believe. And I never thought I'd ever do anything like this either—but don't worry. I will do it. I want to do it."

"Yeah, okay. I understand, I guess. If that's what you want, I'll follow you up."

"But don't come in with me, Manfred. This has to be a private farewell."

On the way back to her Uncle and Aunt's home, her uncle said, "Your aunt and I certainly wish you weren't going to live with Andreotti, Imogen."

"I know, Uncle, I know," said Imogen. "I'm troubled too," she said, "but somehow, I have to do it."

"I don't see why. It makes no sense."

"It doesn't, I know, but I just have to, Uncle. I can't explain."

"It just doesn't seem like you, dear," said her aunt.

"I know, Aunty, I know. Nothing I do these days seems like me. I'm sorry to hurt you, but it seems I have to explore some sides of life that I've never experienced—that I never even knew were there."

"This man has some strange power over you, Imogen," said her uncle."

"Perhaps, Uncle—yes—but I think I also have some power over him."

"Have we been so hard on you that you have to kick over the traces like this?" asked her uncle, his hurt sounding in his voice.

"Oh Uncle!" she said, tears filling her eyes. "No, no. It's not that. It's not that! I'm sorry. As I said, I can't explain it."

"We just can't understand, Imogen," said her aunt.

"I know, Aunty. I know. I can't understand myself. But I have to see—or maybe it's just that I want to see—another side of life."

"Have we failed so badly in the way we brought you up, Imogen?" asked her aunt.

"You've not failed at all, Aunty," said Imogen turning to her, tears in her eyes. "If anyone has failed, it's I. I know it must seem to you that I'm throwing up everything you taught me, but I feel I have to go and live with him. Maybe I just have to get it out of my system."

"This could be very costly to you, Imogen," said her uncle.

"Yes, Uncle, I know. I know the risks. But I'm prepared to take them."

"Well—you're old enough to make your own choices, and we can't control your life, Imogen—so I guess there's nothing we can do. But we still don't understand and are not happy."

"Uncle, Aunty—underneath it all—in spite of everything—I'm still your Imogen. I'm still your niece."

"We love you, Imogen," said her Aunt. "It's because we love you that we're so upset."

"I know, Aunty, I know. And I love you. It really upsets me to be doing this, because I know it hurts you—but I have to do it. That's all I can say."

"And all we can say, Imogen," said her uncle as they drew up to the house, "is we still can't understand why."

"Yes, Uncle, I know. I'm sorry to be upsetting you so."

When they had entered the house, Imogen said, "I'll just change out of my gown first."

She ran to her bedroom where she changed to the dress she had worn on her first date with Manfred.

Before leaving, she looked about the room.

—Will I ever sleep in this room again? she wondered. I have a strange feeling I never will.

She picked up the photograph of her parents' wedding, and looked at it a minute or two.

—Should I take this with me? No. No. It should stay in the world they knew. When you went out on that night that you were killed, Mom and Dad, I'm sure you never thought the little daughter you left with Aunt and Uncle would ever go to live with a gangster. Why, indeed, am I doing this? Is my dark side gaining the ascendancy? Oh God forgive me! But how can you when I have no intention of turning away from what I'm doing. So Imogen! Into the abyss!

She replaced the photograph on the dresser and returned to her uncle and aunt in the living room. Tearfully, they embraced.

"Oh Imogen!" cried her aunt as soon as she saw her niece. "I wish this weren't happening!"

"Aunty, I know it's not much to say I'm sorry—but for your sakes, I am."

"I share your aunt's sentiments, Imogen," said her uncle. "I find it very hard to accept. Neither of us can be happy about it."

"Oh, Uncle! Please, please remember that—no matter what—I love you, and I always will. Please don't ever stop loving me."

"Imogen, you know we won't do that."

"I do know Uncle—and I hate causing that love so much pain, but—"

A flood of tears overcame her so that she was unable to speak. Then she kissed them both long and lingeringly, tore herself away from them and, throwing a cashmere stole over her bare shoulders, ran out the door and down the path to the waiting convoy of cars.

"Okay?" asked Manfred coming forward to meet her.

"No—no, Manfred. It will never be okay. But there's no turning back. So let's go and get it over with."

In the limousine, Manfred put his arm about her shoulder and drew her to him. She leaned her head against him as they drove away.

"That was a great evening," he said. "You really played well."

"Thank you, Manfred," she said, smiling in spite of her sadness and apprehension. "I'm pleased you thought so." Then she fell silent.

"Why so quiet?" he asked after they'd gone a few blocks.

"I—I was thinking, Manfred."

"About Susan? About your uncle and aunt?"

"Uh—yes—sort of. I'll miss Susan—and Uncle and Aunt, whom I never wanted to hurt are, devastated. My mind is in a whirl with all that's been happening lately—it's all confusing, unsettling and daunting—but, for better or worse, I'm doing what I want to do."

"Hey! And I'm glad you're coming to live with me—and I promise, you won't regret it. You won't be unhappy! Mama and Papa and Ana-Maria all think you're just the greatest. They'll do everything to make you feel at home."

"Oh, I know, Manfred. But it's still a big step for me—one I never thought I'd take."

"Hey, Imogen! You're sure making me happy by coming to live with me."

She was silent for a while. Then she said, "I'm happy, too, Manfred, but I can't help my misgivings. I don't think Uncle and Aunt will ever accept what I've done."

"They'll get used to it. My family's sure happy. They've arranged a little welcoming party. It's Ana-Maria's and Mama's idea."

"Oh—how very nice of them! I'll enjoy being with Ana-Maria. I like her very much. You too, of course, you big gorilla," she said, wiping away the last of her tears and smiling teasingly, trying to put aside her misgivings.

"You tease a lot, don't you?"

"It's a survival mechanism, Manfred, to keep you in your place," she responded, half teasingly, half seriously.

"You changed out of your gown," said Manfred.

"Yes. I've left behind the life that dress represents. This is the one I wore on our first date. It represents the life I'm entering now."

"You make too big a thing of this."

"Isn't it a big thing, Manfred?"

"Hey! People do it all the time."

"It's a big thing for me, Manfred—and a hard thing for Uncle and Aunt. But it's my choice to do it. I want to live with you. So there's an end to it."

"You didn't want to go with me at first, so—not that I'm complaining— but why the change?"

"Because I've become a lewd, sex-starved whore because of you, that's why, Manfred, you old lecher!" she teased as she pressed against him. "You aroused my lust and I need you to satisfy it."

"You blame me for everything."

"I'm not blaming you for anything, Manfred. I'm happy you've aroused me sexually and made me feel like a woman. As you said, I didn't know what I was missing." Then, running her hand into his crotch, she said, "Lady Jane can't live without John Thomas."

"Huh? What's this Lady Jane John Thomas stuff?"

"Cunt and cock, Manfred. Haven't you read Lady Chatterly's Lover?"

"Isn't that some kind of a dirty book? I didn't think you read that sort of thing."

"It's not a dirty book; it's an honest exploration of human sexuality and human sexual relations—though in some people's view it's sexist—and it did shock some smug sensibilities and some innocent ones—including mine once. Yes I do read things like that. Do I shock you?"

"You surprise me, sometimes. I never thought I'd hear you say 'cunt' and 'cock'. You've never talked or acted like this before."

"I've come to recognize that I have an earthy side. I thought you'd be happy that I've made the discovery."

"I never thought you'd get that earthy!"

"Oh, it's partly an act, Manfred, but only partly. I have discovered things about myself I hadn't known before. Life is full of surprises, and I've had quite a few since I met you."

"But is sex all you want? You always say you want to be liked for yourself. Do you like me for myself?"

"Yes, Manfred, I do like you for yourself, you big two-bit crook!

The convoy which had been progressing across the city now came to a halt at the gateway to the Andreotti estate. A guard, pistol drawn, stepped from the gate house to investigate.

"That you, Boss?" he asked.

Manfred lowered the window, and called, "Yeah. Who'd you think it was? Santa Claus?"

"Uh—just making sure, Boss." Turning to his fellow guard in the gate house, he said, "Okay, Mike. Open up. It's the boss."

"Sorry, Tony. I was forgetting you're new. Keep up the good work. Have a good evening."

"Thanks, Boss. Evening, Miss. Nice to see you."

"Thank you, Tony," said Imogen. "And the same to you." Then to Manfred she said, "That was very considerate of you, Manfred—apologizing to Tony."

"Hey! You're having a good influence on me."

Again, however, Imogen had a moment of recognition that she was entering a very frightening world where there had to be people on guard to protect other people from still other people.

They stopped before of the great white mansion and Manfred handed her from the limousine.

"I think on such occasions as this," he said, "the man is supposed to carry the woman up the stairs and over the threshold."

"The groom carries his new bride over the threshold, Manfred, but I suppose we can stretch the point for living together," said Imogen, smiling at him despite her apprehensiveness.

"Sure. Who wants to be sticky over rules?"

"Not you, certainly," she replied mischievously. "and, I guess, nor do I any more."

"Huh? Yeah, okay. Come on then," he said, lifting her into his arms.

"Oh! You're so big and strong!" she teased. "How romantic!"

"You're no burden—or, if you are one, the nicest burden I've ever carried."

"Well, if I'm so much trouble," she teased, "you don't have to carry me, Manfred."

"Hey! I want to."

On entering the grand foyer, they were greeted by Ana-Maria who came running to embrace Imogen as soon as Manfred had let her down from his arms.

"Imogen!" she exclaimed. "I came running when I saw the limo drive up! How wonderful that you're going to live here! I've been so looking forward to your company!"

"Thank you, Ana-Maria," Imogen replied. "I'm happy that I'll have you for company, too."

"I just know we'll be friends! We'll have so much to talk about!"

"Yeah," said Manfred. "You two should have great times together yacking away."

"Manfred," said Ana-Maria reproachfully, "that's sexist."

"Hey, Sis! You should know me by now."

"That's the trouble, Manfred; I do know you."

"Hey! Ask Imogen if I'm sexist.

"I'm working on him, Ana-Maria," said Imogen. "He's progressing."

Just then Luigi came rushing in calling, "Immy-jean! Immy-jean! Immy-jean!"

"Luigi!" cried Imogen, kneeling down to him, folding him into her arms and kissing him. "How nice to see you! How's my favorite little man?"

"Oh Immy-jean! You look so boo'ful!"

"My greatest admirer!" she said. Then suddenly remembering Rosina's hostility, she let him go and rose to her feet. "Oh dear! I suppose I mustn't do that. Your mommy doesn't like it."

"Why, Immy-jean?" cried the little boy. "I like you, Immy-jean."

"I like you too, Luigi, but I think probably your mommy's jealous."

"What's jeal's?"

Before Imogen could think of an answer the boy would understand, Manfred interrupted. "Aw, hell! Forget about Rosina. Her bark's worse than her bite."

Imogen turned to him, her brow furrowed. "I wish I could believe that, Manfred."

"I do too," said Ana-Maria, "but it's little enough affection the poor kid gets. Give him all you can, Imogen."

"I don't know," responded Imogen. "I don't want to create trouble—"

"Aw hell!" said Manfred. "You're not creating any trouble."

"There seemed to be plenty last time I was here."

"Yeah, well, I'll make sure there isn't any this time."

Just then Giorgio, Rosina's husband, entered the great hallway. Imogen instinctively drew into herself and stepped closer to Manfred.

"Hey-hey! So the lady's here!" called Giorgio. "And looking really gorgeous, if I may say so."

"You may not say so, Giorgio," said Manfred almost menacingly. "Remember, Imogen's my woman, and you got a wife."

"Hey! A cat can look at a queen. So why should it mean I can't appreciate a beautiful woman when I see her?"

"When she's my woman you can't."

"Hey, *Manfredo*! What's the problem? No need to get touchy."

"I'm not touchy," he said, putting his arm around Imogen's waist and drawing her to him, "but this woman is very special to me, and I don't like you casting your lecherous eyes on her."

"Oh! please, Manfred!" interjected Imogen. "Please! let's not have a lot of quarreling. It seems I'm always the cause of trouble when I come here. I almost wish now I hadn't come."

"It's not your fault, Imogen," said Ana-Maria, coming to her side. "It's this bloody ape and his wife who cause the trouble."

At that moment Rosina entered.

"Well, so you've brought the little working class slut into our home to give an egalitarian tone to the family!"

"Well, well! Darling Rosina! How lovely to see you! But who are you calling a slut, Rosina?" demanded Manfred coming to Imogen's defence. "I met Imogen at the opera, remember. Last time you went to anything cultural, you fell asleep, and we had to wake you up to stop you snoring."

"You know, Rosina," protested Ana-Maria, "there are times when I hate to have to admit that you're my sister."

"Well! I'm not all that happy about having you as a sibling either!" snarled Rosina.

"Manfred! Please take me back home," pleaded Imogen. "I don't fit in here."

"It's not you that don't fit in," growled Manfred. "It's these creeps— Rosina and her lecherous wimp of a husband!"

"It is their home, Manfred, and if they don't want me—"

"Who doesn't want you, *Imogena?*" demanded Manred's mother who at that moment entered the foyer. "Rosina? Are you making trouble? *Imogena's* a very nice, polite, well mannered, well spoken lady who speaks Italian. She makes *Manfredo* happier than I've ever known him to be, so she is welcome here. Papa wants her here. I want her here. Ana-Maria wants her here. Most of all *Manfredo* wants her here. You will not speak against her, Rosina."

And to Imogen's surprise, *Signora Andreotti* came over to her, embraced her and gave her a kiss of welcome. "*Benvenuto a nostra casa Andreotti, Imogena,*" she said.

"*Grazie, Signora,*" replied Imogen. "I just don't want to be the cause of tension, that's all."

"There will be no tension, Imogena. You're Manfredo's lady. You belong here with him and with us."

"*Sono felice fare Manfredo felice,*" exclaimed Imogen, her amazement unbounded. "*Grazie, Signora, per me fare benvenuta.*"

"*Tu sei molta benvenuta.*"

Imogen couldn't help noticing the Signora's use of the informal and familial "*tu.*"

"There, Rosina!" exulted Manfred. "Mama makes her welcome. You got no cause for complaint."

The elder sister scowled and said nothing.

"You come this way, *Imogena,*" said *Senora Andreotti.* "*Manfredo*, give your arm to your lady. Papa's been waiting impatiently all evening for you. Ana-Maria, tell Giovanni to bring in the champagne."

Leading her to the family room, Manfred said, "Right this way, *Signorina Imogena.* Welcome—*benvenuta a la casa Andreotti.*"

"*Grazie, Signor,*" she replied managing a smile despite the tension and apprehension she still felt.

Ana-Maria drew along side of her.

"I'm so glad you've come, Imogen. So very glad."

"Thank you, Ana-Maria," said Imogen turning to her and smiling. "I'm glad you're here."

* * * * *

Later that night when she came naked to him in bed, he looked at her and said, "No mask tonight?"

"No, Manfred. And never again. I've come into your life and your home and become part of your world; so there should be nothing between us. I've lost my inhibitions that the mask helped me put aside. The mask is inappropriate now. But no high heels, either. There's no need either for fetishes and gimmicks. No more kinky sex."

She lay down beside him and he enfolded her into his arms.

"It's wonderful to have you here, Imogen."

She eagerly pressed herself against him.

CHAPTER EIGHTEEN

The adjustment to living in Manfred's home had not been easy. Since her arrival, both because the atmosphere at the library had become quite unpleasant and because Manfred wished it, Imogen had relinquished her job there. She, did not however, like being idle.

And so one morning soon after her arrival as Manfred was leaving, she said, "I wish I could come with you."

"Come with me?" he said in some dismay. "What for?"

"Well, for something to do—"

"Something to do? You've got the piano and Ana-Maria's company."

"I know, and I appreciate both, but I want to be part of your life, Manfred."

"Part of my life? In the Syndicate, what the men do and what their women do are totally separate."

"I don't want you to tell me Syndicate secrets, Manfred, or how you run your business, but I've given up a lot to come to live with you, and I don't want just to sit around waiting while you're out and about on your rounds. And some times you're back very late. I don't know, Manfred, I feel rather left out—neg lected. Even though I enjoy being with Ana-Maria and playing that splendid *Boesendorfer* piano, I often feel lonely. I came here to be with you."

He held her by the shoulders and stared at her.

"I take you out to nice places as often as I can. Don't you like that?" he said after some moments.

"Of course I do, Manfred, but life's more than just being entertained all the time."

"Geez! You're sure not like other women!"

"You say that's one of the reasons you like me."

"Yeah, yeah, it is, and I guess I understand—sort of—but the godfather wouldn't like it if I took you along. It's just not done."

"I guess I'm asking too much, Manfred," she sighed. "I'm sorry. I don't want to get you into trouble."

Again he stared at her in silence.

"Geez!" he said at last. "You know I'd do anything for you, but—"

"I shouldn't have brought it up, Manfred. Please forgive me."

She turned her face away to hide her tears.

"Aw geez, Imogen!" he said clasping her in his arms. "Geez! I donno. If—"

"Forget I even mentioned it, Manfred. I'll be all right. I'll manage. As you say, I've got Ana-Maria and the piano."

"Yeah—yeah. Anyway, I gotta go."

"I know. Take care."

He held her close, kissed her warmly, then broke away.

"Geez!" he muttered as he left the house. "Geez!"

As she turned away sadly to go to the salon to find solace in playing the piano, *Signora Andreotti* saw her and called her aside into her private sitting room.

"Sit down, *Imogena*," she said, "and let us have a talk."

"Oh—" said Imogen, a bit apprehensively, wondering, as she seated herself on the sofa beside Manfred's mother in her comfortably furnished sitting room, whether she had done something to give offence. "Certainly, Signora Andreotti."

"Please, *Imogena*. Call me Mama. And *Signor Andreotti* wants you to call him Papa. You're Manfred's lady, and Papa and I think of you as a daughter. Ana-Maria even talks about you as her sister."

"Oh—I—I'm flattered—honored. Th—thank you—Mama Andreotti."

"That's better," said the Signora reaching across and patting Imogen's hand. "But it's not been easy for you to come here, *Imogena*."

"I have to confess," she said, looking down at her lap, "that it has seemed a strange thing for me to do, and it has been a difficult adjustment, but you've all been very kind to me."

"We've tried to make you welcome, Imogena, but I know this is not your world."

"Well, no—no, it's not. I—I sort of wish I could be a litle more a part of Manfred's—life—than I am."

"I know what you must be feeling," said the older woman, again taking Imogen's hand. Imogen looked up at her appreciatively. "Syndicate women have no real involvement in their men's lives. I know what it is like for you, for I went through the same feelings long ago. This was not my world either. You know I am the daughter of an Italian count, brought up to belong to the world of the nobility?"

"Yes. Manfred told me the night of your anniversary."

"Perhaps he also told you how the marriage was arranged?"

"Yes, something. I was really horrified that you could be forced to marry like that."

"Well, it was the tradition of the Italian nobility to arrange their children's marriages, but I was in love with Papa Andreotti and already carrying his child—Rosina—and so I was not unhappy. I was very happy to be having Papa Andreotti's child, for it was the child of our love, but still, I wondered what kind of a world I was entering and bringing a child into."

"I—I'm not pregnant, but I had similar feelings too. I wondered what kind of world I was entering when I first became Manfred's girl friend."

"I've never known just how that came about, Imogena. He said he met you at the opera, but it seemed a while before you started to go with him. He didn't threaten you?"

"N—no—he—he didn't."

"There's something you're not telling me, Imogena. Even though he is so very fond of you, somehow I think he must have put some pressure on you to make you agree to be his woman. Don't be afraid to tell me. I will be discreet."

"I told Ana-Maria, but she said I should never tell anyone how it happened—especially not Signor Andreotti—Papa Andreotti."

"Oh? Because she thought Papa would not approve?"

"Well—"

"Manfredo, I know, has a soft spot in his heart. Personally, I'm glad of it."

"So am I, Mama Andreotti. I know he thinks very highly of you, and I think in some ways he rather takes after you."

"*Grazie,* Cara. I have tried to have some influence on him. But please tell me how it all happened. I started meeting secretly with Papa Andreotti—who could be very charming—partly to flout my family, and

I fell in love with him. And Papa, though not always loyal, has always been good to me. Manfred, too, can be very charming, but you are a strong, sensible girl, and I don't think it was just his charm that won you. Also, from what I hear, your uncle and aunt are very kind people. So I don't think you were flouting your family. I don't think you and he came together in the same way Papa and I came together."

"No—no, it didn't happen like that. My uncle and aunt are indeed very kind, and I care very much for them. Please don't take it unkindly, but they are very upset by my relationship with Manfred."

"I understand, cara. My family were not happy either with mine with Papa—but my pregnancy and their need for Papa's money—and the hold he had over them—were persuasive. But, since it was not like that with you, how did it come about?"

"Well, initially I wanted to prevent some old and dear friends from having to pay protection money. Manfred didn't exactly threaten me, but he said I could help my friends if I became his girl friend."

"I see. No, Papa would not like him letting people off like that, but I will never tell him what you've just told me, Imogena. But has Manfredo kept his word? I think he would do anything for you, and in his own way, he is a man of honor."

"Yes, Mama, he has kept his word. I respect him for that."

"That is good. I'm sorry, though, that Manfredo put that kind of pressure on you, but I know he did it because you are someone very special. He loves you very much, you know."

"Y—yes—I—I believe he does."

"But you do not love him—perhaps you cannot love him?"

"I—I—I've grown to like Manfred much more than I ever thought I could." Suddenly Imogen burst into tears. "Oh! Oh dear!"

"There, there, cara," said Signora Andreotti taking Imogen into her arms. "I'm sorry. I should not have pressed you."

"It's not that, Mama Andreotti. In fact, I'm glad you know. It's just that at times I feel so terribly confused. I do like Manfred, but—but—"

"No need to explain, cara. I understand."

"Thank you, Mama," said Imogen, drying her eyes. "You've been very kind—kinder than I ever imagined."

"As I said, Imogena, you are like a daughter to me, so please always feel you can come and talk to me."

"*Grazie,* Mama Andreotti."

—How strange, thought Imogen, when she left Manfred's mother and made her way to the large salon where the piano stood. How strange to find, with Rosina's exception, such a warm welcome into a crime family. How strange that Ana-Maria and her mother care so much for me. Even more strange is Manfred's kindness and genuine affection for me. Even now, he seemed to understand my feelings though he couldn't yield to them. What are my feelings for him?

Later that afternoon, again seated at the piano in the salon, Imogen turned to the piece she had been working hard to master, Beethoven's "Appassionata" Sonata. During the furious finale, absorbed as she was in her playing, she did not notice Ana-Maria and Luigi enter the salon and seat themselves on a sofa to listen, nor, a little while afterward, did she notice Manfred's entry. When she had hurtled through cascading arpeggios of the Presto conclusion and hammered out the final chords, Manfred cried, "Bravo!"

"Oh!" she said, looking up in surprise. "Manfred! I didn't see you come in. You're home early. Oh—and Ana-Maria and Luigi! I didn't realize I had such an audience."

"Oh Immy-jean!" cried Luigi, rushing over to her, "Dat was won-iful! You play p'ano won-iful!"

"Why, thank you Luigi!" said Imogen, enfolding him in a hug. "I can always count on you for appreciation!"

"And me, too, don't forget," said Manfred.

"And also me," said Ana-Maria. "You're great, Imogen!"

"No, Ana-Maria, not great. Good, yes, but not great."

"You're great in my book!" said Manfred. "You know I always love to hear you play."

"I know, Manfred, and thank you. I appreciate that you do. But you're liking my playing doesn't make it great."

"Well, I wish I could play like that," said Ana-Maria. "You really get absorbed in your music, don't you?"

"I guess I do, Ana-Maria. It's a very important part of my life. It has always been one of my greatest joys—perhaps the greatest."

"Hey!" said Manfred. "I feel jealous."

"Well, some times I feel jealous of your work, Manfred—because—because you can't share it with me. I guess my music is to me what your work is to you—but I can share my music with you."

"Yeah? Hm" he mused. "Yeah. But, hey! This is kind of nice—sort of a family gathering—part of the family, anyway."

"Yes, it is nice, isn't it?" said Ana-Maria. "We, the four of us, are a family."

"Yeah," said Manfred, "we are. Isn't that right, Imogen?"

Imogen hesitated before replying. "I—I'm beginning to feel a little more that we are, Manfred. Certainly you've all been very kind and made me feel welcome."

"Oh Imogen!" exclaimed Ana-Maria. "I for one am glad you're one of us."

"Thank you, Ana-Maria. You've really helped make me feel at home."

"Yeah?" said Manfred. "And what about me?"

"Oh, you too, of course, you big oaf, but your work keeps you away so much."

"Hey! I'll try to be more considerate. But things get involved and complicated some times."

"It's the syndicate woman's lot," said Ana-Maria ruefully, "to stay home, Imogen, and to be kept in ignorance—pampered and babied, but never involved."

"That's very old fashioned and sexist," said Imogen, "but I guess you can't break with tradition."

Manfred stared off into space, seemingly lost in thought.

"Hm," he said after some moments. "The Syndicate doesn't run my personal life. Let me think about it."

"Thank you Manfred," she whispered. "That's all I can ask."

CHAPTER NINETEEN

A few days day after they had talked with Ana-Maria in the salon, Manfred asked Imogen before he left the house if she'd like to go out dancing that evening.

"See," he said, "I'm trying to be more considerate.

"You sweetheart, Manfred. I'd love to." She paused a moment, reflecting; then said, "Perhaps—is there any place different, unusual—some place out of the ordinary—we might go to?"

He paused for a moment, thinking, then asked, "Have you ever been to the the Gemini Club?"

"The Gemini Club?" she said. "No. What's the attraction?"

"It's sort of a place for the locals in a lower class neighborhood, you might say, but a lot of rich folks like to go slumming there. It's a place where almost anything goes. Their slogan is 'Come as you are, or as the person you want to be.' A lot of people go in costume, some of them pretty skimpy. You could go there in a mask, if you wanted to. Many do. But you can go any way you like. You can go just as yourself, as far as that goes. You don't have to dress up."

"It sounds very interesting. Do you go down there yourself?"

"Not as often as I used to. I wouldn't mind going again."

"Hm," mused Imogen, seemingly engrossed. "Any way you like, you say?"

"Yeah. So would you like to go?"

She made no reply, and stood for some minutes, lost in thought. Then she said, "Yes—I think I would very much like to go. While you're away, I'll think about how I want to go."

"Okay. But I guess I had better be on my way," he said and took her in his arms to kiss her good-bye. "And by the way, I am thinking about what you asked the other day about taking you more into my confidence."

"Why, thank you, Manfred!" she exclaimed and reached up to kiss him again. "You really are a sweetheart! Now, take care and be sure you come back safely!"

"Hey! Don't worry! But it's nice to know you care."

He leaned down and kissed her again and then left.

—Yes, I do care, Manfred. You've been good to me, which I never expected you would be, and you've brought me out of myself and brought glamor and excitement into my life—qualities I never thought I wanted—or perhaps I was just denying that I wanted them. Anyway, now that you've given them to me, I enjoy them. I'm a different person because of you.

She stood bemused for a while.

—Do I dare do what I'm thinking? she asked herself after a few moments. Yes! Yes, I do! Oh, what has come over me? What a naughty girl I've become! Yes, you really have brought me out of myself!

That evening, when Manfred arrived home, Imogen awaited him stark naked in their apartment and when he entered, threw herself into his arms.

"Hey!" he cried. "What the hell is going on? Why are you naked?"

"What do you think is going on? Make love to me you big galoot! Why else do you think I'm naked?"

"You never cease to amaze me. You're certainly not the girl I first went out with."

"That's what makes me so fascinating."

"Hey!" he said, looking down at her. "What happened to your pussy?"

"I had all my body hair removed. I thought you might like it. But stop stalling and make love to me."

Imogen's participation in the love-making was eager, hot, wild, even fierce.

"Wow!" exclaimed Manfred when it was over. "Wow!"

"Yes, wow. Now you get dressed and we'll go down to dinner."

Over dinner, whenever Manfred looked her way, she smirked and looked away.

"What's eating you?" he asked finally.

"Oh, nothing," she said. "You'll see."

"Nothing? I'll see? What kind of an answer is that?"

"The only one you're going to get just now," she replied.

"You've got something very strange up your sleeve," he said.

"Maybe I have," she said.

"You're being very mysterious."

"Also part of my fascination,"

After supper, she said, "Wait for me in the foyer. I want to go upstairs for a minute or two. I've a surprise for you." She rushed up the stairs and entered the bedroom and stood looking at her self in the mirror..

—What a change has come over you, Imogen Edwards! A few months ago you would never have thought you'd be capable of doing what you're going to do now, but now...! Well, here goes!

She undressed and bent down and strapped on a pair of gold high-heeled sandals, took a pair of tear-drop earrings from a jewel box on the dresser and attached them to her ears which she'd had pierced when Manfred gave them to her.

—There. I'm ready. She hesitated a moment and picked up the gold mask Manfred had had made for her, thought for a moment or two then said to herself, No. No mask. I'll go as the brazen Imogen Edwards I've become.

With her long dark hair falling to her shoulders, she walked to the door and stepped out naked onto the gallery and slowly descended the stairs to the foyer.

Manfred looked up at her flabbergasted.

"Imogen! Holy shit! What the hell? You're going naked to the Gemini Club!"

"I told you I had a surprise for you. This is it. You said their motto is come as you are or as the person you want to be."

"Geez! Geez! I never thought you'd have the nerve to do something like this! You amaze me. You're sure not the uptight woman I took for coffee that night."

"No, I'm not, and it's the risk you took when you made me your girl friend, Manfred. Remember that first night we went out of coffee? You thought I was over-dressed—too buttoned up—and I asked if you'd like me to come nude? You said you thought that would be okay? Well, tonight I'm obliging you. I'm feeling rather wild tonight, Darling, and throwing discretion to the winds. You could say it's my coming out party." She threw her arms about him and kissed him. "I never expected to become the mistress of the crime boss of East Clintwood, but since I have, you've brought out in me a whole new personality."

"Yeah, but I wish you'd stop calling yourself my mistress!"

"I am your mistress, Manfred, and I like the notoriety of the word. I like the naughty sound of it, and I like being your mistress. Besides, I'm known as your mistress all over town So since I'm the scandal of the community, I might as well act scandalously. But, let's be on our way, I can hardly wait to see the Gemini Club."

She put her arm in his and leaned against his shoulder.

"Okay," he said. "Here goes nothing, I guess."

"Never were truer words spoken," she said with a whimsical laugh.

When Al and Joe who stood waiting for them at the limousine saw her, their mouths dropped open and their eyes fairly popped out of their heads.

"Holy . . . !" gasped Al.

"Geez, Miss!" exclaimed Joe

"Okay you guys!" said Manfred sternly. "Stuff your eyeballs back in their sockets before they fall to the ground."

"Oh don't be such and old meany, Manfred," said Imogen. "What would we do without Al and Joe?" Then turning to the two henchmen and kissed each of them on the cheek "You're really sweet guys, Al and Joe."

"Geez, Miss!" spluttered Joe in wide-eyed surprise.

"That's to make amends for the first time we met when I kicked you both."

"Aw heck, Miss! "said Al. "We kinda roughed you up a bit. You was just defendin' yerself. But you're the nicest girl friend the Boss has ever had. None of the others treated us like you. You're aces in my books!"

"That goes for me too, Miss," said Joe. "You're the best."

"Al and Joe, you say the nicest things."

"Hey," said Manfred, "you'll spoil the boys."

"Oh Manfred!" protested Imogen. "Joe and Al have been my good friends, and deserve to be shown some appreciation and gratitude."

"Yeah, yeah, okay, yeah. But maybe one of these nice guys would open the door for us, and another'd be so good as to drive us to the Gemini Club"

About half an hour later, the limousine drew up before the Gemini Club in East Clintwood's factory district where shabby houses nestled among warehouses, mills and shops. Leaning against Manfred's shoulder, Imogen said, a bit taken aback, "I've never been down here before."

"Like I said," responded Manfred, "the Gemini club isn't exactly in the best part of town. You sure you want to go in?"

"I didn't come all this way not to, Manfred."

"Okay, if you really want to."

"I do want to."

Al opened the door, and, as the few people on the sidewalk gawked, Imogen walked nude on Manfred's arm to the entrance.

"Oh my gosh, Mr. Andreotti!" exclaimed the astonished doorman, holding the door for them. "Your girl friend's naked!"

"Aren't you the observant one! This is Miss Edwards, Johnny. And stop gawking."

"Uh—yeah. Uh. Golly! Uh—nice to meet you, Miss Edwards."

"It's nice to meet you too, Johnny," she said. "And please, just call me Imogen."

"Oh—uh—yeah—Nice to meet you—Imogen. Gee! Some women have come here in pretty skimpy costumes or ones you can see through, but noone's ever come naked before!"

"There's a first time for everything, Johnny. Maybe I'll start a trend."

As they entered the rotunda of the club, the manager and the receptionist stared dumbfounded.

"Good Lord!" exclaimed the receptionist. "That woman's naked!"

"G—gosh!" exclaimed the manager.

"Geez!" said Manfred sarcastically. "How observant everybody is tonight! This is my girl friend, Imogen Edwards. Imogen, these people with their mouths hanging open are Jake and Judy."

"Hello Jake and Judy it's nice to meet you.

"I—it's nice to meet you, M—Miss Edwards," stammered the manager.

"Thank you Jake. And please, as I said to Johnny, call me Imogen."

"Oh—uh—yes—Imogen."

"And Judy, I'm nude. An unclad person in public is nude."

"There she goes," said Manfred, "Always insisting on the correct word."

"Oh, tut-tut, Manfred," she said, snuggling up to him, placing her arm in his. "But shall we go in?"

"As you said," he replied "that's why we came."

Imogen waved to Jake and Judy who still stared wide-eyed and open-mouthed and walked with Manfred to the entrance of the main room of the club where she parted the curtain that separated the foyer from the club proper, and they walked down the short flight of three steps into a space lit only by candles and surrounded by booths where the patrons sat talking, smoking and drinking. On their entry, glasses clattered to the floor or table tops, spilling their contents, and conversation suddenly ceased; then a voice spoke out: "Hey! That woman's naked!"

"Strange how everyone keeps noticing that," said Imogen turning to Manfred with a whimsical smile.

Then after a few moments, hoots and whistles broke out, another voice exclaimed, "Wow! Is she ever stacked! Geez!"

"Yeah," responded another. "Built like that, she can pull anything off!"

"Real horrorshow groodies!" said another male voice. "She's one horrorshow devotchka,"

"I don't know what that means," said another, "but she's one hell of a dame with a pair of great hooters!"

"Didn't you see the movie *A Clockwork Orange?*" said the previous speaker, "I said what you just did in Nadsat."

Then a woman's voice exclaimed, "What gall! How does the brazen hussy dare come like that?"

"She's with Manfred Andreotti," said her male companion. "She can get away with anything."

"Oh! So that's the notorious Imogen Edwards!"

"With a body like that—" someone began.

"Keep the lewd comments to yourself!" shouted Manfred. "If my girl wants to come here nude, it's her privilege and none of your business, and I ain't complaining. So shut up!"

"Why, thank you, Manfred. *Tu es tres gallant,*" said Imogen, dropping a curtsy. "But you see, I am quite notorious, so I might as well behave notoriously." Then, blowing kisses to the patrons, she called out, "*Bon soir, mesdames, messieurs—mes amis!*"

After Manfred's rebuke, the patron's of the club fell silent for a few moments, but a whispered undercurrent of commentary soon began to buzz around the club as Manfred beckoned with his hand and called out, "Hey Terri! over here."

An attractive young waitress, nude to the waist and in a very short skirt, approached.

"Oh my gosh!" she exclaimed, flabbergasted. "I—I know we say 'Anything goes' here, but I didn't think anyone would go this far! Gosh!"

"Well, Terri, you come pretty close!" said the completely nude Imogen. "But hi. I'm Imogen. And you look very nice."

"Uh—hi, I—Imogen—and M—Mr. Andreotti—

"Okay, get ahold of yourself, Terri and show us to my reserved booth down in the corner," said Manfred. When they were seated, he said, "We're hidden away a bit here."

"Aw! Poor darling! Do I embarrass you?"

"No, I always sit here—and you don't want to be on display all the time."

"I'm always on display when I'm with the Crime Boss of East Clintwood, so I might as well be really on display—and Manfred, this is a circular table. Why don't you move around beside me—if you're not too embarrassed?"

"Oh—yeah—No, I ain't—I'm not too embarrassed."

"Wh—what can I get you?" asked Terri.

"I'll have a Scotch on the rocks," said Imogen.

"Scotch on the rocks!" exclaimed Manfred. "You hardly more than sipped half a glass of champagne when we first went out!"

"See what a bad effect you have on me, Manfred?" said Imogen, giving him an impish smile. "Because of you I'm becoming a lush."

"She blames me for everything," said Manfred.

"Whom else should I blame, Manfred," Imogen teased. "I'd never have done anything like this if I'd never met you."

"Hey! I've introduced you to some different things," he said, "but I'm not sure I have to take the blame for all the outlandish things you do."

"Oh heavens, Manfred! Surely you should know by now when I'm teasing you."

"You do a lot of that. I think you enjoy making fun of me."

"It's a mistress's privilege. I do it to keep a naughty boy of whom I'm very fond from taking himself too seriously and becoming a stuffed shirt. So, you'll just have to learn to live with it."

"I could do without all the surprises, though."

"Surprises are what make life interesting, Manfred. And isn't this a nice one? But I think Terri would like to know what you want to drink, Manfred."

"Huh? Oh—yeah. Make mine the same, Terri."

"Two Scotch on the rocks coming right up," said Terri.

She left them and in a very few minutes returned with their drinks.

"You have nice breasts, Terri," said Imogen as the young waitress placed the glasses on the table before them.

"Oh—uh—gee, thanks—but not like yours! Yours are great—spectacular!"

"So everyone tells me."

"Uh—yeah—Will—will there be anything else?"

"Not just now, Terri," said Manfred.

"Thank you, Terri," said Imogen as the waitress departed. Then taking a sip of her drink, she exclaimed, "Oh! So that's the spirit that won the Empire! Rather rough, but I like it!"

"I never thought of Scotch as your kind of drink. But, yeah," Manfred said as he took a swallow, "it's okay."

"You mean you've never had Scotch?"

"I usually drink Bourbon. I don't know, maybe I like this better," he said taking another swig.

"There now, Manfred! I've introduced you to something new. Oh! This is so much fun! Thank you for bringing me here! Aren't you having fun, too, you old prude?"

"Yeah, yeah, I am. But you still surprise me."

"Now you wouldn't want me to be totally predictable, would you? That would be boring. Besides," she teased, "adapting to a role I never expected to have to play requires imagination. So, here's to my imaginative and exciting life with you, Manfred," she said, touching her glass to his.

"Yeah," he responded. "We have had a lot of great times together."

"And, as you said on our first date, let's hope there'll be many more of them. My whole time with you has been more exciting and enjoyable that I ever thought my life could be."

"Well, you're making my life pretty damned exciting tonight!"

"Oh! Wondrous woman who can do that for the Crime Boss of East Clintwood! But you know, Manfred, I don't think I can ever again be the woman I was. The Imogen who has come here tonight nude is the new Imogen"

At that moment the band in front of the stage began to play a rather ragged version of Offenbach's "Can-can."

"Oh?" said Imogen. "What's happening now? Oh my!"

The stage curtains parted as she spoke, and, to the hoots, shouts, and whistles of the audience—with many a glance in Imogen's direction—ten women clad only in top hats, high-heeled dancing shoes and G-strings high-kicked their way onto the stage. "I suppose," said Imogen after they had sat watching the dancers for a while, "that is the sort of thing that gives the Gemini Club the reputation of being sleazy—that and my coming here nude. But as far as I can see, the only difference between those women and me is that they are on stage and I'm not and, perhaps, that I'm nude because I want to be, not from necessity—not out of a need for money. Otherwise, there's no difference."

"There you go getting philosophical again," said Manfred.

"Oh! Poor Manfred!" she said, and pulled a long face in mock solemnity. "I'm sorry, you old stick-in-the-mud."

"And I wish you'd stop teasing all the time."

"Oh my poor darling!" she said, smiling and laying her hand on his. "You're terribly thin-skinned for a crime boss, and you make life awfully hard for me—but you're a sweetheart, all the same. And who knows, maybe those women too are nude because they like too be."

When the can-can dancers high-kicked their way off the stage, the band began to play regular dance music and couples got up to dance.

"Oh! Let's dance, Manfred," said Imogen, sliding to the edge of the banquette and standing up and holding out her hand to him. "That's what we came for, and it's also something you taught me to enjoy. It will be your first dance with a naked woman—at least I hope it is."

"Don't worry, it is."

Almost dragging Manfred after her, she stepped out into plain view of the customers. "*Signor? Le piacerebe a ballare?*"

"Hey!" came a voice from the crowd. "She's getting up to dance! The naked dame's going to dance!"

"She should have been up on the stage with them other broads."

"There, you see!" said Imogen. "No difference."

"There's every bit of difference," said Manfred. "You're Imogen!"

"Why, thank you, kind sir!"

She led Manfred to the middle of the dance floor where, in sheer delight, she first turned a pirouette before, as all eyes turned on them, she placed her arms around his neck, and for the first time, she led him in the dance.

"Now, isn't this fun, Manfred!"

"Yeah, it is—strange, but fun. Like a dream."

"Or an adolescent fantasy?"

"Huh? Yeah, maybe."

Just then a voice at Imogen's left said, "Well, you and I are exact opposites."

Imogen turned to see, accompanied by rather shy-looking young man, a woman clad in the black cat suit with black gloves and a black cowl revealing only her blue eyes and her ruby-glossed lips, her ensemble completed by red high heels and a wide red belt which hung over her hips, dramatically setting off the blackness of her basic costume.

"Why—yes, you're right. We are, aren't we?" said Imogen. "You look quite striking."

"Not nearly as striking as you," said the mysterious stranger. "You're spectacular! Actually, I've rather hoped to come here nude some day myself—but you've beaten me to it."

"I'm sorry, but good for you! I'm glad to know I'm not the only one with naughty ideas. But why—if I may ask—do you wear that all-concealing cowl?"

"Oh, I like being a woman of mystery."

"Stella's a woman of great mystery," said the cowled woman's boy friend.

"Oh!" said Imogen. "Your mysterious friend is called Stella."

"That's what I call her. You see, I'm Philip Sidney. Perhaps, though you don't understand the allusion?"

"Oh I understand all right. I'm an English major. So you're Astrophil and Stella. Wonderful!"

"Yes, that's who we are," said the black clad woman. "And you called your boy friend Manfred—Manfred Andreotti, I suspect. So you must be Imogen Edwards."

"The news is out, I see" said Imogen. "Right on both counts."

"But you," said Manfred, staring Stella straight in the eyes, "I bet I know who you are."

"Oh! Wha—you—you do?" said Stella, taken aback and seeming somewhat distressed.

"What's this, Stella?" exclaimed Philip.

"I don't know *who* you are," said Manfred, "but I know *what* you are—but I won't embarrass you in front of your boy friend."

"I rather think you already have, Manfred. You've embarrassed Stella and unsettled Philip."

"Huh?"

"You've put questions in his mind."

"Not to worry," said Stella. "It's time Philip knew the truth about me. When we're back at our table Philip, I'll tell you what I've always meant to tell when the time was ripe, and I guess now the time is ripe."

"Gee, Stella. Whatever it is, it won't make any difference to me."

"Oh, I hope not, Philip. I really hope not. But it has been nice meeting you Imogen—and you, too, Mr. Andreotti. And don't worry. In some ways, by forcing the issue, you've simply made things easier for me. Come on, Philip."

When they had left, Imogen said, "Manfred, you must learn to be more sensitive. I think you've really disturbed a happy relationship."

"Well, geez! How was I to know?"

"I'm sure you didn't mean any harm—but there are some things better left unsaid."

"You're the one who's always telling me to speak the truth."

"Between ourselves, Manfred, not when it might hurt others."

"Yeah, well, she said it was something she had to tell him anyway. Mebbe I've just made her be honest with her boy friend."

"I just hope whatever it is doesn't cause them to break up their relationship—but, yes, you're right. A relationship can't be based on dishonesty. But—but—and here I'm being nosy—who—or what—is it you think she is?"

"A cat burglar who's been making heists all over the two Clintwoods."

"A cat burglar! Well I'll be—! You mean to say," she teased, "there are thieves in this town besides you and ones whom you don't control?"

"Ah!" he snorted. "Peanuts. Small potatoes."

Just then Imogen heard a voice near at hand exclaim, "Imogen! Is—is that really you?"

Imogen turned to see her friend from university.

"Betty!" Imogen cried.

"You're—you're naked!"

"Nude, Betty," said Imogen. "Have you forgotten your McLuhan. One is naked in the bedroom, nude in public."

"You're here with nothing on, and you're concerned about the right word for it!" said Betty.

"Yeah, that's what I say," said Manfred. "Who cares what it's called?"

"Another country heard from!" said Imogen. "You remember Betty, don't you Manfred? You danced with her at the graduation ball."

"Yeah, I remember. Nice to see you again, Betty. How've you been?"

"Oh! yes, Mr. Andre—Manfred. I—I'm fine—and—and I really enjoyed dancing with you—"

"It was fun dancing with you, Betty."

"I think you and I should be jealous, Geoff," said Imogen, turning to Betty's partner who stood by gawking in open-mouthed, wide-eyed embarrassment.

"Uh—uh—y—yeah. I mean, no. I mean—uh—nice to see you again—Imogen—and Mr. Andreotti."

"Surely you're not embarrassed, Geoff! After all, you and I danced together too," teased Imogen.

"Uh—yeah—uh—yeah. But then you weren't—you were wearing—"

"I was wearing a dress that exposed quite a lot of me—almost all of me above the waist. *Mais oui, ce soir je suis completement en deshabille, comment Mademoiselle Betty a été si perspicace à remarquer.* But I've never known you to be embarrassed or to be at such a loss for words before, Geoff," said Imogen. "I'm the same person nude as clad. But," she asked, turning again to Betty, "what brings the two of you to East Clintwood and the Gemini Club?"

"I might ask what you are doing here nak—nude, if you insist, Imogen. You're the last person—"

"That's what Manfred keeps saying, Betty, but since becoming Manfred's girl friend I've lost the inhibitions I had when you knew me as an undergraduate."

"You sure have!" exclaimed Betty.

"Perhaps, Manfred," said Imogen, "we could ask Betty and Geoff to join us at our table for drinks?"

"Yeah. Sure. Glad to have you join us."

"Well—" began Betty, hesitantly.

"Please, Betty. For old times" sake," said Imogen. "I thought after graduation I'd probably never meet any of my fellow students again, and here I've met you and Geoff."

"Well, okay I guess. Geoff?"

"Uh—yeah—uh—okay. I—I—uh—okay."

"You've such a way with words, Geoff!" teased Imogen. "So articulate."

"Over this way," said Manfred and, with the eyes of nearly everyone in the club on Imogen, they returned to their table. Turning to Geoff he said under his breath, "Stuff your eyeballs back in, Geoff—if you can—before they pop out and roll around on the floor."

"Well," said Imogen as they all sat down, "a nice little secluded corner, as Manfred said. What would you all like to drink? I'd like a Scotch again."

"Imogen!" exclaimed Betty. "Good heavens! Not only are you here nude—but you're drinking hard liquor! You never touched anything alcoholic at school. This is a night for surprises. "

"Manfred has introduced me to some of the finer things in life," replied Imogen, winking at her lover, "but I've never drunk Scotch before tonight. Now that I have, I realize I didn't know what I was missing. And I think I may have converted Manfred."

"What would you like to drink, Betty?" asked Manfred.

"Oh—white wine, I guess—please."

"And you Geoff?"

"Uh—I'll have a Bourbon and branch—thanks—if it's okay."

"Why not?" said Manfred. With a gesture he summoned Terri. Then, as they waited for their drinks to arrive, Imogen said, "You still haven't told me why you're here in East Clintwood, Betty."

"Oh—yes. Geoff," she said, inclining her head toward her partner who blushed and turned his gaze away from Imogen, "is working for his dad and had to come up here on business, so he invited me along. We heard that this place is one where anything goes and thought we'd like to see it—and you've certainly proved that anything does go here, Imogen!"

At that moment Terri returned with their drinks. Manfred paid her and everyone thanked her.

Then Betty continued when Terri departed, "If you've come here nude, Imogen, you must come here often."

"No, it's my first visit," said Imogen. "I wanted to go somewhere different—and do something a bit daring!"

"A *bit* daring!"

"Very daring if you like, Betty. I decided to kick over the traces as far as I could kick them."

"I'd hardly have expected you'd have done something this daring!"

"Neither would I have a month ago, but as I quoted Conrad's Marlow to Manfred, it's always the unexpected that happens." She leaned back into the plush upholstery of the banquette and continued, "And he says I'm always forcing him to think and complains bitterly about it. He's not used to it, and it's a real strain for him. I guess 'Where ignorance is bliss, 'tis folly to be wise.'"

"Alexander Pope," said Betty.

"You see, Manfred," said Imogen, "I'm not the only one who knows her poets."

"Yeah?" said Manfred. "Well, Imogen's always got a quote for every occasion. Actually, I admire her for her brains and her education, but sometimes I wish she could forget it and let up for a while."

"Just too literary for my own good, I guess," laughed Imogen. "But I should think I've let up a bit tonight, don't you think?"

"You sure have!" said Betty.

For a while they sat in silence sipping their drinks, Geoff torn between his desire to look at Imogen and his embarrassment in doing so and fear of alienating Betty.

"So, what have you been doing with yourself since graduation, Betty?" Imogen asked after a while.

"Oh, an awful lot of parties and receptions. Seeing Geoff a lot. What about you?"

"Well, seeing Manfred a lot," she said, turning to smile at her lover. "I worked at the library for a while before I came to live with Manfred...."

"You're living with Manfred!" exclaimed Betty.

"Oh, yes. It's the going thing now, after all. And the Andreottis have a magnificent Bosendoerfer piano for me to play; so I've been practicing a lot. I played for my friend Susan Van Alstyne's last recital before she left for London."

"I hear she's a really good singer."

"She's a *great* singer—a marvelous singer. She'll be world famous one day."

"And Imogen's a great piano player," interjected Manfred.

"Yes," said Betty. "I've heard you are very good."

"She's terrific," said Manfred.

"My greatest fan!" said Imogen, leaning across the table to place her hand on Manfred's arm. "But I'm not as fine a pianist as Susan is a singer."

Just then, a voice over the PA system announced, "Ladies and gentlemen, Salome," and, almost drowned out by the shouts and whistles of the audience, the band, whose only stringed instrument was a double bass, blared out a raucous approximation of "The Dance of the Seven Veils" from Richard Strauss's opera, and a dusky skinned woman, veiled and in harem costume, hands held above her head to jingle her finger bells, danced sensuously onto the stage.

After watching her routine for a while, Imogen exclaimed, "That's a genuine Egyptian belly dance! Perhaps she really is Egyptian—though Salome was probably Syrian or Idumean."

"I don't know about any of that stuff," said Manfred, "but she's sure good! And who the hell was Salome anyway?"

"Read Mark chapter six—though it was Josephus in *The Jewish Wars* who identified her as Salome. This music they're trying to play is from RIchard Strauss's opera *Salome* based on Oscar Wilde's play which is based—with elaborations—on the story in Mark."

"Well now I know!" exclaimed Manfred sarcastically. "Actually, I'm way out in left field on that one."

"Ah yes! There I go again! Sorry, Manfred. I'll explain later."

"Yeah. I should know better by now than to ask you a question. You always answer it—in Spades."

"I know what you mean," said Betty.

"Yeah," said Manfred.

But before anyone could say anything more, the dancer began one by one to shed her garments.

"Oh my!" exclaimed Imogen. "She's combining belly dance with striptease! What a novel idea—unless, of course, that's what Salome actually did; certainly it's what happens in Strauss's opera."

Finally, down to only her G-string, high-heeled slippers with turned up toes, a few bangles and her veil, the dancer, gently swaying to the music, faced the audience. Then slowly she raised her hands to her veil, paused a moment, teasing the audience's expectations, and then with a quick movement, tore it from her face, stood a brief moment nude and unveiled, and then, to wild applause, ran from the stage.

"Wow!" said Imogen. "That was beautifully seductive! I wonder if, rather like me, she is a woman escaping from the constraints of her culture and upbringing?"

"There she goes thinking out loud and raising questions again," said Manfred. "And again, I don't know why the hell she can't just enjoy something!"

"But I did enjoy her, Manfred."

"But you always have to make some kind of learned comment. But hey! There's the regular dance music again. Want to dance again, Imogen?"

"Why, Signor Andreotti! I'd love to dance with you," she said. "Betty? Geoff? What about you?"

"Uh—yes—I think we will too," said Betty. "Geoff?"

"Uh—yeah—yeah. Okay."

"And then I think we'd better leave you two alone," Betty said looking with a jaundiced eye at Geoff, "but thanks for inviting us to your table, Mr. Andre—Manfred—and for the drinks. It's been really pleasant."

"Hey! our pleasure!" responded Manfred.

"And," said Imogen, "it has been wonderful seeing you both again."

"Uh—yes, and you, too, Imogen—and Manfred," said Betty. "All the best."

"And he best of everything to both of you," said Imogen.

"Thanks, Imogen, and—well—come on, Geoff," Betty said, tugging hard at the arm of her partner to get him follow her to the dance floor and to stop gawking at Imogen.

Then as she and Manfred began to dance, Imogen said, "I never expected to meet Betty here. She's okay—not as snobbish as most of my classmates."

"Yeah? She does seem like a nice girl—not as nice as you though."

"It's a good thing you said that," said Imogen, affecting jealous anger, "or I'd never have forgiven you, you old libertine!" Then she pressed close to him and lay her head on his shoulder.

They danced very close like that a number of times before the evening was over. At last Imogen said, "Well, I've had my fun. Maybe it's time to go."

"Okay," he said. "Maybe we'd better."

As she walked on Manfred's arm to the exit, whistles and catcalls again followed them.

"One thing I'll say for that woman," said someone, "she's got guts coming here naked like that."

"It wasn't her guts I noticed," said another.

As she and Manfred parted the curtains to leave the Club, Imogen again turned and blew a kiss to the crowd and called out, "*Bon soir, mes amis. Arrividerci amici!*" Then as they left the Club she called out, "*Merci bien, Jake et Judy! Au revoir!*"

Once again out on the street Imogen said, "I hope I didn't upset you too much, Manfred. For me, it was fun."

"Yeah, well it was different, but I don't know how I let you get away with some of the stunts you pull."

"It's that old black magic, Manfred," she said, stroking his cheek, "my wicked womanly wiles—and you like them."

"Yeah, yeah. I do." said Manfred as they approached the limousine, "Hey! Al and Joe, stop gawking and open the door for us."

"Uh—yeah, Boss. Sorry," stammered Al.

"Oh Manfred! don't be so hard on poor Al and Joe. They are men, and I, after all, am a beautiful naked woman."

"Geez, Miss!" said Al. "Maybe it ain't for us to say, but we—like me an' Joe an' all the Boys—always did think you was—uh—very pretty, Miss—"

"Why thank you, Al!" said Imogen giving him a sweet smile and, to his great embarrassment, stroking his cheek. "That's one of the nicest compliments I've ever received!"

"Yeah, Miss," said Joe. "You're the best, the best lookin' woman an' the nicest the Boss ever had."

"Geez!" said Manfred. "Compliments flowing thick and fast!"

"Well, I think they're very nice compliments—and sincere, Manfred," said Imogen as she stroked Joe's cheek. "Thank you Joe, and thank you Al. You're good guys, both of you." And then once again she leaned over and kissed them both on the cheek. "For a couple of nice guys," she said.

"Aw geez! Golly!" said Al, blushing in spite of himself. "And you know, there ain't nothin' we wouldn't do for you, Miss, none of us."

"Why, thank you, Al and Joe. But," said Imogen, turning to Manfred, "though it might be pleasant, Manfred, to go for a moonlight stroll, I suppose we should really go home."

"Yeah, okay. And I'm glad you think of our place as home."

"Home is with you now, Manfred," she said, and stopped in her tracks a moment and stood naked at the open door of the limo, bemused.

"Hey!" said Manfred. "What is it?"

"Wha—? Oh—nothing, nothing. I—I was just thinking how strange it all is—all that's happened since that night at the opera."

"Yeah? Well tonight has sure been strange, but let's be on our way."

As Manfred handed her into the limousine, Al, probably thinking Imogen couldn't hear, said, "Miss Imogen sure is the best, Joe"

"Yeah," said Joe. "And she's got the Boss wrapped around her little finger. He'll do anything she wants him to do."

"It ain't just the Boss, Joe," responded Al. "She's got us all eating outa her hand—and like the Boss, we all like it, too, an' like you said, I'd do anything for her. I'd kill for her if she asked me."

"Yeah, Al. Me too."

As she settled herself down beside Manfred, Al's and Joe's words gave her a strange sense of foreboding, and she shuddered.

"What's the matter, Imogen?" asked Manfred.

"Wh—Oh—nothing. Felt a bit of chill. I am naked, after all."

"Well, I'll soon warm you up," he said, putting his arms around her naked shoulders and drawing her close to him.

"I can certainly take this kind of warming," she said, but, despite her teasing manner, she felt strangely apprehensive and vaguely troubled.

CHAPTER TWENTY

Not long after the escapade at the Gemini Club, Manfred agreed to take Imogen along with him occasionally on his rounds.

"If I take you every day it'll look suspicious," he told her, "but maybe once a week we can say I'm taking you to see your uncle and aunt."

As they were driving home after on one such episode, Manfred said, "Maybe tonight we might go out for dinner and dancing—some place more formal."

"Oh!" exclaimed Imogen with a kind of mock seriousness. "You want me to wear clothes!"

"Well—not that I don't like to see you naked—though I prefer it when we're by ourselves—but I like to see you nicely dressed."

"And I like to see you in a tuxedo, Manfred. You look so very handsome."

"I also love to take you out to dinner and dancing. We haven't done that for a while."

"No we haven't, Manfred," she said. "I'd love to."

A bit later, as they dressed in Manfred's suite, Imogen asked, "On our way, could we pay a visit to the Martinellis? I feel guilty that I've not been back since—since that fateful night."

"Huh?" he exclaimed. "Oh—yeah. Sure. No problem."

So not long afterwards, they arrived in front of the Martinellis' confectionery in Little Italy. Imogen, dressed in an emerald green evening gown, long white gloves and gold shoes, an ermine stole about her bare shoulders, and carrying a gold handbag, stepped out of the limousine and took Manfred's arm to enter the store.

Mr. Martinelli looked up as they entered.

"Gena!" he cried. "Is thatta really you? My, you looka beautiful—but we thought you forget us."

"I'm sorry, Papa Martinelli," she responded, running to embrace him. "So much has happened—but I could never forget you and Mama Martinelli."

"Mama she outa da back, I call her. Mama!" he called, turning his head toward the door to the kitchen. "Coma see who'sa here!" Then turning to Manfred he said, without enthusiasm, "Howa you do, Mr. Andreotti?"

"Hi there, Mr. Martinelli! I'm fine. How are things with you folks?"

"Oh, is-a fine," he said without enthusiasm. Si. Okay."

Just then Mrs. Martinelli emerged from the back of the store and, seeing Imogen, ran to embrace her.

"Gena! Oh Gena! Is-a so gooda to see you! Oh! You looka so very beautiful—lika you shoulda look!"

"It's all thanks to Manfred, Mama."

"*Ah, si,*" said Signora Martinelli, turning toward Manfred. "*Buona sera, Signor Andreotti.*"

"*Buona sera, Signora.* Didn't I tell you I'd make Imogen look like a princess—like the princess she is?"

"*Si—si, We approva. Si, is gooda. Imogena beautiful younga lady*"

"So how's everything been with you?"

"Is-a fine. *Si.* Everythinga fine. Gena! You all right? We worry. Everything okay witha you?"

"Yes, I'm fine Mama Martinelli, and everything *is* all right. Manfred treats me very well—much too well in some ways—as you can see. But I have to say now that I like looking glamorous. But Mama and Papa, you're fine? Everything has been going well?"

"Oh, fina. *Si,* everything fina," Mr. Martinelli responded flatly.

Imogen looked searchingly into Mrs. Martinelli's eyes and then across to Mr. Martinelli, for their tone of voice and their facial expressions both suggested matters were not fine.

"Are you sure? I sense something is bothering you."

"No, no," protested Mr. Martinelli. "Everything alla righta."

"It should be," said Manfred, somewhat reproachfully. "I've taken good care of Imogen, and I've kept my word to you. No one's bothered you. You should be on top of the world."

"*Si, si.*"

"But something *is* wrong," said Imogen. "I can tell. You're not yourselves. Can't you tell me what it is? Perhaps if Manfred stepped outside for a few min—"

"No, no. Maybe we better tell. Is abouta Mr. Andreotti," said Mr. Martinelli.

"About Manfred!" exclaimed Imogen, turning to look at him, surprised and somewhat reproachful.

"Me!" exclaimed Manfred, also greatly surprised. "Why me? I swear, Imogen, I have kept my word. I've done nothing I said I wouldn't do or that I said I would. So I don't know what their problem is. Imogen, you know I always keep my promises."

"I believe you Manfred, I believe you. You have always kept your promises to me, certainly," said Imogen, and she turned in puzzlement back to the Martinellis.

"You know I've kept my word, folks, don't you?" Manfred continued to protest. "I've not put any pressure on you."

"*Si, si,*" said Mr. Martinelli. "You keepa you word. No pressure."

"Then what's wrong, Mama and Papa?" asked Imogen.

"*Si, si.* Mr. Andreotti he keepa his word," said Mrs. Martinelli. "Thatsa da problema."

"Manfred's keeping his word is a problem, Mama?" said Imogen, bewildered. "This is a mystery. Please tell us what's wrong."

"*Si, si,*" said Mr. Martinelli. "Gena, you maka da bigga sacrifice-a for us alla for nothing."

"I—I don't understand. I thought—"

"*Si,*" said Mrs. Martinelli. "You meana well. You thinka you do us da favor. But is not favor. Everybody angry at us."

"Angry at you! Why?"

"People in Little Italy find out. They see you at Gabrielli's with Mr. Andreotti. They start aska da question. Soon they finda out."

"But—but surely they would be happy that Manfred is not demanding protection money from them!"

"*Si,* you thinka so. But they not."

"They're not?" Imogen exclaimed, her perplexity deepening. "I don't understand."

"They say because we notta pay Mr. Andreotti, because you maka him promisa notta aska da money from everyone, they notta get alla da good things Mr. Andreotti do for other people in other districts. We notta getta gymnasium, we notta getta community hall, we notta getta playground."

Imogen stared back and forth from the Martinellis to Manfred. Manfred merely shrugged his shoulders and spread out his hands as though to say, "There's no pleasing some people."

"Mr. Andreotti," said Mr. Martinelli. "We pay. You letta Imogena go.

"*Si*, we pay," said Mrs. Martinelli. "Everybody in Little Italy pay. Gena, you not hava be his-a girla frienda any more. Everybody be happy."

Completely dumbfounded, Imogen was able only to stammer. "I—I—"

"Imogen?" said Manfred, turning to her, his face calm, but his eyes full of misgiving, even sadness and looking at her as though to read her mind. "It's up to you. I gave my word."

Again she found that she could only stammer. "I—I—don't—This is—I—hardly expected—"

"Imogen?" he queried and again he looked at her, his face now betraying the intensity of his feeling.

A lump came into her throat, but she managed to speak. "Maybe we—Perhaps Manfred—could—couldn't you work something out—some sort of agreement—some compromise—some token arrangement?"

"Gena!" cried Mrs. Martinelli. "Whatta you saying?"

"*Si, si,*" echoed her husband. "Gena, you notta hava do this any more."

"I—I—" she began. "It's all right, Mama, Papa. Don't worry. I want to do it." Manfred stared at her in amazement, but with the light of joy dawning in his eyes, as she turned again to speak to him. "Manfred, surely—? Perhaps if I stepped outside for a few minutes—"

"Yeah, yeah. Sure," he said, his whole face brightening. "Sure. We can work something out."

"Gena—!" exclaimed Signor and Signora Martinelli together.

"No, Mama and Papa. It really is all right. Please don't be upset. I'll see you again in a few minutes."

She ran to kiss them both, and then turned and ran out of the confectionery. Outside she began to pace up and down under the street light.

—What's happening to me? Why am I acting this way? He was actually willing to let me go! A month or so ago, I'd have jumped at the chance, but now—I don't want to leave him. What does this mean? Is it that I—

"Miss," called Eddie, one of the guards interrupting her muings. "Stay in the light where we can see you."

"Oh," she said, realizing that she had walked out of the circle of light from the street lamp. "I'm sorry Eddie," she said turning back. "I—I forgot. I was thinking about something."

—This life is so full of stress and danger, and I'm always under surveillance—always have to be guarded—but—but—in spite of everything, I don't want to leave him. I—I—I don't understand. Or do I? It seems so strange, bizarre, impossible, but—but—

Just at that moment Manfred, emerged from the confectionery.

"It's all settled," he said. "We worked out an agreement—like you say, a token arrangement."

"Oh, Manfred!" she said, running to him, throwing her arms around his neck and kissing him. "You are wonderful!"

"Hey! Thanks! But you're acting very strange."

"I'm feeling very strange. But just give me a minute to say good-bye to the Martinellis, and I'll be right back."

"Well—Okay. Yeah. Sure."

She rushed into the little confectionery where the Martinellis stared at her in perplexity.

"Gena!" began Mrs. Martinelli. "We see you giva Mr. Andreotti bigga kiss. Whatsa—"?

"I can't explain now, Mama, Papa. All I know is that I want to stay with him—that I *must* stay with him."

"He threaten you?" asked Mr. Martinelli.

"No, no. He never threatens. He's always very kind to me. So, don't worry. I've been all right with him, and I *will* be all right with him."

"We notta understanda—" Mrs. Martinelli began.

"I hardly understand myself," Imogen, interrupted, "but please believe me, it's all right."

"Is-a harda believa that, Gena," said Mr. Martinelli.

"I'm sure it is, Papa, but I'm no longer afraid. He really cares about me and I—I trust him."

The old couple looked at her dumbfounded, unable to speak. Imogen ran around the counter and embraced and kissed them each in turn.

"Mama, Papa. Don't worry. Please don't worry. Nothing will happen to me. I'll be fine. So—so, *arrivederci, a piu tardi.* I'll be back to see you again. And as I said, don't worry. *Arrivederci.*"

Again she kissed them both and ran from the store as the still perplexed Martinellis called after her, "*Arrivederci,* Imogena. Taka care, Gena. Taka care!"

She ran to the limousine where Manfred stood waiting for her at the open door.

Again she threw her arms about his neck.

"Oh Manfred! Manfred!" she cried, throwing her arms about his neck and kissing him long and hard.

"Hey! I like this, but what's got over you all of a sudden? Just because I made a deal with your friends..."

"No. No. It's not that. Well, I'm glad you did, but let's get in the car. Quick! I'll tell then."

She slid in and Manfred followed her, and immediately she snuggled up to him.

"Oh Manfred! Manfred! I—I've been so slow to understand, but suddenly, when I had the chance to break away and be free, I realized I didn't want to. Oh Manfred! You've been right all along! Manfred—I love you!"

"You—! Imogen!" He clasped her into his arms and his mouth came down hard on hers as she threw her arms about him. "Imogen! My darling!"

"Oh Manfred—darling! Let's go to your apartment. I want to make love!"

"Me too! Eddie," he called into the intercom. "Take us to the Imperial Hotel."

"Not the restaurant, Boss?" asked Eddie.

"Phone and tell them we'll be late."

"Tell them to cancel Manfred!" cried Imogen. "We can order up room service at the hotel. Oh Manfred! I could almost make love right here, right now. Tell Eddie to hurry."

"Yeah. Fast as you can, Eddie—and cancel the reservation."

"Oh Manfred!" she said, leaning against him, her arms about him, and finding his lips. "I can hardly believe what has happened! But oh, I'm so happy!"

"I find it hard to believe too," he said, "even though I always knew it would happen. What made you love me all of a sudden?"

"Oh darling! I don't think it was all of a sudden. It was the realization that was sudden. I've been falling in love with you—I don't know for how long—without realizing it—or accepting it because—because—"

"Because of what I do for a living."

"Manfred, I know you don't like to hear it, but between lovers there should be no pretense. I didn't want to love a gangster—but I do. I love you! I love Manfred—and I'm happy."

"So are you saying you think it's okay now?"

"That you're a gangster? No, but because I love you I accept what you are." She looked at him a few moments in silence before she said, "What you do is part of what and who you are. I don't think you could—I know you could not be anything else. I love who you are, Manfred and accept what you are—if that makes any sense—just as, I've come to realize, you've accepted me for what I am. I'm sure that's part of my reason—if one needs a reason—for loving you. But really, I love you simply because you're Manfred."

"And I love you because you're Imogen. But geez! You've sort of got me going in circles."

"Oh, I know. I'm not making much sense—but maybe love itself doesn't make a lot of sense. I love you because you've been kind to me and respectful of me and because you appreciate my piano playing—and because you've been a wonderful lover in bed and taught me to enjoy making love. I love you for making me realize—or to accept—that I'm beautiful and for making me feel like a woman. I'd never have believed, when you first approached me, Manfred, that you could be so kind to as you have been, or respect me as you have—or that you could be such a wonderful lover!"

"Yeah, well it wasn't long before you became a pretty damn good lover yourself!"

"Thank you, Manfred! Thank you! I suddenly realized how much I needed—wanted to be a lover. And," she added with a teasing smile, "how could I possibly not love a man who'd take me nude to the Gemini Club. But can't you make them go any faster?"

"We're almost there," he said.

They arrived at the hotel, and Imogen, in her eagerness, fairly rushed Manfred across the lobby to the elevator. Once it began to move, the guards trying very hard to pretend they were not looking, she threw her arms about him, pressed herself against him and rubbed her left leg sensually against his right one. Once in the suite, she grabbed his hand and dragged him toward the bedroom, her other hand pushing the thin, macaroni straps of her gown from her shoulders.

"Hey! Hey!" he called out. "What's come over you?"

"As I said before, you've come over me. You've awakened the wanton, sensual woman in me, and she's very much in love with you and wants to make love. So hurry up."

"I'm coming! I'm coming! You don't need to pull me off my feet!"

"You're supposed to drag me by the hair saying, 'Me Tarzan, you Jane'."

Within seconds, it seemed, they were tumbling together naked in bed.

* * * * *

"Oh Manfred! Manfred!" she cried as he withdrew from her. "Oh Manfred! This has been the most wonderful love making! Did I ever tell you what a wonderful lover you are?"

"Yeah, back there in the limo."

"Oh! I should have told you sooner, because you are—a great lover! And did I ever tell you how handsome you are?"

"Yeah, you did."

"Well, I can't tell you often enough! Remember that night when we first met at the opera, Manfred? I thought, when I first noticed you looking at me, that you were the most handsome man I'd ever seen, and I broke out in goose bumps because so handsome a man had noticed me."

"Yeah? I sort of thought maybe you'd been pleased. That's partly why I knew you'd fall in love with me."

"You conceited, egotistical, male chauvinist!" she said, both her eyes and lips smiling as she spoke. "You think no woman can resist you!"

"I guess I did. But there's only one I don't want to resist me now."

"You wanted me just for my big boobs and because I played hard to get!" she teased.

"You have breasts, not boobs, darling, but yes, I guess the fact that you did stand up to me made you just that more desirable, because I could tell you were special and were not mercenary—not like any other woman I'd ever known."

"I didn't believe at first that you when you said you loved me, but you did—you do—and you're the first man who ever has loved me. I didn't want ever to go to bed with a man I didn't love—that's why I wore the mask at first—but you made that first night far more pleasant than I'd ever expected it would be, and maybe that's when I began to change my feelings about you. And all the time I thought I was just engaging in sex like an exuberant whore when I was really making love to the man I love!"

"Yeah! Well, you've taught me something. Sex is much better when you're in love. I never realized it before tonight, for tonight was the best of all!"

"And it can only get better, darling!" she said snuggling up to him.

"I wish now there never had been other women before you—and there were too many of them—but believe me, you are the only woman I've ever really loved!"

"I believe you darling. And those other women are in the past, and that's a good place to leave them. Oh Manfred! I wish this moment could last forever! I never knew it was possible be so happy!"

"I didn't either," he said. "I never knew what happiness was till I met you. Like Mama says, you've made me happier than I've ever been in my life!"

And he brought his mouth down hard on hers.

"I'm so glad you have this place," she said when he removed his lips from hers. "I wish we could be on a desert island, Manfred," she said, "with no one but ourselves, where we could be naked all the time, and I could have you beside me always and inside me whenever I wanted, and we could just forget the world. "

"Yeah, me too."

"At least we have this place when we want to be alone—really alone."

Then suddenly, she jumped from the bed and ran to the closet, took down a long sheer black robe, put it on over her naked body and slipped her feet into a pair of mules. "There!" she said, turning to him. "Now, come out to the piano, darling! I want to play for you."

Throwing on a robe, he followed her to the living room where she seated herself at the keyboard.

"This is for you, Manfred," she said smiling up at him as he came to stand beside the piano. "For us!" she said as she began to play.

"Liebestraume!" he exclaimed. "My favorite!"

"Yes," she said smiling at him, her fingers caressing the keys softly at first, then using her forearms and shoulders, increasing the volume and raising the music to a high intensity at the climax. Her fingers rippled over the keys in the cadenza, and then at the end caressed them softly again for the quiet close. She raised her hands from the keyboard after the last hushed chord and sat silently looking up at Manfred whose eyes shone with pleasure and adoration.

"That was beautiful!" he said and sat down beside her on the piano bench.

"When you first asked me to play it, I felt terribly embarrassed, and I didn't really want to, but now I'll play it for you any time you want. I was inspired tonight by our love. I don't think I've ever played it so well."

"You're wonderful," he said and enfolded her in his arms and kissed her. "And beautiful."

"You're pretty gorgeous yourself," she said.

* * * * *

Later, much later after they had ordered up a meal from room service and again made rapturous love, they fell asleep in each other's arms. But after they had slept a while, Imogen cried out suddenly in her sleep and awoke with a start.

"Wh—?" said Manfred, waking and turning to her. "What's the matter Imogen?"

"Oh Manfred! I had a bad dream!"

"A bad dream on a night like this?"

"Oh—I know. It seems so inappropriate—unseemly. I—I guess it's because everything has seemed so—so sudden and so strange. I'm sure it's that. Don't worry. Go back to sleep—but hold me."

"What was the dream? You really cried out."

"It was—I'm sure it can't have been anything really serious, because now I've forgotten."

"Yeah?" he said, dubiously.

"Yes—it really was nothing—but do hold me, Manfred."

He took her into his arms and clasped her to him.

"Well, if this is what happens every time," he said, "have all the bad dreams you want."

—No, Manfred, no! she thought. Not like that one! I dreamt that I was holding you dead in my arms!

CHAPTER TWENTY-ONE

About two weeks after her declaration of love to Manfred, Imogen awoke with a queasy feeling in her stomach and a sour taste in her throat. Throwing the bed clothes from her naked body and, leaving Manfred lying asleep, she ran to the bathroom, retched, but brought nothing up.

—Oh no! she thought. Oh no! I can't be—I always take—we always take—But—Oh Lord! That night when I told Manfred I loved him—we were so eager, so much in love—I'm going to bear the child of our love! How wonderful to have a child by the man I love!

Just then Manfred knocked on the bathroom door.

"What's the matter, Imogen?" he called. "Are you sick?"

"In a way," she said, opening the door to him.

"What do you mean 'In a way'? Either you're sick or you're not."

"Well," she said, going to him and throwing her arms about him, "it's a kind of sickness you might be happy to hear about."

"Happy to hear about—" he began, a puzzled expression on his face, but then as he realized the import of what she was saying, he cried happily, "Imogen!"

"Yes, darling," she said, embracing him. "I think it's morning sickness. I think I'm pregnant."

"Imogen! Imogen!" he cried clasping her to him. "You're wonderful! You're going to bear my child!"

"Our child, Manfred, you old male chauvinist—the child of our love."

"Oh, yes! Yes! Our child, Imogen! Did it happen that night do you think?"

"I'm sure of it, Manfred. In my joy and my enthusiasm, I forgot—we forgot about birth control. But I'm happy, Manfred, darling, and I'm glad you're happy!"

"Happy! I'm ecstatic! To have fathered a child by you, Imogen—by the woman I love! I wouldn't want now to have a child by anyone else! Oh Imogen! We're going to have a child! I'm going to be a father again and have a son to bring up and do all sorts of wonderful things with!"

"Oh you men! How do you know it won't be a girl?"

"Oh—yeah. I suppose it could be, couldn't it. Well, if she looks like you, I certainly won't complain."

"Girls have a funny way of turning out to look like their fathers, you know. But with such a handsome father, she'd be a real beauty. Still, for your sake I'd like it to be a boy to take the place of the boy you never see."

"Yeah, yeah. A boy would be great. Thanks, Imogen, for thinking of that. But this is a very happy moment!"

"Oh, yes, it is, Manfred." Then suddenly Imogen turned very serious. "Suddenly I feel both honored and humbled to know there may be a new life within me. It's a great responsibility."

"Yeah—yeah. It is, I guess. But to have a child by you—I'll love him—or her—all the more because you're its mother!"

"Thank you Manfred, darling. And I will love him or her all the more because you are its father."

"Imogen! My darling!" he said, and brought his lips down on hers. Then after a while he asked, "How are you feeling now, by the way? Do you think you'll be okay for the party for the godfather next week?"

"Oh, I think so. But how are you going to feel when I start getting bigger and look like the Goodyear Blimp? And you know," she added with a twinkle in her eye, "these much vaunted boobs that you like so much are going to get big as basketballs or prize-winning pumpkins! So how do you like them apples, Mr. Crime Boss of East Clintwood? "

"You'll never look anything but beautiful to me. You'll look more beautiful pregnant than you ever looked."

"Why thank you, darling!" she laughed.

"Geez Imogen!" he exclaimed. "I can hardly wait to tell people!"

Imogen pondered Manfred's words a moment and then said, "Could we just wait a while—until I get used to the idea? Suddenly, now, life seems more serious."

"Huh? Yeah—yeah—I guess it is. Okay, if you want—but it'll be hard to keep from bursting out with it, I'm so happy! And Imogen, I know I'm a crook—like you say, there's no point between ourselves pretending anything else—but I'll be a good father."

"Somehow, Manfred, I know you will. But I guess we should get dressed and go down for breakfast—though I don't feel very much like eating."

"But you're eating for two now, remember."

"That's a bit of a fallacy; but don't worry, I won't waste away. My body just has to adjust."

In the breakfast room, Imogen found the odor of coffee nauseating and asked if she could have tea.

"Tea!" Rosina, who had since Imogen's arrival been sullenly quiescent, now suddenly exploded. "Nobody in this house drinks tea! Now she wants special privileges as if she owned the place! She seems to think that because she's Manfred's woman she rules the roost around here!"

"I made only a request, Rosina," responded Imogen. "If there's no tea, I'll have just a glass of water. I don't want to make trouble or cause a fuss."

"It's really not such a horrible thing to ask," said Ana-Maria. "Surely the kitchen staff can find some tea somewhere."

Signora Andreotti looked searchingly at Imogen. Then she said to the attending maid, "Si, Maria. You tell Raoul to find some tea. If there is none, we'll get it. If Imogena wants tea, she can have it."

"There! See what I mean?" said Rosina. Then after a pause during which see stared critically at Imogen, she burst out, "I bet the trollop's pregnant! She's going to bring a bastard into the family!"

"Who are you calling a trollop!" demanded Manfred, turning sharply on his elder sister. "And if Papa hadn't married Mama, you'd have been a bastard yourself. You happened because Mama and Papa loved each other, and, yes, Imogen's pregnant, and she's pregnant because she and I love each other! Geez! You call her a trollop again and our child a bastard, you'll regret it to the end of your days—which won't be very many!"

"Manfred! Rosina! Stop it!" shouted Signora Andreotti. Then coming to Imogen and taking her arm, she said, "Imogena? Are you pregnant?"

"I think I might be, Mama Andreotti. I was sick this morning and the smell of coffee upsets me."

"Hey!" shouted Signor Andreotti to one of the servants. "You taka da coffee away! We not upsetta Imogena! Imogena? You going to maka me a grandpapa?"

"As I say Papa Andreotti, I think so. There'll have to be tests before I'm sure, of course, but the signs all point that way."

"Hey! Thatsa wonderful!"

"Yeah, that's what I think too, even if old sour puss here," said Manfred, glaring at Rosina, "doesn't. It's the most wonderful thing that's ever happened to me—to have a child by the only woman I ever loved—or ever will."

Imogen looked up at him and smiled happily.

"Oh Imogen!" cried Ana-Maria coming over and embracing her. "I'm overjoyed! This is indeed wonderful!"

"Thank you Ana-Maria. I knew you'd be happy for me."

"Hmph!" snorted Rosina.

"Rosina, why are you such a spoil-sport?" demanded Ana-Maria of her older sister.

"Ah, it's her nature. She was born with a rusty spoon in her mouth!" said Manfred.

"You bring into this house this proletarian trollop, this working class slut, and now you say you're proud to be having a child by her—!"

Imogen stepped forward and resoundingly slapped Rosina's face. "Proletarian trollop!" she cried. "Working-class slut! I'm not ashamed of my background! If I'm ashamed of anything it's of becoming part of this criminal world of yours, Rosina! You're the one who should be ashamed of your background, not me. My family gain their living by honest effort!"

"Why you—!"

"Stop! Stop!" cried Signora Andreotti, interposing herself between her daughter and Imogen. "Enough! Rosina! You apologize!"

"After what she called us!"

"I'm sorry, Mama Andreotti," said Imogen, very shame-faced. "I should not have said what I did. You've been so very kind to me..."

"That's all right, *Cara*," soothed Signora Andreotti. "Rosina had no right to speak like that to you."

"And it's true, Rosina," said Ana-Maria. "What are we if not a family of crooks." She buried her face in her hands. "I would to God we were not."

"You don't seem to mind all the good things it brings you," said Rosina. "And neither does she," she added indicating Imogen. "She's certainly got a good thing going for herself."

"I'm here because of Manfred and for no other reason," said Imogen. "He's the man I love!"

Ana-Maria dropped her hands from her face and impulsively embraced Imogen. "Oh Imogen!" she exclaimed. "I'm so happy to hear you say that. Manfred needs you to love him."

"And, Ana-Maria, I was slow to realize it, but I need him—and I'm happy, very happy. We all need love, and Manfred has given it to me."

"Yes," said Ana-Maria sadly, "we all do need love."

"Oh Ana-Maria!" said Imogen taking her hand. "I'm so sorry. That was insensitive of me—but your time will come. There's someone out there for you as Manfred was for me."

"Crook though I am," said Manfred.

"Crook that you are, Manfred," said Imogen smiling at him. "I accept you for yourself. You know that."

"And for all the money he spends on you, and all the fine clothes he dresses you in!" snorted Rosina.

"I do like the things he does for me, yes. By dressing me well, he's made me appreciate my beauty," said Imogen. "But that's only partly why I love him. I love him for himself."

Just then Maria returned with a pot of tea.

"There was some, *Signora*," she said. "We have it for guests who like it."

"And Imogen," said *Signora* Andreotti, "is our guest—more than a guest now; she's family—our daughter."

"Thank you, Mama Andreotti," said Imogen, embracing Manfred's mother, "and thank you, Maria, for the tea."

"Why, you're welcome, Miss," said the servant. "You always appreciate what we do."

"And that's something we could learn form Imogen," said Manfred. "Good manners."

"Yes," said Ana-Maria. "Imogen may be from the working class, as you call it, Rosina, but she has the manners of a lady."

"*Si! Si!*" said *Signora* Andreotti. "Imogena is a lady. And Imogena, I'm so happy my Manfredo is to have a child by you."

"Thank you, Mama Andreotti," responded Imogen. "So am I."

"And I bet nobody's happier that I am," crowed Manfred. "So, I think maybe the majority is all in favor, Rosina, so you better get used to the idea."

"Yes," said Ana-Maria. "Apart from you, Rosina, we all like Imogen. She's the best thing that's ever happened to Manfred—and to all of us."

Rosina scowled, and saying nothing, stomped out of the room.

"Anyway," said Manfred, quickly finishing a croissant and gulping down his coffee, "it's time for me to get going."

"I'll see you to your car, darling. I'm not visiting Uncle and Aunt today," said Imogen with a wink only Manfred could see.

"I won't complain about that," said Manfred, smiling at her.

Manfred embraced his mother and Ana-Maria and bent down to give his father a hug.

"You runna da business good, Manfredo," he said. "I'ma prouda you."

"Thanks, Papa. You taught me well, and left it in good shape. All I have to do now is mention the Andreotti name, and everyone jumps to attention. You made my work easy."

"But you notta slacka off," his father warned.

"Don't worry, Papa. But come on, Imogen. I gotta get going."

"Yes, darling."

"You feeling okay?" he asked as they left the breakfast room.

"Oh—yes—I'm fine. The wooziness has gone—though it will come back tomorrow no doubt."

"Yeah, I'm sorry you have to put up with that, but I just can't get over the fact that we're going to have a child!"

"It's a great responsibility, Manfred, and, perhaps because it's a new experience for me, in many ways it's frightening."

"Hey! Don't worry. You'll be looked after okay and so will the baby. You'll both get everything you need. You can count on it."

"Yes, Manfred, I'm sure I can, but even with the best of care and attention and provision, it's still a big risk and a big responsibility having a child."

"Yeah—yeah, I guess you're right. You always are."

"Oh, I don't know about that." They were now at the waiting limousine, and Manfred took her into his arms. "I wish Rosina were not so hostile," she said.

"Ah, don't worry about Rosina! Like I said, she was born crabby."

"I do worry about her, Manfred."

"Aw! She isn't any danger."

"I hope you're right."

"Like I said, don't worry about her. That's just the way she is. But I gotta go now."

"Manfred—"

"Yeah?"

"I know I call you a crook—even though now it's in jest, but, Manfred, you're different, and I think our relationship is different from other Syndicate relationships, and now in a very deep and special way, so—so I want you to take care of yourself. My whole life depends on you now."

"Hey! You know I always do! And I got the boys to take care of me too. So don't you worry about me, darling. I'll be okay. Right now, I gotta be on my way." He gave her a long, lingering kiss. "See you tonight. And you take care of yourself. You're the best thing that's ever happened to me."

"And you the best thing that's ever happened to me. So do take care! As your Papa says, don't slack off."

"Hey! I won't, don't worry."

"And I'll take care of myself."

Again they embraced, and Manfred got into the limo. She stood and watched the convoy of cars drive away and then walked up to the long, wide, porticoed veranda and sat down on one of the lounges.

—Good Lord! she thought. I'm to be a mother in a world in which I never expected to live, much less in which to raise a child, a world, I'd have never have chosen, and, were it not for my love for Manfred, one where I'd not wish to remain. What will it be to bring up a child in this world of crime? If it is a boy, will he grow up like his father to run the local branch of the Syndicate—to be a criminal? It's not what I'd have wanted—not what I want—but can I prevent it? For better or worse, I'm committed to Manfred, and I've no desire not to be. And now, by this child and by my love for Manfred, I'm committed to this world and this life. His world is now my world, his life my life.

She rose to go back into the house and saw Louie, one of the "boys", coming across the lawn. She waved at him. "Hi Louie!" she said.

"Oh—yeah—uh—Hi, Miss. I—uh—I wasn't expecting to see *you* there."

"I was just enjoying the morning air for a minute."

"Uh—yeah, it's a real nice morning."

"Well, try to enjoy it yourself, Louie. See you again."

"Uh—yeah, right, Miss. Yeah." he turned about. "I gotta get back."

Imogen turned to walk to the door and caught a glimpse of Rosina making as though to come out, then turning away suddenly and reentering the house.

—That's strange, she thought. Wonder what she was up to? Spying on me? Why? What goes on in that dark mind of hers? And why did Louie emphasize "you"?

CHAPTER TWENTY-TWO

On the morning after Manfred's party for the godfather and the heads of the New Jersey syndicate at which Imogen, nude and gilded, had presided as shockingly seductively hostess, she and Manfred—his Glock 19 handgun near at hand on the table—sat on the terrace of his West Clintwood apartment, drinking his last cup of breakfast coffee, Imogen, sipping her tea, quite careless of how her light robe fell open to expose her flesh to the warmth of the morning sun.

"You were great last night," he said. "You sure dazzled everyone. People just couldn't take their eyes off you—it would have been hard for them not to. No one looks as good nude as you do. And boy, you sure gave the godfather's daughter-in-law in her see-through gown her come-uppance.

"That," she responded, smiling mischievously at him, "was my whole purpose. I've become a really awful girl, haven't I?"

"Well, you're certainly not the up-tight woman you were I first met you."

"Yes, I've come a long way, Baby—though that's not what the Woman's Movement means by the expression. But I'm afraid last night will probably be the last time for a several months that I'll be able to appear in such a brazen manner. I'll soon begin to become rather large about the middle. Too bad. I rather enjoy being wicked."

"Hey, you're not a wicked woman."

"Well, Manfred, I've certainly changed—so much so that I don't think I can ever return to my old life. Uncle and Aunt will be terribly upset, I know, but I've fallen in love with you, and I'm going to have a child by you; so whatever the consequences, I'm part of your life and your world. But even before I realized I loved you and became pregnant with your child, I came to enjoy being your mistress."

"I wish you'd just call yourself my woman, not my mistress."

"Oh, I don't know. 'Mistress' has a naughty ring to it that I like. As I said before, I enjoy, even glory in, the notoriety of being the mistress of the Crime Boss of the two Clintwoods."

"Well, I'm sure happy to have you with me—naughty or not. You're a better—and better looking—woman than anyone else in the Syndicate."

"Certainly a naughtier, more brazen one. But you know, Manfred, you're not like the others—as I said once before. I'm not sure I understand why or how—perhaps it has something to do with your mother's influence—but you are different. Oh, you can strut and pose and blow out your chest and play the role of big time crook the same way they do, but with you it is just a pose which you can throw off. With them, the pose has become the reality. You can drop the pose and be a human being, and I guess," she said, smiling and placing her hand on his, "that has a lot to do with why I love you."

"Hey! I guess that's compliment! Thanks. But yeah, they're a bunch of cruds all right; but I gotta butter them up from time to time. And having a good looking woman around helps with the buttering. But like I said, mainly I just want you for yourself."

"I know, Manfred. That's the most important reason why I love you."

"And I'm sure glad you do. But I'm glad you didn't tell the godfather about me starting to take you with me on my rounds."

"I'd never betray you, Manfred. But I'm very happy you are taking me with you. You don't know how much it means to me that you trust me like that. I feel I'm part of your life."

"Yeah. And it's nice having you—and," he added with a laugh, "soon you might even get to know the business well enough to run it if anything ever happened to me."

"Don't say that, Manfred!" she cried, real distress in her voice, a chill running through her as she remembered her dream of the night of her confession of love. "Please don't say that!"

"Hey! Hey! I was just joking. Don't worry. Nothing will happen to me."

"Don't even joke about it, Manfred!"

"Okay, okay, but it's nothing to worry about."

"I certainly hope not." Then looking out across the river toward East Clintwood, she said, "There's a helicopter coming over the horizon."

"Lots of them fly around the Clintwoods," Manfred said, and gulped down the rest of his coffee and set down his cup. "But now, all this has been leading up to something really important I want to say. Like I said, Imogen, I want you with me always; so come hell or high water, by whatever it takes, I'm going to get a divorce so we can get married."

Completely taken aback, Imogen stared at him in open mouthed astonishment.

"Manfred!" she exclaimed at last. "Manfred! My darling! Do you really mean that?"

"Do I ever say anything I don't mean?"

"No—not to me, anyway. Oh Manfred!" She threw herself into his arms and kissed him passionately. "You are the most wonderful man in the world!"

"Anyway, even though nothing's official yet," he said reaching into the pocket of his jacket and taking out a small velvet-covered box and presenting it to her, "I want you to wear this."

"Oh Manfred!" she exclaimed. What—?" He opened it for her to see a large diamond solitaire mounted on an intricately patterned gold ring. "Oh my goodness, Manfred! It's beautiful! You wonderful man!" Again she threw her arms about him. Then, holding the box with the ring out to him, and extending the fourth finger of her left hand, she said "You put it on my finger for me, Manfred." He did so, and again she kissed him warmly, gratefully, lovingly. "Oh Manfred! I can hardly believe this is happening!"

"And I can hardly believe that I'd ever meet a woman like you, much less be asking her to marry me. Like I said, you're the best thing that's ever come into my life, Imogen."

"Oh Manfred! My darling! My love!" Then holding her left hand out in front of her, spreading her fingers and gazing at the ring she said, "It really is beautiful, Manfred, and as usual, it's too much, but I've come to realize that's your way of saying you care. I'll wear this gift with pride!"

"Nothing's too much for the most beautiful woman in the world."

"Oh Manfred!" she said. "Please stop calling me that—but I have to confess I'm getting to like hearing it."

"And I'm in seventh heaven that you love me."

"And I—That helicopter's coming awfully close," she said, looking up as as the noise of the rotors grew louder.

"Yeah, and it's damn noisy" he said, rising. "Let's go inside. Anyhow it's time we were on our way." He picked up the Glock from the table. "So get dressed, and we'll visit a few of some of our wealthier clients."

"Yes, but you forget, Mr. Crime Boss," she shouted over the noise of the flapping rotors, "that I came here naked under my leopard skin coat."

"Oh—yeah. Well, just wear that and your high heels. You said you liked being risque."

"Oh, well, if you—"

"Hey!" Manfred shouted suddenly. "That helicopter's swinging around!"

At the same time shooting broke out and Al shouted from the corner of the gallery, "Boss! Miss! Look out! Get down!"

"Get down Imogen!" cried Manfred as he got off a shot, and pushed her to the terrace and fell on top of her.

Bullets whined and smashed onto the gallery floor and into the gallery's glass doors. The helicopter veered away with Eddie on the roof and Al at the far corner of the gallery continuing to fire at it.

"Boss! Boss! Miss!" cried Al, running toward them as Eddie jumped down from the roof. "Are you okay?"

Manfred's only response was a groan.

"Manfred!" cried Imogen as she struggled out from beneath him. "Manfred! Are you all—!" Then seeing the blood flowing from great wounds at the base of his neck and in his back, she cried, "Oh my God! Al! Quick!" she shouted. "Get the hotel doctor!"

As Al rushed to the phone inside the suite, Joe, who with his partner Jimmy had been on guard in the hallway pounded on the door calling out. "Boss! Al! Miss! What's happening?" Eddie rushed to let them in. "What's happened?" Jimmy asked.

"Helicopter. The Boss's been shot," cried Eddie.

"Oh my God! He ain't dead?"

"No, but he's hurt bad."

"And Miss Imogen?"

"She's okay, but real upset at what's happened to the boss."

"Geez yeah! The Boss! Jimmy! Go get the house doctor! Quick!"

"I just called," said Al, "but you go anyway, Jimmy, and hurry him up! They had to call him up from the dining room where he' having breakfast."

Joe followed by Eddie rushed to the gallery where Imogen bent over Manfred whom she had rolled onto his back, pressing with her thumbs on the wounds to try to staunch the flow of blood where the bullets had passed through his chest.

"Manfred!" she cried. "Oh Manfred! My darling! Speak to me! Are you all right?"

"Imogen," he barely whispered. "You—all—right?"

"Yes, yes, Manfred. Yes, darling, I'm all right, but you—?"

"Doctor's on his way up," said Eddie.

"Oh!" cried Imogen. "I hope he won't be too late! Manfred! Manfred!" she cried again, seizing his hand.

"Imogen—hold me—Don't—let—me—go," he whispered.

"I won't darling! I won't!"

"You—seem—so—far—away," he said, his voice almost inaudible.

"I'm here, Manfred! Manfred!" she cried frantically. "My darling! Please don't die on me! Darling! Please! Hold on! Look at me! The doctor's coming!"

"I—love—you—"

"Oh Manfred! I love you!"

"Al—Joe—Eddie—You—there?"

"Yeah, Boss. Yeah! We're here. You hang on!" said Al.

"I'm—going—Take—care—of—Imogen. Do—every—thing—she—says."

"We will, Boss, but you're gonna be okay!" said Al.

"No—Getting—very—dark. Imogen—sorry—messed—up—your—life—"

"Oh no, Manfred! No, you made me happy. You—" As she spoke, he gave a sudden gasp, his eyes rolled back and his hand in hers went limp. "Manfred! Manfred! Oh no! Manfred! No!" she cried and fell over him, seizing his body in her arms. "Oh God! Oh God! No!"

"He ain't dead!" cried Al.

"Oh God!" cried Imogen. "This is horrible! Manfred! Manfred! Please don't go! Please come back!" Then she slumped down over her lover's body. "Oh God! Why? Oh Al! Eddie! Joe! He's gone! He's gone! He's gone!"

"No, Miss, no!" cried Eddie. "This can't be! Not the Boss!"

"Oh no, Eddie! He's gone! Oh Manfred! Manfred!" Then suddenly she straightened up, clenched her fists, looked to the sky where the helicopter had disappeared and said, "Manfred! I swear to you I'll make whoever did this pay. I'll get whoever's responsible. I swear it! I swear it! Al, Joe, Eddie—you promised Manfred you'd support me—because if you won't, kill me now."

"Hey, Miss!" exclaimed Al. "We'd never do that! We promised the Boss."

"That goes for me too," said Eddie.

"For all of us," said Al. "Me an' the Boys're with you hundred percent. We'll get whoever done this! You can bet on that.

Imogen looked up at him and forced a smile.

"Thank you, Al. Thank you Joe, Eddie. Thank you."

Just then Jimmy came onto the gallery.

"Here's the doctor—Oh my God! He ain't dead?"

"Yes, Jimmy, he is."

"But we're gonna help Miss Imogen get the killer," said Eddie.

Jimmy stared for a moment at Eddie and Al, and then said, "Yeah! Yeah! Right on, Eddie. You can count on us, Miss."

"Uh—excuse me, young lady," said the doctor to Imogen as he came onto the gallery. "If I might have a look—"

"What do you need to look for, doctor!" snapped Imogen, her eyes flashing anger through her tears. "Can't you see he's dead! You're too late!"

"I came as fast as I could, Miss—" said the physician stooping down to feel for a pulse in Manfred's neck, "but I'm afraid you're right. Judging by the wounds, I don't think anyone could have helped him. I'm sorry," he said, rising.

"You're sorry!" Imogen fairly screamed. "My lover—my fiance—is dead and all you can say is you're sorry! What good is it to be sorry!—Oh God!"

She fell into Al's arms.

"Don't know what else I can say, Miss. But I understand—I can appreciate your grief."

"No you can't!" she protested. Then softening and disengaging herself from Al, she turned to the physician and said, "I'm sorry, doctor. It was my grief and bitterness that spoke. I'm sure you did come as quickly as you could, and no, I don't think that you could have done anything."

"No, but—but—I don't like to have to inject mundane practical business into your grief, but I'm afraid I have to call the authorities—if someone will direct me to the phone?"

"In there, Doc," said Eddie, indicating the living room behind the now shattered glass doors of the gallery.

"Geez, Miss! Geez!" said Al when the physician had left the gallery. "It all happened so fast. We shoulda been quicker to suspect that bloody helicopter."

"Oh Al!" she exclaimed. "I wish you had—but Al," she said, changing her tone and placing her hand on his shoulder, "don't blame yourself. Some things just aren't under our control, no matter what we do. But oh," she cried, breaking into tears again and burying her face in her hands, "I wish there could have been something!"

"Who the hell could have done this?" asked Joe.

Suddenly, with a gasp, her eyes opening wide, Imogen remembered Louie's approach to the house and Rosina's immediate disappearance.

"I think I know Al!" she said, clenching her fists. "I'm sure I know! Rosina!"

"Rosina!" exclaimed Al. "Miz Pacelli! Not the Boss's own sister!"

"Yes, Al, Rosina. She never really liked him and she hates me! Thinks I have—I had—too much influence on Manfred—and she's ambitious. She wants to run things herself. And now that I'm to have Manfred's baby—Oh God! My child will have no father!"

Again she buried her face in her hands and burst into tears.

"Uh—yeah, Miss," said Al. "That's rough—but yeah! Yeah! Now that you mention it, I wouldn't put it past the bitch to do a thing like this. There ain't none of us likes her."

But before anyone could say anything more, a voice from the hallway shouted, "Police!"

"Oh! Quick!" cried Imogen, wiping away her tears. "Give me Manfred's gun!"

"You ain't gonna—?"

"No, Al, but I want for it later."

Just as Al grabbed up the automatic, an officer wearing sergeant's stripes appeared on the gallery demanding, "Okay, okay! What happened here?"

"Mr. Andreotti's been killed," Imogen flared as she clutched her robe about her. "Can't you see?"

"Huh! Andreotti! Dead!"

"What the hell does it look like?" demanded Al.

"Okay okay! I can see. I can see. How'd it happen?"

"Yeah, well," answered Al, "like, the Boss—Mr. Andreotti—and Miss Imogen here was just finishing breakfast when this helicopter flew over and someone started shooting, and the Boss was hit."

"That what you say, Miss?" demanded the sergeant. "The shooting came from the helicopter?"

"Of course!" Imogen flared. "Do you think we started it? Manfred—Mr. Andreotti—got in the way of the bullets to protect me. Oh God! Manfred! Manfred!" she cried, again bursting into tears, suddenly realizing the full import of what had happened. "You died saving my life!"

"Uh—yeah. Sorry, Miss," interjected the policeman, "but I gotta ask, just what was your relationship to Andreotti?"

Imogen turned and glared at him. "Everyone knows my relationship to Mr. Andreotti, Sergeant!" she snapped. "I'm the notorious Imogen Edwards. His mistress—his lover—his whore!"

"Okay! Okay! Okay, Miss! Look, I know you're upset. I'm just doing my job, and I got to make a complete interrogation. I gotta ask questions. Anyone get any identification on the helicopter?"

"It all happened too fast," said Al.

"It was blue, I think," said Eddie. "'D'—some—thing on the side. About all I got."

"Not a hell of a lot to go on," said the sergeant. "Any idea who mighta been behind this?"

Imogen glanced sideways at Al, giving an ever so slight negative nod," and Al gave a slight nod of recognition.

"No, Sergeant," she said. "I've no idea. I'm sure Mr. Andreotti had many enemies."

"You say you were his girl friend. You sure you don't know?" demanded the policeman.

"He didn't discuss his affairs with me. The Syndicate keep their business separate from their private lives."

"Yeah, yeah. I know. *Omerta*. The code of silence. So I guess that's all I'm going to get out of anyone here." He looked from one to the other and then said, "Okay. I'll be on my way. We'll need some one in the family to come into the station later and make a statement and to give an identification."

"Good God!" cried Imogen. "Don't you know who he is!"

"Gotta make it official, Miss. I'll send someone up to take the body to the coroner."

"The house doc's already taken care of that," said Eddie.

"Uh—yeah. Okay. Don't nobody leave town."

When the sergeant had left, Imogen turned to Al and the others. "I know Rosina's behind this. But I didn't want to say so to the police. Even if they did take her in, her lawyer would get her off—that and the old Padrone's money and influence. I have to act on my own. But Al, Joe, Eddie, Jimmy—are you sure you're with me? Are you really on my side?"

"Hey Miss," said Al. "We're with you all the way like we promised the Boss. Ain't that right Joe? Eddie? Jimmy?"

"Hundred percent!" said Eddie. "Even if the Boss hadn't made us promise, we'd be with you, Miss. There ain't none of us like Miz Pacelli, and like Al said, you're aces with us."

"Even, if need be, against the old Padrone—Signor Andreotti?"

The men were silent for a few seconds, then Al said, "Yeah, Miss, even against him."

Imogen's eyes narrowed, an unaccustomed coldness and hardness in her voice, Manfred's murder seeming to have summoned from her unbidden a new ruthlessness.

"Good, because I mean to do whatever I have to do to survive and to get to the bottom of this. Those bullets were meant for me as much as for Manfred, so I've got to take control of the organization—and if the Padrone's not with us, we'll have to kill him."

Al, Joe, Eddie and Jimmy started, staring at her in open mouthed amazement.

Then Al said, "Right Miss! Don't let nothin' stand in your way! The old Padrone's a has been anyway. And don't worry. We won't let nothin' happen to you."

"I don't intend to let anything happen to me, Al, and," she said, "Rosina will not live out the day." Imogen shuddered at her own cold bloodedness, but she was resolved not to flinch. "Can I count on the others?" she asked.

"They'll be on your side, Miss, don't worry," said Al. "You're aces with all of us and none of us likes Miz Pacelli. Besides, they'll do whatever I tell 'em to, an' I'll tell 'em to back you. You're our new Boss, Miss, and we're with you all the way."

"Manfred—Mr. Andreotti—was the Boss, Al," said Imogen. "Let's honor him by leaving him his title. 'Miss' will be my title from now on. And thanks Boys—Men—and you'll all be well rewarded for your support. Now, do you know anything about Rosina's dealings with Louie?"

"Louie, Miss?" asked Al in amazement.

Briefly she recounted the episode of a few days previously on the portico of the Andreotti mansion.

"Hey! Yeah!" exclaimed Eddie. "It coulda been Louie in that helicopter. He's usually one of Miz Pacelli's body guards and a good shot with a rifle. Them shots came from a rapid fire rifle."

"Me and Al told the Boss we should have a few of them," said Joe, "but he kept putting it off. Said anyone who wanted to kill him would have to get real close and would never get past us anyway. Guess he never thought of no helicopter."

Just then morgue officials arrived to remove Manfred's body. As they lifted him, Imogen ran over to embrace her dead lover one last time.

"Oh Manfred! Manfred darling!" she cried. And then as they carried him out, she said, "Good-bye, Manfred! Good-bye! Oh God! I can't believe you're gone!" Again she burst into tears, but when the official had left, she quickly got control of herself, stood erect and turning to the men, said, "This is no time for tears. Tears won't avenge his death. We've got work to do. Where's Manfred gun?"

"Here, Miss," said Al reaching into his jacket pocket and handing it to her.

"Good. I'll get my coat and then let's get back to the estate."

"It's a nice light gun, Miss. If you have to use it, just point and shoot—but squeeze the trigger—don't pull it," said Al.

"That's what Manfred told me once, but thanks for reminding me, Al, for I intend to use it," she said coldly.

"Hey, Miss! You're handlin' everything just great! You won't have no trouble getting the boys behind you." Then, Al's pager began to beep. "Yeah?" he said, taking it from his pocket and speaking into it. "Huh? Yeah, Tony the Boss is dead, but not Miss Imogen. And she's in charge now, not Signora Pacelli. We take orders from Miss Imogen now—all of us. Got it?"

"Let me speak to Tony, Al," said Imogen grabbing the pager from him. "Tony? This is Imogen—Miss. What's happening there?"

"Miz Pacelli's saying you and the Boss are dead and she's in charge now," came Tony's voice through the device. "She's got Miss Ana-Maria under guard and is ordering the old Padrone and the Padrona around and giving everybody else orders—or trying to. We ain't sure what to do."

"Do not obey her orders, Tony. Tell the Boys—the Men—that I'm in charge now. Take some of them—as many as you need—and take control of Signora Pacelli and her husband and hold them till I get there. Understood?"

"Understood, Miss. Uh—sorry about the Boss, Miss, but I'm glad you're okay, and so'll the boys be. Miz Pacelli's got some of her own guys around her—"

"Kill them if you have to," commanded Imogen, "but I want Rosina alive. And don't let anything happen to Signorina Ana-Maria or little Luigi, or to the Padrone and Padrona. Get Orietta and Maria to look after the little boy. And also I want Louie."

"Yeah, Miss. Something fishy there. The Boss had Miz Pacelli's phone bugged, and it seems it was Louie who phoned to say you and the Boss was dead. He ain't back yet, but we'll hold him when he is."

"Good. And take careful note of how Signora Pacelli reacts when she hears I'm still alive. I'm sure she's behind all this and that Louie fired the shots."

"We'll find out if he did, Miss don't worry."

"Use whatever means you have to. We're on our way, so get on with it."

Then handing the pager back to Al, she said, "I think we've got all the evidence we need, so, Al—Joe—Eddie—Jimmy—let's get going. Call up the cars while I get my coat."

She rushed to the bedroom.

—Oh Manfred! she cried inwardly. I'll mourn for you later! Right now I have to avenge your death!

She slipped her feet into her gold stilettos and slipped off her robe.

—I think I left my red squined mask here. She opend the drawer of the bedside table. Yes, here it is.

She took up the mask, held it to her face, then put it on.

—Imogen Edwards is no more. When Manfred died, she died too.

She walked to the closet for her leopard skin coat, donned it, dropped Manfred's pistol into the pocket and returned to the living room where the assembled men stared in astonishment at seeing her masked.

"From now on," she said, "no one will see me unmasked. I'm not who I was. I'm no longer Imogen but Miss, head of the the Clintwoods syndicate, and woe betide anyone who gets in my way!"

Her announcement was greeted with shocked surprise.

Then at last Al spoke. "Yeah, Miss! We're right behind you."

"Good. Al, Eddie, Joe and Jimmy, you are my right hand men. Now, let's be on our way. Eddie, you lead the way, Al and Joe on either side of me, and Jimmy behind me. Tell the others to spread out and be ready for anything—everyone," she said as she drew the pistol from her coat pocket, "with guns drawn ready for use."

"Miss," said Al, "like I said, you're handling this real great—just like the Boss would! Mebbe better."

"If so, Al, it's because I learned from him."

CHAPTER TWENTY-THREE

Imogen and her body guards descended by the elevator to the rotunda of the hotel where, the men taking up the positions she had assigned to them, she strode to the door and out to the limousine where the some of the other men, also puzzled by her mask, held the door for her.

"Geez, Miss! That's really horrible about the Boss. Sorry."

"Yes," she said as she stepped into the limo, "it is horrible, but now's not the time for sorrow. There are more important matters to attend to. To the Andreotti mansion."

Within moments, they drove off.

Tony met them at the gate when they arrived at the estate.

"Everything's under control, Miss," he said after his initial surprise at seeing Imogen masked when she let down the dark, one-way vision window of the limousine and leaned toward him. "Only a little trouble. Most of the boys came round when they heard you was in charge."

"Good work, Tony—and thanks. And give my thanks to all the men for me. I'll thank them myself when we've seen all this through. Get in with Joe in the front car and come up to the house with us. We might need you."

"Right you are, Miss. An' Miz Pacelli looked pretty shocked when she heard you wasn't dead."

"I rather thought she would," said Imogen.

When, Glock in hand and accompanied by Al, Joe and the other men with their weapons drawn, she entered the mansion, Ana-Maria came running toward her, then stopped short on seeing her masked.

"Oh Imogen! What is this? Why are you wearing a mask?"

"I'm no longer Imogen Edwards, Ana-Maria. I'm now the head of the crime syndicate."

"Oh Imogen! Surely not!"

"Yes, Ana-Maria. Desperate circumstances call for desperate remedies."

"But oh Imogen! This is so horrible. But is Manfred really dead?"

"Yes, Ana-Maria," she said, her voice choking, "I'm afraid he is."

The two women fell into each other's arms and the tears flowed, but Imogen quickly recovered her composure and said, "There'll be time for crying later, Ana-Maria. Right now there are matters to be dealt with. Is Luigi safe?"

"Yes. He's with Maria and Orietta."

"Good. I don't want him to see what happens. How are Mama and Papa Andreotti taking it?"

"They're terribly distraught. And Imogen, is Rosina really behind this? Is that why she's being held? They say you've ordered it."

"Yes, she is, and yes I ordered it. Manfred's death must be avenged."

"Oh Imogen—! What are you going to do?"

"I've got to stop Rosina to protect my life—and yours, Ana-Maria. Neither of us would survive long if she's allowed to get away with this. Now," she commanded, turning toward the men, "where is that snake? Bring her to me."

Tony, accompanied by Eddie, left briefly and returned dragging in Rosina, her hands bound, squirming, twisting and protesting vehemently, her husband Giorgio, clearly frightened, dragged in behind her. Old Signor Andreotti in his wheel chair, his wife at his side, rolled himself in behind them.

"Imogena!" cried the Padrone. "Whatsa go on here? Whya you weara da mask?"

"I've taken charge, Padrone, and I intend to avenge Manfred."

"Manfredo notta dead! Is notta true. No, is notta true! Is notta true! Manfredo notta dead."

"I wish it were not so, Papa Andreotti, but I'm sorry to say it is," said Imogen.

"Oh God! No!" cried Signora Andreotti. "It can't be true! Not my Manfredo!"

Imogen ran to her and embraced her. "I'm so sorry, Mama Andreotti. You've lost your son; I've lost my lover—my husband, for just before he was killed him, he gave me this," she said holding out her hand with the engagement ring.

"Oh Cara!" cried the Padrona. "Oh Imogena! How horrible for you!"

"Horrible for all of us. We suffer this together, Mama Andreotti. Manfred belonged to both of us. And to you too, Padrone," she said, laying a hand on his shoulder. "And to Ana-Maria. But the culprit is in your own household, a member of your own family."

"Notta Rosina!" exclaimed the old Padrone. "She'sa his sister! She not killa her brother! Rosina! Say itsa notta true."

"Of course it's not!" snapped Rosina. "Papa, you're not going to believe this little minx who struts in here wearing that stupid mask. You're not going to let her push us all around as though she's running the operation. As the eldest, I'm in charge!"

"That's what you've always wanted, isn't it, Rosina—power, control?" said Imogen, "You've never had much sisterly affection for Manfred that I could ever see, and certainly you hate me. You had to get Manfred and his overbearing slut of a mistress out of the way—and their child who'd have succeeded him. But no, you're not in charge of the operation, Rosina. I am," said Imogen. "I've taken control, and for my own good I intend to stay in control."

"Imogena," said old Signor Andreotti, "by whatta right you taka control and giva orders? "

"By the right of self-preservation, Padrone, and by the right of the gun," she said, brandishing the Glock, "and in Manfred's name as his woman—his wife. Those bullets were meant for me, and Manfred put himself between them and me to save my life. That's how he was killed. So, 'For my own good all causes shall give way'" she said, remembering Macbeth's line. "No one will stand in my way, Padrone—not you, not even the godfather himself. Ere I perish, others will perish."

The old man stared at her incredulously.

"She has to have that mask to talk like that!" snarled Rosina. "Just who do you think you are anyway talking so big and so tough!"

"I'm the woman whom Manfred loved and who loved him in return, and you've taken him away from me and left like this," she said, and, to the gasps of everyone present, shrugged off her coat, "bereft and desolate— naked!"

"Oh my! Aren't we melodramatic! Going about naked seems a real penchant with you, from what I hear. Al! Joe!" shouted Rosina. "Get rid of this little naked gutter snipe!"

"We work for Miss Imogen," said Al, "not you."

Suddenly Rosina's arrogance gave way to a look of real fear.

"Papa!" she cried. "Are you going to allow this!"

"I'm in charge here, Rosina," said Imogen, "not your papa. And as you can see, the power and the guns are on my side."

"What proof," Rosina demanded, desperation in her voice, "do you have for this preposterous accusation that I killed Manfred and tried to kill you!"

"How did you know so soon that Manfred was dead—and thought I was too—unless you planned it? And why did ou immediately start throwing your weight around here, unless that was what you had in mind all along?"

"Yes, Rosina," demanded Ana-Maria. "How do you answer that?"

"*Si, si!*" exclaimed the old Padrone, the light of understanding beginning to dawn in him. "How you explaina dat?"

"And why did you want to see Louie the other day, Rosina," demanded Imogen, "when you disappeared from the veranda so suddenly on seeing me?"

"What are you talking about?"

"I'm talking about a conspiracy to kill Manfred and me."

"You tried to kill Imogena?" cried Signora Andreotti.

"Yes, she did," said Imogen and then turned to Al, Joe and Eddie. "Has Louie shown up yet?"

"Yeah, Miss," said Eddie. "He's outside. The boys been working him over."

"Bring him in."

"Rosina?" demanded the old man. "Whatta you say? Is-a whatta Imogena saya right?" Then reproachfully he said, "I not lika the looka inna you eyesa."

"For heaven's sake, Papa and Mama!" she cried, but avoided her father's eyes, "Surely you don't think that I had anything to do with killing Manfred? And I don't have to answer anything—certainly not the preposterous charges of this naked slut that Manfred inflicted on this family!"

"No, you don't have to answer, Rosina," said Imogen, "because I know you did it. I've all the evidence I need, but I want to hear what Louie has to say."

At that moment Eddie and one of the other henchmen brought in Louie bound, bruised and bleeding.

Watching him closely, Imogen caught his furtive glance across at Rosina before he quickly turned to her, his eyes popping and his jaw dropping at the sight of her nakedness, but he forced a smile.

"Geez, Miss!" he said. "Tell these guys to let me go. I didn't do nothin'. I come back—it was my day off, like—as as soon as I heard them rumors about you and the Boss was dead—and Geez! I'm glad you're okay. The Boss ain't really dead is he?"

"You should know, Louie," said Imogen coldly.

"Hey Miss! How should I know? The Boys been tryin' t' make me say I done it, but like I said, it's my day off, so, like, so I wasn't around."

"And how did you spend your day off, Louie? Going hunting in a helicopter?"

Louie's eyes told Imogen that she had found him out, but he continued to deny his involvement.

"Geez, Miss. I don't know what you're talking about!"

"How much did she pay you, Louie? What did she promise you? Money? Her body? A share in the action?"

"Who Miss? I don't know what—?"

"Stop lying to me Louie!" Imogen flared at him and whacked him across the face with her pistol. "You were in that helicopter this morning, and you fired those shots that killed Manfred and would have killed me if he hadn't got in the way. It was you who phoned here to tell Rosina we were dead—but I'm not dead, Louie, because Manfred gave his life for me! And I won't let you get away with this!"

She leveled the Glock at Louie's heart.

"Miss! Miss!" he screamed. "Don't shoot me! Yeah, yeah! I shot the Boss! Miz Pacelli she bribed me, and yeah, she slept with me—"

"What!" shouted Giorgio, who had kept silent through everything up until now. "Rosina! You—!"

"I had to get it somewhere, you useless wimp!" retorted Rosina.

"Poor Giorgio!" said Imogen sarcastically. "That lechery is all an act. But let's hear the rest of your story, Louie. What else did she offer you?"

"Yeah, yeah! She said when she took over, she'd put me in Al's place as leader of the boys. She's the one, Miss! It was all her doing!"

"But you were her willing accomplice, Louie!" cried Imogen. "And you must have had an accomplice. Who piloted the helicopter or held the gun at the pilot's head?"

"I—uh—"

"Tell Miss what she's askin' yuh, rat," snarled Al menacingly, "if yah don't want my boot in yer groin."

"It—it was Danny, Miss!" cried Louie. "There. I've told you everything. I've come clean. So please, Miss—"

"Stop your sniveling!" snapped Imogen. "Al, Joe, Eddie? Is Danny around?"

"Don't think so, Miss," interjected Jimmy, "but I'm pretty sure I know where t' find him."

"Then take as many men as you need, Jimmy, and get him."

"You wanna see him, Miss?"

"Not in this life, Jimmy."

Jimmy hesitated a moment, puzzled; then, suddenly understanding her meaning, he said, "He's dead, Miss."

"Good, Jimmy. Thanks. Now, for you Louie!"

She aimed the pistol at his heart.

"Please, Miss! Please!" cried Louie as Imogen hesitated a moment, her hands trembling as she considered the enormity of what she intended,. "It was all Miz Pacelli's doing! I—"

"Oh shut up!"

Remembering Manfred's throwing himself on her to receive the bullets Louie meant for her, with great inner effort Imogen steadied her hand and fired. Uttering a loud cry, Louie grasped his stomach. Taking better aim, Imogen put the next bullet into his chest, and Louie staggered forward and crashed to the floor.

The onlookers gasped and then fell silent, stunned by what they had witnessed. Then Ana-Maria cried, "Imogen! What have you done!"

"Executed a murderer," responded Imogen coldly.

"Good work, Miss!" exclaimed Al. "The rat deserved it!"

"He did," said Imogen. "And now, Rosina—" she said, turning menacingly toward Manfred's sister who was now trembling.

"Rosina!" cried Signora Andreotti whose eyes had been darting from one speaker to the other through all the preceding interchange. "Rosina! You—? *Madre di Dio!*" she cried, giving way to her pent up feelings. "*Mio Manfredo!* You killed my Manfredo!"

"And my Manfred!" cried Imogen. "My Manfred! My husband, Rosina, and the father of my child—who because of you won't have a father!"

"And you tried to kill Imogena! Why? Why?" demanded Signora Andreotti.

"Because she's a snake in the grass!" cried Rosina, desperately. "She's slithered her way into everyone's affections and was getting too much control and influence over Manfred! And now she's going to have a bastard who'll inherit the business! I had to get rid of her to keep everything in the family. If you have any eyes you'll see I'm right and stop her!"

"Oh, Rosina! How can you say that!" interjected Ana-Maria. "Imogen didn't even want to be Manfred's woman at first, but when she accepted, she made Manfred's life happy for the first time in years. For that you hate her. You hate her because Manfred loved her!" She paused a moment, then said, "You hated her on sight when Manfred brought her to Mama and Papa's anniversary party."

"Bull shit!"

"Enough!" said Imogen. Then, a catch in her voice, she continued, "You can't deny you killed Manfred or that you want the business for yourself. You tried to kill me and my child to get it, and you'll try again if I let you live. I don't need anymore evidence. I never hated you Rosina— until now!" Then leveling her pistol at Rosina's chest, she asked, "Is there a heart in there, murderer?"

"Papa! Make her stop!" cried Rosina.

"You killa Manfredo—" the old man began, but before he could utter another word Imogen squeezed the trigger, the Glock spoke loudly and the bullet struck Rosina between her breasts. Clasping her hand to her chest, Rosina gasped, staggered backwards, then crashed forward to the floor.

"Oh God!" cried Signora Andreotti.

"She notta deserva live, Mama!" cried the old man.

"Yeah. Good work, Miss!" cried Al. "The bitch deserved it!"

"Oh Imogen! Imogen!" cried Ana-Maria. "I can't believe this! Tell me it's not happening!"

"It's finished, Ana-Maria," Imogen responded, lowering her weapon, her voice flat from emotional exhaustion. "My bloodlust is satisfied. I've had my revenge."

At that moment, Giorgio, who had been cowering in the back—ground, stepped forward. "Yeah! Good work, Imogen! Like Al said, she was a bitch. I hated her," he said. "And you know, I never had nothin' to do with this."

"No, Giorgio!" flared Imogen, her anger returning. "You wouldn't have had the guts, you despicable, disgusting, leering, lecherous contemptible excuse for a human being! I ought to make a eunuch of you!" she said, aiming her pistol at his crotch.

"No! Imogen! Please! Not that!" he cried clutching his genitals as though somehow doing so would save him. "Like I said, I never had nothin' to do with this. I—"

"Get him out of here, Al, Joe, Eddie, some of you," snapped Imogen, "before I do with him what I did to Rosina! I never again want to see his drooling face! Get some of the men to take him to New York and use whatever force, threats, or bribery they need to get him on a plane to some place on another continent—Africa or Central Asia. Mongolia would be good."

"Oh Geez, Imogen—" cried Giorgio.

"Don't you dare call me Imogen! Because of that demon wife of your, Imogen is dead. I'm Miss from now on!"

"Miss—Miss—Please! Don't do this!"

"Don't you ever show up around here again, Giorgio, if you know what's good for you. If you do, it will be the last thing you ever do. Now, get him out of here!"

"You got it, Miss," said Eddie, grasping Giorgio and pushing him toward two of the men who grabbed him and began dragging him out. "Take this creep outa here like Miss says. He ain't wanted around here. And like Miss says, Pacelli, you come anywheres within miles of East Clintwood, you'll end up in a pair of concrete shoes at the bottom of the Clintwood River."

"Now," said Imogen when they had taken Giorgio away, "take way the bodies and do what has to be done and clean the blood off the floor."

As the bodies of Louie and Rosina were being removed and a pair of trembling maids came to wash the blood from the marble floor of the rotunda, there was a beep on Al's communicator.

"Lootenant Wolinski's outside, Miss."

"Oh—All right. Clean the place up quickly and then tell the men to let him come in. I'll go upstairs for a minute, but I'll be right down again." She turned to mount the stairs. "Oh Manfred, darling!" she cried, giving way to her grief. "Forgive me for seeming so unfeeling! I've avenged your death, but I have so much to do to keep your work going. All in good time I'll mourn for you!"

She disappeared along the hallway and into the suite she had shared with Manfred just as Lieutenant Wolinski entered the foyer.

"What's this I hear?" he demanded. "Manfred Andreotti's dead? Shot?"

"Yes, Lootenant," said Ana-Maria, "he's dead. He was shot just this morning at his suite in West Clintwood."

"Yeah? How did it happen?"

"Here comes the one who can tell you," said Ana-Maria as down the stairs came Imogen wearing a gown of black net over her naked body and the diamond trimmed gold mask Manfed had given her and gold high heels.

"What—? Miss Edwards—Imogen—is that you?"

"Yes, Lieutenant," said Imogen, "it is I—but I'm no longer Imogen but Miss, head of the crime syndicate."

"What!"

"Manfred's work goes on. I carry it on for the man I loved—"

"The man you loved! Andreotti!"

"Yes, Lieutenant, I loved him, and for his sake I now head the syndicate's operations in the Clintwoods."

"What—!" exclaimed Wolinski. "You can't mean that!"

"Yes, Lieutenant, I can and do mean exactly that."

"What! Imogen! You!"

"Miss, Lieutenant. I'm not the person I was. And you had better believe what I say."

"But—but—! This is incredible."

"Yes, I suppose it is. But it's true nevertheless. And I intend to lean very heavily on you, Lieutenant. You are too good a policeman to have around here. You're a threat to me and my operation of the syndicate. I suggest you look for another job somewhere else before I force you to."

"What! Are you threatening me?"

"Yes, I am, Lieutenant. And I will carry out my threat if you don't do as I say. So, take heed, Lieutenant Wolinski. My threats are not idle. Remember that I've got your chief in my pocket. A corrupt chief is exactly what I need—so I intend to keep him corrupt."

"Is-a da righta way, Imogena!" cried old Signor Andreotti from his wheel chair. "She putta you inna you place, Lootenant!"

"Now, Lieutenant," said Imogen menacingly, "you've learned what you came to learn, so there's no need for you to stay around. Please be so good as to leave. Joe, Eddie—see the Lieutenant out."

The men closed in on the police officer, and Joe said, "This way, Lootenant."

"I warn you, Imogen—" Wolinski called back over his shoulder.

"And I warn you, Lieutenant," Imogen interrupted. "You would not want anything to happen to your attractive wife, would you?"

"You wouldn't dare!"

"Oh yes, I would, Lieutenant. Manfred was not ruthless enough. I intend to be very ruthless. You were Manfred's enemy; now you're mine."

"Imogen!" exclaimed Ana-Maria. "I can't believe this is really you speaking."

"As I said, Ana-Maria, I'm Miss now. Imogen died when Manfred died. And you remember that too, Lieutenant."

As the lieutenant, torn between anger and perplexity, was forcibly and unceremoniously escorted outside, Imogen turned to Al and said, "Al, get me the police chief on the phone."

"You bet, Miss."

Just then a maid entered.

"There's a call for the Padrone—from the godfather."

"I'll take it," said Imogen. "Padrone, you come with me in case I need your confirmation." It was a command, not a request. "Al, get the police chief on another line and tell him that nothing has changed, but that, if he values his job, he'd better get over here pronto. Also, get word out to the business community that it's business as usual and that I want to see all the heads of companies here Monday morning at ten o'clock sharp. Also, I want Manfred's financial people up here ASAP. And I want to talk to the men in here immediately after I've talked to the godfather. They need their orders, and when I know the financial situation, there'll be raises for everyone—and I've not forgotten what you and Joe and Eddie and Jimmy have done today. You'll be well rewarded. Come and see me a bit later. Now, Padrone, we'll talk to the godfather—and remember, I understand Italian."

"Hey, Imogena!" cried the old man. "You-a gonna do alla righta."

"I intend to, Padrone. I fully intend to."

After she had talked to the police chief and had given the henchmen her orders, now at last, overcome with tension and fatigue, Imogen sought out Ana-Maria.

"Oh, Ana-Maria," she said. "Manfred is dead, and I've hardly had time to mourn for him. Oh God! Oh God! What a horrible day this has been!" She fell onto Ana-Maria's shoulder, buried her masked face in it and gave way to tears. "Oh God, Ana-Maria! He's gone! He's gone! How can I live without him?"

"I don't know how you've stood up to everything, Imogen," said Ana-Maria. "I don't know how you've been able to do what you've done, to become what you've become—I find it hard to accept. I can't understand how you can—"

"I had to do what I did, Ana-Maria. I've had to become what I've become. That's all there is to it," Imogen said, looking up and holding Ana-Maria at arms' length. "I had to fight for my life. I had to be hard and ruthless. If I hadn't, Ana-Maria, I doubt if either of us would be alive now to talk about it. But above all, I had to avenge Manfred's death."

"But—"

"There are no buts, Ana-Maria. I'm committed."

* * * *

The following evening, Ana-Maria answered the knock at her door to find Imogen standing before her wearing a body stocking of black net and black high heeled boots, the Glock tucked into the garter on her thigh, a death's head mask concealing her face, a black hooded cloak over her arm.

"Oh my God!" exclaimed Ana-Maria, almost horrified at the sight. "Imogen! You startled me! You—you look so horrible like that!"

"I am horrible. I look like I am, Ana-Maria," said Imogen, her voice deadened by her mask. "But may I come in?"

"Oh—yes. Of course. Come in." She stepped aside and Imogen entered the room.

"Is Luigi all right?"

"He's asleep."

"Poor little fellow. But I'm glad he's with you."

"I've tried to keep him occupied and not think about what's happened, But won't you sit down? "

"Thank you, but I'll remain standing. And I'll remain masked, for as I said the other day, I'm no longer the person I was. The mask is who I am now."

"Oh Imogen! Do—do you really mean to go through with this—to run the organization?"

"What else can I do, Ana-Maria? I can't go back to what I was. I've killed two people and ordered the death of a third. As far as I'm concerned, they deserved to die, but under the law, I've committed murder. My only other choice, and what I probably deserve, is a state administered lethal injection. But this is your chance for freedom, Ana-Maria. I want you to take Luigi and leave here. You'll be a far better mother to him than Rosina ever was. I don't want him to be living always in the presence of the knowledge that it was his Immy-Jean who killed his mother, and of what she's become. This is no world for the little boy. I want him to have a chance for a real life."

"It's no world for you, Imogen."

"I've made it my world, Ana-Maria, and it became my world, I now realize, the moment I became Manfred's woman—but I no longer regret that, for his love for me has been the best thing in my life. But you have the opportunity to get out of a life you hate. You'll be well looked after, I'll see to that. If you want to set up that fashion boutique you once mentioned to me, I'll help you to do that."

"But Imogen, I don't want to leave you. You're the best friend I ever had."

"You've been a wonderful friend to me, Ana-Maria, but I'm no longer the girl you met at the opera. I'm the head of the crime syndicate in the Clintwoods and the killer of your sister."

"I'm not indifferent, Imogen, but I loved Manfred too. He was my brother as well as your lover, and Rosina killed him. No, I'm not indifferent, but, as Papa said, she deserved it."

"Oh Ana-Maria! I know you feel for him—that you loved him too, and he loved you! Our loves were horribly violated. But nevertheless, I'm sorry that it was I who killed your sister and Papa and Mama Andreotti's daughter. But I had to act as I did."

"I don't blame you, Imogen, but I still can't believe what you're doing. Do you really know what you're getting yourself into?"

"I've a pretty good idea, and I don't like it, but when I came back here to kill Rosina and Louie, I crossed my Rubicon. There's no turning back."

"This just isn't happening, Imogen. This just isn't happening."

"It is, Ana-Maria. But as I said, this is your opportunity, and I urge you to take it. I demand you take it. It's the only way I have of repaying all your kindness to me—but I will miss you."

Just then a knock came at the door.

"Who—who is it?" called Ana-Maria.

"It's Eddie, Ms. Ana-Maria. Is Miss there?"

"Miss—? Oh—yes—she is." Turning to Imogen she said, "I—I'll have a hard time not calling you Imogen."

"You still may, Ana-Maria," Imogen answered. Then raising her voice, she to called Eddie, "I'll be right with you, Eddie." Then to Ana-Maria she said, "Think about what I say, Ana-Maria. Good night." Donning her cloak, she walked to the door. Then she turned back and spoke again to Ana-Maria. "Will you take my uncle and aunt with you? I want them to be safe and not to have to be reminded constantly at first hand what their niece has become. They'll be heartbroken enough as it is. And again, I'll provide for everything."

"If—if that's what you want, Imogen. Of course, yes, I'd be happy to have them with me for your sake—and for company for me."

"And when my baby is born, will you take him or her too? I don't want my child to grow up in an atmosphere of crime. I want him to have a normal life—and again, I'll pay for everything."

"Again, Imogen, if it's what you want..."

"It is, and once you're free of this life, Ana-Maria, who knows—"

"I doubt if I can ever be free of the taint of—"

"Nor I, Ana-Maria. There's no turning away for me, but there is for you."

"Oh Imogen! I wish—"

"There's no use wishing Ana-Maria," said Imogen. "There is no place for sentiment any more. You once said Manfred lacked that last bit of ruthlessness necessary to run a criminal organization. You were right. There was too much nice guy about Manfred—which is what made me love him, but look what it got him. He should have dealt with Rosina long ago. I have, and henceforth I intend to be be utterly ruthless."

"You seem so cold, so unfeeling, Imogen. The person I'm hearing just doesn't seem like you."

"As I said, Ana-Maria, I'm not the person I was. That person is dead." And again she turned to leave.

"Imogen—"

"Yes?" she said, again turning back.

"Good—good night, Imogen," said Ana-Maria, her eyes full of tears, "and—and good-bye."

"Good bye, Ana-Maria. Thank you for being my friend."

Imogen turned and, without a backward glance, walked from the room.

* * **

About an hour later, after a trip over back roads, Imogen, in her black cloak, stood by the limousine looking up toward the abandoned railway bridge over the tributary of the Clintwood River where the men had driven a van. As she watched, they unloaded three concrete blocks containing the bodies of Rosina, Louie and Danny and dumped them one after the other into the river. As the last block splashed into the water, Imogen quickly pushed away her mask, turned aside and retched violently.

"You'll get used to this kinda business, Miss," said Al as she straightened up, brought the heaving of her stomach under control, caught her breath, and readjusted her mask.

"That's what frightens me, Al," she said. "I'm afraid I will, but that's the price the mistress of a crime organization must pay."

"Uh—yeah, Miss? Yeah. I guess. But they deserved what they got, Miss."

"Yes, I know, Al—but what do I deserve?" She paused a moment listening to the last waves from the disturbance of the river's surface lap against the bank. Then turning her masked face to Al as he held open the limousine door for her, she said, "But there's no point thinking about that. So, now that we've done what we came to do, let's go home again—until the next time."

EPILOGUE

Following her triumphant home-coming recital and reception, Susan Van Alstyne, in her emerald green strapless gown, blond hair arranged in a chignon, cloak over her arm, emerged from her backstage dressing room at the East Clintwood Auditorium to return to where her parents waited for her in the rotunda, when three black clad women, their faces partly obscured by their hair combed over their left eyes, suddenly stepped from the shadows and two of them grasped her arms.

"Let me go!" cried the frightened soprano, struggling in vain to free herself from the women's firm grasp. "Who are you?"

"Who we are does not matter," said the third of the three women. "Just come with us. Miss wants to see you."

"Miss? Who is Miss? Is it...?"

"If Miss wants you to know you who she is, she will tell you. Come along quietly and you'll be perfectly safe. Your parents have been informed that you'll be delivered safely to their home, and they'll know they can trust the sender of the message."

"Then it must be—"

"As I said, Miss will tell you if she wishes you to know," the strange woman broke in. "Just come along."

Walking briskly in their high heels, their long legs flashing through the slits in their calf-length skirts, the three women propelled Susan against her will to the backstage entrance of the concert hall. Parked in the shadows stood a black limousine. A hard-faced man in black standing beside the vehicle spoke into a cell phone and after only a moment, apparently on receiving a response from inside the vehicle, opened the door.

From inside the limousine a voice once very familiar called, "Come in, Susan. It has been a long time."

Hesitantly, Susan stooped to look into the limousine where, by the dome light, she saw, seated in the far corner of the richly upholstered forward-facing seat, a seductively mysterious and sinisterly magnificent woman, a gold half-mask trimmed with glittering diamonds over her face, an open, leopard skin coat over her shoulders and a gown of black lace woven in spider's web patterns clinging to every curve of her voluptuous body fully visible beneath it, a thin gold belt like a two-headed snake about her waist and on her feet gold shoes with five-inch stiletto heels and double, diamond-studded ankle straps. On the fourth finger of her left hand she wore a diamond ring. Tucked into a black garter on the smooth thigh of her shapely right leg was a Glock 19 handgun reachable through long slit in the skirt. Her long, dark hair fell to her shoulders, a sad smile played over her full sensual lips, and through the openings of her mask she fixed her sad dark eyes on Susan.

"Imogen?" exclaimed Susan as she slid hesitantly onto the rear-facing seat opposite the masked woman.

"*You* may call me Imogen, Susan," the masked woman replied. She raised her hands to her mask and removed it to reveal her beautiful but sad face. "And for you, but for no one else, I unmask. The girl you once knew—Imogen Edwards—is no more. Hence my mask."

"But—but surely almost everyone knows who you are, Imogen!"

"Oh, of course they do. The mask is not to conceal *who* I am—or I should say, who I was—but to proclaim *what* I am, the Crime Queen of the Clintwoods." Then into the intercom she said, "Joe, take us to the Van Alstyne residence, but go slowly."

"Yes Miss," the voice came back.

"Thanks, Joe," she said. Then to Susan she said, "We all wear masks, Susan. Perhaps my life as Imogen Edwards was a masquerade. Perhaps the Crime Queen lurked behind the mask of Imogen Edwards. Now I am Miss, and I have made it a word that evokes fear in the Clintwoods."

Susan stared in dumbfounded amazement.

"You predicted, Susan," Imogen continued, "when I became Manfred's mistress that I would come out on top. Well, I have, but not in the way you expected." She fingered her gold belt with the double snakeheads. "No doubt it's melodramatic, but I wear the belt of Ayesha in Haggard's *She* as a reminder to everyone that here in the Clintwoods I am She-who-must-be-obeyed." Then abruptly changing the subject, she said, "Enough of that.

I'm really happy to see you now that your singing career is well launched, Susan, and that everything is working out so wonderfully for you. You sang beautifully tonight as you always do and as I fully expected you would."

"You—you were there?" asked Susan in astonishment.

"I wouldn't have missed your recital for anything, Susan."

"Surely you didn't come," Susan said, "wearing your mask and that see-through dress!"

"No, though I could have, for I can do anything I want in the Clintwoods. But on the rare occasions when I go out for pleasure, I prefer to be incognito, and so I wear these," she said, taking up from the seat beside her a realistic latex mask of a woman's face, and a blond wig, "and," she said with a wry smile, indicating a grey suit lying on the seat beside her, "to be very simply attired, rather like dowdy Imogen Edwards."

"That ring on your left hand," said Susan. "It—it looks like an engagement ring, but surely..."

"It *is* and engagement ring, Susan," Imogen replied choking back tears as she stretched out her hand to contemplate the ring. "Manfred gave it to me only moments before he was killed. He wanted me to be his wife."

"He—he wanted you to marry him?"

"Oh yes. And I would have married him had he not been killed. As you know, I wouldn't believe it at first, but I came to realize he really did love me—very much—and I fell in love with him." Her eyes filled with tears. "Oh Susan! How deeply—how deeply I loved him!"

"Imogen—!"

"Yes, I know," she said, drying her eyes, "it must seem strange to you, especially since he coerced me into being his mistress. But Manfred respected and appreciated me and treated me well—and he made my life exciting and made me feel like a woman. Now I would not for anything have missed knowing him." Again she broke into tears. "Oh that I had realized I loved him sooner than I did! Now he's gone—he's gone!" Suddenly the tears flooded down her cheeks and she buried her face in her hands. "Oh Susan!" she cried. "Oh Susan! How I ache for him!"

"Oh Imogen!" Susan exclaimed, reaching across to touch her. "I'm so sorry!"

"How horrible, Susan," said, Imogen looking up again, "to have him die in my arms and to know that he died saving my life, for some of the bullets that killed him were meant for me! I still have nightmares about it!"

"Oh Imogen!" said Susan. "How dreadfully horrible for you!! You must have been devastated!"

"I was—I still am. So," she said, again drying her eyes, "if you're wondering how it could have come about how I've become the Crime Queen of the Clintwoods, now you know."

Both fell silent and Susan withdrew her hand.

At last Imogen said, "I imagine you have heard all sorts of horrid things about me, Susan."

"I heard that—that when Manfred Andreotti was killed you had his sister and her accomplice killed. I guess I can understand why, but—"

"I didn't *have* them killed, Susan," Imogen interrupted.

Susan stared at Imogen a moment in uncomprehending silence, and then, on realizing the import of her word's, she gasped.

"Oh God, Imogen! You didn't—?"

"Yes, Susan, I killed them myself. I know," she said, seeing the look of horror on Susan's face, "we were taught 'Vengence is mine, I will repay saith the LORD,' but in my grief and anger all I could think of was revenge on those who had taken the man I loved from me—whom I had only just come to realize I loved and who wanted me to be his wife. I shot Rosina through the heart—for she had broken mine."

"Oh God, Imogen! Oh God!" Now Susan buried her face in her hands.

"I know, Susan. It's horrid to think that your friend could do such a thing—could be a murderess."

Susan fell silent in shock and horror at the word murderess. Then at last she looked up and said, "It—is hard, Imogen—"

"As Manfred's mistress," Imogen said, "I experienced aspects of my personality I never knew existed, and, as with Stevenson's Henry Jekyll, my dark side gained the upper hand."

"I—I find that so hard to understand, Imogen."

"So do I, Susan. I know only that I loved Manfred, and because of that love I am now, for better or for worse, and most probably the latter, the Crime Queen of the Clintwoods. I've jeopardized my soul, and I can never again be the person I was. I can never again be Imogen."

"God's mercy and forgiveness are great, Imogen. If you were to talk to Father Daniels—"

"How I can I face Father Daniels after what I've become? He tried so hard to help me at the beginning, but I've betrayed his trust, first by the pleasure I took in being Manfred's mistress and now by committing myself to this life of crime. I no longer attend church. Evil as I am, I'm not a hypocrite. I can obtain forgiveness only if I accept the consequences of my deeds and their just punishment, and perhaps some day I will but for now, for Manfred's sake, I'm committed to continuing his work. I did not ask to be where I am, but now I am there, I will stop at nothing to remain there."

Susan, stared wide-eyed at her friend but could say nothing.

"Oh," resumed Imogen, "as Manfred did, I give to charities and cultural organizations and provide recreational facilities for the people in the poor neighborhoods, but none of that excuses what I am or what I do. It does not excuse or justify me that I try to insure that drug addicts have clean needles and that the product is pure, and that, though the house never loses, there's no cheating in my gambling casinos, and that I've made conditions decent and comfortable, even pleasant, for the prostitutes in my brothels—if the life of selling one's body can ever be considered pleasant—and that I insure that the women get most of the money they receive for their services, for there's only one pimp now—me. I rule the Clintwoods through extortion, intimidation, terror and exploitation—and where necessary, murder—and I have to confess that I find a perverse kind of pleasure in the power I wield. Henry Kissinger is right—power is an aphrodisiac."

Susan shuddered and cried out, "Oh Imogen! What you're saying is so horrible!"

"Yes, Susan, it is. I have no illusions and make no excuses."

Again Susan fell silent for some moments before asking, "But—but why did Rosina want to kill you?"

"She hated me from the first, and I feel sure that when she knew I was to have a child by Manfred she decided to act. That child was in the way of her own ambitions."

"You had a child by Manfred! My parents never mentioned..."

"Not many knew, but yes, I did—a little boy. In him, Manfred lives on."

"And—and is he with you?"

"No. He's with Ana-Maria, Manfred's other sister, in a town out West far away from here. It was hard to give him up, but I did not want him to grow up in an atmosphere of criminality. I want him to have a normal life."

Susan sat in the dim light inside the limousine staring for some moments in silence at her so drastically transformed friend, incredulous of all she had been hearing. At last she asked, "Wh—what about your uncle and aunt? How do they—?"

"They're devastated, of course, and I can hardly blame them. They could never understand how I could love Manfred and that because of my love for him, I avenged his death and now carry on his work. Now they're with Ana-Maria in that Western city where I hope they'll be safe. I feel very sad when I think about them—very sad—for I've brought such shame on people I love and to whom I owe so much."

"Do—do you ever see them?"

"No. It's best they not be involved in my new life, nor do I want them to be a means for others to get at me. I hope that in Ana-Maria and Manfred's little nephew Luigi and my little boy they have some compensation for losing me."

"Daddy said you forced Lieutenant Wolinski to leave town."

"Yes. I think that, despite interference of the corrupt chief, he may have been getting close to catching Manfred. So I had his evidence destroyed, and by a bit of intimidation—I had his wife's car blown up just after she'd got out of it one day—"

"Imogen! Surely not!"

"She was not hurt—I didn't intend she would be—not then—but I let the lieutenant know that it was only a warning—"

"Oh God Imogen! You wouldn't have—!"

"If I'd had to. The head of a criminal organization must be ruthless and can have no conscience. But fortunately for him and his wife—since he's my uncle's and your family's friend—I was able to avoid doing anything more drastic. He was offered the position of chief of police in the city where Ana-Maria and my aunt and uncle are. I urged him to accept and he did. I'm glad he's there. He's a good policeman, and he provides some extra protection for them. And where he is now, his efforts are not frustrated by a corrupt chief in the pay of the Crime Queen. But a good policeman I don't want and a corrupt police chief I do."

Again Susan fell silent for some time before she asked, "Wh—what about Manfred's parents?"

"They still live at the Andreotti mansion—though it is mine now in all but name, for I make all the decisions. I think the old Padrone thought he could dominate me, but once I got the hang of things, I pushed him aside. Not long ago he suffered a stroke. Neither of them has ever got over Manfred's death, and they are both now only hollow shells of their former selves."

Just then Joe's voice came through the intercom. "Here's the Van Alstyne place, Miss."

"Oh—yes. Thanks, Joe," said Imogen. Then to her friend she said, "Oh Susan! It has been so good to see you! Please, please—try to remember me as I was, not as I've become—" She stopped short and paused reflectively for a moment. "But it's silly to say that. How can you forget what I've become? This is what I am," she said, resuming her mask, "the masked Crime Queen. Imogen is dead. But I treasure the memory of our friendship, Susan. After Manfred's love, it is one of the best things—one of the few really good things—in my life, and I'll never forget how good you and your family always were to me when I was just a poor girl from a working class neighborhood. That's why I exempt your father—who is very decent and honorable in his business dealings—from any payments to me. For the same reason, I make no demands on the Martinellis and the other people of Little Italy. There are no other exceptions." Then suddenly she released Susan's hands and pushed them from her. "But enough of that, and I mustn't hold you. My touch will only taint you. My hands, like Macbeth's, are forever steeped in blood, and not all the waters in all the oceans will wash them clean. "

"Oh Imogen! Imogen! I—" But sobs cut off her response.

"Don't cry for me, Susan. I've acted with full knowledge of what I'm doing. This is good-bye, my dearest friend. We can no longer be part of one another's lives, for my influence will only harm you. Like James's Christina Light, the Princess Casamassima, 'I am corrupt, corrupting, corruption.'"

"Oh Imogen! Imogen!" said Susan reaching forward to try to enfold her friend in her arms. "I can't bear to think that. Underneath, you're still the Imogen I knew!"

"No, Susan! No, I'm not!" objected Imogen vehemently as she pushed Susan away. "I am Miss, the feared Crime Queen of the Clintwoods. I must take myself out of your life and you must put me out of your thoughts!"

"Oh God, Imogen!" cried Susan, falling back into the seat. "What will become of you?"

"There will be retribution some day, somehow. One day probably I'll stop a bullet. Gunning me down won't solve the problem of crime in the Clintwoods, but the world will be well rid of me."

"Oh Imogen!" exclaimed Susan, her voice sympathetic, leaning over to touch Imogen's hand. "It's too horrible to think of!"

"Maybe it won't happen. Lots of gangsters have died quietly in their beds. What I do know is that Manfred was my first and now my only love, for I'll never know love again. What decent person would want me? I have only the memory of his love."

"This is all so sad, Imogen! I feel so sorry for you!"

"Don't be, Susan," said Imogen briefly placing her hand over her friend's.

"I wish I'd never taken you to the opera that night!"

"Don't blame yourself, Susan. We can't foretell the outcomes of our actions, and sometimes, no matter how well intentioned, as yours was, they come out badly. But that night led me to Manfred, and the life I had with him has been the best thing that ever happened to me. I'll never, never regret my love for him, and if it has led to this—well—so be it. I will live with the consequences. The Crime Queen deserves no pity. So don't cry over her."

"But I do cry for you Imogen—for the girl I grew up with, the girl who was my best friend and my talented accompanist who helped launch me on my career."

"Yes, that was one of the best things I did, and it makes me happy to think I helped you. But as I said, Susan, that girl dead. Think instead of this masked woman who terrorizes the Clintwoods, and you won't feel so upset."

"It's that woman—the Crime Queen—I weep for, Imogen, for I know the girl I knew still lives inside her."

"No, Susan. But now, this is our final good-bye, not because I want it, but because, for your sake, it must be. I'll miss you, but it's for the best."

"Oh Imogen!" Susan broke into deep convulsive sobs, and Imogen turned away her masked face, but at the same time she leaned across and opened the limousine door.

"Let's not prolong the agony, Susan. No," she said, pushing her old friend away from her as she tried again to embrace her. "Don't try to hug or kiss me. My touch is contamination, so this is good-bye—good-bye forever, dearest friend. I'll never forget you, Susan, and though the thief is not penitent—not yet, anyway—I don't think her sincere and genuine petition will be rejected: God bless you and keep you."

Tears streaming down her face, Susan stepped out of the limousine. "G—good-bye, Imogen," she gulped.

"Good-bye, Susan," said Imogen, tears flowing down her cheeks from under her mask.

She closed the door, and the limousine drove away into the night.

Almost blinded by her tears, Susan stood transfixed as the dearest friend of her youth and young adulthood passed forever from her life.

"Good-bye, Imogen," she sobbed. "As you say, good-bye forever."